Dang

Clint had been standing there for over an hour, hiding in the dark corner, watching her, trying to watch those around her, and wondering how the hell he was going to manage to convince her to lay low for a while. Morganna was stubborn as hell, and Reno had warned him that it wouldn't be easy to convince her to give up her nightlife.

He frowned as he remembered his friend's words. The subtle warning in Reno's voice, the feeling that the other man suspected more than he was saying as he gave Clint the names of the clubs she frequented.

Did she have a lover? He watched the men who seemed to flock around her like wolves. She didn't seem to pay attention to one more than the other, and as she ordered a drink from the waitress, he could have sworn he caught a glimpse of weariness in her face.

He grimaced at his overactive imagination. Morganna had been a social butterfly even before she came of age. She was one of those women perfectly at home in the middle of a crowd, finding her sense of purpose in the number of so-called friends she could gather around her at any one time.

It would drive him crazy. It was driving him crazy now, watching the men who were drawn to her like flies to honey, their hands touching her bare shoulder, her satiny arm, trying to feel that ribbon of silk she called her hair.

He set his jaw in determination as he straightened from the wall, shrugging the muscles of his shoulders, uncomfortable as he prepared for this new battle. He'd rather face an army of terrorists than one tiny, delicate woman. It was pathetic.

St. Martin's Paperbacks Titles by Lora Leigh

Dangerous Games

Lora Leigh

St. Martin's Paperbacks

This is a work of fiction. All of the characters, organizations, and events portrayed in this novel are either products of the author's imagination or are used fictitiously.

DANGEROUS GAMES

Copyright © 2006 by Lora Leigh.

Cover photo © Shirley Green

For information address St. Martin's Press, 175 Fifth Avenue, New York, NY 10010.

ISBN: 0-312-36580-2
EAN: 978-0-312-36580-6

Printed in the United States of America

St. Martin's Paperbacks edition / February 2007

St. Martin's Paperbacks are published by St. Martin's Press, 175 Fifth Avenue, New York, NY 10010.

10 9 8 7

For Dad and Mom, because they put up with endless hours of listening to the stories; and my husband, Tony, for always believing in me.

For Patricia Rasey, Beth Anderson, Lyn Morgan, Mama Sue, and Stacey, because they were there in the beginning and helped immeasurably; the Ladies of the Lora Leigh Forum; and the readers who have e-mailed and written; you keep me going.

For my advanced readers, for putting up with more than one copy of the same story and for kicking my butt when it was needed.

For Scheme, my music finder, idea instigator, and chocolate source. Thanks for everything.

And for my editor, Monique, thanks for the chance.

Diva's, Merlin's, and the Roundtable and their adjoining underground clubs are all a product of my imagination only. Within the Tempting SEALs series, I've tried to set up what I would envision as the most interesting fringe clubs rather than what my research has found for BDSM (Bondage–Domination–Submission–Masochism) clubs. Male dominance, a hypersexuality, and an awareness of a woman's pleasure are what my heroes have in common, and it's what the members of the clubs within my books have in common as well, no matter their extremity. And I hope you enjoy reading Clint and Morganna's adventure as much as I enjoyed writing it.

Prologue

CLINT MCINTYRE, TWENTY-FIVE YEARS OLD. A Navy SEAL. A fully grown, sensual, dominant male. He was a man whom other men looked to in respect. A man who had grown in confidence and in power. He wasn't a child fighting to hide the abuse he had suffered any longer. He was a man who tolerated nothing less than his best from himself and the men he fought alongside.

But he was a man who nearly came to his knees that night at the sight of one small teenage Lolita decked out in a short skirt, a thin pale blue blouse, and high heels. Dark brown hair flowed around her in a multitude of curls, and gray eyes sparkled back at him with a hint of laughter and interest. Too much interest.

He was a grown man, aware of his sexuality, his tastes, and his hungers. To even consider the beginning pulses of awareness he could feel moving through him was a crime. One he refused to allow to take hold.

She was his best friend's sister. She was his sister's best friend. And normally she was the bane of his existence.

Morganna Chavez had been tormenting him in one form or another since the day she learned how to walk and toddled to him to smack him on his eleven-year-old head with her bottle to get his attention. She had been getting his attention in one form or another ever since.

He hadn't expected this, though. That glimmer of awareness. The way he noticed the full, high breasts beneath her thin blouse and the long, shapely legs beneath the short skirt. Pink lips glistening with a soft gloss and gray eyes that looked smoky, seductive, rather than immature and filled with child-like wonder.

He deserved to be shot.

"So, are you going to stand there like a knot on a log or are you going to dance with me?" She propped one hand on her hip and smiled slowly. "It is my birthday after all."

His lips twitched at her flirtatiousness. She had been flirting with him for as long as he could remember, too.

He stared around the backyard; the lights strung through the trees cast a soft glow over the thirty-some teenagers enjoying the party her brother had allowed.

Reno had lost his mind this year. Clint glanced across the yard to where his best friend, Morganna's brother, was testing the punch bowl for alcohol, to the laughing amusement of the kids gathered around the table.

They were kids. Morganna was a kid.

"Go dance with one of your friends, brat." Clint smiled to soften the rejection. He didn't have to fake his affection for her; she was as much a part of his life as his sister was, when he was home. He did care for Morganna. Deeply.

"Coward." She flicked him an amused look from beneath her lashes. A look far too mature for her years and far too knowing.

No man he knew would ever call him a coward. He was fierce. Strong. Deadly. He was scared to death to be within a hundred feet of her.

He shook his head and laughed at her. A soft, indulgent laugh that had her brows drawing together and her gray eyes dimming with a hint of vulnerability.

"Go play, Morganna," he told her gently as he turned away. "Leave the grown-ups alone."

He should have never agreed to chaperone the party. He wouldn't have if he had known what he would face, if he had even suspected that for even a second in time he would see Morganna as anything other than his best friend's sister. Or his sister's best friend.

TWO YEARS LATER

She was eighteen. Tall and lithe, a gypsy, a hellion, the most beautiful woman he had ever laid his eyes on. Two years, a multitude of lectures, and endless nights of dreams he should have been shot for, and the awareness of her had only grown.

Sexy, sensual Morganna.

"When are you leaving?" They were on the back porch of her home, the home she had shared with her brother, Reno, since the deaths of their parents.

The elderly aunt who had once stayed with Morganna while Clint was on assignment hadn't arrived, but there was no reason to wait for her. Was there? Yet Clint was standing there waiting on her for Reno, who had been forced to leave earlier than usual to take command of the small force of Navy SEALs he was leading into a mission. Reno was comfortable leaving Morganna home alone this time. Clint wasn't.

He also wasn't comfortable sitting on the back porch, his jeans tighter than normal, his skin too sensitive. The situation was getting out of control. Two years he had fought this awareness of her, and it was only growing rather than dimming. He was only growing hungrier, and that scared the hell out of him.

"Earth to Clint," Morganna announced when he hadn't answered her, waving her hand in front of his face as he shifted in his chair and thanked God she couldn't see the erection swelling mindlessly beneath his jeans.

"I head out day after tomorrow." He shot her an irritated glare as she leaned against the post directly in front of his porch chair.

Right in front of him, where he could see the rise of her full breasts against the soft cotton shirt she wore and received the full effect of those long, gorgeous legs encased in snug denim.

"Everyone's leaving me," she said softly, staring over his shoulder with a wistful expression. "Raven's got her internship in the art design school this fall; she'll not even be in the state. You and Reno will be gone. It's going to be lonely here."

Morganna had accepted a scholarship at Atlanta University to stay close to home.

"You have your friends," he reminded her, forcing back a grimace at the thought of the pimple-faced boys she ran with in that crowd.

"Yeah." She nodded firmly. "I do. I'll be fine."

He watched her inhale slowly, deeply, and tightened his jaw at the realization that he had managed to hurt her. Though how he didn't have a clue.

"Aunt Beth remarked that this is the last time she'll have to stay with me," Morganna said then, her tone a little too bright. "Reno was a little slow on this one. I think he's afraid I'll burn the house down or something."

"Reno worries about you being alone." Clint worried. God, did he worry.

"You could stay with me," she said softly. "You have two more days before you leave. I could call Aunt Beth. She would be happy to be able to stay home with her flowers and her neighbors."

His gaze sharpened on Morganna's face as he swallowed tightly and rose quickly from his chair.

"Won't work, brat." He forced the words past his throat. "I have to get ready to head out."

"Yeah. Sure." She nodded quickly, pushing away from the post as she moved to go around him. "Look, head on back to that rinky-dink little apartment of yours and whatever flavor of the week you have in your bed. I'm sick of watching you track each vehicle down the road praying it's Aunt Beth. I'll be fine without you."

He caught her arm as she moved for the back door, pulling her around and making the biggest damned mistake of his life. Because he saw her tears. Because he saw the hurt in her eyes as she turned away.

"I know what you're doing," he said softly. "I know what you're offering, Morganna. Don't make me hurt you. I don't want to do that."

Her expression twisted, determination, defiance, and, God help him, adoration filling her eyes. She saw him as some damned knight there to fulfill all her girlish dreams. He was a bastard for even daring to consider touching her. And he wasn't, he assured himself. He wanted to touch her, but he was old enough that wants wouldn't hurt him.

"I love you," she whispered. "I've always loved you, Clint."

"No." He shook his head firmly, maintaining his hold on her arm as his other hand lifted to touch her cheek gently. His thumb slid over her lips, just because he needed to know if they were as soft as they looked. "You have a crush on me. I'm the only man you can't twist around your little finger." He smiled gently. "That's all, Morganna. And nothing can come of it. Nothing can happen but the loss of something I cherish. Your friendship."

"I can't pretend," she whispered passionately. "You still see me as a child. I'm not a child."

"Then don't act like one," he suggested in return.

Pain flared in her eyes a second before he saw something more. Determination, yes. But something shocking, something almost frightening. He saw hunger. Sexual, intense, and more than he ever wanted to see in her eyes.

"Just kiss me good-bye then." Her breath hitched. "Just a little kiss."

"Morganna." He held her still, staring down at her in regret. Regret for more than she could ever understand. Then he made the mistake of stroking over those soft lips once again.

They parted, the warmth of her mouth searing his flesh as her tongue peeked out to swipe over his thumb before her lips parted and her sharp little teeth nipped at the pad.

And he lost his mind. Hell, he couldn't even claim insanity, because even a crazy man would have walked away. Instead, in less than a second he had her in his arms, his hand snagging her hair at the back of her neck to pull her head back and his lips covering hers.

She was innocent. He tasted it in her kiss. Felt it in the shock that stiffened her body as he gave her a man's kiss. A man's hunger. Slanting his lips over hers, he fought to consume, in one kiss, all the hunger, the sweetness, and the insane need possible. To hold inside his memories.

Sharp, hard kisses parted her lips. His tongue licked over them, before thrusting inside, before possessing her in a way he knew he should have never attempted.

Because she was sweeter than sweet. Hot as hell. And the pleasure ripped through his senses like a cascading explosion as she moaned against his mouth.

As quickly as he had taken her lips, he released her, jerking back to glare down at her as she stared back in shock, in a pleasure that darkened her gray eyes and flushed her heart-shaped face.

"It's never going to happen," he snapped, gripping her shoulders to give her a little shake that he prayed would instill some common sense inside her. "Little party girls and Navy SEALs don't work out, Morganna. Stick to the little boys you run with and leave the men alone. You'll be a hell of a lot safer that way."

Before she could argue, and he knew she would argue, he turned and strode quickly from the porch and across the yard to the car he had left parked in the back lot. Staying with her any longer was out of the question.

MORGANNA AT TWENTY-ONE

Being alone sucked. Morganna stared around the living room of the house she had once shared with her parents and her brother. Her parents were dead, her brother was gone more often than he was home, and one day he wouldn't be here at all.

Her best friend, Raven, spent most of her evenings and nights studying the graphic design she had grown so adept at, and Morganna was stuck in an office job she hated.

And she was alone. Because she didn't have the common sense to let go of a dream and a man who didn't want her.

She walked through the living room, moving to the shelf of pictures she kept and the memories they brought.

Clint was in most of them. With her, her brother, and her parents. Handsome. Tough. Hard. Clint had always been harder than he should have been, tougher than anyone else around him. And he had ruined her heart for any other man.

But she was still alone.

Tucked between two of the pictures were the pamphlets she had kept from the Academy. The Law Enforcement Academy was accepting applicants.

She had meant to discuss it with Reno when he was home the week before, but the stay had been a brief one, and he had been exhausted. He had slept the two days he had been home, only to have to leave again.

She laid her head against the shelf and closed her eyes. He would worry if he knew anyway. And Clint, jerk that he was, would do everything to stop her. And he could stop her. He had connections in Atlanta, connections she couldn't afford to let him use. As long as no one knew she was Reno Chavez's sister, then there wasn't a chance of anyone saying anything to Clint. And what were the chances that the guys at the Academy would really care to call Reno and let him know jack? Especially if his name wasn't on her list of contacts.

She tapped her nail against the papers.

She was bored and she was alone. She wanted more than a secretarial job going nowhere and a silent house every night. Like Reno, she wanted to make a difference. She wanted more than to keep dreaming of something that didn't exist.

She sighed wearily. Restlessly. She was tired of just being Reno's sister. Or Clint McIntyre's responsibility when Reno wasn't around. She was tired of being put on a shelf and taken down to perform when they decided to visit.

She was strong enough to be who and what she wanted to be. And she didn't want to wait for Clint any longer.

She pulled the papers from the shelf, shoved them in her purse, and grabbed her car keys. She wasn't waiting any longer.

Chapter 1

CLINT STOOD IN THE SHADOWS of one of his favorite clubs, his eyes narrowed on the dance floor. He liked Diva's for a variety of reasons. The music was a mix of tracks. A little hard rock, a little Goth, a little pure fun. The women were the same mix, but he had found they all went for one thing in particular. The darker edge of sex. The dominance games, the harder, powerful sensations to be found with a man willing to push their limits. He hadn't expected to find Morganna here.

The music playing now, he imagined, was meant to be pure fun. It should have been causing a riot.

A mix of fury, disbelief, and wild hunger filled him as he watched the witchy little woman on the dance floor strut some daring stuff. She had his body tense, his cock engorged. A man only thought about one thing when he watched a woman dance like that, and it wasn't how concerned he should be with her safety. A man thought about sex when he watched her, and when he watched her dancing like a wanton, the need for sex overrode all else.

The song was a fast-paced rock version of a messed-up line dance, he guessed. The dance floor was packed with women and a few men, laughingly following the singer's direction. Hell if he had ever heard of the guy. Casper? Clint shook his head in disgust. Diva's had an interesting mix of music some nights. The point being to get the women on the dance floor. On display.

This music wasn't his thing, but Morganna was.

Unfortunately.

There she was, dressed in a little hip-hugger girls'-school skirt that barely covered her curvy little ass. Her ass nothing, the top of the skirt barely kept her decent. He swore if it dipped just a breath, then there would be no secrets left to bare between those pretty, shapely thighs.

The white tank top she wore might at first thought have been considered demure. On the rack it might have been decent. On Morganna, it was a crime. It barely reached her belly button, flashing an indecent amount of skin, not to mention that damned gold belly ring he didn't know she had. When the hell had she had her belly button pierced? Raven hadn't said anything about that, and his sister was usually a font of information where Morganna was concerned.

The top was thin; thankfully, it looked like she might be wearing a bra. He couldn't be sure from this distance. She wore a pair of black-and-white girl's shoes on her dainty feet but a pair of over-the-knee white stockings on her sexy legs. Those stockings were going to be the death of him. He could see her stretched out on his bed, her hands tied to the headboard with the silky hose while he stretched between her thighs and drove her crazy with his mouth. The image almost had him panting in anticipation. Oh yeah, he knew exactly how to use those stockings.

Long, long, nut-brown hair rippled down her back as she tilted her hips forward, placed one dainty foot in front of her, and shook her ass in a move that had a cold sweat popping up on his brow. His dick was ecstatic. If she could dance like that, then those sweet hips moving, rotating, thrusting, would play hell on a man's sanity in the bed.

And to top the entire outfit off was a thin black leather collar buckled around her neck.

Sweet God have mercy, Clint prayed silently as he watched her, his eyes narrowed, his muscles tense. And the truly frightening part was that she was actually having fun. He could see it in her face, in her exotically tilted laughing gray eyes. In the way she moved.

If she put half as much effort into fucking a man as she did into driving them crazy on that dance floor, then Clint was in trouble. Deep, deep doo-doo, as his dad once used to say.

As the song came to an end, she shook her head, causing that long skein of hair to ripple and sway again as the leather-clad man beside her lifted her in his arms and swung her around with a laugh.

If his hand had slipped down so much as a thought farther than it had toward her shapely ass, then he would have gone on the endangered-species list. Because Clint knew he would have tried to kill him.

She patted the man's shoulder, making a laughing comment as she turned away and headed back to the crowded table she had been sitting at. The chairs were taken, but rather than taking the offer one of the men made as he patted his knee, her hip bumped at one of the women, who moved over a few scant inches on her own, allowing Morganna to perch on the edge.

She crossed her legs as she leaned forward, listening to something the heavily Goth-dressed woman beside her was relating with an animated wave of her hands.

Clint wiped the sweat from his brow and took a deep, steadying breath. He felt as though he had run a marathon. His heart was pounding in his chest, blood pooling between his thighs, torturing his cock. And it was all Morganna's fault.

He glared back at her, not even bothering to rein in the crash of male irritation the thought brought. What the hell was she doing here? The women who came to Diva's knew the score, knew what they wanted, but even more, they knew what the men wanted. Sex. Wild, often extreme, sometimes not so sober, sex.

He shifted his shoulders, flexing the muscles in an effort to relax, at least marginally, to find the strength to pull his eyes from the sight of the leather-clad man who had embraced her moments ago, bending close to her, his hand lying intimately on her shoulder.

Clint had been standing there for over an hour, hiding in the dark corner, watching her, trying to watch those around her.

He had come there to find a woman to help relieve the dark restlessness growing in his gut since he had been home. And he had found the woman. Despite the objections his conscience threw out at him and against all common sense, he was going to take her.

From all appearances she knew the crowd she was running with well, which meant she had progressed past fairy tales and daydreams and into reality. He could fuck her and walk away, just as he had with every other woman he had taken to his bed. There would be no tears, no recriminations, no dreams of happily ever after.

Did she have a lover? He watched the men who seemed to flock around her like wolves. She wore a collar around her neck with no adornments, no leash. It meant here, within Diva's, she was unclaimed. No other Dom held her loyalty and no Dom could be penalized with the loss of membership by disappearing with her.

Clint watched the men around her. That didn't mean she didn't have a lover. Not that he cared at the moment. Not that he would care later.

She didn't seem to pay attention to one man more than the other, and as she ordered a drink from the waitress, Clint could have sworn he caught a glimpse of weariness in Morganna's face.

He grimaced at his overactive imagination. Morganna had been a social butterfly even before she came of age. She was one of those women perfectly at home in the middle of a crowd, finding her sense of purpose in the number of so-called friends she could gather around her at any one time. It shouldn't have surprised him that she had stepped into this lifestyle. The fact that it did caused a moment's worry.

It was driving him crazy, watching the men who were drawn to her like flies to honey, their hands touching her bare shoulder, her satiny arm, trying to feel that ribbon of silk she called her hair.

For eight years he had fought to stay away from her, to keep from sinking into that sweet, curvy body and destroying both of them. The two years before she turned eighteen didn't count. Seeing her as a woman and reacting to her as a woman, as he had just after she turned eighteen, were two different things.

He had convinced himself she was innocent, too soft for his sexuality, too gentle for a dead-end relationship. Because Clint had learned years ago, at the brutality of his father's fists and his mother's faithlessness, that happy ever afters just didn't exist.

And he didn't want to hurt Morganna. He had no desire to break her tender heart or to see her soft gray eyes fill with tears. But if she was here, enmeshed in the seedy sexuality of the club scene, then she surely knew the score.

He could have her. Just once. Maybe twice. And he could walk away without risking his soul.

He set his jaw in determination as he straightened from the wall and began moving toward her. The crowd parted before him. In a room of male Dom wannabes, Clint knew he stood out in the crowd. He wasn't a wannabe. He was strong enough to take what he wanted and make it stick. The crowd here knew him, understood him.

He shrugged away the feminine hands that reached out as he passed by them. Women he had known in the past or those who had wanted a ride. He knew them, too. They craved the adventure, the excitement, the dark, carnal excesses that could only be found with a certain type man. He had a reputation for being just such a man. As Morganna was soon to find out.

ORGANNA STILLED HER IMPATIENCE, THE instinctive irritation at having so many people around her, so many men trying to touch. You'd think they'd never touched a woman before. Sweaty hands running over her hair, her arm, and even worse were the ones who thought they could start at her knee and she would never notice their hands attempting to slide to her thigh and beyond.

Twits. She gripped the wrist of yet another, glancing up at him as she attempted a polite smile.

"I just washed," she informed him with what she hoped was a decent facsimile of a smile.

A husky chuckle sounded in her ear before the bozo gripped the curve of her shoulder and arm and squeezed intimately. As though she knew him.

Thankfully, the waitress chose that moment to arrive with their drinks, forcing him to move.

Twit.

Morganna took the soda she had ordered, sipping at it gratefully as the band shot into a dark, primal number that sent the energy level in the room pulsing. Lowering her glass but keeping it in her hand, she stared around casually, paying particular attention to the tables around them.

She couldn't see her mark. She had glimpsed him earlier as he made his way across the room, a short Latino in black leather, his hand casually gripping a short dog chain. She knew what he was looking for. A woman who would allow him to leash her, to dominate her. He was also suspected to be one of the men involved in the drugging and kidnapping of six women who had turned up dead in the area. The new date rape drug was rumored to be under strict control until the suppliers could determine its worth on the streets. It was making them a fortune in the pornographic rape videos they were making; that was a certainty.

Morganna suspected this man was the supplier whom the two men Joe Merino and his teams had arrested last week had refused to name. Adonis Santos had also been arrested last week when Morganna witnessed him tapping the powdered drug into a young woman's drink as two of his friends kept her occupied. The arrests of the three men had been a major break in the case Morganna had been assigned to in her first assignment with the Atlanta division of the DEA.

"Hey, Morg, we need to hit this song." Jenna Lancaster, a secretary from the office Morganna worked at, bounded from her seat when another teeth-jarring set began.

Morganna lifted her drink as she shook her head firmly. Hell no. She was out for a while. She hit the glass for another long swallow, wondering at the tingling at the back of her neck. Reaching back, she rubbed at the skin beneath her hair, looking around casually, wondering why she was suddenly so uncomfortable.

She drained the soda, setting the glass on the table as it began to vacate, nominally, as the crowd moved for the floor.

Pulling her hair over her shoulder, she sighed in relief at the brush of a breeze over her nape.

"Another drink, Morganna?" Sandoval Mitchell watched her with dark eyes, his expression somber, watchful. He was like that. Always so serious it made her wonder why he even came here. He didn't dance much, rarely flirted. He just seemed to enjoy being on the outskirts of the crowd, always watching.

Morganna knew most of the people gathered around her. It would be the same no matter which club she hit in town. Most were regulars, and some were even harmless. But mixed in were a few deadly individuals intent on destroying lives. It was the deadly Morganna was looking for.

"No, thank you, Sandy." She smiled back at him warmly as she leaned back in the chair, taking the seat Jenna had vacated. "I think I'm good for the night."

His dark eyes flashed with disappointment. He was kind of cute, in an immature way. He was a player here, not really into the scene in any serious way. He dressed the part with the black leather pants, leather vest, and boots but just didn't quite pull it off.

"Would you like to dance?" The request was made with

charming politeness. He was one of the few men there who wasn't a wolf.

As she opened her lips to speak, she froze, staring over Sandy's shoulder in shock and amazement. It couldn't be Clint.

She watched as the tall, broad body moved through the crowd, wide shoulders displayed perfectly in the snug black T-shirt he wore, the muscles of his arms bulging, the tight, hard abs flexing. Long, muscular legs ate up the distance, encased in snug denim, cupping a bulge that drove her imagination wild and made her mouth water.

His black hair was longer than it had been last time she saw him, but it was still fairly short, brushed back from his face and emphasizing the strong, fierce features that had haunted so many of her nights. And his eyes. Deep, almost black, a midnight blue that made her heart beat faster, made her hungry in a way no other man could.

What the hell was he doing here?

She had no intention of waiting around to find out. There were a few things that Clint didn't know about her life, and Morganna found that she liked it that way. It kept her life running much smoother and without the hassle of worrying about him poking his nose into a career choice that had turned out to be exactly what she was looking for.

Moving quickly to her feet, Morganna headed in the opposite direction, hoping to make it to the ladies' room before he caught sight of her or caught her. She wasn't stupid; he was coming for her and she knew it. She could feel it.

She pushed through the throng, glancing behind her and feeling a start of apprehension sear her chest at the intent, primal expression on his face. Yep, he was after her, and he was gaining on her fast. Too fast.

She pushed harder at the bodies blocking her way, weaving her way through the crowd as she fought to get to the bathroom. Once she was there it would be simple to send out an SOS to her backup and get Clint off her back. She couldn't risk it now, not while she could be seen, heard.

The primal beat of the music emphasized the pounding of her heart as she glanced behind her again. He was closer, stalking her, his expression intent, carnal. Dangerous.

She broke through the mass of bodies and streaked toward the long hallway that led to the bathrooms as well as the private rooms reserved for sexual play. Too bad she hadn't thought to reserve one; she could have locked herself in. But the bathroom was just ahead, the small neon light clearly lit over the doorway.

Her hand touched the door as she went to lean her weight into opening it, but hard hands gripped her hips, nearly picked her up from the floor, and began to propel her forward.

"You should have headed for the exit," Clint said into her ear. "You might have actually escaped then. What the hell are you doing here?"

Shock held her speechless as he paused at one of the private rooms, swiped a card through the security lock, and propelled her through the open door.

It wasn't a bedroom; there was no sleeping done here. This was a sex room.

A large box bed sat in the middle of the room. There were shelves of sex toys, a wall hung with small whips and quirts. Manacles hung from the wall over the bed and chains with leather straps led from the floor at each corner of the bed.

And Clint had a key to it. Which meant he knew what the hell went on in here. Even more, this was his personal room, reserved for him alone. He would have placed the toys here, the manacles, the accoutrements of the erotic and extreme.

Shock plunged through her body. She had known he was dominant, highly sexual. But she had never suspected this.

"Fancy seeing you here." She swung around, opening her eyes guilelessly as she stared back at him, fighting to calm her racing heart. "And you're not wearing leather, either. Aren't you breaking some kind of unwritten Dom rule?"

He stared back at her. Morganna fought to keep her expression a bit mocking, rather than slack with amazement. And here she had thought she knew everything there was to know about her best friend's brother.

"Is that look a permanent part of your expression? I don't think I've seen a change in years," she accused him lightly when he didn't speak. "Most people try for a little variety sometimes, you know?"

"Is complete insanity a part of your personality?" he asked in turn. "I'm starting to think I should have let Reno tan your backside when he caught you slipping from your bedroom window years ago."

Morganna rolled her eyes and fought to keep from showing her nervousness. "Reno wasn't going to 'tan my backside' then any more than he would now. He was all bluff."

His lips tightened. Clint wasn't all bluff, and she knew it.

"You need to be spanked," he growled, shooting her a brooding look as he strode to the small bar.

She stared around the room again. "Well, if punishment were my thing, then you would be the man to come to. Tell me, do you really use this stuff?"

He glanced over his shoulder, his gaze moving to the toys and sexual paraphernalia.

"Sometimes." He shrugged. "Some subs almost require it."

She raised her brows. "Does it turn you on?"

His gaze flickered as it returned to her. "Would you like to find out?"

It didn't turn him on. She could see it in his eyes, in his voice. Sometimes she knew Clint better than she knew herself. And she knew the look in his eyes as he answered her. A look of wary regret.

"I think I'll pass tonight." She smiled back. But when he turned away from her, Morganna jumped for the door. The knob wouldn't turn.

"You need a key," he informed her calmly as he poured a drink before turning back to her.

Damn, he looked like a Dom. Brooding sexuality swirled around him as he lifted the short glass to his lips and tipped it back. When he lowered it again, his blue eyes seemed to burn into her.

"I asked you a question. Answer me."

She crossed her arms beneath her breasts as she faced him challengingly. "What do you think I'm doing here, Clint? It's a club, isn't it?"

His jaw bunched before he brought the glass to his lips again and finished the drink. He looked even less pleased than normal. But he did look sexy. Hell, he always looked sexy.

"You know what kind of club it is." His voice was hard, dark. The hunger slipping into it had her nipples peaking beneath her top, the flesh between her thighs moistening

"So I do." She fought to control her breathing, as well as her reaction to him.

She knew exactly what kind of club it was and she knew the type of men who reserved those rooms. Realizing that Clint was one of those men had both fear and excitement racing through her.

"So I'm asking you again. What are you doing here?"

She had never heard that tone of voice before from him. Rasping, filled with lust. It shook her to her core. "Now, Clint, why do you think I'm here?" She cocked her hip and propped her hand on it, watching his eyes flare and loving the response. This was a side of him she had never seen. A side that fascinated her, drew her. Shocked her.

"That's what I was asking you," he finally snapped. "Honestly, Morganna, I can't come up with a single reason why you would be here."

"Of course not—you're too busy trying to convince yourself I'm complexly nonsexual and therefore unthreatening." She shrugged. "I'm not responsible for your self-delusions."

Daring him was never a good idea, but she couldn't seem to help herself. Some imp of self-destruction was lodged in her brain and playing hell with her sense of self-preservation.

He set the glass on the bar then, and before her stunned gaze he sat down in the plush chair beside it and stared back at her.

His expression was so filled with lust, with carnal knowledge, that the fires burning in her body since she first caught sight of him began to flame higher.

"Sexual, are you?" He flashed her a hard look. "Since when?"

"I don't kiss and tell," she informed him with a polite smile. "A girl needs to have a little mystery, Clint."

His blue eyes gleamed in assessment. Oh, now that look was interesting. If a little scary.

God, why hadn't she known this about him?

"Come over here."

His voice was lower, darker, suggestive. His tall frame slouched in the chair, his legs splayed out before him as he stared back at her with that brooding, hot look. So hot it made her flush, made her breathe in nervously as she gathered her courage and stepped closer.

"Closer." He lifted a hand from the chair arm, his fingers beckoning her closer.

"Why?" She didn't trust this new Clint in any way whatsoever.

"So I can show you why little girls shouldn't play grownup games," he growled. "Come on, Morganna; show me how grown-up you think you are."

Chapter 2

MORGANNA FELT HER HEART RACING, a fine sweat breaking out over her skin. She hadn't expected this from Clint, not in a million years. In her deepest fantasies, he played a lot of little sex games with her, but she had to admit, she would have never expected the dominant, forceful imaginings to meet with reality.

"This isn't a good idea." She fought to breathe, to push the words past the constriction in her throat and the arousal pulsing through her.

"We're agreed." His eyes narrowed further. "Don't make me come and get you, Morganna. Come here now."

Come here now. The rough demand sent her senses careening.

As she tensed to move, a soft voice sounded in her ear, interrupting the sensual spell building in her head.

"Do you need backup?"

Agent Joe Merino and his team was her backup. A crack four-man DEA unit that she had worked with for the past six months. She was the bait on this assignment. Something that it really wouldn't be a good idea to let Clint know. And Merino was listening to every word said.

"No." She kept her voice firm as she stared back at Clint, a hint of defiance in her face. She could feel a flush building in her face at the thought of the ears listening.

Clint couldn't see the small receiver in her ear, but that didn't mean she was safe. It wouldn't take a genius to realize what it was if he got close enough, and he was intent on getting real damned close. She could see it in his eyes, in his expression; she could feel it in the hunger building in her own body.

Clint quirked his lips, certain she was talking to him. And perhaps in a way she was. The eroticism of the room, the sheer disbelief that she was in it with him, blew her mind. Clint was a Dom? It was almost too much to believe. And she had been defying him for as long as she could remember, challenging him, daring him to take what she had always sensed he desired. She just had no idea how intent he could become on what he wanted.

"I couldn't believe it when I saw you out on that dance floor," he murmured, his gaze going over her slowly, sending flames licking over her body wherever he touched. "Dressed like a man's greatest sexual fantasy, an innocent little schoolgirl, ready and willing to be used. Scared now, little girl?"

More than he knew.

"Perhaps uninterested," she answered instead. "I didn't accept an invitation into this room, Clint. You pushed me into it. I believe that's against the rules."

She heard Merino curse in her ear. He knew Clint, and he knew the whole operation was at risk now. Just as she did. How she played this out could mean the difference between success and failure.

And she couldn't forget Merino was listening. She was frantic to get out of the room before Clint actually touched her. He had the ability to make her mindless. Good God, she couldn't afford to be mindless while Joe and his entire team were listening. She would never live it down.

She stepped back from Clint then, turning to allow her gaze to rove over the small room. She had to get out of there, fast. All Clint would have to do was touch her and she would be putty in his hands.

"Morganna, you're playing a very dangerous game with the wrong man," Merino hissed in her ear. As though she didn't already know that.

"Morganna, don't play with me. You won't like the consequences," Clint's voice overrode Merino's as Morganna bit her lip at the insanity of the situation.

She turned at the bottom of the bed, facing Clint once again. "Unlock the door."

"No."

Her heart raced at the answer, at the brooding carnality of his expression.

Morganna licked her lips nervously. There was no way to get rid of the receiver at her ear.

"Why?" She barely managed to keep her voice firm, to keep herself from stuttering with shock and nerves.

"Because I'm going to lay you back on that bed and show you exactly what you're asking for by being at this club. Then I'm going to paddle that pretty little ass for giving me the chance." His answer shocked her, but her body's response shocked her more.

"And should I cry 'Daddy' or 'Uncle' while you try?" She arched her brow mockingly.

"'Master' will work," he growled. Master? Oh, she so didn't think so. Taking the clothes off? She would have loved to. Under different circumstances, of course.

"This is getting out of control. I'm sending Craig in, Morganna. He'll get you out. Just play along with it."

Shit. Shit. This was going to get ugly. She had to get out of there before Craig showed up.

"Unlock the door, Clint," she ordered, frantically fighting for a way out of the situation. Damn her luck, it was starting to suck fast. "I'm not in the mood for you or your games tonight."

He rose from the chair, six feet, four inches of sheer male muscle, primal animal, and began to stalk toward her. There was no place to run. No way to evade him. And her legs didn't want to move anyway. She could feel her body tensing, preparing for him, anticipating his touch.

Craig Tyler would be here in a minute. The burly ex-Marine could play the outraged Dom like nobody's business. Clint wasn't a man to attempt to poach on another's territory. At least, not staked territory. Her collar proclaimed her a free agent, an unrestrained submissive, free to choose a Dom. Craig's cover of the Dom attempting to acquire her wasn't going to work here.

"Do you know how long I've been dying to fuck you?" Clint stopped before her, his hands settling on her bare hips as she stared back at him in shock. Her hands gripped his forearms as the heat of his fingers sank into her flesh.

"Well, you sure could have fooled me," she gasped. "You are the same man who has run from me at every opportunity. Right?"

She hadn't expected this, couldn't believe she was standing here with him, his eyes burning down at her rather than freezing her with dismissal.

"I can have you now, can't I, baby?" he whispered, his voice immeasurably gentle as he watched her. "You're learning the rules of the game. Happily ever afters don't happen here."

A wave of pain suffused her senses as his whispered words processed in her brain. He hadn't taken her before because he had known what she wanted? Because he knew she loved him? But he could take her now because he thought she was a whore? He thought she was available to any bozo willing to give her the fix he thought she was looking for?

She stared back at him in shock as her hand flew toward his face in a violence she hadn't known she was capable of. He caught her hand. Inches from his face, his gaze igniting as she glared back at him.

"I don't want you now," she said, fighting the tears that threatened to flood her eyes. "Not even on a bet." She jerked at her arm, enraged by his arrogance. "You're a jerk, Clint. A complete vicious, dirty jerk."

Surprise flickered across his expression as he let her go. "If you're not part of the scene, then what the hell are you doing here?" His eyes narrowed on her as she stilled before him.

"Who says I'm not part of the scene?" she bit out. "I said

I didn't want *you.* Sorry, Clint, but just any Dom willing to play the game isn't enough," she informed him rashly, furious, using the only weapon she had left now. "You had your chance how many times over the past few years? You turned them down. Remember?"

"And now I'm picking them up."

Morganna's eyes widened and she felt fear slam into her as he reached for her. If he touched her, if he did as the hunger in his gaze warned her he was going to do, then she was screwed. She had fought to get on Joe's team, pulling every string she could think of to work this assignment.

If she showed a weakness now, then Joe would have her replaced so fast it would make her head spin. He hadn't been comfortable with her on the team to begin with. But she was the only recruit he had who was a regular at the Masters clubs.

"Clint, no." "No" meant no.

He paused, his eyes narrowed, his chest heaving, as she backed away from him slowly.

"Unlock the door and let me out of here. Don't force me to lodge a complaint with Masters."

Drage Masters, the owner of the club, did not take kindly to patrons forcing anything from the members. His rules were strict, and everyone knew it.

"Lodge all the complaints you want," Clint said. "I want answers, Morganna, and one way or the other, I am going to get them."

He took a step closer and Morganna knew the game was up.

"Morganna Chavez, I'm going to whip your ass red," a drunken voice yelled from the other side of the door. "Open this door, you little wildcat. I told you no other men until we've settled our deal. Period."

Her eyes widened in shock as she watched rage transform Clint's features. It wasn't just anger; it was a killing rage that terrified her.

"Open this door!" Craig yelled, pounding at the metal panel again. "Did you think I wouldn't find you?"

Oh God. Wrong move. Surely they knew better than this: Merino couldn't be so insane as to send one of his best men in like this, at this moment. It was like sending a baby into a war zone. Clint was going to mow right through him.

"He's dead." Clint's voice vibrated with wrath as he pushed her aside and headed for the door.

"Clint, wait!" Morganna cried out as he swiped the card through the lock and jerked the door open.

His hand latched onto Craig's throat before Morganna could yell out in warning, pushing him across the hall and slamming him into the wall.

Years of backbreaking training and SEAL maneuvers had hardened Clint's body, turning it into a living weapon of mass destruction when needed.

"Back off!" Clint snarled into Craig's amazed expression.

The DEA agent was decked out in an overabundance of leather and chains that sang in an unholy jangle as Clint seemed to shake him without effort.

"Clint, dammit, let him go!" Morganna grabbed Clint's arm, her nails biting into his forearm as Craig's body tensed to fight.

"Get back, Morganna, before I rip your pansy-assed boyfriend in half," Clint snapped.

"You're crazy!" she yelled, attempting to shake him loose. "Let him go."

"Is this how you get your jollies?" he snarled back at her. "Does Reno know where you go for fun, Morganna?"

The threat. There it was. That familiar warning that assured her Reno was going to get a phone call.

"I don't know; does he know how you have your fun?" she sneered back. "Go ahead and rat me out like you always do and I'll tell him what you had in mind for me before you were interrupted. Now let him go." She slapped at Clint's arm, furious, terrified. Craig was starting to turn blue.

Clint jerked his arm away, turning back to her, the primal danger she glimpsed in his eyes taking her breath. It wasn't violence; it was lust. Pure, hot, unadulterated lust.

"Get out of here." His voice was hoarse, his hands balling into fists as he faced her. "Get out of this club and get your ass home. Now. Right now, Morganna, or God help us both if I get my hands on you again."

She jumped back, watching as Craig quickly moved around him. Craig's hazel eyes were concerned, his wavy hair disheveled, as he gripped her arm and began pulling her backward down the hallway.

She stared back at Clint and knew it wasn't over. Not by a long shot. The look in his eyes promised her he would come after her. Soon.

"Move it, girl," Craig muttered as he dragged her behind him. "Merino is having fits in the van. This has fucked the entire night up."

No shit. Morganna turned and followed him through the throng of dancers, nearly stumbling more than once as she fought to make her limbs cooperate. She could still feel Clint's touch, still ached for his kiss. She wanted to look back, see if he was following, but she knew he was. She could feel him.

"He's behind us," she informed Craig as they moved through the front door.

"Tough," Craig growled as the warm night air washed over them, the sultry South Carolina heat reminding her of Clint's touch. "Get in your car and head home. We'll meet up with you at the house later."

"You can't do that," she snapped as they moved into the parking lot. "I'm telling you, he's going to follow me to the house; he'll have a fit. You've got to give me time to explain."

"You get out of here; Merino will take care of the SEAL."

Morganna turned on Craig. She jerked her arm away from him before slamming her hands into his chest and pushing him back.

"I said no," she repeated furiously, aware that Clint would be turning the corner into the parking lot at any minute. "I'll come in tomorrow and that's final. Merino can wait on me this time."

This was too important to allow male ego and pride to suddenly mess it up. If Clint found out what she was doing, he would fly to Hawaii himself to tell Reno all about it. Clint had always been a damned tattletale, ratting her out every chance he got. There was no way he would let this pass. And once he did tell, Reno would hit the roof.

What made her think she could keep this from her brother or Clint, she had no idea.

"Don't mess this up, Morganna," Craig hissed as he checked the parking lot for curious ears. "You know what's at stake."

"Then don't you mess it up." Her furious whisper was followed by her finger poking into his chest as she turned on him. "I told you when we'll meet and that's it. Because trust me when I tell you blood will be shed if he finds you at the house tonight. And it won't be his."

She didn't wait for an answer. She turned away from Craig stiffly, moving across the driveway and heading for her car. She turned to glare back at him, barely catching the sudden alarm on his expression before she heard the squeal of tires.

Morganna turned, blinded by a sudden light flaring in front of her eyes as her ears filled with the screech of tires and the sudden awareness of danger.

She heard Clint scream her name a second before something, somebody, hooked her around the waist and slammed her through the air. Gunfire echoed around her. It had to be gunfire, blazing across her senses as time slowed, inching by as she felt herself falling, aware of the hard pavement that would meet the end of her journey.

A thousand thoughts blazed through her mind; uppermost was the fact that it was Clint's arm hooked around her waist, then Clint's hard body bracing hers as they hit the ground and rolled. She could hear his curses in her ear, explicit, enraged, as he took the brunt of the impact before rolling her beneath his body. One hand cupped the side of her head as the ping of bullets pelted around them.

She could hear car alarms shrieking now as shattered glass rained over her. Clint was using his larger body to shield her, holding her in place as she fought to escape the bullets, to get him out of the line of fire.

"Move it!" He lifted her to her feet and with a surge of motion dragged her between the nearby cars, pressing her into the side of the nearest vehicle as sparks flew from the pavement.

The sound of gunfire filled the night again as he grabbed her around the waist and forced her into a ducking run to avoid the bullets firing toward them.

"Son of a bitch!" he cursed as he rushed her deeper into the line of cars and farther from the vehicle now tearing from the parking lot. "Damn it to hell, Morganna, what are you mixed up in?"

Tires screamed in the distance as the sound of frightened cries echoed from behind them and male curses raged around her. She couldn't tell if it was Merino or Clint. Or maybe both.

Chapter 3

"WHAT THE HELL IS GOING ON?" Clint's voice had Morganna flinching at the pure, undiluted rage that filled it as he pushed her into his apartment, slamming the door closed.

He hadn't waited around at the club for the police to arrive. He had pulled her straight to his truck, unlocked the driver's side door, and stuffed her in before crowding in beside her.

The drive to his apartment had been quick and short. Morganna had kept her mouth shut, using the time to come up with an explanation. She was in trouble and she knew it. Clint wasn't stupid, and he wasn't a man known for his patience.

"You're asking me?" She still hadn't come up with an explanation as she faced him, opening her eyes wide. She didn't have to force the fear that she was certain shadowed her expression. "Ask the bozo who was shooting at us."

Clint stalked to her, one hand jerking out to push through her hair and lift it, revealing a damning piece of evidence. The receiver she had worn in her ear earlier.

Before she could stop herself her hand flew to her ear. Yep, it was hers. The betraying action had his deep blue eyes burning with renewed rage as his teeth bared in a snarl.

"Oh yes, baby, it's yours." His voice was hoarse with his anger now. "What the hell are you doing with it?"

Morganna licked her lips nervously. She had never seen Clint so angry. His eyes burned with it, his arrogant, sharp features tight with it. The harshly defined cheekbones stood out clearly as his lips tightened to a harsh line.

"Get off!" She slapped her hands into his hard chest, desperate to get him away from her now. He loomed over her like an angel of retribution and sent her heart racing with trepidation. And arousal. She hated how aroused she was, hated knowing that despite the past few years, despite her fight to forget him, to get over him, he could still affect her. Even when he was this damned mad.

Morganna gasped as he threw the receiver with a vicious movement. "What are you doing with it, Morganna? Don't play me for a damned fool here. I almost watched you die before my eyes. Do think I enjoyed it?"

The emotion blazing in his eyes shocked her. They were dark, tortured, his expression a furious grimace as he stared back at her.

"I can't imagine it would cause you a sleepless night," she yelled back at him, tugging at the hold he had on her hair. "Now let go of me."

He was breathing as hard as she was. "Not on your life, sweetheart. By God, you'll answer me or you'll answer to Reno. Take your choice."

"I don't answer to either one of you." She was panting with her own anger now. Anger and arousal. The anger she could understand; the arousal infuriated her.

She watched his eyes widen at her response.

"There is where you are so wrong." This was more nerve-wracking than being shot at. Clint looked ready to commit murder.

"Oh my God, you have so lost it." She pushed at his chest; unfortunately, it was like shoving at a boulder. "Who the hell do you think you are? What I do is none of your business. And how do you know the bastard playing with guns wasn't after you? I could see someone wanting to kill you. I fantasize about it often." She glared back at him, anger surging through her system.

"Answers, Morganna. Now."

She hated it when he got like this. When he decided he was the law, that she was answerable to him just because that was what he decided.

"I have no answers for you, Clint. Even if you did deserve them. Which you don't." She kept her voice low, despite her anger, despite the fact that she had intended to attempt to explain things to him earlier. The look on his face assured her that no explanations were going to help. There was the potential of making things worse.

She lifted her chin defiantly, refusing to back down, even as she refused to admit that his rage sparked more than just her answering anger.

But it wasn't just rage. For the first time, she saw emotion. It shadowed his eyes, roughened his voice, and she had to tamp back the hope flaring inside her at the evidence that somehow he might very well care for her.

"Why doesn't this surprise me?" he shouted to no one in particular as he jerked away from her, his dark glower causing her to watch him with wary suspicion. "Why, Morganna, doesn't it surprise me that you're doing something stupid?"

"Stupid?" She stared back at him incredulously. "Excuse me, Clint? What do you do for a living here? I was just having a good night at a nice little club. Honestly, I'm beginning to suspect that car was after you. What did you do, manhandle the wrong woman?"

He snarled as he cast her a fulminating look, his eyes burning with anger. "I knew you were up to something. I told Reno last year you were up to something. You've been acting sneaky as hell for years now."

"You are so paranoid." She jutted her hip and braced her hand on the bare flesh with a mocking laugh. "Really. Just because I'm not chasing after you day and night anymore doesn't mean I'm up to something."

God was going to get her for that lie. The day she had stopped watching the door for him, had decided to get a life, it was as though he had known. But instead of accepting what she felt for him, he had automatically assumed she was up to something.

And perhaps she was. She had a life. A productive one. One that gave her purpose.

He turned on her, crossing his arms over his chest, narrowing his eyes as they went over her body. And she didn't look bad; she knew she didn't. She had worked hard over the last four years to make certain her body was in peak shape, that the clothes she wore enhanced her figure, and that the makeup enhanced her role. Though she was pretty certain the makeup had worn off when he'd pushed her face into the truck seat earlier.

"What were you doing at Diva's?" he demanded. "Dressed like that and flashing your body to every damned pervert there? And don't lie to me, Morganna. I have friends there. I'll find out the truth."

Now why didn't that surprise her?

"So asks the man that owns his own private room," she snorted. "Clint, I know exactly how much those rooms cost per year. And it's more than obvious you use it. Does that make you a pervert as well?" She arched her brow mockingly.

"The worst kind."

Her breath slammed from her throat as his gaze became more intent, touching over the flesh bared by her clothing, reminding her of his touch, the dominance in his kiss.

"Well, at least you're honest," she breathed out. "Now, if you'll be so kind as to call me a cab . . ."

"Explain the receiver." Cold fury filled his lowered voice. He was no longer pissed; now he was dangerous.

She arched her brow.

"I'll track it to the other side, Morganna. I'll find out who's on the other end and I'll start by questioning that leather-toting Dom wannabe first. You want to see his pretty face messed up?"

Could Craig take him in a fight? Morganna knew in a heartbeat he couldn't. Clint had nearly killed him in the hallway earlier.

She lifted her chin defiantly.

"I don't owe you explanations, Clint. I don't owe you anything. Now I'm ready to go home."

"Now isn't that just too bad," he drawled, his expression shifting, lust mixing with the anger as he continued to watch her. "You know, Morganna, I have that room there for a reason. I don't know who you think you're playing with, but it's not a fake Dom willing to let you play your little games. Is that what you were hoping for? That this game you're playing would get you into my bed?"

No. She didn't. But the subtle throb of arousal in his voice had her sex clenching in response, her juices gathering, weeping from her aching vagina.

This was a part of Clint she had never seen before. A part that filled her with trepidation and excitement.

"And who says I'm going to end up in your bed?" She tried to forget how much she wanted to be there.

Every cell in her body was throbbing in need. She remembered his kiss. One brief, possessive melding of lips when she had been eighteen and he was twenty-seven. His hands had held her to him, his lips had possessed her, and she had never forgotten it. Now, ten years later, she still remembered. She wanted his lips on her again, anywhere, everywhere.

"Oh, you're going to end up there," he assured her smoothly. Morganna swallowed tightly.

"Why now?" She had ached for him for years. Done everything she could think of to make him see her, make him want her. And now, when she had given up, he wanted to play sex games. Talk about lousy damned timing.

The tight smile that creased his lips wasn't comforting.

"If I had known the games you liked, Morganna, I wouldn't have denied myself. The submissive scene doesn't cater to happily ever afters, does it, baby? Maybe you're not the starry-eyed little dreamer I thought you were. There's no room in my life for dreamers. Just the sex. And that I can give you plenty of."

Her heart wasn't breaking, Morganna assured herself as she stared back at him. The pain splintering her soul wasn't the result of the cold, unemotional declaration he had just made.

"And you think all I want is the sex?" she asked him, fighting to cover her pain as she watched him with a bitterness she knew she couldn't hide.

For a moment, compassion flashed in his eyes.

"You're young," he said. "You think the nasty little games you're involved in have something to do with your heart? That hunger inside you is a search for love? It's not." He dropped his arms from his chest and paced closer, wrapping her in his warmth and his own bitterness. "Don't make that mistake," he whispered as he moved behind her, his chest pressing against her back as he lifted his hands to draw her hair back from her neck.

"Forget it." She jerked from him again, pacing several feet away from him before turning back to face him. "It doesn't work that way, Clint. If you didn't notice earlier, I already have a lover. Why would I need you?"

Craig wasn't her lover. It was a role they played, nothing more.

Clint laughed at her declaration. "He's never touched you." He shook his head knowingly. "He's never tied you down and driven you crazy with his touch. He's never spanked that tight little ass or fucked it. I'd bet my life on it."

Morganna felt her face flame, first with embarrassment, then with a need that bordered on violence. The image of her strapped to the bed in that room as Clint did all those things to her had her nearly climaxing in anticipation.

"God, your nipples just spiked beneath that shirt you're wearing," he said, staring. "You want it, baby. And you'll get it. But I'll get what I want first."

"Not in this lifetime," she snapped, turning and heading for the door. "Take your threats and shove them—"

She made it to the door; her hand even gripped the knob a

second before a hard, forceful body pinned her against the metal panel. Her breath slammed from her chest at the feel of his erection pressing into her lower back, the sound of his breathing, hard and rough at her ear.

"You think you're just going to walk out of here?" His hands gripped her wrists, forcing them above her head until he could grip both with his long fingers.

"Stop this, Clint."

"Not on your life, Morganna," his voice rumbled at her ear a second before his teeth gripped the lobe with a heated little nip.

What his teeth were doing was nothing compared to where his other hand had moved. To her thigh. He was pushing her skirt above her legs, his palm sliding over sensitive flesh until it cupped the hot, damp core weeping with need.

"Damn, you're soaking wet." His voice was almost a groan as she whimpered, pressing her head into the door and fighting for control. "You like to push me, don't you? How many years have you been doing this, Morganna? Pushing me, growing wet and hot every time we've fought? Almost as wet as I am hard. You've been making my dick hard for nearly ten years now."

His fingers were burrowing beneath the elastic of her panties, uncaring when it snapped from the force. Morganna didn't care, either. Using one foot between hers, he forced her legs wider as his fingers moved to the saturated folds of flesh he found there.

Bare, smooth, recently waxed, every sensitive cell of her flesh shouted in pleasure as his fingers ran through the narrow slit, circled her swollen clit, then slid back to the aching entrance of her vagina.

She arched against him, frantic now as pleasure seared her nerve endings. It would take so little to bring release, a release that she knew for a while would ease the aching knot of hunger that burned for him.

"So sweet and hot," he whispered, his mouth moving to

the sensitive cord of her neck as his fingers massaged the small opening, encouraging the wet heat to flow harder from her core. "I bet you could come so easy for me, couldn't you, baby? One hard thrust inside that tight little pussy and you'd explode like the Fourth of July. Do you want to explode, sweetheart?"

She did. Oh God, she did. She needed to. If she didn't, she was going to die. She panted in anticipation as she felt his fingers move again, felt the touch of not one fingertip against her entrance but two. Oh yes, she was going to come so hard. Just one thrust. One hard, searing thrust and the hunger would be quenched.

But he didn't thrust hard. He eased in. Morganna heard her own shattered cry as she felt the slow, heated stretching of her pussy, felt his fingers working into her with practiced, diabolical skill.

"God, you feel like silk. Hot, slick silk, Morganna."

He continued to ease inside, filling her, burning her, driving the heat higher, hotter, but never stilling the flames.

"Please . . ." She couldn't still the weak plea as he filled her, felt his fingers crooking a second before he began to rub that spot she could never seem to effectively manipulate.

But he was. With just the calloused pad of his fingertip he was sending blistering shards of nearing rapture to shoot through her nerve endings.

"You're so close, Morganna," he whispered. "I'm going to have you in my bed, those pretty thighs spread and my cock stretching you more."

His fingers were wicked. Carnal. Destructive.

He slid them back, nearly pulling free before he moved inside her again. The same steady, slow entrance, the same diabolical caress when they reached the depths of her vagina.

She was shaking, shuddering with need now. Lust was a demon devouring her mind, the need to orgasm so pervasive, so imperative, now that she knew she was fighting a losing battle.

"I can feel you rippling around my fingers, milking them. Wouldn't it feel so good, Morganna? Climaxing for me? Filling my hand with your sweet warmth?"

"Not fair. . . ." She was reaching blindly for that release, so close, so desperate for it that she felt as though she would shatter without it.

"No. Not fair is seeing you nearly run down by that car." Rage filled his voice as his body pressed her harder into the door. "Not fair is feeling those bullets pelt around you, knowing you could die." His fingers jerked inside her, as though he couldn't resist thrusting, just a little, almost enough.

Enough to have her crying out, arching to her tiptoes, then falling back, fighting desperately to find that final sensation needed to pitch her over the edge.

"You almost died in front of my eyes, damn you," he snarled before his teeth raked over her neck, his fingers flexing inside her. "For God's sake, Morganna, why?"

She opened her mouth to speak, to spill every secret she had been trusted with. The information couldn't be bought, but, oh God, it could be had. As she was drawing in the breath to confide every morsel of information, a hard knock vibrated against her cheek with enough force to shock her.

Clint stilled behind her as the knock came again, harder this time.

"If that's your leather-clad Lothario, I'm going to kill him."

She whimpered as Clint's fingers slid from the aching depths of her pussy and he pulled her back as he stepped aside. He didn't give her time to recover, didn't give her the option to leave the room. He looked through the peephole as he released Morganna, pushing her slowly behind him as she stumbled, fighting to regain her balance, cursed, then swung the door open to face the four plainclothes DEA agents she worked with.

Joe Merino was no one's fool. She saw the knowledge of what had been going on behind the door narrow his eyes as Craig's muttered curse echoed behind him.

Joe flipped open the small wallet that carried his badge and identification. The DEA seal was clear, as were the others who stood around him.

"Clint, we need to talk." Joe's gaze flickered to Morganna before a tight smile curved his rough face. "If you don't mind."

"Well, well, well," Clint drawled, glancing at her over his shoulder. "It looks like your cavalry is here. Do you think they'll have my answers?"

CLINT WAS MORE FURIOUS THAN he could remember ever being in his life. And there were times he had been damned mad. It wasn't bad enough that he had learned the innocence that shone so bright in her eyes was false. No woman who embraced the submissive lifestyle could claim the degree of sexual innocence he had fooled himself into believing he saw within Morganna.

But added to that was the knowledge that she had managed to get herself tangled into a web so dangerous, it made his guts cramp in fear. Son of a bitch, he was going to kill Merino. If it was the last thing he managed to do in his life, the man was dead.

After the four men moved into the room, Clint gripped the side of the door and slammed it closed with a force that had Morganna flinching in surprise. His gaze sliced to her wide gray eyes, his jaw bunching with the effort not to put his arms around her, to hold her to him. To know she was safe.

"Buy insurance, Merino," he growled as he turned from Morganna. "Good insurance. You don't want your family to be out too much when they have to bury you."

Joe Merino's mobile lips kicked up in a cool grin as his brown eyes gleamed with wary amusement. "Come on, Clint; chill out, man. I had no idea she belonged to you." He flashed Morganna a chastising look.

"Oh God, does this sound like a trashy novel or what?" Morganna piped up, her voice filled with disgust.

"I want to hear the explanations. I'm going to assume you're working on the date rape case, and pray I'm wrong, because if I'm not, there's going to be hell to pay once Reno finds out," Clint ordered tersely

"Tattletale," she grumbled.

He ignored her, merely staring back at Merino with narrowed eyes.

Joe shook his head mockingly as he stared back at Morganna. "Does your family even know what you do?" he finally asked her.

She pressed her lips tightly together.

Hell no, they didn't.

Joe sighed. "She's a DEA agent, Clint. One of the best rookies we have. I don't know where that attack came from tonight, or who's behind it, but this is Morganna's first case and she hasn't had time to draw that kind of notice yet."

"It was probably a hit against him," Morganna said. "I keep telling him he's going to piss off the wrong person."

"You set her up as bait," Clint said, continuing to ignore her. Right now, it was his safest bet.

He couldn't believe it. Morganna working with the DEA? That wasn't possible. She couldn't pull something like that off without Reno's knowledge. And sure to God, Reno would have told him.

She couldn't be doing this. She was too soft, too fragile. A man protected women like her; he didn't allow them to be drawn into the middle of a nightmare.

"We're investigating the hit," Merino sighed as he pushed his hands into his slacks pockets and stared back at Clint consideringly. "I'm here out of consideration to you. Because I respect you. But Morganna is an agent with this force, Clint. I can't have you jerking her out of the arena every chance you get."

Joe Merino was one tough son of a bitch, despite the designer clothes he wore. He had resigned his commission with the SEALs five years before, after his wife's death, and gone to work with the DEA instead. He was snake-mean when dealing with criminals and not much nicer when dealing with friendlies.

But he was a damned good agent, and Clint had once believed his judgment to be sound. Pulling Morganna in on this was not sound judgment. Because he should have known that even if Reno didn't kill him, Clint would. Agent or no agent, this was no place for Morganna.

He turned to Morganna, barely restraining the agonizing fear for her as she stared back at him. It tightened every muscle in his body and left him struggling to pull enough oxygen into his lungs to breathe.

She was deliberately risking her life. She was risking his sanity, his very survival, with this madness.

"You didn't tell me? Did Raven know?" He was surprised at the hurt that clenched his chest at the thought.

"Raven only knew that I was back in school until my actual graduation. Reno still doesn't know any differently," she finally revealed. "Come on, Clint, I didn't want to be jerked out before I even had a chance to graduate from the Law Enforcement Academy."

"You didn't need to be there!" he exclaimed, aware of the horror in his voice. "For God's sake, Morganna. Merino is going to get you killed."

She stared back at Clint in determination, defiant courage lighting her eyes. "I'm good at what I do."

He turned to Merino. "And what made you think you could place her in this kind of danger?" he snarled. "Reno will take you out for this, Joe, and you know it."

"Reno will accept it the same way you will—"

"Exactly, because I'm going to kill you first." Clint clenched his fists as he fought to restrain the need to kill the bastard now. "Slowly. Reno can have what's left."

Merino snorted mockingly. "Give it up, Clint. We approached you months ago about working this case because of your experience and your reputation on the BDSM scene.

You turned it down, so your opinion doesn't carry any weight here."

"I have a job, remember?" Clint pointed out sarcastically. "It does kind of require a steady amount of time."

Merino grimaced. "You're on leave for six more weeks," he pointed out. "We could wrap this up within that time with your help. Your reputation as a powerful Dom, combined with the reputation Craig has gained from chasing after Morganna this year, could give us the ace we need—"

"Forget it."

"Everyone knows her; they know you. Craig is considered new on the scene. He's barely been in a year—"

Clint swung his gaze to Morganna. "How long have you been involved in this?"

She lifted her chin, her eyes glittering in challenge. "The club scene, for more than three years now. The agency, six months."

Fuck. Fuck. "And I missed you at those clubs, how?" he demanded.

"I don't know." She shrugged her shoulders, crossing her arms beneath her breasts and drawing his gaze to the hard-tipped mounds. "I guess you just weren't at the right club at the right time, Clint. Or maybe you just weren't paying enough attention to me." Her eyes rounded in mock innocence. "I guess it could have been either one."

Either one? He turned from her slowly. He needed to kill; since he would never consider hurting so much as a hair on her head, that left Merino.

"Forget the insurance," Clint said softly. "I won't leave enough of you to bury."

Chapter 4

THE SETUP WAS ENOUGH TO make Clint clench his teeth and fight back an explosion he knew would land him in prison. Killing a cop was bad, even if the cop did deserve to die. And no one deserved it like Merino did.

Morganna had been working the case more than a year.

Fresh out of a Law Enforcement Academy that Clint hadn't even known she attended; hell, he'd thought she was in secretarial school. After graduation, she had gone to Joe and requested to be part of his task force. She knew the scene, knew the people, and she had the training he needed for an agent.

Clint was aware of the case. Two years ago, a new, specially synthesized date rape drug had come onto the market. A stimulant with the capabilities of rendering victims unable to remember anything but the haziest details while turning them into sex machines for hours at a time. It affected men and women; the powerful aphrodisiac also had the unfortunate side effect of killing the victim in many cases.

The sale of the drug had been controlled by the suppliers, resulting in the inability to identify where it had come from or who was using it. The majority of the women dosed with it disappeared for days at a time and, if they lived, turned up brutalized.

Many hadn't lived. But the videos made of their rapes had turned up to make millions on the black market. The sexual exploitation of those women was horrendous. Those who survived lived a waking nightmare of knowing the crimes committed against them were being sold, enjoyed. The resulting suicides hadn't been a surprise.

Not that women had been the only victims. There had been a few men, though those occasions weren't as numerous.

Clint managed to drag the details out of Merino once the other man understood that death was in his immediate future. Morganna's part in the case had been small. She had already been part of the club scene, evidently had been for years. She had been careful, though, staying home when Clint was in town or going to the less extreme clubs that he didn't associate with.

Diva's, Merlin's, and the Roundtable were his favorites. They were also the upper-scale, more expensive BDSM clubs on the eastern seaboard and just happened to operate in the same general vicinity of Atlanta.

Morganna didn't confine herself to the BDSM clubs until she began working with Joe's team. She played a very careful game of a woman hovering on the edge of submission. Or one fighting her Domme tendencies. Morganna was a dare to every male Dominant in those clubs.

Clint watched Morganna keep a careful distance from him as Merino and the others provided the details of the case. And through it, he learned that Morganna was the bait.

Several of the Doms who inhabited the clubs were sniffing around her. She hadn't settled on a lover yet, hadn't used the private rooms, other than Craig's for meetings, and she played the untouchable challenge. Eager to step into the lifestyle of a sexual submissive, but unwilling to settle on one man to do so.

She kept a close eye on the dealers suspected of handling the drug, as well as informing Merino and his men if any of the women acted drugged or seemed to need help leaving.

In the months Morganna had been working with the team, two women had disappeared, turning up days later, dead. Several more had been rescued from their fate by the team's intervention, with only three arrests, and those just here lately.

So far, Morganna had been personally responsible for the arrests of the three men suspected of drugging and kidnapping the women and was now on the lookout for their supplier.

"They've targeted the BDSM community because of the more unrestrained sexual atmosphere and the participants' general secretiveness about the double lives they lead," Joe finished up. "If we could get the group drugging and raping these women here, then we could find the location of the lab or labs being used."

"The Fuentes Cartel created the drug." Morganna spoke up then. "Their stronghold was destroyed last year, but we suspect several of the family members survived. We do know from the intel we've received that the cartel is fractured now and only one lab is currently working. The drug hasn't hit the streets yet; so far, it's just being used for the underground rape videos and, we suspect, is being perfected."

Clint stared back at her, hiding the shock he could feel racing through his system as he watched her. She was speaking of the Fuentes Cartel as though they were your regular, run-of-the-mill drug runners.

They were killers. And the thought of them targeting Morganna had the blood freezing in Clint's veins.

"Do you have idea what you're getting into here?" he ground out. "Any idea just how fucking dangerous the Fuentes people could be?"

She stared back at him calmly. "This drug has to be destroyed, Clint."

"Not by you." God, she had no idea what she was getting into. "Not if Fuentes is involved."

"Fuentes' survival or lack thereof isn't the problem. The supplier and the source are. We can get the suppliers if we get a strong enough Dom in to appear determined to tame the shrew no matter the cost or moral objection." Joe cast a smug look toward Morganna. "So far, we haven't found one. Morganna isn't the easiest woman to work with."

Clint watched her expression closely. Of course she wasn't, and he would have killed any of the four men if they had convinced her to do what would have been required. If he didn't kill them anyway for involving her.

"Are you aware of what they're asking you to do?" he asked her furiously.

She shrugged mockingly. "I'm just waiting on them to present a viable candidate."

The challenge she was presenting to the Dominants within the club was bad enough. Some of them had fewer scruples than an alley cat. But even worse, she was daring some bastard to attempt to drug her, to force her into submission.

Clint had followed the news reports of the women who had been drugged. Those found dead as well as those who'd survived. They had presented a challenge. Women who didn't bow to the submissive lifestyle but who enjoyed watching from the sidelines and socializing within the fringe clubs such as Masters provided.

And Morganna was just waiting for Joe to find a viable candidate to push the bastards into drugging her?

Clint's outraged anger edged higher.

"And you think you could handle working with a full Dom?" He shook his head. "You can't keep from arguing over a damned grocery list. There's no way in hell you can pull it off."

"Of course I can." She waved the furious retort away with a graceful flip of her hand. "I can be a very good actress when I need to be."

"You've lost your ever-lovin' mind." He stared back at her. His southern drawl had slowly eased over the years of learning other languages, being in other nations, but at times of stress it slipped out. And his stress level was nearing stroke stage.

"For God's sake, Morganna, the private rooms are just for the more extreme acts. I know you're not blind." And that wasn't even counting the underground club—the sexual extremities there had been known to make even him uncomfortable.

"Stop acting like an outraged father." She stared back at

him defiantly. "I don't have to ask your permission to do this."

His fists clenched in an effort to control himself, to hold back the lust and the anger and the driving need to protect her. Even if that protection was from herself. Or him.

"Most of our agency Doms won't fool with her past the first hour," Merino snickered as he sat down. "Morganna has a bad habit of trying to tell them how to do their jobs. I believe she even informed one of them that her vibrator was more fun to play with."

Clint watched her face flush as she lifted her eyes, staring at the ceiling rather than the five men now currently discussing her sex life.

"A woman can't fake walking with a plug up her ass," Clint snapped then, seeing the shock as her eyes flew back to his. "Just as she can't fake her demeanor after leaving one of those rooms with a real Dom. Half the time, I've never used the room." He watched her closely as he delivered his next piece of information. "Have you ever fucked in the middle of a crowd, Morganna? Sat on your Dom's lap and had his cock slide up your pussy? That's what we're talking here. Not playtime, dammit."

He saw her flinch, then watched the heat that filled those dark stormy gray eyes. It turned her on, almost as much as it turned him on.

The agents watching them weren't unaffected.

Clint turned to Merino and glimpsed the lust in several of the agents' eyes. Some Doms shared their women easily and with pleasure. Clint wasn't willing to share this woman, but would Morganna's sexuality allow her to let another man touch her?

The need to know consumed Clint, even as the knowledge that he would kill the bastard who took her in front of him filled his mind.

Clint's gaze flew back to Morganna. She was watching him

with dazed lust, the kind that filled a woman's eyes when her sexuality was at its peak, the need to be touched, taken, filling every particle of her mind.

And she needed. He knew she needed.

"Fine, you want to be my sub?" He narrowed his eyes as he watched her. "Let's see how submissive you can be. Come here." He lifted his hand, waving his fingers back toward himself in invitation.

Morganna arched her brow mockingly even as fluttering warnings of danger vibrated in her stomach. Clint was not a man to be played with when he had that look in his eyes. Cold ice-blue, like Alaskan waters, freezing her to the pit of her soul with trepidation.

He wouldn't hurt her . . . well, not without pleasure being involved. But that look meant she was not going to like what was coming.

"I don't think so." She stood her ground, and so help her, if he got out of that chair and came after her, she was going to throw something at him.

Joe snorted from where he sat. "See what I mean? She's too confrontational to be a sub."

"Says who?"

"That would have earned you a ball gag," Clint said.

"You'd have to be willing to die to put it there first." She smiled with chilling politeness as he paced to the other side of the room, one hand rubbing at his neck as he glared back at her.

"You guys are taking this way too seriously." She shook her head as she stared back at them. "We've caught three of the dealers. Craig will score as soon as we get another Dom in."

"Until you get to the part where we can't find a Dom willing to work with you," Joe reminded her. "We haven't been able to find a suitable couple familiar to the scene, either. And whoever is supplying this shit seems to smell damned agents. Which leaves us where we are. We have two more months left to find a break in the case before we're going to be forced to abandon it."

Morganna clenched her teeth at the thought of that. "We have a list of suspected players—"

"Enough!" Clint's voice sliced through the room as she turned back to him. How did she know he would be the one to protest? "Just to begin with, the players would more likely put a bullet through your head. Hence tonight's attack. In case they didn't, though, just how the hell do you think you're going to fake disinterest in me?"

She let her gaze rove over his body this time. Her mouth watered at the sight of that bulge in the front of his jeans. She forced herself to move on, lifting her brow disdainfully as she reached his gaze once again.

"I should point out, Morganna, at this moment, you are showing anything but disinterest," Joe pointed out drolly. "Bang, baby, you're dead."

"Who says there can't be attraction? Just because a woman is reluctant doesn't mean she has to be uninterested," she snapped back at him. "You're trying to make this more complicated than what it is."

"We're trying to make this safe," Joe argued.

"I can't believe you're trying to argue with her." Clint shook his head in exasperation. "I learned better than that years ago. No, Morganna!" His voice sliced across the room, causing her lips to flatten in frustration as she glared back at him.

"Damn, she's not arguing with him," Craig muttered moments later. "He's good."

Satisfaction glittered in Clint's gaze. One of these days, she was going to learn to ignore that tone of voice.

"Our original problem hasn't been solved," Joe pointed out. "You're getting no place fast this way. No dealers means no suppliers. All we have are the three men we caught last week, none of whom seem to know shit about where the lab is located. All we have is this monster drug Fuentes created, and women who are going to keep dying while those fucking videos are going to keep selling."

"Your original idea is a good one." Clint clenched his teeth as he pushed his fingers through his hair. "Your problem is your female agent."

"That's your problem," she broke in.

"You're pushing me, Morganna," he said as she smiled innocently, batting her eyelashes just because she knew it pissed him off. She received a glare in return.

"I'm just waiting for words of wisdom to spout from your golden lips." She smiled innocently. "Figured you'd take offense."

He ignored her, turning to Joe instead. "They won't sell to someone they can't vet thoroughly. Your men are good men, but I'm betting they weren't a part of the scene before two years ago."

"Not in this area." Joe shook his head firmly. "We pulled several in from New York and one from California, though. They have solid reputations in the bondage community."

"But whoever is testing this drug here is damned careful," Clint pointed out. "You need someone he knows, someone he can vet easily. Someone known for his dominance as well as the fact that no one has ever said no to him. But also a male careful enough to want to dose his woman himself, to be sure she stays safe. Pull in a female agent strong enough to work the part, I'll work with her."

Morganna felt the slow, steady burn of betrayal begin to consume her. He wouldn't do this to her, surely?

"This is my assignment, Clint."

"You're not involved." The edge of command in his voice vibrated through the room. "I have six weeks' leave. Pull her off the case and I'll work with you."

"You can't do that," she cried out painfully.

She turned to the agents she had worked with for the past year and with a sense of failure realized she had lost. "Do you really think you can find an agent experienced enough to say no to him?"

"Willing to fuck and willing to submit are two different things, as you point out, Morganna," Joe argued. "A man wanting submission is not going to settle for just a roll in the sheets. Especially a well-known Dom."

"Morganna, arguing over this isn't going to help," Clint replied in return. "They need a dependable Dom that fits into this area more than they need you at present. My terms are that you go off the case."

She blinked back at him in shock and pain. "You can keep using Craig to push for the drug." She turned to Joe for support. There was none. "He's been there long enough, Joe. Anyone who knows Clint knows he's a SEAL. They'll never go for it."

"Anyone who knows me knows a hell of a lot more about me than you do, Morganna," he pointed out, his voice soft. "I don't take no for an answer. It would be in my character to take what I want. However I had to."

"This is so bogus." She forced back her pain, her knowledge that she was losing, as she turned to Joe again. "You're going to go along with this, aren't you?"

It was there in their faces. They would hear any argument she had, but they had what they'd wanted all along, a local Dom they could trust.

Six months wasted, and this was what she had to show for it, Clint walking in and throwing her out.

She dropped her arms as she stared back at all of them, aware of Clint's waiting stillness, the tension that zapped around him.

"Morganna, it's better this way—" Joe met her gaze, his eyes narrowed, his expression thoughtful.

"Save the apologies," she snapped, catching the satisfaction that shimmered in Clint's eyes. "I've had enough of the five of you. I'm going home. I'll lodge my protest with the commander Monday morning."

"We're not finished," Clint reminded her, his voice dark, furious, as she turned and stalked to the door.

As she gripped the door handle she turned back to him, a bright, false smile tipping her lips.

"Oh, you mean the fucking thing?" she asked with false innocence. "Thanks, but no thanks. See if your pretty little submissive agent can give you what you need, because I'll be damned if you have anything I want."

WHAT HAD GOTTEN INTO HER? Clint cursed in four different languages as he followed Morganna's cab at a sedate distance until it pulled up on her street. He continued on to the alley behind her house, turned off his truck lights, and pulled into the back driveway he knew was never used.

Would she be pissed enough to look to see if he was sitting there? He doubted if she would see him if she did. The overhang of the old garage Reno's father used to tinker in before his and his wife's deaths would hide the vehicle from the second story, and the lawn furniture directly ahead of Clint would shield him from the back unless she turned on the porch light.

He rolled down his window, listening as the front door slammed and lights flipped on through the house.

Why couldn't he just leave it alone? he asked himself as he stared at the house. Joe Merino and Grant Samuels had promised to take watch out front on her tonight; it wasn't like Clint needed to be there. Still, he couldn't help himself.

He watched as the kitchen light flared and her silhouette moved through the room. Graceful, slender.

Clint leaned his arms on the steering wheel as he sighed wearily.

He hadn't expected that steel core of defiance that lit her eyes tonight, and he sure as hell hadn't expected his response to it. Morganna had been able to make his dick hard for eight years now. But she had never really tested his control until tonight. Tonight he had been close to taking her against the door of his apartment with no consideration for her comfort.

She moved from the kitchen, the light blinking off behind her. Minutes later, the light flared in her bedroom. Unlike in the kitchen, her silhouette lasted for only seconds before she closed the heavy curtains, blackening his view into the bedroom.

He leaned back in the pickup and stared back at the house thoughtfully. He was going to have to call Reno. Despite her accusation that he simply tattled on her for the hell of it, that wasn't exactly true.

Reno and Clint had made a pact years ago. They knew their sisters and knew the trouble they could get into if left unattended. Both men swore the two girls, precious to them, would never lose themselves as so many other young women had.

The two men ratted to each other in the spirit of love and protection, Clint thought with a grunt as he pulled his cell phone from the holder at his hip.

Bullshit. If Reno wasn't around as a buffer, then only God knew what Clint was going to end up doing to that sweet, hot little body of Morganna's. And in doing so, he would end up breaking them both.

THE ISLAND OF OAHU, HAWAII

Raven answered the cell phone on the third silent vibration, casting a wary glance to the bathroom as she kept her attention on the sound of running water.

"Hey, Clint. What's up?" she answered cheerfully.

Her brother's number popping up on the caller ID couldn't mean anything good.

"Hey there, Sis. How's the honeymoon going? Have you killed him yet?" Clint's voice was smooth, real smooth. It was a dead giveaway. He was madder than hell.

"Oh, like any other honeymoon." She pretended indifference. "Lots of time in bed and a little sightseeing. Reno is balking over the snorkeling and doesn't want to hike into a volcano. Go figure."

"Go figure," Clint muttered in return. "He wouldn't be available for a quick chat, would he? Just to make sure he's still living and all."

Uh-huh, she believed that one.

"Is anyone dead?" she asked suspiciously.

"No," Clint drawled carefully.

"Then you can't talk to him. Every time you've called him in the past six months he's gone running out of the house and hasn't returned for hours. It's my honeymoon. I am not coming home." And she wasn't going to let Reno make Morganna's life hell right now.

Raven didn't exactly agree with her friend's decision when she joined the Law Enforcement Academy without telling Reno, but she supported her. Morganna needed an identity outside her brother, a life of her own, and if that was the life she chose for herself, then she had the right to live it.

Clint's voice hardened over the line. "I'm not a fool, sweetheart. I know you're blocking my calls to Reno. You know I'll get there eventually."

"Clint . . ." She bit her lip before sighing deeply. "We've all left Morganna. She's alone now; you can't expect her to live her life in a way that's comfortable for the rest of us. If you can't help her, and if she needs us, then she'll let me know and I'll tell Reno."

She could feel Clint's fury rolling over the phone line now.

"She's going to get her ass killed, Raven. Some bastard nearly ran her over for her efforts in whatever the hell she's involved in."

Raven's heart thickened in her chest. "Is she okay?"

"Do you care?"

"Don't give me that, Clinton McIntyre," she hissed. "How

many times have you been shot that I don't know about? How many times was Reno hurt that Morganna and I were never informed of? Don't you try to guilt me; just tell me if she's okay."

"She's fine," he snapped. "Now put Reno on the phone."

"No."

"No?" Male outrage filled his voice. "Raven, don't make me fly out there."

"And if you fly out here, who's going to watch Morganna?" she pointed out. "If you think she needs protection, then protect her. Stop whining to Reno over everything. You just do it so you can avoid her, which really doesn't make sense. If you don't care anything for her, then why care what the hell she's doing?"

Raven was sick of watching her friend eat her heart out over Clint's stupid male pride. Morganna loved Clint until nothing or no one else would do, and despite Clint's frozen seeming disregard, he did care. If he didn't, he wouldn't take such pleasure in driving Reno crazy every time he thought she was doing something wrong.

"Raven, this isn't a game." His voice roughened with his anger. "She's going to get killed."

"And you can't help her?" Was she wrong about him? "Do you really have to worry Reno to the point that I have to cancel my honeymoon because you can't do what Reno would do? Reno would have protected me. He wouldn't have called you home, Clint."

"Reno loved you, Raven." He sighed. "He always has. There's a difference."

"And you don't love Morganna? Even a little, Clint? Enough to give her just a little of what you would give a total stranger if you were on a mission? What happened to you, Clint, that you hate her so much?"

"I don't hate her." He ground the words through the phone line.

No, he didn't hate Morganna, and Raven knew it. Just as

she once had, he was fighting everything he felt, everything he wanted. Reno had broken through that fight, though, and it made her realize how much she was missing out on by missing out on him. She thanked God every day that he had done so.

"Reno will jerk her to a safe house, and he'll stand guard over her like the terrified brother he'll be," she murmured.

"Hell yeah," Clint snapped. "Why do you think I'm calling?"

"And in doing so, he'll alienate his sister forever, taking the last tie she has to a family. She'll never forgive him, Clint. And she'll never forgive you if you do it, either. Please don't hurt her like that. Don't steal her dreams, Clint."

"Party girls shouldn't play grown-up games," he snarled. "She isn't experienced enough for this."

"And you know Morganna now about as well as you knew her when she was a teenager," Raven said sadly. "Why not try looking past the makeup and pretty clothes, brother mine? You might be surprised at what you find."

As the shower shut off, she disconnected the phone and tucked it back in her purse, then she breathed in a hard, desperate breath. God, if anything happened to Morganna, Reno would never, ever forgive her. Morganna was the last family tie he had left, and he worshipped his sister. Raged at her sometimes, rarely understood her, but he loved her, as only an older brother could.

And Raven knew she would never forgive herself, either. Morganna was the closest thing to a sister that Raven had ever known. If anything happened to Morganna, Raven would always know that by telling her husband the truth she could have saved her.

"Raven?" She jerked as Reno's voice, soft, inquiring, spoke behind her.

She turned to him, amazed anew at the man who was now her husband. She had sworn she would never marry a SEAL, that she would never trust her heart to a man in such a dangerous profession. He had changed her mind. He had shown her how much she truly did need him. For as long as she could hold him.

"That was fast." She tightened the belt of her robe and walked into his arms, feeling the strength and hardness of his arms enfolding her.

"I missed you in there with me. What was so important out here?"

"Checking up on my brother." She hid her face against his chest. "Making sure he wasn't causing any trouble."

"And is he?" His voice was gentle, curious. Suspicious.

"About normal." Her arms twined around his neck as her lips pressed against his chest. "And it's my honeymoon. He's not allowed to ruin my honeymoon."

"No one is allowed to ruin your honeymoon." He kissed her head gently. "But you know, Raven, sometimes your husband isn't as thickheaded as you think he might be."

She stilled in his arms.

"I've known about Morganna since she joined the Academy," he whispered at Raven's ear. "And unbeknownst to both of you, I attended her graduation and watched her take that diploma with pride. And, sweet wife, I am receiving regular updates on her progress."

She jerked back, narrowing her eyes before slapping at his bare arm and baring her teeth at him furiously.

He laughed, concern lurking behind the amusement in his gaze.

"Don't worry." He winked. "I promise not to let Clint get hold of me for a while. Okay?"

"That is so mean." She pouted. "I can't believe you hid this from me."

"You hid it from me," he pointed out. "I'm just sick of watching you worry about her on our honeymoon." Then he sobered, his eyes darkening in worry. "I know she grew up, Raven, and I know she has to make a life for herself. I'll head home if she needs me, but as long as Clint's there, she's safe."

Now Raven just prayed Clint didn't break her friend's heart and that he realized how easy it would be to do just that.

Reno pulled her back into his arms, controlling her struggles as his erection pressed against her stomach, firing her arousal.

"Now come here, wife. Let's enjoy our honeymoon."

Chapter 5

JOE MERINO PULLED THE BLACK surveillance van into a parking spot within sight of Morganna's house and stared at the dimly lit upper window thoughtfully.

She was home safe and sound, no tails, no problems. So why was the hair on the back of his neck tingling? It was never a good sign.

Beside him sat the one true friend he had ever claimed and the only man he trusted with his life.

Grant Samuels was slouched in his seat, nursing a steaming cup of coffee and bleary eyes. His ever-present University of Southern Carolina baseball cap was pulled down over his eyes and his dark T-shirt stained with some painting project his wife had pulled him into months ago. And he was scowling. This was his third night away from his comfortable matrimonial bed, and he was starting to get damned cranky.

A cranky Grant wasn't anyone's idea of a fun time, either. Even his best friend's.

"Think he'll do it?" Grant finally mumbled as he lifted the coffee cup to his lips again.

Grant was as addicted to his coffee as he was to his wife.

"He'll do it."

"What makes you think so?" Grant yawned through the question.

Joe stared back at the house, seeing the slender female shadow as it passed by the curtains in the living room before the lights flipped out. He was going to have to mention windows and shadows before some son of a bitch put a bead on her through that window.

"She's his weakness." He nodded to the house. "Every

woman he's had in the last five years resembles her. She's not going to obey him like a good little girl, no matter how much he wishes she would. She'll defy him, and then he won't have a choice."

Joe understood that kind of weakness; he could even respect it in a pitying sort of way. When a man loved a woman like that, then the betrayal, if and when it came, ripped his soul apart.

"He has a strange way of showing it," Grant muttered. "And he's not the smartest good ole boy I ever met, Joe. You don't piss a woman off like that; she'll cut your balls off for it. And she's crazy about him. I swear I heard her heart break when he talked about working with another woman."

Yeah, Grant, poor sap that he was, had kept his eyes lowered, his expression filled with sympathy, as Clint pushed the girl. Grant had actually muttered an "amen" when she stalked from the apartment.

"She reminded me of Maggie," Grant sighed. "Full of fire."

Joe grunted absently, watching the house. Clint McIntyre was one hard-ass. He was one of the regulars at the upper-scale bondage clubs and well-known for his extreme tastes in sex. Spanking, toys, butt fucking. He was good to the women, but he pushed them, pushed the limits of their sexuality as well as their endurance.

Some of the women he'd had in the last few years said he could fuck for hours without breaking pace and then start again with only a light nap. Hell, Joe hadn't done that since he was eighteen. McIntyre's testosterone level must be off the damned charts. That or he was trying to screw a hunger out of his system that wouldn't die. Joe understood that one. He understood that one too well.

"So why are we here?" Grant shifted in his seat, working to get more comfortable. "Clint's in the back watching the house, and I can't see where we're needed."

"That attempted hit bothers me, man," Joe finally admitted. "Her cover couldn't have been cracked. No way in hell."

"There's never no way in hell," Grant pointed out wearily. "Anything's possible."

Yeah, no shit. It wasn't something Joe should have forgotten. Hell, he hadn't forgotten; that was why Grant was here missing out on his wife and bitching over it. Joe didn't have the same trust in the others.

Joe shook his head. "I have a bad feeling about this one, brother. A bad feeling all the way around."

"Not good," Grant muttered.

No, it wasn't good. Joe lived his life by his gut; he always had. It was one of the reasons he'd left the SEALs, one of the reasons he'd taken command of this task force.

"So why are we here?" Grant asked again. "I could be curled around my Maggie, sleeping peacefully, Joe. McIntyre ain't stupid. He'll watch her tonight."

That was Joe's intention. Clint needed time to assess the situation, to think about things awhile without interference. If that hit was against Morganna and another came too soon, then he'd jerk her out of the assignment and cart her off gagged and bound. Joe couldn't afford that. He needed the other man in this assignment fast.

"We'll help him watch her awhile," Joe murmured. "You can sleep tomorrow."

"Man, Maggie ain't in the bed through the day. You suck, Joe," Grant griped.

Yeah, yeah, yeah. Grant was missing one pitiful night with his wife. So what? Joe was missing every night with his.

"If I were that mean-assed SEAL, I'd cart little Morganna off as hard and fast as possible and tell you to kiss my ass," Grant continued. "What makes you think he won't?"

"She won't let him." A tight smile curved Joe's lips. "She's had a taste of adrenaline, Grant. A taste of danger. She likes it. She likes it real well. And she's damned good at the job."

He knew the signs, knew the fire that burned in the eyes and in the soul. It made her careful, but it pushed her, made her eager for the job. Given a few more years, a little balance and experience, she would be a damned good agent.

"You're a bastard, Joe," Grant accused, his voice low, sad. "You've really sunk, man. You knew what you were doing when you let her come in, didn't you?"

"Did I know McIntyre would follow?" he asked knowingly. "Yeah, I knew. Just like I made sure she was in the right place at the right time when I needed him. I'm good like that." Maneuvering it had been a bitch, though.

"You're evil like that." It wasn't a compliment. "He'll kill you if he finds out."

"So?" If McIntyre found it, then it meant the operation had been completed successfully. That was all that mattered. Nothing mattered but the mission.

"You scare me sometimes, buddy," Grant whispered. "Sometimes you really, really scare me."

"I'll watch your ass." That one was a given. Always.

"I'll watch yours," Grant promised. "But, brother, one day, payback is gonna be hell."

Joe was already paying.

MORGANNA SAW THE SHIMMER OF color just beneath the awning of the small shed out back and knew that Clint was parked there.

He was watching over her. A sad smile reflected in the window as Morganna sat tucked into the wide frame, knowing he couldn't see her, that he was unaware that she was watching him even as he was watching her house. And she bet he didn't even know why he was sitting out there.

Clint would excuse it, just as he always did, but in his eyes she would see the truth. He was as helpless against what he felt for her as she was against her emotions for him.

Maybe in a way she could almost understand his determination to keep her out of the line of fire, away from danger. If she could keep him home and safe, then she would have done it years ago. But the one thing she understood about

Clint was the fact that he was a warrior. He believed in what he did; all the way to the bottom of his soul he believed in it.

Just as she believed in what she was doing.

Clint may have made certain she was no longer working this case. Morganna had no doubt that Commander O'Reilly wouldn't prefer a trained SEAL, familiar with the role he was playing, working it. But he would place Morganna somewhere else.

Perhaps it was time to request an assignment outside of Atlanta, she mused sorrowfully. She could tell Reno what she was doing now; it was too late for him to stop her. He wouldn't like it, it would hurt him, but he would accept it.

And if she left Atlanta, then the chances of seeing Clint again would be nearly zero. At least slim enough that maybe she could find a life outside the constant hope she managed to keep alive in her heart.

She loved him. She had long ago grown used to the fact that she would always love him.

And she was terribly afraid Clint would never change. He would always fight what he could feel for her. And he would always insist on attempting to save her from herself. As though she were a child rather than the woman who ached for him nightly.

She touched her hand to the window, her gaze never leaving the dull shimmer of color beneath the awning. He had shown her more of himself tonight than she had ever seen in him before. She had felt his kiss, his touch, his passion, and the need for more burned inside her with a ferocity she couldn't fight.

She had fought too long to allow Clint to take this from her, though. This was different from the parties he had dragged her away from and the boyfriends he had frightened off. This was her life, and if he didn't want to share it with her, then he could step aside and let her live it in peace.

Even if it meant she had to eventually leave Atlanta herself.

"Good night, Clint," she finally whispered, pressing her lips to her fingers before placing them against the glass once again.

Then with a self-mocking little snort she moved from the window, shed the robe she had donned, and climbed into her empty, lonely bed.

Chapter 6

"WHY AM I SO NOT surprised to see you here?" Morganna muttered as she followed the scent of freshly ground and brewed coffee from her bedroom to the kitchen.

There were few people capable of making decent coffee. Clint was one of the best.

He was sitting at her kitchen table reading the newspaper. Dressed to kill in well-worn jeans and a white shirt that begged her to unbutton it and strip it off his wide shoulders. If she weren't so damned mad at him, then she would have tried.

Her one concession to modesty herself was the loose light cotton pajama bottoms with Kiss This written across the rear and a rosy pink camisole top that left a swath of creamy bare skin from just above her belly button to the band of her pj's that lay below her hips.

"I brought donuts. They're probably still warm." His voice was soft, almost conciliatory, as he laid the paper down and picked up his own steaming cup of coffee.

"Cream-filled?"

"Would I bother with anything else?" Amusement laced his voice.

Okay, so her habit was pretty well-known. Krispy Kreme cream-filled glazed. She opened the box and inhaled as a shiver of pleasure washed over her. Forget sex with grouch-ass. She would drown her sorrows in fluffy cream filling and melt-in-your-mouth sweet perfection.

"Why are you here?" She shuffled over to the coffeepot and picked up the waiting cup.

She heard his sigh behind her. She didn't trust Clint when he was being nice. Which said something about their non-relationship.

It sucked.

"I promised Reno I'd look after you while he was gone." Clint cleared his throat with uncharacteristic nervousness.

She restrained the urge to throw the cup of coffee at him.

"I'll lie for you and tell him what a great job you did when he gets home." And in the meantime she would figure out how to heal the lacerations he was inflicting on her heart.

"Morganna . . ."

She turned, watching as he wiped his hand over his face, his expression somber as he lifted his eyes to her. Not just somber, his blue eyes were dark with emotion, with a rare tenderness that never failed to clench her heart.

God, she loved him. And at times it just seemed so hopeless.

"Look, I just want to talk sensibly. Can we do that? Just once?" he asked.

"I always talk sensibly, Clint. You can just never get past the fact that while I'm doing so, I'm making you hard," she pointed out sadly. "That's not my fault."

He lowered his head, rubbing fiercely between his eyes as he grimaced.

"I'm trying here, Morganna. Can't you?" The irritation faded from his expression as he stared back at her sincerely. "Just for a few minutes?"

"Have you changed your mind about working with me?" That betrayal was the worst he had dealt her so far.

"I can't do that." Regret filled his voice.

She breathed in roughly, fighting past the pain that rose in her chest, thickened her throat.

"Then we don't have anything to talk about," she told him evenly. "You wasted your time this morning, Clint. The donuts were a nice try, though."

She moved to the box of donuts, lifting the lid and removing one as she glanced back at him. He was watching her silently, calculating.

Damn him, he knew how she felt, knew how weak she

was toward him. Surely he wouldn't try to use that against her now?

She knew Clint, to the bottom of her soul. What he couldn't get yelling at her he would try to "reason" her into. Sadly, his male reasoning sucked, which meant she wasn't in any danger of agreeing with him. He hadn't tried sexual coercion. Yet.

Moving back to her coffee, she leaned against the counter, crossed her ankles, and bit into the near-orgasmically delightful confection. His eyes followed every move.

"You're not going to even try to understand, are you?" he asked quietly.

"That you're being unreasonable?" She licked the thick, fluffy cream from her lip with a flick of her tongue. "I understand that completely, Clint. I actually expect it from you."

A frown marred his brow. "What the hell does that mean?"

"It means that since the moment you caught me wearing makeup and dressing like a girl instead of a tomboy, you've resented me. You see me as a pretty, worthless party girl without a brain in her little head. Unfortunately, I'm not willing to play into your image of that forever. I've actually grown quite sick of it."

Morganna picked up her coffee, sipping at the hot brew as she watched his expression closely.

"That's not true."

"Of course it's true." She smiled gently, inhaling a ragged breath. "You think I'm just like your mother. Unable to settle down or care for her children while her husband is off fighting wars."

There. It was out in the open. Morganna steeled herself against the hard expression that came over his face, the ice in his eyes. God, she hated it when he looked at her like that.

"This has nothing to do with her."

"Of course it does. It always has." She shrugged, fighting back the tears, the pain. "Do you think I haven't realized what the problem was all along, Clint? You believe I'll screw around on you while you're gone, simply because I wear makeup and like to dance. Because she did. As far as you're concerned, I have no more honor than she did."

"You're reaching, Morganna." He shook his head.

"Am I?" Her smile was forced, as was the calm edge of her voice. "I don't know, Clint. The evidence is pretty over-whelming from where I sit. We were getting along fine when I was a little tomboy chasing after you. Once I started wear-ing makeup and having a life outside you, you hated me."

"I don't hate you."

"You can't keep your hands off me and you hate yourself as well as me for it."

Her heart was racing as his brows lowered ominously, his expression becoming darker. "Morganna. That has nothing to do with this operation—"

"Of course it does." She lifted her chin defiantly. She was not going to cry over him again. She had spent weeks crying a year ago when she made the mistake of going to his apartment to comfort him after his buddy's death. "It has everything to do with it. How can a party girl, one step above a tramp, pos-sibly contribute anything worthwhile to such an important cause? I'm a hazard to the entire operation, aren't I, Clint? It doesn't matter that I've been training for this for years. That I fought for this assignment and that it means something to me. All that matters to you is that you can't handle it."

"Because you're inexperienced and that will get you killed." His jaw clenched almost violently. "You're not cut out for this life."

She stared back at him silently for long moments. She didn't fight the pain he could cause her. It would rise and ebb, like the tide. What tore at her heart now would ease to no more than a dull ache in a few weeks.

"Taking me off this assignment isn't going to make a difference," she finally said. "When I return to the agency, the commander will find me something else. Perhaps not something that means as much to me, but something I believe in. What will you do then, Clint?"

He didn't answer her. Clint rose slowly from his chair instead, his expression blank, though his eyes churned with emotion as he watched her.

"Don't make the mistake of coming back to one of those clubs tonight," he announced, his voice hard.

She tossed the donut to the top of the box as she stiffened defiantly. "Don't make orders you can't enforce, Clint. It is a free country here, you know."

"Don't you underestimate me, Morganna." He towered over her, glowering down at her from his lofty height with arrogant confidence. "I will put a stop to this."

"Why?" Her fists clenched as anger enveloped her. "Why do you even care, Clint?"

"Because it's no more than I would expect from Reno if it were Raven acting so damned foolishly," he growled. "I won't let you risk your life, Morganna."

"And you don't? Has either Raven or I demanded that you leave the military and take a nice safe little job shuffling papers? Your double standards suck, Clint."

"Then they suck," he retorted, his voice harsh. "Dammit, Morganna, you're asking too much of me."

"And you're a liar," she raged back rashly. "This isn't about Reno, or friendship, or anything else. The fact of the matter is that you can't admit how much you care about me, so you're just going to jerk me out of something I've worked my ass off for. Your selfishness amazes me, Clint."

"Bullshit!"

"The hell it is." She was in his face and didn't even realize how she'd gotten there. Her finger jabbed into his chest as she stared up at him challengingly. "You won't work with me because you know if you did, you couldn't keep your hands off me or your stone-cold heart safe. That's your problem. Walk away like you always do. But no, you have to destroy my dreams while you're at it."

"My problem is spoiled little girls who think they're bulletproof," he snarled, catching her wrist and holding it in the manacle of his fingers. "My problem is your damned stubbornness. I can't even talk to you."

"Because you never see anything beyond your own needs," she cried out raggedly. "You think you can lay down laws and I'll obey you like I did when I was a child. I'm not a child anymore."

"That's more than obvious every time you parade around half-dressed in one of those fucking clubs," he bit out. "You're a walking, talking signal for sex and you know it."

"And you hate it because you can't ignore me. Because it just makes you hungrier. You can't stand it, Clint, because you want me just as bad as I want you. Until it's like a sickness you can't get rid of."

"Damn you," he groaned. "God damn you, Morganna."

He jerked her into his arms, his lips slamming down on hers, grinding against her as the breath tore from her chest. Desperation fueled his kiss, desperation and fury. She could understand that. She had enough of it herself.

Rather than fighting him, her arms wrapped around his shoulders as she arched to him, certain she could crawl right beneath his flesh if he continued to consume her with his lips as he was doing.

She moaned with aching need as a growl of hunger tore from his chest. His hands were on her hips, lifting her to him as her back met the wall and his cock notched heatedly between her thighs.

The rough denim of his jeans and the fragile material of her pajama bottoms did nothing to protect her from the hard shaft pressing against her. She could feel the dampness flowing from her, the tight clench of her vaginal muscles, and the flaming need that overtook her.

Morganna wrapped her arms around his neck, her hands spearing into his hair to hold him closer to her, to relish every inch of the hard body pressed into hers and the calloused palms clenching against her rear.

"Open," he growled against her lips as she held them closed. "Now."

His tongue pressed against the seam of her lips before one hand left her rear, his fingers gripping her jaw and exerting just enough pressure to force her teeth open.

A shiver of debilitating arousal shot through her at the dominant forcefulness. She shuddered in his grip as his tongue forged past her lips and sent fire rushing through her body The heat of his touch, his kiss, seared her, tore through her senses, and enveloped her in a need so intense she didn't know if she would survive it.

She wrapped her legs around his lean hips as they ground against her, moving her body in counterpoint to his, the friction against her clit sending impulses of pleasure so intense throughout her body that she knew climax was only seconds away.

His lips devoured hers, slanting against them as his tongue fed from her. Morganna met his kiss with a greater demand of her own. Years of aching, unslaked arousal were like an animal clawing at her womb. She needed him, helplessly, desperately.

"You make me crazy," he groaned as his lips tore from hers, his hands moving against her as his body held her firmly in place against the wall.

His hands pushed beneath her sleep top, jerking it above her breasts as his palms covered them, drawing an incoherent cry from her lips as she writhed against him, determined to find release before he changed his mind. Again.

"I love your breasts. They get so tight and hard for my touch, your nipples flushing that pretty ruby red." His head lowered as the fierce throb of lust in his voice sent tremors quaking through her.

When his lips surrounded one hard point, Morganna saw

stars. He wasn't gentle, but she didn't want gentle. She didn't need gentle. She needed this, his teeth gripping the hard point, nipping at it erotically before his lips surrounded it, his cheeks drawing on her with a friction that slammed pulse points of pleasure through her vagina. She needed to come. She needed just a moment of release, just one driving orgasm from his touch, and she could go on, because she was smart enough, intuitive enough, to know Clint would never give in this easily.

H E WAS DROWNING IN HER. What was it about Morganna that destroyed his self-control, that tore through his determination to be patient, to be calm with her? What made her so different from any other woman?

Whatever it was, it went to his head faster than the strongest liquor. It made him crave the taste of her, the feel of her. Her hands tearing at the collar of his shirt so her sharp little teeth could rake across the column of his neck, her hot hands pulling the material of his shirt to give her better access.

Driving lust bit into his balls as his cock surged with an edge of hunger so keen, so violent, it sent shock waves racing through his mind, further eroding his control.

He released the swollen tip of her breast to ease back, holding her in place with his hips as he jerked his shirt from his pants, her hands moving for the buttons.

"Just a few more minutes," she whispered desperately, panting for air as her stormy eyes met his. "Just a few more minutes, Clint. Please. Please don't stop yet."

The need he saw in her reflection destroyed him. Had a woman ever stared back at him with such stark hunger, with such desperation? Her face was flushed with it, her lips swollen, her expression tight with her race to orgasm as she ground the hot mound of her sex against the ridge of his cock.

He should stop now. He knew he should stop now. As her hand tore at the buttons of his shirt, some releasing, some popping free, and the edges spread to her inquisitive little hands, he knew he should stop.

Instead, his lips were lowering to hers, taking them fiercely as her nails bit into his muscles, raking across them with fiery heat.

He couldn't leave her aching, but he couldn't take her. His hands clenched on her hips as his lips and tongue tasted hers, and he fell deeper into the intoxicating sensations he found only with her.

He ground himself tighter between her thighs, feeling the moist heat echoing against his erection. God, he needed her. He needed inside her, driving deep and hard into the wet, hot depths of her pussy. Just once, the animal lust howled inside him. Just one time. But he knew one time would never be enough.

"Come here." He tore his lips from hers, snarling with the demand he could feel rising between them.

He loosened her thighs, forcing her to lower her legs to the floor despite her whimper, and went to his knees before her.

He was met with the sight of that silky bare skin between the top and her pajama bottoms. Her shallow belly button, glistening with the gold of her belly ring. He pressed his cheek against the heated flesh, then turned his head until his lips were opening on it. Soft, sweet Morganna. He licked at her, blowing his breath over the damp flesh as she shivered in his grip.

His tongue laved the soft skin; his hands clenched in the elastic band of the bottoms and slowly pulled them down her thighs. He had to taste her. How many times had he dreamed of it? Of feeling the hot syrup of her desire against his tongue as she unraveled in his hold?

Her bare mound glistened with her juices as he forced her legs apart, his fingers spreading the soft folds for his mouth.

"I have a bed," she cried out, even as her hips arched to him. "Oh God, Clint, I won't be able to stand up."

"I'll hold you up," he muttered, moving a hand between her thighs as his tongue arrowed in on the ripe flesh awaiting him.

Her keening cry filled his senses as the soft, sweet taste of her exploded against his tongue and the tight, hot grip of her sex began to surround his questing fingers. She was a wet, silken vise around the two fingers he began to work inside her, drenching them with the heated slide of her juices. Beneath his tongue, her clit swelled in anticipation, and her hips writhed against his touch.

"Come for me, baby," he whispered, dying to feel her convulse around his fingers, to taste the pleasure he could hear echoing in her cries. "I want to feel you come for me."

His lips moved over her clit, catching it in the gentle suction of his mouth as his tongue began to flicker over her. His fingers moved inside her, stretching her, filling her completely, before bending and finding the sensitive spot inside, just behind her clit.

The pads of his fingers rubbed gently as he increased the friction on her clit. She was close. So close her hands were tangled in his hair, pulling at it as her body began to tighten.

She was going to come. Morganna fought to breathe as the pleasure overwhelmed her, stole her sense of self, and merged her with Clint. Whatever the hell he was doing with his fingers was destroying her. They didn't just stretch her, didn't just fill her with pulses of fiery sensation. But he was rubbing against something, making her clit pulse in warning, swell, and demand relief.

She fought against his hold, desperate to feel his fingers pumping inside her, but the arm wrapped around her hips held her carefully in place. She wasn't moving, but she was getting ready to fly. She could feel it building, tightening in her womb, in the ecstatic pulses pounding in her clitoris.

She arched tighter to him, feeling the pressure from his mouth increase, feeling the sizzle of impending orgasm rush along her spine. So close. Her fingers dug into his hair as he suckled at her clit, harder, faster, his tongue massaging her with fast, rapid strokes until she splintered.

Her own screams echoed in her head as the orgasm slammed through her, rocking through her system, jerking her with hard, brutal spasms as her sex convulsed around his fingers and tightened almost painfully before releasing again, jerking the strength from her legs and leaving her helpless in his grip.

Stars exploded through her head as space and time warped around her. Clint was wringing every last ounce of pleasure from her helpless body and stealing her breath, her reality, with his touch.

When she finally slumped against the wall, he began to release her. Slowly. His head lifted from her oversensitive flesh as his fingers eased slowly from her vagina, pulling back as the muscles protested with a last, violent spasm that sent shudders slamming through her.

His hands were gentle as he pulled her pajamas back into place, sat her in the chair he had vacated earlier, and pulled her top over her naked breasts.

It was over. She could see it in the tight lines of his face, the raging, unquenched lust in his eyes. He wouldn't go any further, despite his own need. And his need raged. She could see it. Feel it.

"It won't go away," she whispered tearfully as he squatted in front of her. "It will only get worse now, Clint."

His fingertips touched her cheek as a grimace contorted his face.

"Stay out of the clubs," he ordered hoarsely. "Stay away from me, Morganna. For both our sakes."

He leaned forward, kissed her lips with such tenderness she felt the first tear fall from her eyes as he stood to his feet.

"Don't make me do something we'll both regret. If you do nothing else to save yourself, baby, do that."

Morganna kept her head down, hid her tears, and fought the anger rising hot and deep inside her. Her fists clenched against the need to scream, to rail, to beg. And she swore she would never do that. She was a fighter, but she wouldn't fight for pity.

She stayed silent until the door closed behind him, until she heard the truck start up in the back driveway with a powerful throb.

Then the tears fell. And she swore she would never cry for him again. Just as she had the last time.

Chapter 7

SHE WAS DOWN, BUT SHE wasn't beaten. Morganna dressed carefully for the night, beginning late in the afternoon to prepare to make her own stand. She couldn't have Clint and she knew it now, but she would die and go to hell before she obeyed him. She had a job to do, and she was determined to finish it.

She wasn't officially off this assignment until her commander gave the order. She had begun working with Joe Merino's team first as a watcher. That was something Morganna had always been good at. She knew how to watch, how to pay attention to body language and pinpoint the women who were acting out of character.

She was well-known in the club scene, so she wasn't a suspected agent. Despite the arrest last week, her cover was still solid. No one knew who had witnessed the three men drugging that woman. And despite the attempted hit the night before, Morganna wasn't convinced her cover was blown. And if it was, then it could work more in the team's favor than against it.

But until she was told differently, she was still an agent here, and her job was still to show up and watch the action playing out.

Drugs worked differently from person to person, as did alcohol. She had been a part of the club scene since she was twenty-one, five years ago. Boredom, disinterest in a permanent relationship with anyone but Clint, and her own curiosity about people in general had drawn her to the pseudo-bondage atmosphere she found at these particular clubs.

They weren't true bondage clubs. At least not the upstairs portions. She had never been invited into the lower rooms.

She remembered the hue and cry, though, when Drage Masters opened his first club seven years ago.

It had been raided monthly when it first opened, the owner arrested just as often, but the club had never lost its license.

The Roundtable catered to alternative lifestyles and was as far removed from the honky-tonks and bars as one could get. It drew in the Goth crowd, the techno, and the extreme sensualists.

And that was the reason the drug was being tested here, the DEA believed. Here the easy camaraderie and familiarity of the honky-tonks weren't present. The crowd could change from night to night, from club to club, with only a few of the regulars remaining at any given hour.

Morganna stared around the interior of the Roundtable now, and she knew why Masters clubs had survived the outcry. The governor's son was a regular there, as were several city and state officials. The private rooms in the back afforded them a certain anonymity in their sexual excesses. If the bar area was raided, for some reason, the police never bothered with the back rooms. And never, at any time, had the basement portion of the club been invaded.

Not that one of the clubs had been raided in years. The influx of differing lifestyles and cultures into Atlanta, and the metropolis atmosphere, had eased the controversy over them. There were more extreme bondage clubs in the area, but Drage's ability to provide a club for the more extreme as well as those wanting to play along the periphery had drawn in all types.

Now the three clubs, Diva's, the Roundtable, and Merlin's, could be some of the most popular clubs in the state.

She moved through the Saturday night crowd slowly, feeling the hard pulse of the music thrumming around her as her gaze probed the crowd.

The slow, sensual beat of Gavin Froome's "Plane Jane" met her, but Morganna knew the house mix could swing just as quickly into the Cure, Depeche Mode, or any of the hard Goth, techno, or tribal beats.

It raged from current to classic at the drop of a hat and filled her blood with the need to dance. She loved dancing, moving, feeling her body come alive to the music. As did most of the other women and a few of the men who moved between the three clubs like a wave, the faces changing through the night as the club-hopping thrill took them over, though there were regular all-nighters specific to each club.

And there were new faces nightly. Plenty of them. Women dipping their toes into the open sexuality afforded them. Men playing at being Doms, finding a vicarious thrill in the openness of the women they found there.

Alcohol flowed like water, and drugs were the dirty little under-the-table side benefit. There was no evidence that the owner supplied the drugs or condoned them. Bouncers made a habit of throwing out the less secretive dealers and users, but for the most part, drugs were easy to come by.

Dressed now in snug leather pants and a half corset with black thin leather cups that covered her breasts, and high-heeled black leather boots, Morganna swayed sensually to the music.

Cinched low on her hips, nearly to her thighs, was her favorite wide black leather belt. She hooked her thumbs into it as she made her way to the bar and her first drink of the night before she let her body go, her gaze staying centered on the crowd.

She had perfected the ability to dance, letting the pulse of the music pound through her, as she watched the crowd and picked up probable victims of the drug she and her team were searching for.

"Morganna, darling. Gorgeous outfit." One of the younger regulars stopped her as she made her way to the bar. Cletus Tomas was a quarterback for the university. A gentle giant with a taste for female Dommes.

"Thanks, Clete." She reached up and patted his cheek, smacking a kiss toward him for the boost in confidence.

"You gonna dance with me, baby?" His wide face creased into a smile, his black eyes dancing with good humor as he stared down at her from his near-seven-foot height with a reverence that never failed to make her laugh.

"Maybe later, sweetie," she yelled over the music. "I need a drink and a chance to settle in first."

He winked as his gaze went over the black leather pants and half corset. At the side of her belt she wore a pair of silver handcuffs and the small leather pouch that carried her essentials.

"Save me a dance then, beautiful." He winked at her slowly. "I could let you learn to use those handcuffs if you like. Just say when."

"They wouldn't fit you," she laughed back. "Go play, Clete. I'll catch up with you later."

He threw his hand up in a farewell as he moved through the crowd, his wide body parting the ocean of humanity like an unerodible boulder.

She shook her head before moving to the bar, sliding in quickly as a bar stool was vacated before smiling in triumph at the line waiting to do the same thing.

"Lawry, I need a drink," she called to the bartender. "The good stuff."

Kentucky whiskey. Something to calm the pulse of fury moving through her blood as she felt the absence of the receiver that Joe hadn't replaced.

The fact that Craig hadn't stopped by the house or been waiting in the parking lot to check her in was telling. The team's black van was in place, though, which meant they were watching something.

She took a hard sip of the glass Lawry set in front of her, then breathed deep against the fire burning to her stomach. That easy, she had been dumped. Because of Clint.

She turned on the stool, holding the glass in one hand as she leaned back against the hardwood bar behind her and stared out over the heads of the crowd packed into the cavernous room. The raised bar floor allowed those at the bar to survey most of the room.

She found Craig first, staring back at her from a slouch against one of the large pillars placed strategically to bear the weight of the roof in such a large area. She followed his gaze then to a table set back from the dance floor but not quite in the shadows.

Clint was impossible to miss. As was the redhead sitting on his knee as he socialized with several of the hard-core Dommes who were a part of the clubs. Men and women Morganna had only watched, never spoken to. Clint obviously knew them well.

She ignored the wave of jealousy that ripped through her at the sight of the woman. Damn him to hell. Morganna couldn't bear the thought of another man touching her now and there he was with a redheaded bimbo perched on his knee like a well-trained bird.

Morganna took another fortifying sip of the whiskey as she pulled her eyes from him. She wasn't here to watch Clint.

"Girlfriend, there you are." Jenna Lancaster hopped onto the stool beside her, her heavy breasts bouncing beneath the silk camisole she wore as her heavily lined eyes stared back at Morganna with rabid curiosity. "Man, did you lose out last night or what? That big bad Dom we've all lusted after that jerked you to the back rooms pulled in a newbie tonight."

Morganna breathed in carefully. "That bad-assed Dom you're talking about is an asshole," she snorted. "She's welcome to him."

Jenna laughed at the description. "Those are the best kind, honey. You sure you don't just have those Domme tendencies Cletus keeps swearing you have?"

Morganna rolled her eyes. "I just like the clothes," she retorted.

"They say he likes full subs, girlfriend." Jenna shook her head. "I think if I were you, I could pretend for a night with a man like that. I hear he can fuck for hours. Have you ever been fucked for hours?"

Only with her vibrator. And what he could do with his lips and tongue alone in five minutes had it beat to hell and back.

"She's welcome to him." Morganna lifted her glass to her lips; her gaze caught when Clint gripped the redhead's hair and held her in place as she started to move.

The woman settled back on his lap, her eyes closing in obvious pleasure. Jealousy struck Morganna in a wave of white-hot hunger, ripping through her chest and tearing into her heart swifter than the sharpest blade.

She pulled her gaze away again, looking for the suspects Joe had on his list, as well as the women they were with. She had a job to finish; if the only part she played was in helping to find the supplier drugging those women, then so be it. At least he was off the streets.

"At least Craig still looks interested," Jenna pointed out, glancing over at him.

Yep, Craig was still watching Morganna, but the bastard hadn't returned her receiver. With it, she could have heard whatever Clint was saying to the passive little sub he had with him.

God, she hated both of them.

She turned from Craig's gaze, deliberately snubbing the questioning look he was giving her.

"Oh, girlfriend, that was cold." Jenna laughed, her expression calculating as she watched the exchange. "I'm telling you, Clete is right. You'd make a much better Domme than you do a sub."

"Jenna, is there a point to this discussion?" Morganna finally asked, turning to the other girl as she lifted her brow coolly.

Jenna giggled, her brown eyes twinkling in fun. "Oh, girl-friend, come spank me. That's such a cool look."

Morganna sighed roughly before finishing the whiskey and turning back to gesture to Lawry for another. It was obviously going to be a trying night.

Jenna sighed gustily as Morganna turned back.

"I was so hoping you would know if Mr. Badass could really last for hours. His subs don't talk."

"I have no idea," Morganna revealed drolly. "Craig wasn't too pleased to find out where I was. He dragged me out."

"Straight into a drive-by shooting, too!" Jenna suddenly exclaimed. "I almost forgot about that."

There was something wrong with the world when the subject of a man's stamina was more important than a supposed friend's near murder.

When this operation was over, it might be time to find a new haunt. These clubs were just getting on Morganna's nerves. Hell, they had been getting on her nerves before Cindy was killed. Morganna loved the dance, but she hated the feeling of being hunted, a slab of meat on the table of sensuality. She sighed at the thought.

"It's nice to know my near demise blipped your radar, Jenna," she laughed. "Why don't you go play? I need to chill out for a while. It's been a killer week."

As Morganna watched the crowd, she was aware of Jenna's probing look.

"You're looking for a new Dom," Jenna piped up. "You've dropped Craig then?"

"Craig never had me; he was just in the running. That's all."

"Who else was in the running?"

Morganna turned back to her, aware that the "mouth of the South" title hadn't been given to Jenna without reason. Her lips quirked. "At the moment, no one. Go play, girlfriend, and let me finish my drink."

Jenna giggled, a sound that really didn't suit the thirty-something legal secretary. She hopped off her bar stool, though, and with a little wiggle of her hips headed back into the throng.

Morganna's gaze slid back to Clint and his little red-headed sub. He was currently caressing her arm absently, running his fingers up and down the slender limb as she clearly telegraphed her arousal, her readiness to fuck.

The perfect little sub. There wasn't a chance she was going to convince a dealer she had to be drugged to accept Clint.

Morganna sighed. There was no way she could sit there so passively beneath his touch. She watched the girl's body language, the obvious sense of waiting, of anticipation. It was completely opposite Clint's. He looked almost bored as he glanced around.

His gaze roved over the dance floor, the crowd, then lifted to the bar. Morganna knew the moment he saw her. His hand paused on the other woman's arm, his eyes narrowing as his jaw clenched.

Morganna lifted her drink mockingly in recognition of his awareness of her and tilted her head in acknowledgment before she turned away from him again. As luck would have it, her gaze locked on a shadowy corner and the couple there.

The guy was big, tall, and broad; his companion, what you could see of her, was short, full-bodied. Her head was thrown back in pleasure as the man bent to her breasts. Morganna could see very little, but she saw enough to know what was going on.

She swirled the liquor in her glass as she watched with open curiosity. Could she do that? It was damned arousing to watch, to see the sexual act playing out, the way the male lifted the woman, aligning his hips with hers, and moved.

The long skirt of the woman's dress hid anything from view, but it was more than obvious what he was doing. For a moment, just a moment, Morganna felt Clint's touch again, his lips at her nipple, his tongue lashing it. His hips between hers, the thick length of his erection grinding against her. The image was broken as someone moved in front of her, then stopped.

She lifted her eyes slowly, amused curiosity filling her as she met the frowning, disapproving gaze of the club's owner.

He was nearly as tall as Reno, classically lean, but there was muscle beneath that white silk shirt and black European trousers. His black hair was pulled back from an aristocratic face, tied at his nape, and fell below his shoulder blades. Green eyes, as dark as moss, were cool, cynical, as they watched her.

He rarely came out. She had expected to hear from him tonight, but not in person, not like this. He was making a statement; she just wished she knew what that statement was.

"Ms. Chavez. Could we talk? Privately." The thick Cajun flavor of his voice was dark rather than sensual, almost deadly.

She almost shivered in trepidation, aware of the gazes locked on them. Swallowing tight, she slid from the bar stool, her gaze searching out Craig's as she followed Masters through a crowd that parted automatically for him.

Craig's eyes tracked them, obviously concerned. She didn't dare look for Clint.

"This way, please." Masters stopped at the entrance to the private hall before stepping aside and extending his hand before him. "My office is just down the hall."

What the hell had she done? Morganna thought frantically to try to come up with a reason for his sudden notice. Hell, she was one of the lower-key members of his clubs. She came to dance, drink a little, and meet with friends, supposedly. Drage only barred the real troublemakers from his clubs, not little nobodies like her. Unless he wanted something else?

"Here we are, *cher.*" He unlocked the door with the electronic card before ushering her in. "I was surprised to see you here tonight. I was making plans to head to your residence when my doorman informed me you had arrived."

"You were?" That one was shocking.

It was all she could do to contain her nervousness as she stepped into the dimly lit, surprisingly old-fashioned office.

"Of course. I had the report you were nearly murdered in my parking lot. I wanted to be certain you were well."

She stood aside as he moved around her and headed for the desk. A bank of monitors were lit beside the desk, more than a dozen showing varied views of the club. Another set below them were blank.

"Please, sit down." He gestured to the comfortable leather chairs in front of the wide, dark cherry office desk as he sat down himself and stared back at her through those deep green eyes.

Morganna took a seat, leaning back with false confidence as she crossed one leg over a knee and allowed her foot to swish back and forth as she stared back at him.

"Very cool," he commented with a slight quirk of full, sensual lips. "You act as though being invited to my office were commonplace. Most women would at least be curious."

"I'm very curious." She shrugged her shoulders, all too aware now of the brevity of the half corset and the way the leather cupped her breasts. "But I've done nothing wrong, so I can't exactly be in trouble."

He leaned back in his chair, steepling his hands in front of him. "I've been asked to revoke your membership for a time." The announcement was delivered with an edge of amusement as she stiffened in response. "I was curious why."

Her lips opened as she breathed in roughly, then licked over her dry lips as she fought to keep her temper under control.

"McIntyre?" she finally asked, clenching her teeth over his name.

Drage's brows arched. "Indeed. He came to me this evening before the club opened. I thought it very odd that he would make such a request, but I rarely question requests from members of his stature. Until now."

Morganna pressed her lips together, glaring back at him. "Am I banned then?" Anger was burning hotter than the whiskey in her belly now.

"I'm not entirely certain," he answered, his amusement obvious. "I'm still trying to figure out why one of my best-paying members would request the barring of one of my favorite members."

Now that one was a surprise.

"One of your favorites?" she questioned. "Since when?"

He glanced at the monitors thoughtfully. "I spend quite a bit of time here alone. You're a delightful addition to any night. You cause no trouble, until last night—"

"I didn't do anything last night," she retorted. "He did."

"You went to the private room with him, angering your Dom—"

"If you watch as you say you do, then you know Craig isn't my Dom; he just likes to think he is."

Drage's gaze swung back to her. "What the hell are you up to in my clubs, Morganna?"

She blinked back in surprise, her eyes widening at the dangerous, rough rasp of his voice.

"Mr. Masters." She kept her voice carefully apologetic. This was not a man she wanted to get on the wrong side of. "Whatever Clint is pissed over, it's personal. I'm sorry if he doesn't want to conduct his sexual exploits with me around, but that's all there is to it."

"His sister married your brother; is she aware of his membership here?"

"It wouldn't matter," Morganna gritted out. "But *I* didn't even know until last night. I assure you, her brother's sex life isn't something we discuss anyway. Besides, it's not exactly a crime and it's rather late to hide the information from me. Banning me won't change that."

"Then tell me why he wants you banned," Drage demanded

smoothly. "Otherwise, as of this moment you leave my establishment tonight, you will be unwelcome in all three clubs."

Damn Clint and his high-handed arrogance.

She pushed herself angrily to her feet. "You do what you have to, Masters, but Clint's using you to do his dirty work. He doesn't approve of my being here. It's that simple. But since his money is better than mine . . ."

"He does pay more," Drage murmured, his gaze considering. "The yearly reserve on the private rooms alone is rather high."

"How high?" She propped her hands on her hips, glaring back at him.

His gaze dropped to her bare midriff. At least they had gone farther than her breasts. Finally, those forest eyes lifted and his eyes narrowed.

"Twenty thousand for the yearly room reserve. Twenty-five for downstairs membership. Forty thousand a year for all of it if you're accepted."

Good God, that was a lot of money. How the hell did Clint afford it?

She sat down in shock. "What's downstairs?" She had only heard rumors of the private club that existed there; she had yet to have them substantiated by any of the club's members.

"A very special club." He was watching her too closely. "A very private Dominants' club."

"I'm not a Domme," she pointed out.

Masters shrugged. "Let's just say, I like you. Forty thousand for full membership, fifteen up front. If I lose a member because of the other, I'd at least like to replace the income."

"And if he ups the amount?" she snapped, holding the cover she had maintained since the assignment began. "I'm a legal secretary, for God's sake. I don't have that kind of money."

"Hmm. That's too bad," he commented. "His money isn't

better than yours, but it is a bit more than entrance fee per year, *cher*."

"No kidding," she breathed, furious. Damn Clint.

"Of course, you could be sponsored." The subtle offer had her staring back at him silently. "There are several of the full-membership Dominants and Dominatrices willing to sponsor you for a period of time under their tutelage. You could train to be either a Dominatrix or a sub, your choice."

"This means?"

He leaned forward slowly, bracing his elbows on the desk as his gaze sharpened. "It means, for a contracted period, *cher*, you would become the lover to one of them. You would rescind your rights to your sexual dependence, and would instead leave the choice of your sexuality up to the Dom sponsoring you. A very simple business arrangement. The question is, is your fondness for the club serious, or merely an amusement? Amusements can be found elsewhere."

Morganna stared back at him quietly. This could be the break the team had been waiting for. If she took this offer to her commander, it could ensure that she remained on the team.

"I've noticed over the past two years that you haven't requested a private room, and from all appearances your visits to Mr. Tyler's have not been productive," Masters pointed out. "You're an exquisite young woman, Morganna. You have fire and passion. The perfect student for whichever level your Dom places you within. Whichever, you would learn exactly what you need to know to excel within it."

What the hell was this? School for the perverted?

"It's your choice." He shrugged negligently as he leaned back in his seat and watched her closely.

"Do I choose my Dom?" she asked.

"You do." He nodded. "But if the relationship doesn't work out for whatever reason, then he can place your contract up for bidding if you cannot buy it back within a specified amount of time. In other words, my dear, you go to auction."

"That's illegal. There's no way to enforce it."

"You haven't seen my contracts. Nor have you seen the men who will uphold them should you decide to sue. Have no doubt, *cher,* I have covered my ass well."

"Clint would know about this?" His knowledge would definitely cause an explosion.

"Of course, he has full membership."

She shook her head and smiled cynically. "You don't know Clint; he would never allow it. And even if he did, he'd tattle straight to my brother and bring hell down on me."

"His contract forbids it. Trust me, McIntyre won't want to lose his membership by doing such a thing. I won't cover just my ass, Morganna, but yours as well."

Morganna stared back at him in surprise. "Meaning?"

"I wouldn't be opposed to sponsoring you myself." His gaze roved over her again, the mossy color darkening in sexual awareness. "But it's your choice."

Interesting. Morganna sat back in her chair, forcing herself to hide the nervousness moving through her. There was enough of it to power a city if it were electrical.

If Clint was considered a prime catch by the women in the clubs, then Drage Masters was considered the ultimate goal. So ultimate that he was rarely reflected upon simply because he never seemed interested.

And the lower levels of the club were only reflected upon. Even Joe wasn't certain what went on there, because so far, no one had even admitted they were there. They were like an urban legend all their own.

"So I can finance my own in—"

"You can finance your application," he amended. "Though honestly, no one is admitted without sponsorship of some sort. And for you, it would demand sexual sponsorship."

"Because I'm a woman?"

He inclined his head in agreement. "Not politically correct, I'm aware, but . . ." A sensual, carnal smile tipped his lips. "A fact nonetheless."

"Sexist," she muttered before biting her lip and cursing her tongue.

Her response was met with a bark of laughter. "Directing all that energy would be a pleasure, Morganna," he said moments later. "Learning to harness all that sexual energy could come in handy for you. It helps balance the rest of your life, helps you to focus."

Oh, she just bet it did.

This sucked. She didn't know Drage Masters, had nothing to go on except his reputation and the sparse details Joe had managed to scrounge up on him. It wasn't enough to instill trust.

"I gather there's not an option for no-ties sponsorship?" She lifted her brow in question.

"Sadly, no." His lips twitched. "And the time constraints are rather strict as well. I'll need to know before you leave the room so I can inform my security personnel of your status."

Oh great. Her eyes strayed to the monitors, hoping to catch a glimpse of Clint so she could glare at him. They widened as she saw him, but in apprehension rather than anger now. He was stalking toward the hall, his brows lowered in a frown, anger glittering in his eyes.

"Yes, I expected him to show up," Drage murmured.

"Asshole," she muttered as a heavy fist landed on the door.

"Your choice?" Drage asked her. "I'm afraid, dear, you are out of time."

"Can he rescind his request?" There had to be a way out of this.

"He can." Drage's lips twitched. "Though I would be surprised were he to do so. Clint rarely changes his mind."

"Yeah, that one's news." She flinched as the next knock came through, loud enough to bring a frown to Drage's dark features.

He leaned forward, pressing a button on a small control panel, then stared back at the door expectantly as it swung open slowly.

Morganna did shiver when Clint walked in. The aura of danger that swirled through the room was almost physical. His deep blue eyes were nearly black, his tall body tense, prepared. For a fight.

"Evenin', Clint," Drage drawled. "I assumed we had concluded our business earlier."

"Why is she still in here?" Ice dripped from his voice.

Drage leaned back in his chair as he turned his gaze to Morganna. "I was informing her of your request as well as her possible choices."

"There are no choices." Clint stepped into the room, his gaze slicing to Drage. "That was my request."

"Your request was her immediate barring from the clubs, which I decided required her the opportunity to counteroffer. We were discussing the details."

"The counteroffer being?"

Morganna held her breath at the calm, incredibly gentle tone of Clint's voice. The situation was getting ready to become explosive, and she knew it.

"Sponsorship, of course." Drage lifted his brow archly. "She was just making her decision. Weren't you, Morganna?"

She narrowed her eyes on Drage. Could she do it? Was what she wanted enough to allow another man to touch her, to hold her?

She looked over at Clint. Hard. Cold. She had waited for ten years for him, and the best he could do was throw her out of an operation she had worked her ass off for. He didn't want her enough to risk that piece of ice he called a heart. And all this after blowing her mind with an orgasm she still hadn't recovered from.

She clenched her teeth. She wasn't a virgin. Other men could arouse her. She'd had other lovers before; she could again.

"I'll need a trial period. Three nights," she bargained. "To be certain we'll suit."

She could feel her stomach tightening in dread at the

thought of another man touching her, even one as handsome and obviously sensual as Drage Masters. She steeled herself against it and thought of the women dying because of that drug. The pictures, the videos, the lives it was destroying.

He inclined his head in agreement. "A cautious lady. I can do that."

"Then I agree."

"Like hell."

Chapter 8

BEFORE MORGANNA COULD FIGHT, SHE was over Clint's
shoulder.

"Damn you, Clint McIntyre," she screamed out in rage
as he stalked from the office.

She kicked against his hold, her fists beating at his back
until a hard hand landed on her ass.

"This is getting so old." She bucked, trying to break his
hold again, only to scream in outrage when his hand landed
against her behind again.

She braced her hands on his lower back, attempting to get a
view of the room. Where the hell was Clete when you needed
him?

Clint shifted his shoulders, breaking her position as she
bounced in his hold, screaming in outrage.

She slapped his ass back with both hands. He didn't so
much as flinch, but she did. The hand that landed on her own
butt burned. Right to her pussy.

Morganna let out a scream of pure frustration and anger
as cool air met her back end and the doors swished closed
behind them.

He moved in a hard, ground-eating stride, obviously ignoring her as he headed for the parking lot. Within seconds they were at his truck and she was bouncing into the
seat.

As she moved to throw herself back out the door, his hands
gripped her shoulders, slamming her back.

She stared at him in shock. It didn't hurt, but the restrained fury in the movement sent her heart racing, her eyes
widening, as she stared back at him.

"If you move, you're fucked. Right here. Right now. In

front of God and everyone. Do you understand me?" His
voice throbbed with power; his eyes blazed with anger.

Morganna swallowed tightly before nodding. There were
times when you just didn't defy Clint. This was the ultimate
of those times.

He moved back, slammed the door with enough force to
rock the truck, then stalked to the other side and climbed in
himself.

The vehicle peeled out of the parking lot, leaving rubber
behind as Morganna fought to buckle her seat belt and waited
for the coming explosion. There was no doubt he was going
to yell. Clint was always yelling when he got pissed.

When he didn't say a word, not a single word, in five
nerve-wracking minutes, she risked a glance toward him. He
was gripping the steering wheel with both hands, his eyes staring straight ahead, his expression forbidding.

So why wasn't he yelling?

"Pulling me out doesn't change anything."

"Open your mouth again and I swear to God I'll strap a
ball gag between your lips."

Morganna flinched. God, she had never heard his voice
like that. Low, brutal. Brooking absolutely no refusal.

"Gagging me won't change anything," she pointed out reasonably. "I'm not a child you can order around, Clint."

He didn't speak. His hands tightened on the wheel until
she wondered if it would snap beneath the pressure.

"I'm twenty-six years old," she continued softly. "You
don't have the right to do this. None of it. You should have
worked with me—"

She breathed in roughly as the truck executed a hard turn,
pulling into a deserted office parking lot on what she swore
was two wheels.

Clint didn't speak. She had no warning before his seat belt
was released, then hers. Her first sign that he had finally lost
control came when he tangled his hand in her hair, jerked her
to him, and slanted his lips over hers.

Morganna fought the grip, fought his kiss, for all of a second. Maybe. His lips were hard and burning, his tongue pressing between her lips, licking at her before his teeth nipped demandingly and he growled. A full-throated, wicked, carnal sound of hunger.

Morganna's lips opened to him, her hands sinking into his hair as he pulled her closer, then lowered her until her back met the wide seat.

Bench seats. You had to love them.

Then anything else she could have thought was wiped away. Clint's kiss changed; it stripped her mind, filled her senses, and stole reason. He devoured her lips, sipped at them, sank into them, his tongue thrusting past them, tangling with hers as she whimpered into the kiss.

Pleasure tore through her as heat wrapped around her senses. His lips were like velvet, rasping and demanding, his tongue carnal, tasting her as his lips ate at hers.

She was consumed by him. Every nerve ending in her body felt the possession and reveled in it. Clenching her hands in his hair, she arched closer, pressing her leather-clad breasts into his chest, whimpering with the need to feel his flesh against hers. Her nipples rasping against the coarse hair on his chest.

"I told you to shut up," he muttered, dragging his lips from hers, his teeth rasping her neck as he raked down it.

His free hand moved between them, loosening her belt, stripping it from her first before working on the closure to her leather pants. Once the material parted, his hand moved farther up her body.

One hand held her head back; the other gripped the thin, elastic edge of the leather cups above the corset and pulled. They raked over her nipples, sending blinding waves of pleasure shrieking through the hard, gold-studded points.

She had worn the thin gold chains she had purchased for the piercings, letting them dangle below her nipples erotically rather than tightening the subtle noose the two connected chains made as they dangled below the hard points.

"God. That has to be the sexiest sight in the world."

His hand cupped the mound, lifting it as he stared down at her, his eyes glittering in the dim light reflecting from the parking-lot lights.

His lips were swollen, parted, as he breathed roughly. His eyes were narrowed, the rough slash of his cheekbones emphasized by the tense set of his expression.

She arched to him, needing his lips on her, his tongue, the feel of his cheeks drawing on the sensitive flesh.

Instead, his thumb and forefinger gripped the point, tightened, sending her awakened senses exploding with heat and pleasure.

Morganna cried out, writhing beneath him as the flash of pleasure-pain tore through her. This was pleasure. The dark edge of ferocity, a hunger that couldn't be controlled. It rose within her like a demon, raking at her womb with merciless fingers, convulsing in her vagina with the warning tremors of nearing orgasm.

"I like the nipple rings, Morganna," he whispered as she stared up at him blindly. His fingers moved from her nipples, gripped the gold chains, and tugged at them gently.

Her head twisted on the rough truck seat, a whimpering cry tearing from her.

"So hot and ready," he whispered. "Would you be this hot with Drage, Morganna? Would one touch have your body twisting in need?"

"No. Oh God, Clint. You. I need you." She was past lying. She knew she would regret it, knew Clint was going to destroy her with her own body, but at this moment nothing mattered but his touch.

"Damn you. Damn you to hell for what you do to me." He may damn her, but his head lowered, his lips covering the hard point and burning her with the sensation.

"Oh God. Yes." The whiplash of heat that suffused her body left her gasping.

The moist suckling heat of his mouth, the lash of his tongue tugging at the gold chains on her nipples, were nearly unbearable. She twisted against him, not knowing if she needed to get closer or escape the electrical impulses of pleasure tearing into her womb as his other hand slid into her pants.

Her fingers clenched in his hair as she felt his fingers rasp over the swollen bud of her clit. She was wet. So damned wet his fingers sank into her juices as they slid through the narrow slit awaiting him.

He played with her. Toyed with her arousal. He circled the throbbing opening of her vagina, his fingertip brushing over the entrance with firm strokes. Hips writhing, her moans echoing in her own head, Morganna fought for penetration. Oh God, she needed penetration.

"Please, Clint." Surely he wouldn't be so cruel as to deny her. To bring her so close, only to pull back.

"So sweet and hot," he muttered against her breast.

"For God's sake, Clint, please . . ."

A strangled scream tore from her throat. He didn't penetrate with just one finger. He used two. Slow. Easy. Stretching her, burning her. She felt her pussy convulsing around his fingers, felt her orgasm close, so close.

"Do you need me, baby?" His voice was torn, rough, thick, and edged with the same hunger that ripped through her. "Tell me what you need, Morganna."

"You."

"What part of me?"

"All of you, Clint," she cried out as his fingers flexed inside her, sliding deeper before withdrawing. "Please. All of you . . ."

He thrust inside her, a hard, long impalement that had her hips lifting, her body reaching for orgasm. She could feel it whipping along her nerve endings, thrumming in her blood, and pounding in her head.

"Son of a bitch." Before she could understand the sudden desertion, Clint was jerking from her. His fingers pulled from the clenching depths of her pussy as he jerked the leather back over her breasts and lifted his eyes. His expression was tight as he stared beyond the window.

"Clint, it's Officer Zane Roland. Is everything okay in there?" There was an edge of suspicion, of amusement, in the voice beyond the door.

"Come on." Clint levered himself from her, quickly helping her sit up before the pounding at the window made sense to her.

He lowered the window enough to glimpse the police officer standing outside before lowering it halfway.

"Thought that was you, Clint." Surprise surprise, he knew the police, too.

The stoic expression of the officer creased into an apologetic smile for a moment.

"We're heading out, Zack," Clint breathed roughly, pushing his fingers through his hair as he slanted the officer a wry smile. "Sorry 'bout that."

"Understandable." Zane nodded, glancing at Morganna as she ducked her head. "Just thought I'd check and make sure everything was okay. I heard about the shooting at Diva's last night."

Clint nodded abruptly. "You're right; this was real dumb." He glanced at Morganna, but his gaze wasn't angry now; it was . . . perplexed maybe. "She goes to a man's head."

"So I see," Zane chuckled. "See you around, Clint, and take care."

"Yeah. I'll do that," Clint grumbled as he hit the electronic lever that raised the window.

Morganna was still fighting to breathe, to pull her emotions and her senses together, when Clint put the truck in gear and pulled out of the parking lot, back into the traffic as she moved to fasten her pants.

He didn't have to warn her to keep her mouth shut now;

she didn't think she could form a coherent thought, let alone produce speech.

What was she going to do about Clint? Her body awakened to him with nothing but a look, and what his kisses did to her should be illegal. It probably was illegal.

She stared through the windshield until he took the turn leading to her house, rather than his apartment. She breathed in slowly, pulling herself together, pushing back the pain she could feel clawing through her.

She had a feeling he had no intention of joining her in her bed. It was a repeat of that morning, except for the orgasm. She would definitely be left wanting tonight.

"We need to talk." The anger wasn't there, only the aching well of sadness she had sometimes glimpsed in him.

"We tried that this morning. It didn't work." Wrapping her arms over her chest did nothing to soothe the aching void inside her. "Besides, Clint, you don't talk; you order, demand, or command. When that doesn't work, you tattle. Why should we break the habit now?"

"God, Morganna, you have no idea what you're getting mixed up in." He sighed, the weariness in his voice pricking her conscience. She knew he had slept in his truck the night before and that couldn't have been restful.

"I can't sit on a shelf and wait for you and Reno to decide to take me down for a visit," she whispered, swallowing tightly. Emptiness stretched ahead of her, years alone, if she didn't do something to change it. And God knew she was so tired of being alone.

"What happened to marriage? Children?" he bit out, his voice rough. "Morganna, what you're doing will get you killed."

"Are you proposing?" she asked as he pulled in front of her house.

"This isn't a joking matter." He jerked his head around, staring at her as he put the truck into park.

"No, it isn't." She shook her head dismally. "Because it

wouldn't matter if you were proposing, Clint. I've found what I want to do." She stared back at him directly. "I found something I believe in. Something that gives me purpose. I won't give that up for you. And it wouldn't work if I did. Because, quite honestly, you don't want me, not really. It wouldn't matter if you were fucking me or that redhead tonight. We would both be the same in your eyes. And I need more from a lover than that."

"And you think Drage Masters is going to give you more?" Clint asked in astonishment. "Do you think you can sell your soul to the devil and walk away later, Morganna?"

"Then rescind your request that I be barred from the clubs," she said gently. She wasn't angry any longer. She was tired. Tired of loving a man who didn't need her. Who didn't truly want her. "Don't take this away from me, Clint. I've worked too hard and too long. Don't force me to choose like this."

"You'd play the whore for him?" He frowned back at her, his expression heavy, set.

"I have to find a life, Clint. A lover. Someone who sees something in me other than his best friend's sister or a responsibility he can't run away from this time," she pointed out, aching inside. "I love you. I've always loved you. For as long as I can remember. But I can't continue to wait on a man who doesn't even respect me enough to work with me. A man willing to steal years of my life for his own selfishness. I've worked for this assignment. I trained for it. And you pushed me out as though what I want, what I need, doesn't even matter."

He said nothing in his defense, no explanation, no denial. The pain of it ate at her heart as the years she had wasted stretched out behind her.

"Good-bye, Clint," she whispered. "Just say good-bye. I don't need a babysitter; I need a lover who's willing to care. Drage might not love me, but he's willing to put effort into some part of me. That's more than you've ever done."

She gripped the latch, pulling it toward her to open her door, when Clint caught her arm. Drawing in a deep breath, she turned back to stare at him.

His eyes blazed from his face, his expression torn and, for the first time, reflecting the conflicting emotions she had always felt raged inside him. Emotions she would have jumped with joy to have seen in the years past. Now it was just too little too late. Clint couldn't change who he was; somehow she had always known that, always sensed it. She had kept their confrontations light, kept from pushing too hard, because of that instinctive knowledge.

She couldn't fight it anymore, though. She couldn't fight him.

"I care. . . ." The words seemed torn from him. They ripped through her chest, tore at her heart with slicing, agonizing blows.

Lifting her hand, she touched his cheek. The growth of beard was sensually rough beneath her fingertips, sending an aching hunger to pulse through every cell of her body.

"Not enough," she whispered tearfully. "Not enough for either of us, Clint."

She pulled free of him before jumping out of the truck and running up the cement steps to the front yard. Now was as good a time as any to say good-bye.

Chapter 9

CLINT HUNG HIS HEAD, HIS jaw clenched, his head pounding with a need that wracked his body. And he was sitting here in this damned truck letting her run away, letting her give up on him. Hell, he had never let her give up, he realized. He had pushed her away with one hand, pulled her back with the other, and tortured them both with the arousal she fired in his blood.

No one could affect him like Morganna, and she terrified him because of it. Terrified him because he had always known that something wild and free beat inside her. She needed a man who could stand at her side, not one who would stand in front of her.

And Clint needed to stand in front of her. He needed to protect her, to shield her. The thought of losing her forever . . . God, it was killing him.

He groaned, a low, torn sound that shocked him. She was giving up on him. He had heard it in her voice, and that affected him more than he would have ever guessed. Affected him, hell. He couldn't do it.

Clint jerked open the door and moved from the truck, striding quickly up the cement steps to the house. He was about to make the biggest mistake of his life. He was about to take a chance on destroying both of them, and he knew it.

The front door was open, but no lights were on. As Clint made it to the porch, every instinct he had ever honed in the SEALs went on full alert.

He heard Morganna's short cry, the sound of something breaking, and fear tore through him. He rushed into the house, his gaze quickly finding her. For a moment, one blinding second in time, Clint knew he had lost her forever.

The dim light seemed to glow around the two figures. The tall, masked form behind her. A leather fist was clenched in her hair, jerking her head back as the other hand lifted, the blade of a wicked knife gleaming in the darkness as Clint rushed for them.

His mind was processing as he rushed for her. The determination in her face, the lack of fear as her arm came up, bent, her elbow slamming into her attacker's solar plexus as she gripped his wrist and twisted with both hands.

Clint managed to grip her arm, jerking her back and throwing himself at her attacker. The sound of a knife clattering on the floor was followed by a heavy male curse as Clint rushed him.

Rage transformed itself, fury and fear; the sight of Morganna within inches of death sent a flash of red before Clint's vision.

Before he could slam his body into the assailant's, before his fists could connect or the bloodletting rage could find an outlet, the dark form threw itself through the window behind him.

The crash of glass and the splintering wail of the home security system shrieked in Clint's head as he jumped through the window frame, landing on the ground in a crouch as gunfire splattered around him.

"You son of a bitch," he snarled as he threw himself to the side, staying low and rushing to the front of the house.

"Gun." Morganna was waiting at the doorway, pushing the .45 into his hands.

"Let's go."

He had to get her out of there. If the intruder was an assassin, he'd definitely have backup. Clint grabbed her arm as he balanced the weapon in his hand and pulled her from the house.

"Stay low." Clint pulled Morganna close to his side as he moved at a run for the truck, rushing to get her out of the line of any fire.

Lights were filling the homes around Morganna's now, and he knew the police would be on their way soon. Jerking the driver's side door open, he pushed her inside before following.

"Get down." He pushed her down in the seat as he twisted the key in the ignition and pushed the gas to the floor.

The truck peeled out of its parking spot, followed by the ping of bullets against the side.

"I'll twist his guts if I find him," Clint growled at the damage to his truck. "Damn bastard. It's a new truck."

He twisted the wheel as he turned the corner, accelerating down the street and heading for the interstate.

Morganna hadn't said a word.

Clint glanced over at her, seeing her wide eyes, her pale face, as she curled up on the seat, her head lying next to his thigh.

"Are you okay, baby?" One hand shot from the wheel, running down her arm, her stomach, her hip. "Did he cut you anywhere?"

Clint leaned over her, checking her for injuries as he raced away from the residential streets. The fear that flooded him at the thought of her wounded, bleeding, cramped his guts in horror.

"I'm fine." She was shuddering, shaking from the shock. "No cuts. Few bruises. I'm fine."

He straightened, jerked his cell phone from the holder at his hip, and punched Joe Merino's speed dial.

"This is Merino. We have a report of a disturbance—" Merino's voice was frantic.

"I have Morganna," Clint snapped. "She was attacked when she walked in the door. Damned rookie. He didn't expect her to fight back."

"Is there a body?"

"Negative. We're taking cover. We'll contact you at zero eight hundred hours."

"Shit," Joe snarled. "I'll contact you if they find anything at the house, and apprise the officer in charge that the owner of the house is safe. And, Clint?"

"Yeah?"

"We had another girl drugged tonight. She was being led to the back entrance when one of Masters' bouncers caught sight of her and went to investigate. The bastard got away."

"The girl?"

"Critical. She's at the hospital now, but she was a little thing and the dose was a good one. She might not make it."

Clint took the exit to the interstate, his eyes narrowed as he checked the rearview mirror. It would be impossible to tell if they were being followed until they managed to get farther from town.

"They're looking for their next mark now." Clint's jaw clenched at the thought.

"My gut is rocking on this one, and I know yours is, too. We don't have much time here. What did you find out tonight?"

"Not enough." Enough to know every fucking Dom in that club had put his name in the hat in case Morganna asked for sponsorship, but that had nothing to do with the drugs or their mark.

"Is Morganna okay?" Joe breathed out roughly across the line, obviously aware that this was not a discussion Clint was ready to have.

"She's fine." Curled at his side like a little cat. "Find out what you can; we'll talk later."

He disconnected the phone before shoving it back into the holder and easing up on the gas. He kept a close eye on the rearview mirror as traffic began to thin and they neared the next exit he was searching for.

"I'm going to find a hotel for the night." He buried his hand in her hair, caressing her scalp. He needed to touch her, to know she was alive.

He felt her nod.

"We'll find some place with room service. You need to eat, to rest. We'll figure this out tomorrow."

"Someone knows," she whispered. "I know I didn't give myself away, Clint. I know I didn't. We weren't even close to finding out who's supplying that drug. All we caught were three of the dealers, and they had no idea I was involved."

Clint swallowed tightly. He agreed. There was no reason for a hit against her, not now, not yet. Unless the suppliers were aware that she *had* been behind the arrests of the dealers. And if any of the Fuentes family were still operating behind the drug, then it would be a matter of personal satisfaction to take Morganna out.

"We'll figure it out." He couldn't stop touching her. Even as she moved to sit up, he pushed her back down.

"Stay down a while longer," he whispered. "If they're looking for us, they're looking for a man and woman together, not just a man. We'll be at the hotel soon."

Her hand curled over his knee as her head rested on his thigh.

"I was scared," she whispered. "I'm glad you came back."

She hadn't looked scared. Determined. Defiant. But she hadn't looked scared.

"I never left." He kept his eyes between the windshield and the mirrors, his body tense as he watched the traffic coming up on them.

He couldn't think about that now. He couldn't think about how close that knife had been to her throat, how easily she could have died in front of his eyes. He couldn't let himself admit, yet, how he had nearly failed her.

He slowed down and the cars behind him passed. He sped up and they fell back. There was no sign that he had been followed, that anyone cared one way or the other about the gray extended-cab pickup heading for the next off-ramp.

The assailant in Morganna's room had been sloppy, but that didn't mean he couldn't track her and Clint. The only thing that had saved Morganna was that her attacker hadn't expected a fight. He had expected a victim. And he hadn't expected Clint. The advantage of surprise had been on their side. This time.

"If I had lost you . . ." He swallowed tightly, his throat tightening at the thought as her hand tightened on his knee.

"I'm okay." But she was still shaking; her voice quivered.

"A miracle." He kept driving. He knew where he was going, but he was determined to take his time getting there.

"Well, I have to admit, it wasn't looking good there for a minute." Her laugh was shaky as she rubbed her cheek against his thigh.

His teeth clenched at the vibration of pleasure that echoed into his rapidly aroused cock. God, he couldn't even keep his head out of his pants long enough to get her to safety.

This was one of his greatest nightmares, that his need for her, his hunger, would affect his better judgment, his training. At the moment, all he could think about was getting her to a hotel, locking the world behind them, and sinking into the soft, blistering heat between her thighs. He had to assure himself she was alive, breathing, whole.

He wanted to hear her scream for him. He wanted to taste the sweet, soft syrup that ran from that tight pussy and become drunk on the taste of her.

He licked his lips, tightened his hand on the wheel, and made another turn. His gaze was never still; his mind assessed every vehicle he passed, every flash of headlights in his rearview mirror. His senses were as alert now as they were in full combat mode, despite the arousal. At least so far.

"Why did you come into the house? I thought you were leaving." She suddenly asked the question he was hoping she wouldn't think of.

Clint inhaled roughly. He could feel the invisible bands of steel tightening around him with the knowledge that it didn't matter what he had told himself over the years. He couldn't walk away from her.

"It's a good thing I did," he grunted, his fingers luxuriating in her thick mass of curls. "You were holding your own, baby, damned good. But he was better than you."

"No kidding," she sighed. "But you didn't answer my question."

Silence filled the truck then. He made another turn as he headed back to the interstate.

"I couldn't walk away," he finally breathed out roughly. "I couldn't."

"Why?"

He knew what she needed to hear, knew what she wanted. He glared at the signs along the interstate that pointed him to his destination.

"I can't answer that, Morganna," he breathed out roughly. "You were right earlier, though. You deserve better. But maybe, we both deserve to know where this could go, too."

She stiffened for a second before he felt her inhale deeply. The tremors still raced through her body, but they were no longer shudders; she was no longer fighting to breathe from terror.

"And the operation?"

He snarled silently. "We'll work together. You were right about that, too; it wasn't fair to take it from you. But you'll follow my rules, my direction. Period."

"You mean that?" The vulnerability in her voice tore at his heart. God, how cruel he had been to her. He had hurt her in so many different ways that her voice echoed with distrust.

"I mean it, baby." He shook his head as he drove into the enclosed parking garage attached to the Sheraton. "Come on. Let's get a room and see if we can figure out what the hell is going on here."

He pulled the truck into one of the upper-level parking spots, a shadowy corner with the elevator and stair entrance shielding it from oncoming vehicles.

"Stay put a minute." He slid from the cab, reaching into the back and pulling free the emergency duffel bag he kept there.

He pulled his wallet from his back pocket and replaced it with the one in the duffel, then pulled the extra license plate from inside and moved to the rear of the truck. A quick change and he was back to the cab and storing the old plate beneath the seat.

"Interesting." She was staring back at him with wide, stormy eyes.

"It should be effective." He shrugged. "They're looking for Fulton County tags, not Cobb. Ready?"

He ran his gaze over her intently. There was no blood, a few scratches, and one of the most gorgeous bodies he had ever seen dressed in leather.

Smooth sun-kissed flesh that he knew needed no sun to darken it. Long, loose curls twisted down her back, fell around her shoulders. And those breasts cupped by leather and held in place by the flimsiest ties were enough to send his blood pressure rocketing. The soft rise of the flesh over the cups tempted him, drew him until his head lowered and he heard her gasp as he breathed a kiss over the closest one.

She was warm and sweet, a bounty of passion and need that he knew he couldn't deny himself any longer.

Raising his head, he stared back at her, realizing his hands were gripping her soft hips, holding her in place where she sat sideways in the seat.

"Ready?" He stepped back, extending his hand to her.

"I'm ready." She slid from the seat, balancing her weight as she drew in a deep breath, her hand gripping his tightly for a moment. "A little shaky, but ready." Her smile was quick, nervous. Her eyes were still big for her pale face, though.

"Let's go then." He gripped her arm as he pulled her to him before slamming the truck door. He hit the automatic lock, then headed for the elevators. "There's a bathroom right as we get off the elevator in the reception area. Hide in there. There's no way to hide all that leather and that curvy little body. I'll get our room and come back for you."

She snorted. "And you think you're easier to forget?"

"There are plenty of dark-haired men in leather," he informed her. "Especially in this area. I have what I need to get the room in another name and hide us for a night or two until I can get this figured out. You, on the other hand . . . every man breathing would notice that outfit. It's distinctive."

"Whatever." She shook her head as he escorted her into the elevator and hit the lobby button. "Just hurry, Clint, because I think I've about had it for the night."

She had been pushed to her limits; he could feel it. She needed to be fed, soothed, and eased into sleep. God help him, he prayed he could soothe her, but he was very much afraid that once he touched her, all bets were off. He was going to love her instead.

Chapter 10

SHE LOOKED LIKE HELL.

Morganna dampened a soft cloth beneath the running water and washed the smudged makeup from her face before grimacing at her pale reflection. There was a scratch on her neck that she had no idea where it came from, a few fingerprint bruises on her bare arms—only God knew if they'd come from Clint jerking her away from the assailant or the assailant himself.

She breathed in deeply. There hadn't been time to be terrified during the attack, but the moment Clint jerked her from the knife heading for her throat, it had set in.

The attack didn't make sense.

She braced her hands on the sink as she lowered her head and fought the weariness washing over her. Through her. Nothing about this operation was making sense now. Why would she be targeted now? And how had anyone learned she was even working the case? Only her commander, Joe's team, and now Clint knew that she was more than a secretary.

The job in the local law firm had gotten her through the Law Enforcement Academy, nothing else. No one had known what she was doing. Not even Raven had known until after the graduation.

It was apparent that someone else did know Morganna was working the case, though.

And what had the attacker said just before Clint came into the room? Something about divine retribution? What the hell was divine retribution?

Shaking her head, she dropped the cloth into the basket under the sink before washing her hands and forcing back the edge of shattered nerves pushing at her mind.

Adrenaline. She recognized it, though it was stronger now than it had ever been. Coming down from it was a pain in the ass.

She was shaking from head to toe, fine tremors more than shudders, a heightened awareness, as well as a heightened arousal. Now that one was different. The arousal was burning inside her, a flaming ache in the center of her sex that refused to be ignored.

"You've lost it, Chavez," she told herself as she lifted her head, staring back at her reflection. "You just can't learn your lesson, can you?"

She knew not to trust Clint. How many times in the past had he allowed her to hope, to dream, only to pull back?

But he had never promised her before.

Clint always kept his promises. He never broke his word. At the least, he wouldn't take this operation from her. The sense of accomplishment that filled her with was overwhelming.

"Morganna, are you okay?" Clint's voice was husky, soft, from the other side of the door.

"I'm fine." She drew in a deep breath before opening the door and coming face-to-face with him.

His expression was concerned, his eyes dark in his sun-tanned face, his big body tense as he towered over her.

"I have to get out of this leather." She moved past him and into the sitting room of the suite he had taken. "I hope you have something I can wear in that bag of tricks you carried up with you."

"I laid it on the bed," he drawled behind her. "I called room service. We'll have something up here to eat soon, then you can shower."

Morganna sat down on the couch, breathing out wearily as she unzipped the high boots and dragged them off her feet. Pleasure eased through her as cool air enveloped her tired feet, the cramped muscles relaxing as she pressed the pads of her feet into the floor.

"That sounds good." She set the boots to the side as she fought to ignore the fact that he was shirtless. That all that bare, powerful muscle was on display and nearly impossible not to look at.

Besides, she wasn't here to have sex, she reminded herself; she was here because someone had decided they wanted her dead.

"I guess tonight clears up whether or not the drive-by shooting the other night was aimed at me." She kept her gaze on the floor, determined not to stare up at him. Not to eat him with her gaze.

"Someone knows what you're doing." He paced across her field of vision, long legs encased in snug leather. "But that's not enough to put out a hit against you. Craig maybe. Joe definitely. But not you. You're just a watcher, and easy enough to avoid if they know who you are."

That was what she thought.

"Then what's going on?" She lifted her eyes wearily, feeling the effects of the late nights, the excitement, the raging emotions she had dealt with over the past two days, catching up with her. "Why risk getting caught? If they know of me, then they know of the team. Why not just move to another club?"

"Arrogance." He shrugged as he leaned against the frame of the entryway across from her. "To make an example of you. There could be several reasons and all could apply. Or none of them." His expression was thoughtful, somber. "They tried to take another girl tonight. One of Drage's men caught up with them before they managed to maneuver her through the back entrance. She was drugged, heavily."

Morganna's eyes widened at the information as she stared back at him in shock. "They moved fast. We just arrested the three suspects attempting to drug that girl last week."

"They have a schedule then," he mused. "The hit bothers me more, and the fact that they waited until you left to drug the girl."

"We move between several clubs in one night, and Joe's team isn't the only one working this. We have three teams on the task force here in Atlanta. The DEA is determined to shut this down now, before the drug goes further. We suspect the sale of the videos is being used to fund terrorist activities, but there's no confirmation on that."

"How many agents?"

She stared back at him with dismay. "There are fifteen agents total working this. But only the individual teams and the commander know the 'watchers' such as myself."

"Watcher, my ass. You're bait. But that doesn't explain why you were targeted with a knife instead of the drug."

"Divine retribution," she muttered, staring back at him. "That's what he said just before you came into the house. Divine retribution."

"Nothing else?" Cold purpose glittered in Clint's eyes.

Morganna shook her head as she moved to her feet, unable to sit still. Rubbing her fingers over her brow, she paced to the small office desk on the other side of the room before stopping and tapping her fingers against the desk softly.

"It was personal," she finally said. "You could hear it in his voice. There was an accent. . . ." She frowned, trying to remember the sound of her attacker's voice. "I can't place it."

God, she wanted to curl into Clint's arms. His broad chest looked wide enough to shelter her, his arms strong enough to hold her. And she needed him to hold her. She had needed it for so long, though, that she wondered if she wasn't more used to the hunger than she would be to easing it.

"We'll rest this weekend." He straightened from the door frame, his arms dropping to the pockets of his pants as he stared back at her. "You'll have to call in to the office you're working at, take next week off while we work on this. Joe had a good idea, setting up in the clubs like that. But the community he's dealing with is far more extensive than he could imagine unless he was part of it. Monday, we'll start making some calls."

"Then you were serious about working together on this?"

His lips quirked. "As much as I needed to keep you out of this for my own peace of mind, whoever's behind it seems more intent on dragging you into it. The only way to keep you safe is to neutralize the threat. And I called Drage while you were in the bathroom and had him rescind the request that you be banned from the clubs. You're now under sponsorship. We know they're after you; we just have to use that to trap the suppliers." It was more than obvious he wasn't pleased with the situation.

"Will you or Craig be set up to buy?"

"Me." His voice was a hard rumble. "You'll not be playing a role. You'll be yourself. By now, everyone will have figured out I'm so damned hot for you that I can't breathe for the hard-on killing me." And he didn't seem pleased by that. "I don't want you to play the submissive. Fight me as you would any other time."

A knock at the door had him whirling away from her as he pulled the .45 from the small of his back and moved in complete silence to the door of the suite.

"Room service," a cheerful voice announced.

Bedroom. Clint turned and mouthed the word at her as he neared the door.

Morganna grabbed her boots and moved hurriedly across the room and ducked into the bedroom, careful to hide along the side of the room. Clint had been adamant that no one, including hotel staff, know that she was in the room with him.

"Good evening, Mr. Sizemore." The waiter's voice moved into the sitting room. "I have your dinner, sir."

The sound of footsteps, then a heavy tray being placed on the wide coffee table in the other room could be heard.

"Is there anything else I can get for you, sir?"

"That will be all." Clint's voice was clipped, businesslike. "Thank you for being so quick."

"Yes, sir!" The waiter's exclamation had her rolling her

eyes. Must have been a helluva tip. "You need anything, sir, you just call right down. We'll take care of you."

"Will do," Clint responded as the steps moved back to the door of the suite.

Seconds later the sound of the door closing and the bolt lock had Morganna moving quickly from the bedroom. The smell of food had her stomach growling. She was starved and she knew for a fact he had ordered enough to feed an army.

He was waiting on her when she walked into the room, his gaze frankly sexual as she moved to the food tray. She hadn't eaten since lunch that day and her stomach was voraciously reminding her of the fact that even that meal had been incredibly small.

She pulled the metal covering from the cheeseburger and fries she had ordered. Being attacked and nearly having one's throat sliced called for calories to celebrate life. Lots of calories.

Clint pulled the nearby chair over to the low table and followed suit as she poured a glass of tea from the pitcher and began to dig in.

She tried to ignore Clint sitting across from her, as well as the implications of what he had implied before the waiter knocked on the door. If Clint intended to take her to his bed, she wouldn't be able to refuse him. Just as she wouldn't be able to protect her own heart. He was her weakness; he had been her weakness for most of her life.

"The girl that was drugged, Cathie Fitzhugh, she worked in the same office complex as you." Clint stated as he slathered mayo over his own hamburger, glancing up at her with steely-eyed purpose as he spoke.

Morganna nodded. "She works in another department, though. That makes three women who worked there and have been drugged by these bastards."

"There could be a link there." He nodded. "Joe is checking it out. Your cover's shot, Morganna. They know who you are."

"And we must be closer to the suppliers than I thought." She shook her head in confusion. "We have a suspect, but nothing concrete. And it would make better sense to attempt to drug me, rather than attacking me at home."

Clint shook his head at that. "The drug can take up to an hour to fully hit the system and make the victim dazed enough that she wouldn't remember who took her out of the club if she did survive the rest of the night. Whoever is watching you is aware that you're being watched as well. They wouldn't have taken that chance."

"The whole damned assignment has been compromised." The reality of that one sucked.

"Not necessarily. They're obviously not willing to move the operation, for whatever reason. That kind of arrogance can weaken any plan. We'll make our own rounds, dig deeper into the lower areas of the club, and see what we come up with. The majority of the women are being hit at Masters' clubs, so we'll concentrate there. Let's see how stupid they can get."

The cold smile that crossed Clint's lips had a chill racing up Morganna's spine. She hadn't realized until now just how furious he was.

"Joe cleared Drage Masters of any involvement with the drugs. They had his clubs staked out for months before I came onto the team. They've also hit a couple of the other more extreme clubs. They're steering clear of the bars and honky-tonks."

"The crowds are larger in the clubs such as Drage's and they're more impersonal. It's easier to strike there." Clint nodded.

"If my cover's been blown, then I'm a liability to the case," she said. "They won't move against me."

"Wrong." His smile was cold, ruthless, but his eyes were shadowed. "They proved that last night, Morganna."

Morganna watched him carefully. "You're angry at me."

She knew that look, knew the controlled line of his lips and the glitter in his eyes.

His jaw bunched. "I've fought for eight years," he finally said. "Thinking you were safe. That what I was doing was keeping you and Raven safe. And I'll be a son of a bitch if you didn't just walk your ass right into danger."

Yep, he was mad. But she hadn't expected anything less.

A smile trembled at her lips as she stared back at him, meeting his gaze head-on.

"I make a difference," she finally whispered, reminding him of the words he had whispered the day he had left for SEAL training.

She had cried because he was leaving again. He had pulled her into his arms as though he couldn't help himself. She had been so young, and he had been a warrior. He still was.

"You're going to be the death of me," he finally said, his voice low, rough. "Because if anything happened to you, Morganna, God's truth, I don't know what I'd do."

DRAGE WATCHED THE VIDEO FEED closely, following the girl's progress backward, hoping to find where she had been drugged and by whom.

Fury ate inside Drage, as the male figure who had attempted to lead her from the club seemed aware of the placement of the video cameras. His face was kept carefully hidden from the all-seeing eyes spread through the ceiling and around the walls of the club. There were very few ways to avoid them, but this bastard had figured it out.

The reverse run of the video followed the girl back to her table, where she had been sitting with several of Morganna Chavez's friends. Jenna Lancaster was there, as were Sandy Mitchell and Craig Tyler. Waitresses had come and gone, and once again the shadowy male had shown up.

Drage watched as the man sat down beside Cathie Fitzhugh. The girl resembled Morganna Chavez a little too closely. Same style of dress, same hair. The drink he held was unobtrusively moved into the place of the drink the waitress had just brought Miss Fitzhugh. Without looking, without checking, she picked up the wrong drink and began to consume it.

Craig Tyler had turned from the table at the same moment, looking out over the crowd. Sandy Mitchell had been flirting with Jenna Lancaster. It was as though the dark figure sitting among them was noticed by no one but the video camera. And then never at an angle to catch either his profile or his full expression.

"He makes it look very easy, doesn't he, Jayne?" he murmured to his head of security, who was currently pacing the room.

Jayne Smith—he almost snorted at the name—was the best money could buy in the security field, but even she had been unable to catch the drugging of the women.

"It's the second attempt, though there are slight differences in build and mannerisms between the two men slipping the drinks in," Smith snapped, her icy blue eyes staring at the screens intently. "We managed to avoid one last week. Sandy feigned accidentally spilling her drink when he noticed it had been switched. But he didn't see who switched it. That bastard . . ." She pointed to the leather-clad shadow slowly moving back from the table as the slow-motion reverse cycle of the feed continued. "Is damned good. He knows the placement of our cameras, your bouncers, and the men watching out just for this. If it hadn't been for the bouncer making a quick, unannounced trip to the men's room, another girl would have disappeared last week."

"Reno isn't going to be pleased with this report," Drage muttered as he kept his eyes on the video. "Have you been able to figure out where McIntyre has Morganna hidden?"

"Not yet." She shook her head, the short strands of silky dark blond hair feathering around her face. "But we're working on it. That attempt on her at the house will spook him. Maybe we'll get lucky and he'll pull her out."

Drage shook his head slowly. "It won't happen. She's

committed to this. We'll wait until the club empties out of employees before we relocate a few of the cameras. Don't let anyone else know what we're doing. We'll do it ourselves. I want to know how that bastard knows my security angles enough to keep his face hidden."

"You and me both." Murder swirled in the dark cadence of Smith's voice. "And I don't know about you, but I'm starting to suspect Agent Merino has a mole in his group. They would know our cameras and their placement after pulling the security tapes last month after one of the women turned up dead."

"Agreed," Drage murmured as he continued to watch the figure move through the club until he exited. The outside cameras picked him up from there.

Two dozen cameras and nothing, not even a profile shot that wasn't shadowed one way or the other, to give a hint to the man's identity. No tags on the plain brown sedan he entered, no marks to identify it.

"Joe definitely has a mole." Drage finally admitted to the suspicion he had tried to deny. "Contact McIntyre when you find him. He called earlier, but his number was blocked. I want to talk to him before he brings her back in."

"He rescinded his request?" Smith guessed.

Drage smiled faintly. "As I expected he would. I didn't expect this attack on her so soon, though. It will only raise suspicion. Merino surely suspects himself now that he has a leak."

Smith shook her head as Drage glanced back at her. She looked like a cuddly little mistress, not the best damned gutter fighter he had ever run across.

"He won't believe it," she said coolly. "He'll point out that the objective was to bring focus to her in the first place. He won't accept one of his men has turned."

"Do we have any reports on who could be behind this yet?" Drage asked.

Smith's nostrils flared as her gaze met his. "A few rumors

are coming in, but nothing I can substantiate. We've had the name of a canceled cartel pop up a few times, but they were taken out two years ago, the entire family neutralized. We have a possible Russian connection, but that one doesn't feel right. I'm still checking into it."

Drage nodded in reply before sighing deeply. "Take the bouncers off scheduled posts. Have them move freely about the club rather than in the formation we've kept them in. I don't want to lose any more women from my clubs, Smith. This is pissing me off."

"You're not alone," she snorted. "What I can't understand is why strike so soon after the three were arrested last week."

"These videos are funding something." His fist clenched as he stared at the video once again. "And they're using my damned clubs to do it."

"Two other women were hit last month at other clubs," she pointed out. "Diva's, Merlin's, and the Roundtable just happen to have the crowd they're looking for. As for what they're funding, I'm guessing their own damned pockets, boss."

He heard the throttled fury in her voice and knew she was just as determined to find the bastards behind this as was he. Jayne looked soft, sweet, like a sex kitten waiting to play. She was a tiger waiting to devour instead. The damage she could do to a man when she wanted to had Drage wincing at the thought. She had nerves of steel and ice water for blood.

"Let me know when you're ready to start moving the cameras," he told her quietly. "I'm going to go over these videos again, see if I can catch anything familiar about this guy."

She was silent. Drage could feel her standing behind him, watching him. And he remembered weeks before, when he had nearly lost her to those bastards. Jayne drugged on Whores Dust wasn't a sight he ever wanted to experience again.

"Be sure to remember to eat," she said, her voice cold as

she headed for the door, obviously offended by his abrupt manner. "Don't make me have to cart it in here to you. I'm not your maid."

Before he could snap out a reply the door was closing quietly behind him and he realized that once again she had managed to get the last word on him. Damn her.

Chapter 11

CLINT PACED THE SUITE AS he listened to the water running in the shower. The dinner plates had been cleared away and set outside, the door carefully bolted. He was sealed inside with her, the scent of her filling his senses as he prowled the room, waiting.

If he could hold the rest of the world at bay for just a few hours, then he could convince himself, to the bone, that she was okay. He pushed his fingers through his hair before gripping his neck in an effort to massage away the tension there.

He couldn't shake the sight of that knife moving for the fragile column of her neck. If she hadn't saved herself, she would have been dead. There was no way he could have gotten to her in time. He tried to tell himself he would have, but he knew better. All the training in the world couldn't make him Superman.

And he still remembered her expression. Determined to live, her eyes bright with anger, her face twisted into a grimace of resolve. She wasn't going to let her assailant kill her, not that easily. She had given Clint those extra few seconds he needed to jerk her out of her assailant's arms and out of harm's way.

That time.

His guts tightened with the thought that just pulling her out of the game wasn't going to pull her out of the danger. She was compromised, for whatever reason, and now she was marked.

The thought of that was enough to make him wish for an empty room and ten minutes alone with the bastards targeting her. He'd show them pain. He'd show the sons of bitches what it was like to hurt, to die in an agony so intense that death was a relief. No one, but no one, was allowed to hurt Morganna.

He had made that rule years ago, and he'd made it stick. The boys who dated her knew that if a single tear was shed over them on her part, then he and Reno came after them. She was heartbreaking when she cried. It was something Clint couldn't handle, not for a second.

Her eyes just got wider, her pouty little lips turned down, and silent tears washed over a heartbroken expression. His hands shook at the thought of dealing with those tears, because he wanted to kiss them away. Then kiss her trembling lips, and from there . . . there would have been no stopping his downfall.

Just as there was no stopping it now. He knew when she walked out of that shower; within seconds he was going to end up tossing her in that bed. And God help her. He hadn't been this damned hot for a woman in years; it might be days before Morganna got to see sunlight again.

Which only added to his frustration. To keep her, he was going to have to save her first. He stopped in the middle of the floor at that thought and raised his eyes to the ceiling, looking for answers where he was certain there were none.

Save her? The minute he managed to pull her ass out of this fire, she'd have the flames licking at her from somewhere else. She was trouble. She wasn't even trouble waiting to happen; she was trouble in progress.

And he was going to work with her?

He ground his teeth together at the thought. It would be more like trying to work just to keep up with her. He knew from experience that keeping up with Morganna was next to impossible.

Damn. He was in trouble and he knew it.

Because in some ways, she had been right that morning. His parents' relationship had colored his belief in love, in women. Morganna was the prettiest thing he had ever laid his eyes on and so filled with life he knew he had no hope of keeping her to himself.

He couldn't lock her away and expect her to be happy. She would always need an adventure, and as she was proving now, that adventure would never be safe.

And the men. God, they flocked around her like flies to honey, hungry to touch her, to possess her. As though the life that burned within her eyes drew them like moths to a flame.

Once he had her, any man who touched her would be taking his life in his own hands. Unlike his father, Clint would never be able to contain his fury if he arrived home to find his woman in bed with another man.

Clint's jaw clenched as anger nearly overwhelmed him. He knew Morganna had known other lovers; hell, he even knew who they were. He could tell, the moment he met them, that they had touched her beautiful body, had lain with her, caressing her, loving her. And he had wanted to kill them. Hell, he still wanted to kill them.

That fury had terrified him. If he felt that way and she didn't even belong to him, what would he do if the loneliness she would live with as his wife became too much? If temptation was too close, the fear and the worry too strong, allowing her to give in to another man?

"You think too much."

He swung around, tension tightening his body at the sight of her leaning against the wall that led to the bathroom. He had heard the shower turn off; he hadn't expected her to leave the bathroom so quickly.

The shirt he had given her was the ugliest one he owned. A pea green combat shirt that had been washed one time too many. It hung to her knees, but first it whispered over her breasts, outlining those damned gold rings centered in her nipples.

Lust sizzled in his groin, torturing his erection, tightening it further. He swore he was harder than he had ever been in his life. "You didn't need the T-shirt."

"Yes, I did." She straightened from the wall, watching him warily. "You surely didn't think I was just going to lay down with you and let you trample all over me again, Clint."

He had wondered how long it would take her to get mad. And she was plenty mad now. The shock from the attack was wearing off, but the adrenaline was still riding high inside her.

"You've been fighting for this for eight years, Morganna." He ground his teeth together in frustration, certain she would end up driving him crazy.

"I stopped fighting tonight, remember?" she pointed out, those stormy eyes biting into him, defying him, challenging him. "I gave up."

"You?" he said, smiling, shaking his head. "You don't give up, baby."

"In this case, I'm reevaluating my options." Slender shoulders shrugged negligently as her arms crossed beneath her breasts, her slender fingers curling into fists as she tucked them out of sight. "I don't want someone who so clearly hates wanting me in return, Clint. Find someone else."

Find someone else?

"I don't think so." There were no options left. "Neither one of us can walk away from this now, Morganna. I think you know that."

Her eyes narrowed, the shifting grays swirling with emotion as they raked over his body. It was almost a caress, tinged with anger, with a forceful determination to strike back at him.

He had hurt her. He knew he had. His own determination to protect her had stripped her down to the base of who and what she was. Stubborn, intent. The shock had worn off and now the woman was emerging, pissed off, wary, and ready to fight.

"*You've* avoided it for eight years, Clint. I can work with you and handle it. You don't have to fuck me to keep me alive." She straightened from the wall, her arms dropping to her sides as he began to pace closer to her.

"No. I have to have you to keep my own sanity," he said softly. "I have to touch you, taste you, possess all the heat and fire before I die inside from the cold, Morganna."

She warmed him and he hadn't even realized it. When he was with her, his emotions, his hungers, all the desperate needs she inspired in him rose to the surface. There was something about Morganna that made him feel. And he had sworn long ago that he would never let that happen.

"You never cared how cold you were before. Why start now?" Her voice was rough with the angry tears he could see she was holding back.

He was almost wary. He had learned how to handle Morganna in every given mood but this one. This one intrigued him the most, though. She was fighting him rather than teasing him. Defying him rather than giving in to him. The complete opposite of the type of woman he had always believed would suit him.

Anticipation licked over his flesh, sending vibrations of awareness to ripple through his cock. He was going to lay her across that damned bed and paddle her ass for making him crazy first. Then he would show her exactly how a true Dom tamed fiery little wildcats like herself.

She stared back at him defiantly as he stopped within inches of her, watching her with narrowed eyes, feeling the waves of anger and desire that whipped around him.

"You're mine." He kept his voice low as he watched her lips tighten in anger.

"And it took a knife at my neck to convince you of that?" She snorted derisively. "Oh really, Clint. You're just horny. Did the redhead turn you on a little too much? I can't believe you would dare to try to touch me after having that bimbo on your lap."

Brilliant points of light fed into the stormy gaze now, the phenomenon mesmerizing him for long minutes. He believed she just might be more pissed than he originally thought.

"She's an agent, Morganna," he reminded her. "That was the role. Remember?"

"As though she convinced anyone she needed to be drugged to fuck," Morganna sneered. "She was so ready to do you it was pathetic. And you were encouraging her." She threw it at him as though the sin were of blasphemous proportions.

She was jealous. Furiously jealous. And seeing it did nothing to still his lust and his need as it would have with any other woman. Instead, if possible, his cock grew harder, his hunger for her rising.

"I'll encourage you harder," he offered. "Come and sit on my knee, Morganna. Let's see if you can show me how it's supposed to be done."

"You bastard!"

He saw her arm move, the upswing of her tight little fist, and held himself still. He could have caught her barreling fist, could have stopped the impact of it before it connected with the side of his lips.

But he didn't. The sharp sting caused him to flinch, but he didn't break eye contact with her. His fingers snapped around her wrist when she drew back, and he watched as shock rounded her eyes, drew the color from her face.

Holding her gaze, he lifted his free hand and wiped the thin trail of blood from the corner of his mouth. He glanced at his fingers, seeing the dark smear across them before he stared back at her.

She gasped as the same finger touched her lips, pressing inside her mouth. Her tongue curled over it, a shiver washing over her as a startled, breathless little cry vibrated from her lips. He brought her fist to his lips then, his tongue licking over the smear of the blood that stained her fragile fingers.

"Kiss it and make it better now," he growled, jerking her to him, feeling the demon of lust that rode his back howling out in hunger as her body came flush with his. "We'll both make it better."

ORGANNA MET CLINT'S LIPS HALFWAY, a cry of hunger and desperation leaving her throat as they came together. It wasn't an easy kiss. It wasn't a gentle kiss. As though the fear of losing him and the aching loss she had dealt with as she left his truck hours before coalesced into a driving, burning conflagration that overtook her mind.

A haze of red filled her vision, even though her eyes were closed. Brilliant pinpricks of color exploded behind her closed lids as dizzying sensations ripped through her mind.

"I can't be around you without craving your taste," he muttered against her lips. "Dying for you, a little bit at a time. Dying to taste and touch . . . Sweet God, Morganna, you make me crazy for you."

His voice was dark and heavy with emotion. Tormented. Filled with need and hunger. A need and hunger that rose inside her, matching his for desperation and intensity as his lips covered hers once again.

His kiss was a marauder intent on submission, and submission had never been Morganna's strong suit. Especially with Clint.

As his lips controlled hers, she was well aware they were controlling her, his tongue moving past hers in well-timed thrusts that mimicked a pleasure her body was rioting for.

His fingertips touched her jaw as he groaned against her lips. Touching her with a gentle, hesitant caress that reinforced the dominance of his kiss.

She nipped at his tongue, only to have his hand cup beneath her chin, his fingers gripping her jaws and holding them open. Oh, she loved that. The forceful domination blew her mind.

He growled into the kiss, the animalistic, primal sound

sending shivers racing down her back as her nails raked over his shoulders while she squirmed against him, bucking in his arms in an attempt to be free of him. She wanted to touch him, devour him. Standing still and in a haze of pleasure beneath his kiss was all very well and good, but she had waited years for this. Fantasized about it. Ached for it. She wanted more than her own submission.

"Stay still. God. Easy, baby . . ." he panted as his hips pressed her against the wall, and leaned back to grab her wrists and shackle them over her head. "Leave me a little self-control here."

"Like hell." She nipped at his lips as they lowered, the swollen sensuality of them making her want to devour them. He had stripped her of her self-control; why should she leave him any?

"I'm going to paddle your ass if you keep this up." His eyes were glittering with lust, his voice thick with it as he stared down at her.

His hands were like manacles on her wrists as she glared back at him, or tried to glare back at him. It was hard to glare when she could feel her juices literally dripping between her thighs and the love she felt for him weakening her knees. God, she loved him. Loved him until she felt seared from the emotion.

"You and whose army?" she taunted with a smug, mocking smile. "Don't make threats, big boy, that you can't uphold."

She was dying to feel his hand on her ass. He had been threatening to spank her since she was eighteen years old, and she had fantasized about it just as long.

His eyes narrowed on her as his chest moved harshly with his breathing. She was panting. She was certain someone was limiting the amount of oxygen in the room.

"I should have packed the ball gag in that damned duffel I brought, instead of the butt plug." A sensual smile tugged at his lips just before his tongue licked over hers. "That would have shut you up."

Her vagina convulsed so heavily, she was certain she was going to orgasm right there on the spot.

"Bring a toy to do a man's job, did you?" She bucked in his arms again.

His rough chuckle was wickedly sensual and set her soul on fire. This was how she had dreamed of him. Sexually dominant, allowing her to challenge him, defy him, and taking pleasure in the game.

"Preparation is everything, baby." He crooned, "And trust me, tonight, you'll find out exactly why the hell I didn't take you up on your very charming offer when you were eighteen."

There was no time for a comeback. Before she could do more than squeak in surprise, he picked her up against his chest, strode into the bedroom, and tossed her onto the mattress.

"Take off the shirt," he ordered her roughly as he jerked the duffel bag to the edge of the bed and pulled the zipper on it, removing several items from it that had her flushing in aroused embarrassment. The tapered sexual toy and tube of lubrication had her blood pressure skyrocketing as well as a small spurt of concern. It just wasn't possible that she could accommodate that thing where no toy had gone before.

"In your dreams." She crouched on the bed, staring back at him as she swiped back the long curls that fell over her face.

She felt empowered. Utterly sensual. Staring back at Clint, seeing the naked hunger and intensity of emotion raging in his eyes, Morganna knew that all their battles had merely been foreplay to this.

His smile as he moved for her proved it. Before Morganna could evade him, Clint gripped the hem of the T-shirt, wrestling it from her as she screeched in outrage.

"Arrogant ass," she accused as he moved back, disposing of his pants just as quickly.

Within seconds he was naked, bronzed flesh rippling over

powerful muscles as his hand lowered to the stalk of his erection, his fingers stroking over it slowly as he stared down at her.

"That is just so not right," she panted, her eyes widening at the sight of the gold ball ring that pierced the underside of his cock, just beneath the thickly flared crest.

God, he was pierced. That was just so wicked.

Her mouth watered to taste him as his fingers gripped the little ring, tugging at it teasingly as the head of his erection pulsed and darkened with arousal. A little bead of pre-come glistened on the tip, tempting her as she licked her lips in hunger.

Staring at the flushed, heavily veined flesh, Morganna was distracted just enough, just for the few precious seconds Clint needed to catch her off guard. Before she could do more than gasp in outrage, he moved, gripping her waist and flipping her to her stomach a second before his hand landed on her rear.

"Damn you!" That felt too good. She was not into that submissive spanking-master stuff, she assured herself, but the sharp little tap to her buttock sent pulses of heat and pleasure rushing through her.

"Stay still." Clint's voice was harsh, hoarse. "God help me, Morganna, I don't know if I can wait."

He pulled her hips up, back, as she braced herself on the mattress and tried to crawl away from him. She was not going to make this easy for him.

"Enough!" One broad hand gripped her hip, holding her in place as his knees bracketed hers.

He shackled her in place. Sort of. She knew she should have been fighting him harder, but the feel of his heavily lubricated fingers moving through the cleft of her rear had her stilling in shock.

"What the hell are you doing?"

"Preparation." She felt the fiery probing of his fingertip against the forbidden entrance and jerked in reflex. She could feel her heart pounding between her breasts in excitement, stealing her breath.

"Clint . . ." She could feel her flesh tightening, stretching around the width of his finger.

"Stay still. Just a minute. . . ." The sudden impalement was shockingly heated, wicked. Carnal.

Slick, cool, his finger slid back, only to be replaced by a second. Shocked lust seared her, as though the tiny prick of burning pleasure were a narcotic.

Her hands fisted in the coverlet as she tried to move, bucking against his hold, the breath strangling in her chest as he held her in place, slowly working his fingers inside her, stretching her, burning.

She should say no. She should protest. She knew she should. She struggled in his grip, but his hand tightened on her hip as his knees held her legs in place. The forceful dominance was more arousing than she could have ever imagined.

"This is depraved." She jerked against him, crying out at the fiery pleasure as the impalement increased. She bucked against him, fighting to free herself, knowing all she had to do was say no, but unable to push the word past her lips.

She wanted to fight him, she realized. She wanted the challenge, the defiance, the loss of control she knew he was experiencing.

"God, the way you stretch around my fingers," he groaned, retreating from her rear, only to return, stretching her further as the cool lubrication eased his way. "I'm going to take you here, Morganna. Eventually. When you're ready. When I have enough control. Until then, you'll have this."

She tried to breathe as his fingers retreated, expecting to feel a more normal caress, a touch to her aching, saturated sex, a heavy thrust into her aching vagina. What she felt instead was the cool tapered end of the thick-based toy he had jerked out of his pack earlier.

"Clint, this is so perverted," she panted as she twisted in

his grip, crying out at the extremity of the sensations tearing through her.

He didn't pause. He made no allowances for the untouched condition of the tiny entrance; he pressed the toy inside her firmly, stretching her with it, sending flames of pleasure so intense it bordered pain, flaring through her body.

It shouldn't feel so good. It shouldn't burn inside her with the force of a wildfire ripping over her nerve endings. Stealing every vestige of control she had ever possessed.

"Take it, baby," he growled, working the shaft in with deep, careful strokes despite her struggles. "God yes, open for me, Morganna, just as I've dreamed."

She screamed as the thickly flared bottom popped inside her anus, the narrower portion at the base locking it inside her. Her upper body collapsed to the bed as she fought to accustom herself to the heavy invasion a second before a deep vibration began to ripple through it.

It was vibrating, massaging the delicate, pleasure-tormented cavity as she writhed with a pleasure so intense she was fighting in earnest to crawl from him now, whimpering at the sensations breaking over her, tearing through her senses as the destructive pleasure-pain tore loose any previous concepts of passion she had ever known.

"Easy, baby." Clint turned her to her back, spreading her thighs before him as he lay between them, holding her in place as he stared up at her.

She cried out, even as her hand locked in his hair, holding him in place. "I can't stand it, Clint."

His hands were ruthless, holding her thighs open, pressing her to the bed, refusing her the need to curl away from him, to accustom herself to the dark pleasure enveloping her.

She had never been invaded anally before. Had never known pleasure and pain could ride so close together.

He didn't answer her plea. Instead, his head lowered, his tongue swiping through the drenched center of her body before lapping at her like a man starved. Over her clitoris, around it, tormenting the already-tortured entrance to her pussy as she pulled at his hair. The vibration in her rear was sending hard, electric pulses of sensation up her spine, into her sex. She was stretched on a rack of sensation so intense she wasn't certain she could survive it.

This was Clint. Touching her. Taking her places she had never imagined with an extremity that canceled reality.

"God, you taste good." His voice was savage, intent, as he suddenly moved from her.

"Don't stop!" Her eyes flared open, desperation tightening her fingers in his hair as they tried to force him back to the weeping flesh burning for his touch.

Clint pulled her hands from his hair. He came over her instead, stretching her arms above her as her fingers formed claws, her hips churning beneath him until she felt his cock, hot, fierce, pressing into her.

Okay. Maybe this was better.

Then, as she felt the entrance struggling against his invasion, her breath caught. Maybe it wasn't.

"It won't fit." She couldn't breathe. The heavy, short thrusts that forced the thick erection inside her had searing waves of pleasure tearing through her vagina.

Pleasure. The pleasure was like a demon, devouring her mind, mixing with the pain, spiking both higher until she was certain she couldn't bear more.

And yet he gave her more. Threw her higher as her vagina tightened convulsively around his invading shaft.

"It will fit. Look at me, Morganna. Damn you, look at me."

His voice was darker, more commanding, than she had ever known it to be. She forced her eyes to his, staring up at him in dazed rapture as she felt him pushing inside her.

His expression was savage. Dark blue eyes glittered with lust and hunger; his features were taut, the flesh stretched tight over his cheekbones as a breathless scream left her lips and he forged into her to the hilt.

She felt tender tissue and muscle part for him, stretching to accommodate him, revealing nerve endings and pleasure her vibrator had never come close to matching. The ball ring slid over her flesh, caressing the internal muscles with a wicked little rasp. He felt huge inside her; the deep throb of heavy veins along his erection pulsed, adding to the heavy throb of the vibrating toy in her rear.

"Fuck yes!" The cords stood out on his neck as his head arched back, his gaze never leaving hers. "You're so damned tight, I'm dying. . . . God yes, baby, milk my cock. Just like that."

Her vagina was spasming with the effort to accommodate him as the heavy vibration in her rear sent sharp talons of electrical impulses to attack her clit, her womb.

"I can't bear it. . . ." She couldn't breathe for the sensations. Every muscle, every cell, in her body was stretched tight, reaching, tortured with a need she couldn't make sense of.

"It's okay, baby." Sweat stood out on his lean face, his shoulders, as he shook his head, his erection still throbbing inside her. "It's okay. We're almost there. Almost there." And he began moving.

One hand held her wrists in place as the other lowered to lift her leg, pulling it to his hips as he drew back, then forged back, hard, fast.

"Clint . . ." Her eyes dazed, her breath strangling in her throat as she began to fight the rising, white-hot impulses of feeling exploding through her. Was it pleasure? Was it pain?

"God yes, baby. Let me have you. All of you. All of you, Morganna." He groaned as he came over her, his hips pumping as sweat coated their flesh, the heat building, rising to the point that she was fighting it, fighting him, fighting the screeching, clawing animal of lust tearing at her womb, tightening it with a ferocity that terrified her.

She could feel every thick vein of his erection in her

overstretched vagina, the slick drag of the golden ring with its center ball, the press of the flared head as it pulled back, raking the violently sensitive spot just beneath her clit.

"Sweet darlin'." His accent deepened. "Take me, baby. There you go. I feel you, darlin', tighten around me. Just like that. Just like that, sweetheart."

Everything inside her was tightening, burning, building.

"There you go, baby." His voice thickened further as his thrusts became faster, stronger. "Come for me, baby. Let me feel you. . . . Let me feel you. . . ."

Liquid flames tore into the center of her body. Morganna tried to scream, to cry out, but no sound would emerge. The conflagration grew, intensified, until his head lowered, his teeth gripping the sensitive cord in her neck as his lips covered it, drew on her, and sent her exploding.

Her teeth locked in his shoulder, and she was certain she tasted blood as she felt the world dissolve around her.

Chapter 12

How long had it been since he'd cried?

He needed to cry now, to ease the emotion tightening his chest.

As Clint eased the plug from Morganna's rear, he could feel the emotion ripping through him, tearing at his soul. She was damned near unconscious, a breathy little moan her only sign of awareness as the sensual toy slipped free of the tight grip her body had on it.

His hand smoothed over the side of her thigh as she lay curled on her side, her hair tangled around her shoulders, back, and face, sweat dampened and gleaming like wet silk. Unblemished. Unmarred. There wasn't a scar on her fragile body, but he could see the bruises rising beneath the creamy flesh.

He had bruised her. And her neck . . . He lifted his gaze to where he had marked her. God, what had he done to her? He raked his hand across his face as he jerked from the bed, pacing to the bathroom, where he ruthlessly washed the plug and stored it in the protective covering he had bought for it.

He braced his hands on the sink when he finished, breathing in deep, hard, before he forced himself to stare back at his reflection.

He was surprised by the mark on his shoulder. Her sharp little teeth had pierced the tough skin in two places, leaving a small smear of blood across the primal mark. He lifted his hand, touching the sensitive spot as a bitter smile touched his lips.

It didn't make up for what he had done to her.

It was more than obvious her sweet rear had never been breached; she had never been taken with a hunger as deep as the one she inspired in him. Her eyes had been dazed, her face pale, but God, she had taken him. Growing wetter, hotter, clasping him inside her until he was certain he couldn't move, could do nothing but pump every ounce of his semen inside her rippling little channel.

Shaking his head, he jerked a washcloth from the side of the sink as he turned on the water with a vicious jerk. He dampened the cloth, wrung it out, and forced himself back to the bed.

He used the heated washrag to clean her gently, to first wash the uncomfortable perspiration from her neck, shoulders, breasts, belly, and back before he moved to her thighs. His semen marred the soft, flushed folds of her sex, slickened her thighs.

As he cleaned her, his throat tightened at the sight of it. He hadn't used protection. But he had never meant to with Morganna. He had been careful all his life; there was no chance of infecting her with anything but his own bitterness and no chance of pregnancy. He could live with his cock spilling inside her on an hourly basis, and she would never risk conceiving his child.

For the first time in years, the thought of it bothered him. He would never see her body ripen with his baby. But on the other hand, no child would ever suffer the hell he had known, either.

"Clint . . ." His name whispered past her lips as he pulled the blankets over her to protect her from the chill of the air conditioner.

She shifted on the mattress before settling in with a little sigh and sleeping again.

God, he couldn't do this.

He jerked a pair of jeans and underwear from his pack and stalked to the bathroom. He showered quickly, drying his body with rough, ruthless movements before dressing and heading back to the sitting room.

The small refrigerator held several hospitality bottles of

liquor. He jerked them all out, uncapped the first, and tossed it back. Shit, he hated vodka.

Pulling his cell phone from its holder, he flipped it open and punched in Joe's number. The bastard better have some answers. He was getting sick of trying to figure out the impossible from this point.

"Hey, Clint." The other man's voice was weary as he answered the phone. "Are you secure?"

A frown darkened his brow. "Secure enough," Clint growled, the cell phone specially designed for secure conversations by a friend with a knack for electronics. "What's up?"

"Hell if I know," Joe snarled across the line. "Drage has closed down for the day and run off all his staff except his head of security. I suspect he's shifting camera angles. He's pretty pissed. Seems our perp knew the angle of the cameras."

"Masters knows about the operation?" His jaw clenched over the question.

"He came to us right after Morganna was assigned to the team," Joe admitted. "As far as we can find out, he's not involved, but we're keeping an eye on him. He's locked up tight this morning, though. He's not letting us in there until he's finished."

"Which tells me what, Joe?" Clint asked carefully, keeping his voice calm, neutral.

"Which tells you I don't know shit," Joe snapped back.

"It tells me you have a mole," Clint informed him, feeling the edge of violence pricking at his temper. "Who is it?"

"Not in my crew—"

"Don't be a fool," he advised Joe softly. "I'm not. Find your mole or I'm going to start looking for him, and you don't want me to have to do that with Morganna in tow. If I have to offend her sense of justice by killing a few DEA agents to get the right one, I'm going to be pissed off, Joe."

It wasn't a threat, and by the silence on the line he knew Joe was aware of that.

"There has to be more to this," Joe finally snapped. "If

they wanted to take someone out, they would have started with me or Craig, not Morganna. Taking her out won't stop the operation."

"She spotted three of their men drugging one of the women there last week. This is revenge. And someone on the inside is helping them." If Joe couldn't get to the bottom of this, then he would. "You can send your female agent home. Morganna will be working with me."

A hard, hissing breath filled the line.

"If she's compromised, they might not try to hit her again."

"They won't stop," Clint snapped. "Pull in all your men except your tech and get them in the bar from here on out. Cover our asses. If anything happens to her, Joe, I'll kill you. You know that, don't you?"

"Agreed," Joe said, his voice rough, frustrated. "I'll pull the team together and we'll meet you tomorrow night—"

"I'll call you before we meet. You and Craig can meet with us, then brief the rest of your team. Now, what did you find at Morganna's house?"

"We found the knife. No prints, but it was manufactured in South America. Bogotá, to be exact. I'm trying to get a trace from other sources now, but it will take a while."

South America. The Fuentes Cartel. He knew it.

Fuentes had used a very exclusive drug to dose the senators' daughters. Clint remembered the sight of those girls the night his team rescued them. Nearly naked, sweat-dampened, their pupils dilated. The oldest girl had been coherent enough to tell Kell that the soldiers were preparing to videotape their rape as incentive for their fathers to do as Fuentes wanted.

"Contact your head office. Get your best computer geek moving on the Fuentes Cartel, or what's left of it. The drug you're chasing was developed by them, so the lab, suppliers, and most likely dealers will be part of this. Someone left from that organization is trying to rebuild it, and they're using the videos to fund it."

"We've been working that angle, but nothing has popped yet." The frustration in the other man's voice was clear. "With Diego Fuentes killed, I'm leaning more toward a rival group than the Fuentes Cartel itself."

"Doesn't mean Fuentes didn't have an enterprising lieutenant smart enough to pull this off. See what you can pull up on the remnants of his cartel. Someone has managed to snag the drug, as well as a corner of his cartel here. Start tracing and see what you come up with. Some intel out of Colombia after we hit Fuentes was that before Diego Fuentes' old man died, his closest advisor, a man who went by his first name only, Saul, went into retirement. After Diego's supposed death, Saul disappeared from his seaside mansion and took a private flight to California. Intelligence lost him there."

"Damn. Intelligence in the DEA has no idea Saul left retirement." Excitement colored his voice now. "This could be the break we're waiting on. How the hell did you know this?"

Interagency collaboration could be a bitch. The CIA had the information on Saul six months ago. Clint had acquired it from a team member currently investigating the rumor that Nathan Malone, the team member lost in Colombia, was still alive.

"Where doesn't matter," Clint murmured. "Fuentes and his men thought women were one step below their dogs. Except for that aberration he called his wife. They worshipped her. Saul shared this view and he knew Fuentes' business inside and out. He could be the key we're looking for."

"Was the Fuentes bitch even female?" Joe grunted. "The reports I read on her suggested otherwise."

"She had a kid," he grunted. "So she was at least equipped physically. Mentally, I'd put her against Genghis Khan. Let me know what you can find out. I'm going to make a few more calls, then catch some sleep. I'll contact you later to see what you've learned."

Dawn was peeking through the sides of the curtains, reminding him exactly how long it had been since he had actually slept.

He disconnected the call, made a few more contacts with friends he knew would spread the word that he was currently trying to tame the shrew, then pocketed the cell phone and muttered a curse.

Damn, this was starting to get sticky. They thought they had taken out enough of Fuentes' network to completely disable the cartel. Who had they missed?

He rose from the couch, pushing the phone back in its holder as he paced back to the bedroom. He just wanted to look at her. Hold her.

He shucked his jeans and underwear before easing slowly onto the bed beside her, careful to stay on top of the blankets that covered her as he curled himself around her.

He buried his face in her hair, inhaling the sweet scent of it, smelling the combined scents of their bodies. Hers warm and tinted with spring, his darker, more forceful. He was sunk and he knew it. Years of secrets, of hiding the truth even from those who knew him best, weighed on his shoulders with backbreaking force. On his back, old scars, long ago healed, stung with a fiery heat.

He flinched at the memory of the belt coming down on his back, the rage in his father's eyes, the violence that tightened his features.

You're the man of the house while I'm gone and you couldn't stop her?

Whoop.

She's a woman, boy; where's your pride? You're going to let them make a whore of your momma?

Whoop.

I'll teach you to do your job right. By God, you'll do it right or I'll kill you.

Whoop.

He had been thirteen years old. It was his responsibility to keep his mother home, to keep her from screwing everyone on the fucking base while his Navy SEAL father was gone. His responsibility.

His father had never beaten Clint's mother. He had never so much as spanked Raven. It was Clint's job to watch them, to protect them, to keep them safe. Even from themselves. If he failed, then the punishment was his. It was the lesson his father had learned from his father, and so on down the line. It was a bitter legacy that would end with Clint.

Clint remembered the day the black car had driven up, his mother's hysteria at the news of his father's death. Clint had known only relief. Soul-destroying, guilty relief that his father wouldn't return. Ever.

Allen McIntyre had been a good husband, despite his wife's infidelities. To Raven he had been a loving, strong figure for a father. But the face he had shown his son had been demonic, and one Clint knew would haunt him forever.

He tucked himself closer to Morganna, pulling her into the cradle of his body as weariness washed over him. He couldn't keep her forever, and he knew it. He couldn't be certain that the insanity that gripped his father wouldn't take hold of him one day as well. He had been given proof of that the first time he met one of Morganna's lovers, years before. He had wanted to kill the bastard. Every instinct inside him had pushed him to kill. And it terrified him.

But while he had her, he would love her. Silently. Stoically. He would love her.

DREAMS WERE CLINT'S WORST FEAR. Each time he closed his eyes he knew the chances of reliving the past were high. Seeing himself in his father's place, his hand raised back, the length of a leather belt clenched in his fist as his blue eyes blazed with fury, was his greatest nightmare.

He knew the child before him was his own flesh and blood. Big for his age, maybe, smart for his age, but still just a child. Tears stood in the boy's eyes, but none fell to his cheeks until the flesh of his back smeared with blood. And still the belt fell, the fury cracking around them with each strike.

It was a dream Clint had never forgotten. Just as he had never forgotten his own beatings.

My father taught me to be a man, boy, Allen McIntyre had raged as he beat Clint. *I'll teach you to be a man. A man doesn't stand by and let others turn his momma into a whore.*

The bastard had idolized his wife. He had worshipped at her feet, fought with her, screamed, and cursed her. The house and Allen's life had revolved around Linda McIntyre.

The dreams poured through Clint's unconscious mind, though this time they grew dimmer, dimmer. Rather than feeling the stripe of his father's leather, Clint felt a soft caress along his arm. The smell of his own blood was pushed away by the scent of summer, of heat and passion.

The smell of Morganna.

He shifted against her touch, knowing this dream better than most. He would feel her touch, light as a butterfly over his body, but never as he needed it. He would awaken, poised at the gates of her glistening, wet flesh, unsated, aching for her.

But the touch was firmer this time. Lips heated rather than merely warm. Her fingertips like silk, the murmur of her arousal against his abdomen as she licked.

He arched to her, rolling to his back, his arms outspread as he relished this touch. A touch from a woman whom he had only had in his dreams. Until now.

Her approval was a stinging little kiss just above his navel. He groaned, the sound piercing his mind as his fists clenched in the blankets. He needed her lower, just a little bit lower. His cock was rising fierce and hot from between his thighs, his balls aching with the need for relief.

Slowly, the knowledge that reality and dream commingled penetrated his mind, sending a harsh flare of horror raging through him. His eyes snapped open as his hand flashed out, catching her wrist as her slender fingers moved to encircle the fiercely throbbing shaft rising so eagerly to her touch.

Her witchy eyes, stormy gray, almost black with arousal, lifted to his. Dark lashes shadowed her cheeks as a wanton smile curved her lips and her pink little tongue swiped over her lips before her head began to lower.

He couldn't speak. Jaw clenched, body aching, his free hand shot out, gripping her hair to hold her back. Her lips were but a breath from the damp, flushed crest rising so eagerly to her lips.

Nothing could stop her tongue. His jaw clenched so hard he wondered it didn't snap as her tongue swiped over the bead of pre-come welling from the tip, then tickled at the gold ring piercing his foreskin.

His hips jerked, involuntarily arching to her lips despite the hold he had on her hair, the desperation in his mind that he hold her back falling beneath the pleasure.

It was so good. So damned good. Her tongue tugging at the little ball ring, sending sparks of heated sensation burning along his cock.

She was so pretty. Naked, flushed, her breasts swollen, the nipples peaked and rosy as she bent to him. His greatest fantasy, his worst fear.

"Let me," she whispered, breathing over the damp head of his erection as he jerked at the lash of pleasure that so simple a caress brought.

His eyes narrowed on her as he took the hand he gripped, wrapping his fingers over hers as he forced her to grip the base of his tortured flesh.

He couldn't speak. God only knew the insanity that would pass his lips if he tried. His other hand tightened in her hair, intent on dragging her rosy lips over the throbbing crest.

A frown snapped between her brows as she leaned back, tugging at the hold on her hair.

Her voice was strong, demanding. "You had your playtime; now it's mine. Let me go, Clint."

He fought to breathe. How the hell was he supposed to allow her the freedom to touch him as she pleased? She would kill him. Didn't she know she was already destroying his soul?

"Let me go." Her voice softened as she continued to stare at him from between his splayed thighs. "I've dreamed of this. Bringing you pleasure. Let me bring you pleasure now."

Her free hand reached up, her fingers gripping his wrist, pulling at it as he forced his fingers to release her. He could see the need in her eyes, the hunger. Just for a minute. He could bear it surely—

"Jesus!" His hand flew to her hair again, gripping the strands as her hot mouth encircled the violently sensitive crest. "No."

Her lips lifted from him as her gaze flashed.

"Don't tell me no." She pulled his hand from her again. "What are you afraid of, big man? How is the puny little girl going to hurt you? Like this . . . ?" Her tongue swiped over him, sending a burst of heat to his loins that damned near stole his breath.

"Morganna." He moved to snag her hair again, only to have her flip her head to the side, anger mantling her cheeks.

"If you grab my hair again, I'm going to bite you." Her teeth raked over the throbbing head of his cock and he nearly shot his release then and there. "Now stay still and let me play, Clinton McIntyre, or I promise, you're going to hurt for a week."

Her tongue snagged the gold ball ring a second before her teeth gripped it, the little pout on her lips assuring him she meant business.

Clint fought to swallow. With every touch, every sweet, silky caress, she was destroying his soul. How the hell was he supposed to let her go when this was finished?

"I need to taste you," she whispered as she licked beneath the crest, her little tongue flickering over the most sensitive area of his cock. "I need to make you feel good, too, Clint."

His hands slapped to the bed, fisting in the blankets as he glared back at her. He couldn't speak. Gibberish would result.

"So gracious you are, too." Her husky laughter breathed over him, torturing him as her delicate hand began to stroke the thick shaft. "That's okay, lover; I'm used to the Grouch. God knows how I could handle the shock if you were actually nice."

Her eyes gleamed with laughter.

He forced himself to stay silent, to brace himself.

There was no bracing himself for her mouth. Her lips surrounding the blazing ache in the head of his erection, sucking it deep into her mouth as her tongue caught and played with the ring that pierced the foreskin.

"Sweet God!" he prayed, feeling the come boiling in his scrotum as he fought for control.

Her moan vibrated against him as her mouth tightened on him. Her lips stretched around him, sending exquisite fingers of electric shock through his penis, straight to his balls. Shit, he wouldn't last a minute like this.

His hips arched again, driving the bloated head deeper as her mouth sucked him firmly. So sweet and hot, velvet-tight. And her face. Her expression was something he knew would be branded in his mind forever.

It glowed. Her sweet, beautiful face glowed before him as her hungry lips consumed him. Heavy-lidded eyes stared up at him; slender fingers stroked his shaft, caressed the taut sac below, and blew his mind.

She was the vision of every sexual fantasy he had ever known in his life. Of course, every sexual fantasy he had ever known *was* Morganna.

"Sweet baby." His lips opened, his voice, so hoarse it shocked him, spilled the words building in his mind. God, he couldn't resist her, couldn't resist the need that had his hips pumping, his erection fucking into her mouth as his loins tightened with a release he wondered if he would survive.

"Perfect." His strangled groan tore from his lips as she tongued the ball ring, tugged at it, licked over the foreskin. Sweet Heaven have mercy on him, he was going to blow his mind with his orgasm.

This wasn't pleasure. This was torture with silken licks, a firm draw of satin cheeks. It was the most incredible torment he had ever known in his life.

"God yes!" His body corded as he felt her take him deeper, felt the sweet, fiery constriction at the back of her throat on the highly sensitive tip of his cock. "Damn you to hell, Morganna!"

He was going to come. His hands moved for her head, only to have her slap them back as the pressure on his cock eased.

"Fuck. Suck me." His hands slammed back to the bed.

He wasn't a fool. If he dared attempt to control this, she would stop. And he couldn't bear that. She was sucking his mind from the tip of his cock and he considered it an acceptable sacrifice. Fiery fingers of exquisite pleasure were tearing up his back, sizzling in the base of his spine, warning him that he couldn't hold off much longer.

He was panting for air. Breathing was almost impossible. Sweat broke out over his body as he gritted his teeth, snarling with the rapture tearing through him.

"Damn you!"

Her mouth tightened.

"Morganna. Baby . . ."

Her tongue flickered, tugged at the ball ring, lashed him with heat, and then as the tip of his erection was sucked to the back of her throat the explosion that resulted had him crying out, when he never cried out.

His hips arched tight, his eyes closed as his head ground into the pillow and his semen burst from the tip of his cock, spilling into the hot depths of her mouth. It was never ending, ripping through him, shuddering through his body, and stealing his soul.

When the last furious pulse of hot liquid was consumed by her greedy lips, he was free. He jerked her to him, rolling her to the bed and pushing in between her thighs.

He was still hard, still hungry. He would never, could never, get enough of her. His hands gripped her hips as he came over her, his thighs widening hers as he pressed into her.

Liquid heat began to surround him. She was so tight he had to work inside her, groaning with each shallow thrust until he filled her, until he could feel every inch of his erection surrounded by her.

And it wasn't enough. He held her as close to his chest as possible, needing her skin to merge with his, to touch her soul despite the fear holding him back.

"Hold me," he growled against her neck.

But she was holding him, her arms tight around his shoulders. And it wasn't enough. He needed more. Needed more of her to still the pain building in his soul.

"Hold me, Morganna." He began to thrust, desperate for her, needing more in ways he couldn't explain. He couldn't get closer to her, it wasn't possible, but still, it wasn't enough. God, it wasn't enough; he was going to die if he couldn't touch her deeper, if she didn't touch him deeper.

Her arms tightened around his shoulders then, her cries echoing in his ear as he pushed her harder, his thrusts gaining in speed, killing them both in pleasure as his desperation drove him harder.

Harder. More. God, he needed more.

"I love you, Clint. . . ." Her cry tore through his head as he felt her tighten around him, felt her orgasm taking her. "I love you. . . ."

And he was there. She was there. Deeper. He buried his head in her neck as his own release swept over him. Pulse after blinding pulse as sanity became hostage to pleasure, and Morganna swept through his soul.

Chapter 13

H E WAS RUNNING SCARED. MORGANNA could feel it. It echoed in the sluggish beat of her heart and the pain that resounded in her soul.

It wasn't a physical escape but mental. Emotional.

"What time are we meeting Joe again?" She forced Clint to turn his gaze to her as she slid a stocking over her toes and pulled it slowly up her leg.

Dressed only in a black thong and black demi-bra, she knew the image she presented. Sex. Seduction. And the effect wasn't lost if that bulge in his pants was anything to go by.

"Four." His answer was quiet, his voice distant.

Morganna ducked her head as she lifted the mate to the black stocking she had just adjusted at her thigh as she sat on the edge of the bed. It went over her opposite foot, sliding it up her leg as his eyes stayed on her. He watched her when she turned away, when she lowered her head, but if she faced him directly his gaze would flicker from her before turning back.

It terrified her. Not because she was scared of him but because the strength of his defense mechanism had come the moment he lifted from her body hours before, stalking to the bathroom, where he had showered for what seemed like hours.

Long enough she was certain his skin was going to prune.

"Would you hurry and dress? We need to get out of here." He was in SEAL mode, as she and Raven called it. Emotionless, all business.

Morganna adjusted the stocking before glancing over at the chair where he sat again. He was sprawled out in all appearance of lazy abandon. Even the appearance of it sucked, though.

"I told you it took a while for me to get ready." She lifted her shoulders in a negligent shrug as she rose to her feet, careful to keep her back to him.

She could feel his eyes on her ass. The intimate knowledge didn't shock her, she had always known when Clint was watching her, but now she knew the difference in the varying intentness of it.

He was eating up the sight of her. Devouring it. Aching for it. And he was holding himself back from her. Pulling away the only way he knew how.

She reached back, adjusting the material that ran from the cleft of her rear along her hips. She heard his indrawn breath and chose to ignore it.

Turning slowly, she moved for the clothes Clint had somehow managed to find earlier. After that long-assed shower, he had disappeared for an hour and returned with the clothes he had informed her she would wear.

"Your taste sucks." She lifted the minuscule black leather skirt and stepped carefully into it.

The edges of her stockings showed, but they looked reasonably sexy. The black silk camisole top wouldn't have been her first choice, though she hadn't argued when she lifted it from the bag earlier.

"It looks okay." His eyes never left her as he rubbed his finger over his chin, his gaze going over her.

She knew what he was doing. He was calculating the best way to keep her out of danger, going over every detail of what they were about to do, and forcing himself to see her as a tool for the job rather than the woman he ached for.

SEAL mode. She hated it.

"Hmm." She pressed her lips together before sliding her feet into her shoes. "I have to stop at the house for makeup. I should have waited till then to dress."

"You don't need the makeup."

"Yes, I do." She smoothed the skirt over her thighs before gazing back at him placidly.

A frown snapped between his heavy brows. "You don't need it and there's no time to stop for it."

"Then there's no time for the meeting with Joe," she informed him calmly. "I don't go anywhere without makeup, Clint; get used to it."

"No."

Okay, she'd had enough of this. She turned, grabbing the bag that held the clothes she had worn the night before, and headed for the hotel room door.

"Where the hell do you think you're going?" His hand slapped against the panel as she reached it, reminding her way too much of the night in his apartment when he had backed her against the door.

She turned to him, feeling the brush of his jeans-covered erection against her lower stomach and trying to ignore the jump in her blood pressure. God, what he had done to her in that bed through the night. Pleasure shouldn't be that good; it shouldn't ride an edge so close to torment, to dreams never imagined.

"I'm going back to my house," she told him softly. "I'm going to dress in my own clothes, and I'm going to put on my makeup. After that, we can make that meeting or you can go to hell. Your choice."

She watched the battle that raged in his eyes, mesmerized by it as she watched anger and emotion struggle for dominance.

"Your clothes kick ass," he finally said, his jaw clenching violently. "It's not a case of what looks best. After we meet with Joe we're going downstairs at Diva's, to the heart of the club. If you don't dress the part, you'll never be accepted there. This isn't about the challenge or control. It's about getting to that drug. Defying me sexually is one thing. Defying me at the basis of the Dom–sub relationship is another."

"And wearing these clothes and no makeup will help that

how?" She frowned back as the feel of his hard body against hers sent her pulse racing.

He breathed in deeply. "By stripping yourself of the makeup and your normal mode of dress, you're showing the others, those not involved with the drugs, that you're interested in submitting. It gains you acceptance, and acceptance gets you information. Where the suppliers or dealers are concerned, it pushes them closer to making a mistake, because they know it's an act. They will know what you're doing, even if no one else does. Men like this see it as a challenge rather than a ploy to force them into a mistake.

"They won't suspect my involvement simply because I am a part of the inner club. I'm also known for choosing women who resemble you. It will make my job easier."

"Because you wanted me," she said roughly, hearing only the admission that his women resembled her. "You went to others when you wanted me." And that bit.

He grimaced, the ice around him melting further.

"Until I couldn't breathe for it," he finally admitted as though the knowledge of it angered him. "I still can't breathe for it, Morganna."

"Clint—" She would have protested the admission, but the finger against her lips halted her words.

"You're like a fire inside me," he said, but the tinge of regret in his voice sliced through her heart. "You think I find you lacking, and that's not true, baby. I'm the one lacking, and when you realize that, you'll understand why I've stayed away from you."

"Lacking in what? The ability to understand that your normally less than charming personality is not why I love you?"

He breathed out heavily as his head lowered, his lips brushing over her shoulder as Morganna fought the heaviness in her heart.

"If I could love anyone," he whispered at her ear seconds later, "it would be you, Morganna. It would always be you."

Another woman might be offended. A part of Morganna assured her she should be offended. Except she knew Clint. As stubborn, impossible to get along with, and arrogant and demanding as he could be, he wasn't lacking in love.

He loved her; she was certain of it. Accepting it might be a different matter for Clint. He saw too many shades of gray sometimes and not enough of the rainbow hues that love could be.

"It is me," she whispered back, refusing to allow him to hide, to lie not just to her, but to himself. "And we both know it, Clint."

As his head lifted, Morganna stared back at him silently.

His lips quirked wryly. "You'll be the death of me."

"Or the life of you." She let her hands fall to his shoulders as he released them, relishing the warmth and power in his broad shoulders.

"Don't you know that you always were the life of me?" he said as he pulled her close, only to facilitate opening the door behind her. "Come on. It's time to show what you've got, wildcat. Let's go see if we can find the bad guys."

She didn't argue with him, but she did know him. Clint had never realized, and perhaps he still didn't, just how well she did know him.

He was still hiding from her.

She frowned as he checked the hallway before drawing her from the room and leading her to the elevators. She had always wondered at the shadow of pain in his eyes, even when he was much younger. She and Raven had discussed it often.

Clint had always been distant with his sister as well, though Morganna and Raven had marked it down to the differences in their ages. He was ten years older than his sister, and his relationship with his parents had always been stormy.

Raven had still been a child the day Clint graduated from high school and joined the Army, and after that, Raven saw her brother only occasionally, when he was at the Chavez home. He rarely appeared at his parents' home. He hadn't attended his father's funeral.

After Raven moved out of her mother's home Clint had seen her more frequently. Often staying at her apartment when he was in town rather than his own. But it was as though he had deliberately placed that distance between himself and his sister. A distance Morganna had always known he regretted.

She glanced up at him as they stopped at the elevator. He stared at the display marking each floor as it passed, his expression blank. Morganna bided her time. The elevator doors opened into the parking garage. She stood silently as he checked the area, then followed sedately behind him as they moved for the pickup.

The soft click of her heels on the cement flooring was the only sound between them as he led her to the truck.

"Stay here." He held her back several feet from the truck before bending and beginning to work his way around it. "Clear," he announced as he jerked open the driver-side door and stood back for her.

"You're kidding." She stared at the running board, several inches higher than her tight skirt was going to allow her to step.

His sigh was long-suffering. Tossing the pack into the backseat, he turned back to her, gripped her waist, and lifted her to the seat.

"You're just going to make me shiver with all those muscles, Mr. McIntyre," she simpered mockingly as she batted her lashes at him before turning and sliding to the middle of the seat.

"Nut," he grunted as he moved beneath the wheel and slammed the door closed. "Scoot over."

His thigh was plastered to hers, his arm lying over her breast, as he slid the vehicle into gear and pulled out.

"No." Morganna wiggled against him, dragging her breasts over the underside of his arm as she felt him grow more tense.

"What do you mean no?" She liked the way his voice throbbed with lust. Oh yeah, he knew what they had, knew what he found with her he wasn't going to find with another woman, and he wanted it. Bad. Again.

"I mean, I'm comfortable. If you want to dress me in clothes guaranteed to invite sex, the least you could do is give me a thrill."

"Last night wasn't enough of a thrill?"

"I liked this morning better." She flicked him a glance from the corner of her eye as he pulled from the parking garage.

"I'm sure you did." His voice cooled marginally.

She barely restrained her sigh. "I actually noticed something vaguely bothersome, though." She lifted her hand, surveying a chipped nail, before looking up at him as he glanced over at her quickly.

"What?" His voice was suspicious.

"You didn't use a condom, big boy," she pointed out sarcastically. "Did you think of that?"

She had.

"Don't worry about it."

She hadn't mistaken the tightening of his body or the way his hands clenched on the steering wheel until his knuckles turned white.

"Don't worry about it?" she asked in amazement. "Clint, I'm not stupid here. I might be on birth control, but it's not one hundred percent effective, as you know. And that's not even considering STDs. How could you so calmly believe I wouldn't eventually worry about it?"

"I used a condom with other women," he growled, flicking her a half-angry look. "You don't have to worry about STDs."

She rolled her eyes mockingly as she scooted to the side enough to click her seat belt and turn to him. "And how can you be so certain I've been safe?"

"Because you weren't raised to be stupid." His jaw bunched as his eyes stayed glued to the road.

She stared back at him, confusion nudging into anger.

"You can be certain of this how?" she asked.

"Drop it, Morganna," he forced past tight lips.

"I'll get an appointment with my doctor next week." She knew that expression on Clint's face. It was the one she usually saw when she learned that he or Reno had put the fear of death into a boyfriend.

"You're not pregnant, Morganna—"

"You can't be certain."

"I'm certain, dammit."

"Prove it."

"Because I had a fucking vasectomy five years ago. I can't get you pregnant."

Morganna stared back at him in shock. An angry snarl curled his lips as he glared over at her briefly, his blue eyes alive with anger.

"Satisfied?" he snapped when she had nothing else to say.

A heavy weight settled in her chest as she stared at him. It wasn't just anger that filled his expression or his gaze. Shadows of bitterness, haunting demons swirled there, and Morganna realized she was only now seeing them for what they were.

What had happened? For whatever reason Clint had held himself back from her, this proved that it wasn't simply because she was a "party" girl. There was something deeper, some darker reason.

"For now," she whispered, turning back in her seat and staring ahead as Clint navigated the Sunday afternoon traffic toward Atlanta and the meeting with Joe.

What the hell had happened to him? Morganna frowned, wondering if Clint had always been this hard, this cold. Had it evolved? In ways it had, but she realized that as long as she had known him, she had realized there was a core of steel-hard strength, not just physical but mental. And there had always been shadows. They had drawn her when she was a child. Made her ache to comfort him the few times she had glimpsed the pain in his gaze.

He had hidden from everyone he had ever known, she thought. So effectively that she had never suspected that the man who had been so tender, so gentle, with others' children would never want one of his own.

Chapter 14

EVERY HEAD IN THE MAIN room of Diva's Downstairs turned when the elevator opened and Morganna stepped into the elaborately furnished room. There had to be fifty pairs of eyes suddenly trained on her, surveying her naked face, the short length of the leather skirt, and the collar at her neck.

The collar had surprised her. It wasn't the traditional leather or studded belt that many of the submissives wore. Clint had surprised her instead with an inch-wide silver choker chain that fitted her perfectly and showed up clearly against her dark skin. Hanging in the center of the chain was a small deep blue sapphire, almost the color of his eyes. A pendant to mark her as his alone.

They paused at a wide, curved dark wood reception counter where Morganna signed the confidentiality statement Clint had warned her would be waiting for her. The six-page agreement involved everything but her firstborn child if she dared divulge the activities seen, practiced, or heard of within what they called Diva's Downstairs, Merlin's Down Under, or the Roundtable Caverns. As Drage had stated before, he covered his ass well.

With his hand at her back, Clint led her into the plushly carpeted room. Moving with relaxed ease, he guided her across the room to a small group seated at the small end.

Drage Masters leaned back in his chair as he watched their progress, a small smile tilting his sensual lips as her gaze flickered over the men and women gathered there.

Good Lord, there was the senator's son. Aaron Hawkins. She had long heard rumors of his excessive tastes in sex, but she hadn't believed them. Beside him, Jayne Smith reclined back in a chair, her exotically tilted eyes following their progress. She wore no collar, which proclaimed her as a Domme rather than a submissive.

Morganna would have much preferred to make her debut here on her own terms, under her own control. Instead . . . She glanced at the women sitting at the feet of their Doms. Jeez, that was going to suck.

She tensed as Clint moved to an empty chair, ignoring the warning flex of his fingers at her back. She wasn't a moron; she knew what she was supposed to do. Be *submissive*. She almost sighed at the thought. That was so not her.

"McIntyre." Drage nodded as Clint took his seat easily, tugging at her hand subtly until she managed to sink down gracefully to the floor at his feet.

With her legs bent, balancing carefully on one hip, she was able to maintain at least a semblance of decency as she did so. She was going to kill Clint when they left here for not warning her what she should expect.

She had expected something similar to the club upstairs. What she found instead was a sanctuary of control. The music was sedate, a soft murmur of classical tunes that throbbed with an undertone of sexual heat. Comfortable seating arrangements were scattered throughout the room, as well as what appeared to be card tables. On the far side was a well-stocked bar, and the waiters and waitresses wore leather and red leather collars with the word "Diva's" emblazoned into them.

The seating arrangement Clint had chosen was eight chairs grouped around a wide, low table. All the chairs were filled, with only Jayne Smith lacking a female companion at her feet. Instead, a heavily muscled male leaned against her chair, his handsome face filled with amusement as he glanced at Morganna.

This was too unreal. Jayne's sub was a very well-known member of society. Excessively wealthy, handsome, and considered one of the state's most sought after bachelors,

Todd Harrington wasn't anyone's idea of a sub. Yet here he sat, dressed in black leather pants, his muscular chest bare, the black leather band at his neck simple and understated but unmistakable with its small silver looped chain that hung from the side. Rather than a full leash or a gem, Jayne had marked her sub with a small, barely four-inch-long, chain.

Morganna's attention turned from the sub as she felt Clint's fingers threading lazily through her hair as he ordered himself a drink, then ordered her a water. Water?

She turned her head and glanced at him from the corner of her eyes. Oh, he was going to pay for that one.

"Good evening, Morganna," Drage finally greeted her as everyone else continued to watch her.

She turned her head, meeting Drage's gaze directly.

"Hello, Drage." She ignored the delicate tensing of Clint's hands in her hair.

Drage's lips twitched as he glanced at Clint. "She's going to be difficult to tame, McIntyre," he informed Clint.

"Eventually she will be." Clint's voice hardened in determination, and though Morganna well understood the act they were involved in, she was suddenly intensely glad it was an act. Because she knew Clint could be a very dangerous man to cross.

"I'm surprised you pulled off making her wear the collar," an older gentleman across from them commented. "She never wears another's mark, nor has she allowed a chain to grace her own neck. Congratulations."

What the hell was she, a trophy? She looked at him through her lashes, memorizing his face. His tone was insulting, his gaze disapproving, as he stared at her.

"I don't make her do anything, Collins," Clint stated with an undertone of exasperation. "Morganna is here by choice, as I assume Velvet is."

Velvet being the twenty-something blonde sitting at the older man's feet, her head lowered. She was dressed in a black velvet dress that hugged her figure and left little to the imagination. Her breasts were nearly bursting from the too-tight bodice, and the slit running up the thigh stopped just shy of her hip.

"Of course she is; aren't you, sweet?" He patted the blond head as though she were a favorite pet.

"Of course," Velvet murmured, her head still lowered.

Morganna placed Collins high on her list of suspects at that point.

Morganna watched the gathering as the discussion moved to county politics, the age-old argument. The waitress brought Clint's drink, then set Morganna's water on the low table. She stared at it. Hard.

A second later Clint reached forward and set his drink on the table beside hers. The whiskey sour just called to her. She bit her lip, glancing away before an imp of less than submissive impulses took hold of her.

She reached out, lifted his drink, and took a fortifying sip as she ignored the flicker of amusement in most of the expressions around her. Everyone's but Collins'.

"Morganna sweetheart, that was mine," Clint said, an edge of steel in his voice. "I may have to punish you."

His fingers tightened sensually in her hair. And that just wasn't fair.

"I'll remember that," she answered in reply, barely holding back a smile at the silence that filled the group for a moment.

"So, Jayne, has your little boy toy managed to suppress his fondness for other women?" Collins asked then, turning to Jayne. "He seemed to take particular pleasure in fucking Hawkins' woman the other night."

Oh man. Morganna's gaze flew to Jayne and her "boy toy." Jayne's fingers ruffled through his black hair.

"It was quite arousing, wasn't it?" she said softly. "He has such a way about him. I believe the girl enjoyed it greatly."

Todd bent his head, kissed Jayne's leather-covered knee, and winked subtly at Morganna.

"If I remember correctly, he took particular delight in helping Clint last month with that girl from Merlin's," Collins piped in as he smirked at Morganna. "Your master enjoys sharing his women, Morganna."

"He *used* to enjoy sharing his women perhaps," she stated calmly. "No longer."

Collins lifted his gaze to Clint. Morganna didn't bother turning to see the fury blazing in Clint's eyes; she knew it was there. It was reaffirmed by the slight paling of Collins' face.

She was also aware of the fact that that the men watching her had suddenly become more intense, their gazes hotter. One in particular, Hawkins, watched her with blistering lust as his hand tightened in his sub's hair. And as Morganna watched, wide-eyed, the woman moved between his thighs, her fingers obviously loosening his pants.

They wouldn't.

They did.

Hawkins stared back at her with narrowed eyes as the brunette eased his erection from his trousers and lowered her head.

Morganna jerked her head around, feeling the heat pouring into her face, all too aware of how closely she was being watched. She forced her hand not to tremble as she snagged Clint's drink again and took a larger, burning drink.

Hawkins was obviously enjoying his lover's attentions if his quiet murmurs of pleasure were anything to go by. Good Lord, didn't these people believe in privacy?

Rising to her feet, Morganna ignored Clint's quiet murmuring of her name as she inhaled deeply and stared back at Jayne.

"Do you have a ladies' room?" Morganna glanced at the woman sucking intently at Hawkins' erection. "Or is that for public view as well?"

Jayne looked over at the couple for a long moment before patting her lover on the shoulder and rising to her feet. "Clint?" She turned to Clint.

"I need his permission to visit the ladies' room?" Morganna was practically burning with embarrassment now. She was going to kill Clint for not warning her.

"With another Domme you do." Jayne laughed. "But he knows he needn't worry. As lovely as you are, dear, women aren't my thing."

Morganna wasn't about to comment.

"Come along then." Jayne indicated a hallway several feet from where Morganna stood. "I need a break myself."

They moved into the hallway, where Morganna came to another bone-jarring stop. The way was lit by windows, but the view wasn't of the outside. It was of small rooms stretching down the hall, one window after another, with varying degrees of sexual acts being played out behind the windows.

"I can see Clint followed the letter of his contract with Drage," Jayne commented as Morganna began to follow her slowly. "Warning you what to expect is expressly forbidden by a member. Until you're accepted by myself and Drage, you aren't allowed down this hallway."

Morganna stopped again, staring through a glass partition with wide eyes. She knew that woman. The TV anchorwoman was bent over and shackled to a bed, her hips raised as a leather-clad man took a paddle to her rear and the woman raised and lowered her hips, working the dildo her lover held inside her with each backward thrust of her hips.

So this was what the confidentiality agreement Morganna had signed when they first entered meant. Sweet mercy.

"The ladies' room is just down the hall." Jayne gripped her arm and pulled her forward. "Why the hell are you here, Morganna? You're obviously not submissive material."

"Says who?" Morganna questioned her absently as she paused again, swallowing deeply at the sight of another couple. If she had ever been curious about anal sex, she was getting an eyeful now.

The toy Clint had used on her the night before didn't even

compare to the sight of the couple engaging in it on the other side of the glass.

"Come on, Morganna," Jayne chuckled as she pulled at her arm again. "You can watch later when Clint's with you. . . ."

Later? With Clint? Good gracious. That very well may not be a very good idea.

Morganna escaped into the ladies' room, breathing in roughly as she tried to plaster herself to the tiled wall just inside the door.

Jayne had excused herself to return to the main room, and to be honest, Morganna was damned glad of it. She hadn't expected this. To be honest, she had expected something darker, rougher, and she could have handled that much more easily. Shadowed rooms and pounding music with a few sexual antics in the corners. That wouldn't have thrown her nerves into a tailspin.

The restrained elegance, controlled lusts, and blatant disregard for the normal rules of sexual privacy were on the verge of freaking her out. Doing something in a shadowed corner or within a large crowd was one thing. The hall of windows into the bedrooms provided for sexual play, and Hawkins' display while calmly sitting within a discussion group, was another.

She knew the role she was there to play. The defiant submissive unwilling to actually submit. And if she wasn't mistaken, she had caught sight of the suspect she had been trying to keep an eye on upstairs several nights before in one of those window rooms.

He didn't appear any nicer to the woman he had facedown on that bed than he had acted upstairs to the uninitiated women dipping their toes into the lifestyle. Morganna was certain Roberto Manuelo was involved with the drugs. He socialized often with the three men who were arrested for dosing the drink last week, and since the arrest he was a shadowy figure rarely seen in the clubs.

The underground clubs Drage ran explained why Manuelo

wasn't seen entering or leaving the main entrance of the building and yet could be glimpsed occasionally on the main floor. The underground private parking would allow him just that sort of entrance as well, but watching it was a hazard. Drage allowed no vehicles to park along the back entrance to the club without permission and it was the only spot to get a proper view of the entrance that led beneath the club.

Shaking her head, Morganna moved to a gleaming porcelain sink and waved her hand beneath the sensor. Warm water sprayed out onto her hands, dampening them before she brought them to her face.

Soft towels were folded to the side, and she shook one out with a snap before drying her face and forcing her equilibrium back where it belonged. Out of her throat. Damn, she never thought she could get so flustered just watching another woman give a blow job. Or another couple having sex. Or anal sex.

Her butt clenched as she braced her hands on the sink and she drew in a deep breath. She had to go back out there.

Oh God. She was not ready for this. She was not this blatant about sex.

Morganna drew in a deep breath, straightened her top, then turned and moved back into the hallway. She was not going to look into those windows.

Four windows down she stopped. Drawing in a deep breath again, she stared into the room, mesmerized by the sight of the couple.

The female half of the duo was tied to the four posts of the bed, spread-eagled and obvious in a world of her own. Between her thighs, her guy was doing some real lip action against her bare pussy. Lips. Tongue. Teeth. He licked, sucked, nibbled, and his lover's lips moved frantically as she pleaded for release.

Morganna was not a voyeur. This should not be turning her into one.

But it was. She could feel the liquid heat between her

thighs as she forced herself to turn away, lower her head, and rush through the hallway. Damn, some things were just wrong. Getting turned on watching a stranger have sex was just so wrong, on so many levels.

As Morganna moved back into the main area, she kept her head down. She wasn't going to look. She didn't want to see sex. She didn't want to think about sex. She wanted to have sex.

As she moved back to Clint he caught her wrist, drawing her to his lap rather than allowing her to sit down once again. She expected to perch on his knees, but when he drew her farther back, lifting her legs over the side of his, she stared back at him in surprise.

He continued his conversation with Drage. Something about a new club Drage was considering? It was hard to keep track of the conversation when Clint's hand was stroking high on her thigh.

God, she needed a drink.

His free hand pressed her head against his shoulder while his hand stroked over the skirt to her hip.

This was so not fair. She was already so hot she was about to go up in flames. She had never had any defenses where his touch was concerned, and it was disconcerting to realize how easy it would be to lie there, to let him touch her, no matter the eyes watching them.

He was relaxed, comfortable, in this setting. And it was obvious he had done this before. Touched a woman as others watched, caressed her. Made her moan.

Morganna jerked at the sound of the soft whimper of desire that passed her lips.

"Clint, that's enough." His hand was moving beneath the edge of her skirt, his fingers caressing in small, mesmerizing circles.

At her words, he paused as his hand tightened in her hair.

"My body," he murmured softly then. "Remember? To do as I please."

"This wasn't the agreement." No, it was the act.

She tightened as his fingers slipped beneath her skirt.

"No." Her legs tightened, her senses aware of the eyes watching.

His hand paused again.

Morganna was aware of the sudden silence of the group around them.

His hand tightened in her hair again; then his head lowered and his lips covered hers. And God, he could kiss. His lips dominated hers, his tongue ravished her mouth, and her nerve endings began to flame in need despite the eyes watching.

Morganna curled her fingers into the material of his shirt as she fought her hunger, her arousal. This wasn't the place. She was his lover, not his toy. In this arena, she would always be a toy. To him. To the men who watched her. And this arena was something Morganna would never submit to. She knew it. Clint knew it. And the enemy knew it.

She jerked back from him, scrambling from his lap as he stared up at her with a dark frown. There were too many eyes watching her. Too much lust whipping around her, inside her. Her own emotions were suddenly frightening, because she knew, to the soles of her feet, that being Clint's toy might not be so bad. And it might be all she could have, unless miracles occurred and the battle she often saw raging in his eyes stilled to acceptance.

Loving her and accepting it would be two different things with Clint. Whereas to her, they had gone hand in hand all her life.

"I said no," she repeated softly. "Not here. Not like this."

She turned on her heel and stalked across the room, back to the elevator and escape. They had discussed this. Gone through the act more than once. But as she stalked away from him, she felt the pervasive little thrill of arousal, the suspicion that perhaps she wouldn't have made a bad submissive, if Clint had been the one teaching her.

♦ ♦ ♦

ROBERTO WATCHED THE COUPLE AS he stood in the shadows of the private hallway that led to the window rooms. He had been finishing the little bitch he had leashed several nights before when he saw her in the hallway.

Morganna Chavez. She had witnessed his men spiking the woman's drink last week and was the reason they now sat in jail, a threat to Diego Fuentes and all he worked for.

Morganna should be dead. If the bastard moving to follow her, his expression enraged, hadn't interrupted them, then she would have died beneath Roberto's knife.

He watched them leave, his eyes narrowed, a sneer twisting his lips. McIntyre wasn't known for allowing a woman to tell him no. He employed every trick he knew to gain his women's cooperation and sexual submission before turning from them to find another.

But none of them had been Morganna. They had resembled her, but they weren't her. Clint McIntyre obviously lusted greatly for this woman.

Diego would be very interested in this, Roberto decided. It was something they could use. McIntyre was known for his sexual excesses; the drug would not offend a sense of morality that wasn't present.

Perhaps it wouldn't be so hard to get rid of the Chavez girl.

A smile twisted Roberto's lips as he moved into the reception area and headed for the elevators himself. He must meet with Diego and see exactly how they should handle this development.

Killing two birds with one stone may well please his boss.

Chapter 15

H E KNEW THE PARTY WAS a mistake; thankfully the small gathering hadn't been too important and Morganna had played her part excellently. Perhaps too well.

She had silently challenged and defied every unwritten rule that governed the Dom(me)/sub lifestyle. And in doing so had every fucking male in the room panting after her. Clint had had to tamp down every possessive instinct he knew to keep from slamming heads together and shoving their eyes back in their heads.

Clint led Morganna into his apartment later that night as he ground his teeth together, fighting to keep his temper.

"That went very well," Morganna commented as she moved to the side of the room, watching as he made his way through the apartment to check it out carefully. "And Manuelo was there. I'm sure I saw him in the other hallway just before we left."

Clint wasn't going to say a damned word. If he did, only God knew what he would say or how he would say it. She made him crazy. How the hell was he supposed to work with her when all he could think about was fucking her? Proving to those jackasses drooling after her exactly who she belonged to.

He stalked into the bedrooms, checked the windows, made sure the clear tape he kept over the seals was still in place. It was. No prints marred it, and the wood around it hadn't been disturbed.

She didn't move from her position beside the door until he came back into the main room, his jaw bunching with the effort to keep his mouth shut as she straightened from the wall and arched her brows at him.

A beer. God, he needed a beer. He stomped into the kitchen, jerking the refrigerator door open and pulling one from the interior. He twisted the cap off with a savage motion before tilting it to his lips.

"So, did you get your cock pierced the same time you got the vasectomy, or did you have to wait?"

He snorted his beer, choking on the bitter dregs as the words slammed into his head. The minute he managed to get his breath he leaned his head against the freezer door, grinding against it as his arms hung slack at his sides. God save him.

He had known she wouldn't be able to hold it in long. He was amazed she had lasted this long.

"The piercing came first. A drunken night in Bangkok with the guys after a mission." He shook his head as he straightened. "Can I take a drink of this beer now or do you have any other questions?"

Her lips pressed together as she glided into the living room. A flip of her wrist tossed her purse to the nearby chair as she moved to where she could see him more clearly.

"Did Raven know about it?" Morganna's eyes were narrowed, her chin lifting defiantly as her gaze met his.

"It didn't exactly come up in conversation," he assured her. "As far as I know, she's unaware of it."

He took a fast draw on the bottle, praying Morganna kept her mouth shut. He needed something stronger; too bad he didn't keep it on hand.

"Why did you do it?"

"That should be obvious," he said as he faced her. He felt like a man facing a firing squad.

He watched as she swallowed tightly, not from nerves; there wasn't a hint of nervousness in her.

"I don't believe you never wanted children," she stated fiercely, her expression tight with suspicion. "You're too good with them."

"I don't want any of my own." He tried to keep his voice

calm, casual. Despite the lie. He would have loved to see her carrying his child, her belly ripe with pregnancy. A perfect little form created from what he knew burned inside him for her. And all he could hear was that child's cries.

"Don't make me ask why again," she warned him softly. "I'll start guessing soon, Clint, and you won't like what I'm coming up with."

He lifted a single brow easily, forcing mockery to his expression, watching the hurt that flashed across her eyes.

"There's no mystery, Morganna," he finally sighed, hating the shadows in her eyes. "I'm rarely home and my job isn't exactly the safest one going. I don't want to leave a child of mine an orphan. Condoms aren't always effective to prevent pregnancy—"

"I hate it when you lie to me," she said, anger thickening her voice as he stared back at her in surprise. "You know, Clint, I overhead Reno and Dad talking one night, a few months before Mom and Dad were killed."

He flinched. "Yeah?" He smirked as he lifted the beer again.

Thankfully she gave him time to fortify himself before she continued.

"Reno thought your father was beating you before he died. Was he?"

Clint stared back at her silently. He hadn't known Reno had suspected. He had thought he kept it hidden so well.

"Every time your father came home and caught your mother out, you would stay 'sick' for days. He was beating you, wasn't he?"

Clint kept his expression bland, his face relaxed. He didn't grit his teeth; he didn't let the fury claw at his guts. He couldn't. Not in front of Morganna.

"Oh God. . . ." Her voice sent a chill up his spine, but her eyes broke his heart. They filled with pain, with tears.

"Don't you fucking cry," he suddenly snarled desperately. "You cry and by God I'm putting you on a plane straight to

Hawaii. You can crash Reno's fucking honeymoon with my damned blessings."

It broke him, those tears. Morganna couldn't cry. And by God, he would not let her cry over him.

"He was beating you." Clint watched her fight for control. "That's why you would spend days in bed. Raven would worry herself sick because you never seemed to run a fever, but you didn't want to move."

He couldn't move. There were times he wondered if the old man had broken bones. Raven, thank God, had been too young to realize exactly what was going on, and Clint's father had always made certain she wasn't home when the beatings took place, and the belt marks were never higher than his shoulders or lower than his hips, so she had never seen them. As young as his little sister had been, she had no idea the hell her teenage brother was enduring at the time. And he wouldn't have had it any other way. He was older by ten years, and at that age he had always feared his father would strike out at the delicate sprite Raven had been if Clint hadn't been there to take his rage out on.

"I couldn't figure it out." Morganna shook her head slowly, her face pale, her eyes like storm clouds, swirling furiously as she stared back at him. "Raven would come to my house when they started fighting, but you stayed. Why? Why didn't you come to Dad?"

"At what cost?" He set the beer on the table before crossing his arms over his chest and staring back at her. He let the ice that filled him each time he thought of the beatings reflect on his face. "He was Rory's commander, Morganna. What would your father have done?"

"He was beating you," she cried furiously. "Dad wouldn't have stood for it."

"He didn't have a choice. And I survived it."

"Did you?" The bitter mockery in her voice sliced across the shield he used to hold back his own rage. "Did you survive it, Clint? You're thirty-five years old. You aren't married, you have no children. You have nothing but an apartment that doesn't even belong to you. You push Raven as far from you as you can, and you screw women you don't even like. What does that say for you?"

"I like *you*," he pointed out calmly.

He could control this, he assured himself. She would run out of steam soon. He knew Morganna; she blew up like a mini-volcano, then settled down. As long as she didn't cry, he could get through it without losing his mind.

"You love me." He flinched at her declaration, watching warily as she moved closer. "You've always loved me," she said. "I bet I know when you got that vasectomy. Let me guess, Clint, the week after I turned twenty. After you walked in on me in the shower while you were visiting."

He had stood shell-shocked, staring at her wet body, hunger eating him alive. Furious, burning lust had torn through him, and he knew he had nearly lost the battle. And if he had, he wouldn't have stopped. He would have pushed her against the wall of the shower and fucked her until he spilled himself inside her.

No condom. He always knew that he would never be able to bear a condom between his flesh and hers.

"Let it go, Morganna."

"Let it go?" she cried out, incredulous.

"You don't know what you're talking about."

"You loved me and you walked away from me. You did something to ensure you were always, always alone and you ran from me every chance you had. Admit it."

"I told you years ago you were chasing rainbows," he yelled back, his control snapping. "Damn you, Morganna, if I wanted you that bad, don't you think I would have taken you?"

She stepped back, almost stumbling.

He raked his fingers through his hair as he glared into her face. "God, I didn't mean that," he finally whispered wearily. "Don't cry, Morganna. I won't make it if you cry."

He moved to her, pulled to her by the pain blazing in her expression, the tears filling her beautiful eyes.

"Look at you, baby. So sweet and innocent, crying over something that wasn't your fault. That you couldn't stop. That you can't stop." He ran his thumbs beneath her eyes, feeling the dampness that marred them as her breath hitched in her throat. "You're right. I've always wanted you. I've wanted you until the want has eaten me alive. Until no matter how many women I had, it wouldn't ease. Until I thought I'd die if I didn't touch you just once. Taste you just for a second."

"Then why?" Her lips trembled as she stared up at him, her eyes darkening with everything he knew she thought she felt for him.

"Because I needed to protect you from myself. Because I'm my father's son, just as he was his father's son, and on through the line. Mom was luckier than Dad's mother was. He didn't beat her, too. Raven was even luckier. Dad would have died and gone to hell before he hit her."

"Clint, you've let him steal your life," Morganna cried hoarsely. "Don't you know you aren't like your father? God, if you were, you would have beaten me and Raven years ago."

"You don't know that. And neither do I," he told her gently. "Accept what we have, Morganna, for now. That's all I can do. Don't ask for things I can't give you."

She pushed back from him, painful anger contorting her features as her gaze raked over him. "Your love? Something more than a hot little fuck whenever the urge hits you?" She laughed, the mockery twisting her face held no amusement, though, only the anger, the fury, he had felt so many years himself.

"Morganna, please—"

"You didn't even say anything." She slapped at his chest, pushing him back as she whirled away from him. A second later she was in his face again, angrier than ever. "You suffered.

You never said anything when you could have, when you could have gotten help. Where the hell was your mother?"

He tried to turn away from Morganna. To keep her from seeing, from knowing. Damn her, she was killing him here.

"Oh my God. She knew," Morganna whispered, horrified, her hands reaching out for him. "She knew."

Her fingers trembled as they touched his face, his neck, then moved to his chest. She touched him as though afraid he would break, as though afraid she would hurt him anew.

"Morganna . . . it's over." It didn't hurt him anymore; he refused to let it hurt now.

Her tears fell. "Oh God, how could she let him?"

Clint had to stop her. He couldn't let her cry like this. He wouldn't allow it. Not over him. Not for him. He had spent too many years protecting her to allow this to happen now.

Clint jerked her into his arms, his fingers tangling in her hair, pulling her head back to cover her lips with his own. She tasted of sweet passion and salty tears. Her lips parted beneath his, her hands pulling at his shirt, popping buttons, touching heated flesh.

"Don't cry, baby," he whispered against her lips. "It's all over, Morganna. See? I'm fine."

He shrugged his shirt off, allowing her hands to whisper over his torso, the soft pads of her fingers glancing his hard, flat nipples. God, she felt good. Like an angel touching him, all silken fire and sweet passion as she made him burn.

"You're not fine." She stared up at him, her eyes misty, cloudy with sadness. "And you never will be, until you let yourself love. Don't you see that?"

He couldn't afford to love her. For both their sakes, he had to protect her. No one had won; they had all lost. Clint had realized that years ago. That didn't mean she was going to keep the upper hand on him. And it sure as hell didn't mean she was allowed to cry *for* him. He had spent too many years keeping the tears out of her pretty gray eyes to allow them to fall now.

"Come here, baby." He lifted her into his arms, ignoring her little gasp as he strode quickly into the bedroom and to the large bed he had dreamed of seeing her in. He was going to have some set ground rules. He was going to have to get control of her before she sent him into cardiac arrest. "I'll show you just how 'fine' I really am."

Morganna stared up at Clint as he laid her carefully in the center of the big bed and proceeded to strip her of her clothes, leaving her clad only in the black fishnet stockings.

She knew what he was doing. Knew he was playing her need for him, his need for her, avoiding the truth at all costs. It just wasn't the time to tell him just how full of crap this whole deal was. He was running scared and she knew it. Not because of his parents, not because he was afraid he was like his father; Clint was running because sometimes being alone was a hell of a lot easier than taking that final risk.

"Damn, you're beautiful." He straightened from the bed, staring down at her, his midnight eyes glowing with hunger as he pulled his boots and socks from his feet.

Her mouth watered as his long fingers moved to the clasp of his belt, working it free before loosening the waist and drawing the material down his legs. When he straightened, his cock stood out stiff and hard from his body, the wink of gold that pierced it flashing beneath the darkly flushed crest.

Morganna came to her knees then, casting him a hungry look from beneath her lashes as she crawled to him, licking her lips in anticipation. She wanted to taste him again, feel him throbbing between her lips, filling her mouth as she held his big body prisoner with a flick of her tongue.

"You wish." He caught her before she could touch him, flipping her to her back once again as he came over her.

"That's not fair," she panted, struggling against him as his muscular legs trapped hers between them, his hands catching her wrists and stretching them above her head.

She watched his face, saw the heat and hunger, and gloried

in it. He was arrogant, totally dominant, and all hers, whether he liked it or not.

"This is my bed," he murmured, his lips quirking with an inherent dominant sexiness that had her nerve endings sizzling.

"So what?"

Her eyes widened at the feel of cool silk and metal snapping around her wrists. She twisted, staring in surprise at the length of chain coming from the headboard and the padded cuffs now imprisoning her wrists.

"So we play by my rules."

Morganna shivered as he pulled his gaze from hers and let it travel over her body. Her upthrust breasts, the flushed mound of her sex, her legs, still encased in the fishnet stockings.

"It's time to set some rules in place." He sighed as his eyes met hers once again and he shook his head as though in chastisement. "You were very naughty today, Morganna."

Okay, that shouldn't turn her on. It sure as hell shouldn't have her womb clenching, knotting like a fist as pleasure rocked through her body.

"I'm always naughty," she informed him, tugging at the cuffs as she stared back at him suspiciously. "It's part of my nature. And this is not gaining you brownie points, Clint. I'm already upset with you."

"You stay upset with me, Morganna," he said as he cupped the breast nearest to him, his thumb flicking over the hard peaks, catching the little gold rings there and tugging at them as heated pleasure rushed from the tips.

Her breath caught in her throat. She was not going to get turned on over this "Me Dom, you sub" stuff, she assured herself. But she could not help but admit she was so turned on, so wet and close to orgasm, that it would take very little to set her off. Swirls of sensation pulsed from her nipple to her vagina, breathtaking jumps of electric hot pleasure that had her eyes threatening to close weakly.

"This is no way . . . ," she gasped as his fingers moved to her other breast, tweaking at the nipple there. "No way to soothe my anger, Clint."

"Who says I want to soothe it, sugar?" he asked, his voice impossibly gentle despite the fire burning in his eyes. "Maybe I want to see it burn hotter, brighter. Maybe your anger turns me on."

That she didn't doubt.

"It's just the challenge." She tried to control her breathing, but it was a hopeless battle. "You're a control freak, Clint. You can't control me."

"Bet me?"

Oh hell. She moaned at the excitement churning through her now.

"Clint, sex is supposed to be a participation thing." She was fighting to breathe, and thinking was quickly giving way to feeling as his fingers began to trail down her belly.

"Hmm. You get to participate, baby." His smile wasn't comforting; it was frankly sexual. "In plenty of ways." His fingers gripped the small gold ring at her belly button.

She stared up at him, seeing the savage features of his face as they planed out, tightened with the hunger that glittered in his eyes. His lips were full, mobile, eatable. God, she needed his kiss, his touch.

Her hips arched from the mattress as he pushed her legs apart, his hands smoothing up the threads of her stockings.

"I'm going to fuck you until you beg for mercy," he growled. "Until you're sweating, reaching, certain release is but a second away. And then I'm going to turn you over, baby, pet that pretty little ass, then show you just how good it can hurt."

She shuddered, feeling her juices spill from between her thighs as she stared back at him, wide-eyed, maybe a little shocked. But definitely aroused. Too aroused.

"Oh God . . ." Her eyes fluttered closed as she felt his fingers slide through the saturated folds of her pussy, felt her clit swelling, her womb clenching. "Don't you torture me, Clint. I'll get you back; you know I will."

His finger pressed against her clit, rotated, and she swore she saw stars.

"It's not nice to threaten your Dom, baby," he growled before his fingers slid down again, then moved slowly inside her.

One. A smooth achingly slow thrust that had her fighting to breathe. He retreated seconds later, only to return with two fingers, stretching her, making her ache for more.

"So sweet and tight," he whispered, kneeling in between her thighs, his cock jutting out heavily, the head almost a ruby red as it throbbed only inches from her desperate, willing flesh.

"Okay, I'll beg." She arched to him, only to have him retreat. "Dammit, Clint, this isn't fair. I'm a novice, remember? You're supposed to go easy on me. Fuck me, damn you."

"Soon." His fingers worked inside her again as his hand twisted, pulling a ragged groan from her chest. A second later it was a cry as his thumb raked her clit.

This was too good. A person could die of pleasure, couldn't she?

"Damn, you're wet, baby." His fingers slid free again. "Hot and sweet and wet. I think you're ready for me."

"Duh!" she snapped in reply, jerking at the cuffs. "God, Clint, let me go. Please let me touch you."

"Watch, Morganna," he crooned as he came closer, his hard hands lifting her hips high before he shoved a pillow beneath them, then another.

She was lifted to him, open, level with the thick length of his cock as the swollen head nudged against the folds of her intimate flesh.

Morganna was panting for air, desperate for oxygen as she felt the hard flesh begin to part her, pushing inside her. Clint's hands tightened on her hips as she watched him begin to slide inside her with slow, careful strokes. The hard wedge of flesh slid easily against her, stretched her until she burned.

"More." Her voice was strangled as her eyes rose to his. "Please. Please, Clint, more. I need more."

"Are you begging, Morganna?" His eyes were narrowed on her.

"Yes. Yes. I'm begging. Please." She would do whatever he wanted. Just one hard thrust. That was all she needed.

"How bad do you need it, baby?" His hands slid to her thighs as he rocked against her, pressing farther into her, sending her senses spinning.

"Bad enough to beg, damn you," she cried out, desperate now.

"Bad enough to stand by my side at those fucking parties?" A short, hard thrust had her head spinning. She needed more. Just a little bit more.

"Yes! I'll stay with you. I'll fetch your damned drinks; I'll simper like melted butter. Just fuck me!"

One hard long thrust filled her to overflowing. She could feel every throbbing vein, every hard, thick inch, as she writhed beneath him, her body tightening, shuddering with the effort to come.

"I promise," she panted, fighting his hold on her hips. "Please, Clint."

He came over her, hard, fierce, his hips moving hard and fast. She should have exploded. She could feel it, building, burning, the need to come raging through her as his cock stroked, plunged, working inside her with thick hot strokes. Uneven strokes. She could feel the sweat pouring from her body, the need racing across her nerve endings, tingling along her spine until she was screaming in need.

Only to have him stop. Her eyes snapped open as he pulled free before quickly turning her to her stomach.

"Clint," she cried out weakly as her hands clenched around the small chain, her hair tangling around her face. "Please. Please don't tease me like this. I promised. You heard me."

His hand landed on her ass, lightly. A soft little sting, controlled, heated. It wasn't a full slap, not even a smack. But it didn't stop. The hard pats delivered a soft burn, over and over again, until the fiery pleasure blooming in her rear spread to her clit. It pulsed, throbbed, pleaded, and demanded.

"Now, for this sweet little rear." His hand smoothed over the hot flesh. "Are you ready for me, baby?"

She was panting, gasping for air, and he expected her to talk?

"Answer me, Morganna, or I'll think you don't want me."

"Yes. Yes." The sound was harsh, hoarse.

"Good girl," he crooned, pulling his hands back.

A second later, he was working the cooling lubrication inside her. Morganna arched back to him as the single finger began to prepare her. It was easy, no burn, no bite. She had to grit her teeth to keep from begging for more.

Then there was more, another finger added to the first, scissoring inside her desperate channel as he worked more, then more of the lubrication inside her.

"So sweet and tight," he groaned as she felt him moving closer to her. "You're allowed to scream for me, Morganna," he whispered at her ear as his cock began to press inside the prepared entrance. "Just as loud as you need to."

Chapter 16

THE FEEL OF HIM TAKING her, possessing her in one of the most forbidden, intimate ways imaginable, sent Morganna's senses reeling. She had fantasized about it, dreamed about it. There wasn't a sex act she knew of that she hadn't imagined Clint participating in with her. But this one, it defied her perceptions of pleasure and pain. It wiped any preconceived notions of acceptance from her mind and replaced them with this.

The feel of him stretching her, slowly easing into her an inch at a time, rasping over nerve endings she couldn't have known she possessed. Even after the experience with the sexual toy that first night, she couldn't have imagined this pleasure. This was blinding, furious arousal. Building. Overtaking her.

Eyes wide, her vision filled with the dark wood of the headboard and the slender chain that held her hands cuffed in place, Morganna fought to hold on to her sanity.

Heat built beneath her flesh, white-hot electrical fingers of sensations whipping from nerve ending to nerve ending as a low, keening moan left her lips.

"Stop fighting me, baby." His lips were at her ear, his voice a hard growl as one hand gripped her hip to hold her in place. "Push out; relax for me, Morganna. You can take me. Every inch, sweetheart." His breathing was as hard, as ragged as hers as he slipped inside more, stretching her until she was certain she couldn't take more, yet she did. Loving it, burning with it.

"Are you mine?"

Her hips jerked at his question, at the black velvet hunger that it reflected. Only here, only within the hunger and arousal he couldn't deny, did she glimpse the needs that raged beneath the surface of his determination to remain alone.

"Are you . . . mine?" She repeated his question back to him, barely able to speak, but unable to hold back her own needs, her own desires.

His hips jerked as his cock pulsed inside her, flaying her tender nerve endings with blinding pleasure as he sank farther inside her, driving in those last inches with a desperate, involuntary thrust.

"Sweet God. Morganna. Sweetheart." His head lay beside hers, his big body shuddering above her as she writhed beneath him. "Don't fight. . . ." His hands were clenching and unclenching at her shoulder and hip as his voice became a harsh, primal growl. "Ah, baby. Don't fight it. . . ."

Morganna heard her own cries echoing around her as liquid heat raced up her spine, sizzling at the base of her skull before surging through her bloodstream. Pleasure tore through her body, sending her senses careening with ecstasy as the blend of fiery heat and exquisite pleasure tore through her womb.

Her hips bucked, driving him deeper, causing a groan to tear from his throat as he began to move. Deep, hard strokes. He wasn't gentle, but she didn't want gentle. She didn't need gentle. Arousal was like a demon clawing at her, throwing her higher, further into the excessive sensations ripping around her. She needed more. She needed all of him.

Tilting her hips, she used her internal muscles to grip his thrusting shaft, to caress him, to hold him to her as he drove inside her.

"Oh yes. There. Sweet baby . . ." His voice was a hard rasp at her ear as she tightened further around him, fighting for orgasm.

He held satisfaction just out of reach, pushing inside her over and over again, his moans, his pleasure echoing at her ear as the hunger spiraled out of control.

"Please. Clint . . . I need . . ." She could feel perspiration building between them, sealing them together as he drove inside her.

"Are you mine? Answer me, Morganna. . . ." His deep voice was desperate, agonized.

Her chest clenched with the pain in his voice, the hunger and need he only loosed when the limits of his own control had been breached. And his limits had been breached.

Morganna arched beneath him, lifting closer, tilting her hips, and pushing her buttocks closer to the stalk of heated flesh pushing into her.

"Answer me. . . ." He was close; she could feel the hard, fierce throb of his flesh inside her, the hunger that beat beneath the silk-covered steel.

"Answer me now. . . ." His hand moved from her hips, tunneling beneath her body, his fingers rasping over the swollen bud of her clitoris.

"You . . . answer me. . . ." She tossed her head, fighting to hold on to her last measure of common sense. She was so close to giving in to him, to giving him what he needed, forgetting what she needed.

His thrusts became harder, delving past delicate tissue, stretching it to reveal hidden nerve endings, stroking them, sending brilliant bursts of light to explode at the edge of her vision as her orgasm grew closer.

His fingers rubbed around her clit, stimulating the already violently sensitive bundle of nerves as he pushed her past the brink of hunger into desperation, greed. If she didn't come she was going to die. She was going to explode; she would never hold on to the last measure of her heart if he succeeded.

"Be mine, Morganna," he groaned, his voice rough. "Sweet Morganna . . ."

She screamed as his fingers trapped her clit, milked the engorged flesh.

"Answer me!" he snarled, his hips moving faster, his breathing harsh. "Now. Tell me, Morganna. Sweet God, tell me. . . ."

"Yes!" she screamed out her answer. "As much yours as you are mine."

His fingers firmed. His strokes gained in depth and in rhythm. Smooth, hard strokes as his hand moved farther between her thighs, two hard fingers fucking into her pussy as the pad of his palm rasped her clit and the thick, hard intrusion in her anus began to swell, to throb.

Release came as a cataclysm that tore through her senses. Aided by the deep, heated jets of his semen spurting into her and the rough growls of desperate male satisfaction against her ear.

Pleasure consumed her entire body, whipped through nerve endings and cells, threw her past sanity and reality, and flung her into a realm of ecstasy she couldn't have believed possible. One she knew she would never know again without Clint.

H E WAS REBORN IN HER. Clint fought to find his breath, to find control that had been lost the minute he sank inside the heated depths of Morganna. The ultimate intimacy, the ultimate trust. And he was lost in her.

She was lax beneath him as he slowly withdrew from her, collapsing beside her as he struggled to breathe. His lungs labored to adjust to the sensations racing through his body—fuck that, his soul. She was touching him. Each time he touched her, each time he took her, she came away with another part of his spirit.

"This is dangerous," he panted, facedown on the bed, boneless, so weak he couldn't lift his middle finger if they were attacked at that moment.

"No, it's not," she muttered. "I'm dead already."

A grunt of laughter pulsed from him, unbidden, involuntary. She could do that to him, make him laugh whether he wanted to or not.

"We're going to kill each other at this rate." He lifted his arm lazily, activating the mechanism that released the cuffs at her wrists. The rattle of the chain against the headboard assured him she was free. But she didn't move.

His hand touched her shoulder, smoothed back to her raised hips. Her skin was like silk, heated silk.

"We need to take a shower." He forced himself to speak when he wanted nothing more than to sleep.

Morganna's irritated little mumble had a smile quirking at his lips.

"Come on, sugar girl." He forced himself to sit up, staring down at her with a little smile as she rolled from the pillows that had lifted her hips to him. "We'll shower and sleep."

"I'm hungry," she grumbled. "You have to feed me."

She rolled to her back, staring up at him with smoky eyes, her expression languid, sated.

"We'll order pizza."

"I want Chinese." A little frown probed at her brow.

He had an odd desire to roll his eyes at her.

"Fine. I'll order myself pizza and you Chinese." He shrugged as he stood up beside the bed.

"I might want a piece of pizza, too." A smile quirked at her swollen lips.

"Minx." He pulled her from the bed, swatting at her very delectable rear as she padded past him. "Shower. We'll argue food later."

"I don't argue," she murmured as she glanced at him over her shoulder, a provocative little wink making his cock twitch. "I win."

Chapter 17

Hᴏᴡ ᴅɪᴅ sʜᴇ ᴅᴏ ɪᴛ? She should have been angry, furious with him. He had forced acknowledgment that she belonged to him without giving anything in return. Without giving her what he knew himself. That he did belong to her. But she wasn't angry. She was . . . herself. Giving. Confident. A complete enigma to him.

It didn't matter how many different ways he asscrtcd his hold on Morganna or how many times she submitted to his touch and his hunger; Clint found himself more owned than owning. And he'd be damned if she acted like a submissive. The only problem with that was the fact that instead of dulling his needs, her defiance kept him challenged, kept him hungry.

She kept him, period. He couldn't remember a time in his sexual life that a woman had sustained his interest past the first few days. Of course, he should have been prepared for it. Morganna had been his greatest sexual fantasy for more years than he was comfortable admitting to. She held a part of him no other woman ever had, and that terrified the shit out of him. That fear of her hold over him was only growing. How was he supposed to walk away later when each day her hold on him only grew stronger?

"Mmm, want a bite?"

He stared down at her, where she reclined against his back, wearing nothing but one of his T-shirts, as she lifted a bit of her Moo Goo Gai Pan to her shoulders and stared back at him.

"It's really good." She waggled her brows comically as he leaned forward and took the bite of chicken and mushroom that she held out to him.

So close, her eyes seemed to be filled with small starlights, glittering, gleaming, within a dark gray velvet backdrop. A small smile tugged at her lips and he knew the emotion he saw in her eyes. The very same emotion he had hidden from for ten long years.

"Very good," he agreed before leaning back and enjoying the feel of her resting against his naked chest.

She was soft, relaxed. The overabundance of silken waves that fell from her head flowed over one of his arms and reminded him of the warmth he had dreamed of whenever he dreamed of her.

"Reno hates Chinese food," she said as she went back to the carton of food. "Steak and potatoes all the way for my brother."

Clint played with a curl of hair as he thought of all the times he and Reno had dreamed of a potato, let alone the steak, on some of the hair-raising missions they had been sent on. Missions on which the thought of a steak urged Reno home and the thought of Morganna urged Clint back.

" 'Nother bite?" She lifted the chopsticks and he leaned forward, taking it slowly.

He should be running like hell and he knew it. He should jump out of the bed, dress, and get drunk enough to ignore the fever raging in his blood. And he would, if he weren't so damned relaxed. If every bone and muscle he possessed weren't just comfortable where they were. Supporting the bundle of dynamite that lounged languorously against him.

"Why did you go into law enforcement, Morganna?" Clint was almost surprised as the question slid past his lips.

The chopsticks paused above the carton as he felt her take a deep breath.

"I wanted to make a difference, too," she said quietly. "I hated secretarial work. Waitressing sucked. Law enforcement was there. And it taught me how to beat up on big, muscley guys." She shot him a smile over her shoulder.

"Reno's not going to be happy when he finds out. If Raven

had done something like that without telling me, I would have been madder than hell." Or would he? Somehow, he wasn't so certain.

"No. You would have been hurt," she said with a thread of regret. "And he might be hurt. But I couldn't take the chance that he would pull me out of it. Or that you would."

And he would have; there was no doubt.

"I think of you sometimes when we're on a mission," he said, his brain seemingly disconnected from his common sense. "I think of you safe and warm, your eyes bright because you're mad at me, or because you're wanting me. I wouldn't have pulled you out because I was pissed. I would have done it because the thought of you hurt . . . upsets me."

The thought of her hurt destroyed him.

Silence filled the bedroom for long moments. The lights were low, the food scattered around the heavy wooden tray they had placed it on at Morganna's side.

"I can't be a pretty little doll that you and Reno take down from the shelf to admire or pick at when you have time to come home," she said, though there was no heat, no ire, in her tone. "The house is dark and empty, and now that Raven's married and she and Reno are trying to start a family, her time is limited as well. I need a life, Clint."

"You could have married. Had babies." He had voiced the same argument once before, while they were fighting, while they were hurting.

"The man sleeping in my bed wouldn't have been you. The babies on my hip wouldn't have been yours." She shrugged easily. "You shouldn't marry and have children if you can't commit all of yourself to that family. I couldn't do that with another man."

She made his chest tight, made his throat sting with the lump of emotion threatening to strangle him.

"I never wanted to hurt you," he finally said. "That's why I stayed away, Morganna. That's why I was cruel, why I tried to make you hate me. I don't want you to cry over me."

"Eh, hell, Clint, it's too late for that." Her laughter was easy, if tinted with regret. "We take one day at a time, right? When you have to leave, I promise I won't cry."

She turned her head to stare back at him as he watched her in confusion.

"At least not while I'm looking?" he asked as he let his fingertips run down her cheek.

Her eyes sparkled with a glimmer of laughter. And how the hell she could be happy right now, he didn't know. But she was, and, he admitted, he was as well. Right here, with her in his arms.

"Yeah." She finally nodded. "Not while you're looking."

She turned back then, digging into her food with gusto as he lifted his beer from the bedside table and drank from it.

"Here. This is good." She lifted a spring roll dipped in duck sauce and leaned forward for a bite.

"I didn't really care much for the Academy," she said then. "I've enjoyed working with Joe, though. And I spent a few months in intelligence gathering here in Atlanta. Processing the information that came in from the agents and fitting it with reports from informants and so forth."

"So why did you take this assignment?" He couldn't believe he had placed so much distance between them that he hadn't even known what she was doing.

He had suspected for years she was up to something he wouldn't like, but to investigate, to delve into it, meant getting involved. Getting involved meant this. While they ate in his bed, Morganna curled against his chest, sinking further into his soul.

"Because I was the only one in place for what they needed. And it mattered," she whispered. "What they're doing to those women . . . Women I socialized with, that I had laughed with. It was too much."

Morganna shook her head with a jerky movement.

Clint tightened his arms around her waist and rested his chin atop her head. "When we lost Nathan, that's how Reno and I felt. Like a part of us had been wounded. No more fake Irish brogues, or practical jokes. No more crowing over the woman that loved him or the life he was going home to." He closed his eyes against the memory.

"That's how I felt." She curled closer in his arms. "I needed to do something to make it better."

Yeah, that was his Morganna, always fighting someone else's battles.

"If something happened to you, a part of me would die," he admitted. "If you were gone, Morganna, what would I have to fight for?"

She stilled in his arms then.

"Raven. The children she'll have." She breathed out roughly. "I don't ask you to quit, Clint. I know you can't quit. It's not a part of you. You're a warrior, and I love all of you, especially the warrior. But I'm not a baby, and I won't stand by and watch you kill yourself alone, because you're too stubborn to love, or to accept love. When this is over, maybe we both have some hard decisions to make. Because I won't go full circle. If you walk away from me, from what we have, then I'll go on. And I won't wait any longer for a man who so obviously loves being miserable more than he loves me."

He frowned down at her, knowing he should be angry, he should be arguing. But her hand was smoothing over his chest with a gentle caress and she was staring up at him with those velvet eyes shining with love.

"So you'll just walk off and find someone else?" he asked with a frown.

"The biggest, meanest, thickest-muscled redneck in the South," she assured him. "Then I'll cry and tell him how mean you were to me and watch him kick your butt."

He laughed. He couldn't help it. She actually looked serious. Staring up at him with that fierce look, her pert little nose wrinkled just the slightest and her lips held in a firm line. Though he was certain there was a hint of a smile there.

"Might as well get a cat while you're at it." He smirked. "You know how much I like cats."

And he did. He loved cats. He'd just never owned one. Unfortunately, most cats really seemed to dislike him.

"I'll get a mean cat," she assured him, and yes, that was definitely a smile tugging at her lips and sparkling in her eyes. "And he'll have really sharp claws. He'll scratch you for being mean to me, Clint."

He chuckled at the threat. If he wasn't mistaken, she had made the same threat when she was eleven and her parents wouldn't allow her to go with him and Reno when they went out one night while home on leave.

She had cried then. Tears running from her eyes as she swore it wasn't fair that she didn't get to see them long enough.

And they had stayed home until she had gone to bed. If he wasn't mistaken, two tough twenty-year-old Special Forces recruits had sat for nearly three hours and played Monopoly with her and Raven.

He shook his head at Morganna as he reached for his beer, only to have her lift it from his hands and bring it to her lips. And he swore it was the damnedest sight in the world, her lips touching the rim as she tilted the bottle back and drank from it.

"Your beer tastes better than mine," she whispered as she then placed it at his lips. "Taste it and see."

And he did. And it did. He could taste Morganna, Sunlight and heat filling his senses until he knew he would never be the same again.

He took the bottle from her and set it back on the table before lifting the tray and pushing it beside the beer. So he could tumble her to the mattress. So his lips could fit over hers and he could taste more of her.

Sweet and addictive, spicy and electric, the feel of her lips beneath his, her tongue stroking over his, tore through him in ways he couldn't bear to acknowledge. Hands as soft as silk caressed his shoulders, his back. Delicate little nails pricked at his flesh; a soft female moan washed over his senses.

There were no words. There was no need for them. As he consumed her kiss, he was consumed in return. As he pushed between her thighs, they parted for him; her legs lifted and clasped his hips in the most intimate of embraces.

She was still snug. Her sweet pussy was tight, hot, and he had to work for what he needed, the full clasp of snug, satin muscles rippling over the full length of his cock.

Short, gentle thrusts worked his flesh inside hers. His hands caressed her and he was caressed in turn until he was seated fully inside her, his senses exploding with pleasure as he began to rock against her.

This was what he fought for, what he dreamed of and ached for: Morganna in his arms, her breathless moans breaking free of their kiss as she arched, tightened, and exploded around him.

And as she milked his cock he followed her. His thrusts lengthened, grew faster, until a shattered cry tore from his lips and his release spilled inside her.

She was his and his soul acknowledged it, even if his mind couldn't.

Chapter 18

THE NEXT NIGHT CLINT SAT sprawled in the leather comfort of his host's living-room couch, his expression carefully bland as he watched the crowd milling about the huge room. The mansion sat on the outskirts of the city, a two-story monstrosity of glass and stone that had always somehow offended his tastes. Though he got along well with its owner.

Trina Blake was an oddity. A Dominatrix with a cruel streak, as well as a record a mile long. Her sexual tastes ran to women rather than men, especially small, willful women. And her gaze was currently tracking Morganna.

His Morganna. The possessiveness rising inside him had the power to bring a measure of fear to his heart. She was changing him and he wasn't certain how he would survive the outcome.

"Forget it, Trina." Clint lifted his drink to his lips, sipping at it as he spoke to the black-haired Cuban-American.

"She's exquisite," she murmured, her maroon lips curling into a smile as she shifted on her chair, her hands playing indolently with the long, coarse strands of her black hair. "I was actually ready to go after her myself when I heard you had carried her from the bar, for the second time." She cast him a mocking glance from black eyes before, oddly, checking the diamond-studded watch on her wrist. "Though she doesn't appear as submissive as I know you like them, Clint."

He turned his gaze back to Morganna. Her back was to him as she sat with several other guests, not all of whom were part of the lifestyle. Where the other submissives were catering to their Doms' needs, Morganna was socializing. Playing her part to the hilt and driving him insane.

"You have no idea what my likes or dislikes are, Trina," he said, pulling his gaze back from Morganna and the small crowd growing around her. She was like a flame, incandescent, fragile.

"I know your women normally hover about you, closer than any others," she drawled maliciously. "That one will bow to no one willingly, Clint."

He grimaced in irritation. No shit.

But he was catching the undercurrents to the conversation. He had known that if Fuentes' drug was involved in this, then the chances of Trina's involvement were high. She had been part of the drug network two years before and had been girlhood friends with Carmelita Fuentes, the viperous bitch who had run Fuentes' cartel at Diego's side with a bloody hand.

"She'll heel." He kept his response clipped. Morganna was playing her role perfectly. And why wouldn't she? he thought with a spurt of inner amusement; defying the rules came so naturally to her.

"Masters members have been watching her quite closely," Trina murmured. "I was so hoping she would apply for sponsorship. There's no way she would have heeled to any of the Doms, which would have put her on auction. I would have made certain of it." She glanced at her watch again, a slight frown furrowing her brow.

"Leave it alone, Trina," he growled.

"If you're sponsoring her, you can put her up for auction, Clint."

"She didn't apply for sponsorship, Trina," he snorted.

"Have you signed an agreement with her?" Her brows lifted questioningly as a hint of amazement showed in her gaze.

Clint didn't bring women to the parties; he picked up women at the parties. He had never shown a willingness to participate in the sort of relationships that existed just under the surface of the atmosphere he partied within.

"No agreement," he admitted, glancing at Morganna again.

Damn her. That skirt molded over her ass perfectly, reminding him of the silky feel of it and the feel of his cock sinking slowly within it. He didn't fight the lust he knew was reflected on his face. Trina would read it. She would process it. . . .

Her chuckle grated on his nerves.

"She is the real one," she said then, drawing his gaze back to her as she tilted her head, watching him with a hint of regret.

"Excuse me?" He narrowed his eyes as he rotated his wrist, swirling his drink in his glass, allowing the ice to clink against the sides.

"Every woman you've had since I've known you has resembled her. But she's not the imitation; she's the one you've always wanted. I'm not the only one who has recognized that."

"What's your point, Trina?" He was aware of the fact that every woman he had bedded for years had reminded him of Morganna. It was the only way to stay away from her, to diffuse the hunger eating at him. He just wasn't aware that anyone else had figured it out.

Catlike calculation filled Trina's angular face as she lowered her chin and watched him through veiled lashes.

"I like you, Clint," she said then, her voice low as she swept the area with her gaze. "Perhaps a bit too much."

That one was a surprise.

"Would you like to clarify, Trina?"

"She has made enemies. Powerful enemies, my friend. Just as you have."

Shit. He tensed at the undertone of her voice.

"When?"

"You know when. And if you're smart, you now know who. Diego isn't dead, Clint." She stood carefully to her feet, leaning closer as irritation flashed in her eyes. "You have five minutes," she whispered. "It's all the head start I can give you. Get out of here, and get your woman out of here, before it's too late."

Fuentes wasn't dead. It should have been a shock, but it wasn't. Clint had never been satisfied with the information that had come through, that the charred remains of Diego Fuentes' body had been found within the hacienda that had burned to the ground that night.

Fuentes would not have gone into that burning building for any reason, and Clint knew he hadn't been trapped inside it when it began burning. Fuentes was behind the drug, and Morganna had stepped in his path when she had witnessed the dealers spiking that woman's drink.

"We're out of here." Clint leaned close to Morganna's ear, whispering the words as his hand tunneled under her hair to the opposite ear and slipped her receiver free.

She was better than he gave her credit for. She didn't argue. She turned to him with a graceful smile, though her gray eyes had darkened, sharpened. She turned with him, moving easily at his side as he curved an arm around her waist and led her quickly through the house and into the darkened kitchen.

As they entered the tiled room she paused only long enough to slip free of her high heels before they headed quickly to the back door.

Pulling the revolver from the small of his back, he was aware of Morganna slipping the snub-nosed pistol from her purse. There was just something wrong about her carrying, he thought distantly as his eyes narrowed, probing the dark shadows beyond the French doors.

"Stay behind me." He eased the door open, ignoring her soft snort.

"Don't worry, baby; I have your back." Her voice was calm, though the thread of amusement had the corner of his lips kicking up in a grin as he led her onto the deck and they worked their way to the ground.

Nothing moved; nothing breathed. The hairs along his nape were tingling with warning, though. They had to hurry. Gripping her free wrist, he pulled her through the shadows toward the front drive as he dropped both their receivers to the ground.

Forget the valet parking. Despite Morganna's grumblings earlier, he had parked close to the exit drive directly in front of the thick brush that bordered the property. He led her into the brush then, aware of her stocking-covered feet and cursing his own ignorance in not thinking of this.

He hadn't expected it to come this soon, he admitted. He hadn't expected them to move so fast. Though he should have. He had just hoped the intel they had received that Diego Fuentes was dead had been correct. He had also hoped his suspicions against Merino's team had been wrong. He had messed up, he admitted. He should have dragged Morganna out of town the first night he'd found her.

She stayed silent as they worked their way to the truck. She moved behind him easily, her breathing steady, following the guidance of his hand on her wrist until they paused in the dark shadows in front of the pickup.

The driveway was well lit closer to the house, but this far down the bright lights were dimmer, the shadows cast by the other vehicles making the truck harder to see.

"Stay put," he whispered as they paused beneath the thick weeping willow branches. "When I give you the go-ahead, stay low and get your ass to the truck."

"Got it." She crouched beside him, and when he glanced back at her, he didn't see fear or excitement. He saw determination.

Gripping the revolver in his hand, he slid from beneath the tree and made his way to the truck. He had seen the black sedan that pulled in front of the house as they neared his truck; he was betting Diego's assassins were already figuring out something was up.

Bending close to the truck, he checked the length of Scotch tape he had placed over the front of the hood. It was still in place. Then he made a quick survey of the undercarriage, checking for surprise packages that would blow them to hell and back.

Moving quickly, he pulled the keys free of his pocket and eased open the driver's side door before motioning her to him.

Pulling back, he helped her into the truck before jumping in behind her, shoving the key into the ignition, and praying before giving it a quick turn.

The engine turned over with a smooth hum. Throwing it into reverse, Clint pulled from the parking spot as he saw the two men rushing from the front of Trina's house.

"Hang on." He shoved the vehicle into drive before accelerating quickly from the parking lot.

"Only Joe's team knew where we were?" Morganna was turned, staring behind them, as he raced back toward town.

She was quick; he had to give her credit for that.

"Yes. They were the only ones."

"Could someone have had time to call from the party?"

"They would have." He nodded. "But it was pre-planned. I was tipped off at the last minute by a friend."

"Hell of a friend," she breathed out roughly. "We have lights rounding the curves behind us."

"I see them." Clint flipped off his own lights, knowing the brake and parking lights would follow suit. The adjustments he had made to his vehicles after the operation in South America were paying off.

He had known something had gone bad there besides Nathan's death; he just wasn't certain what.

With a quick jerk of the wheel he turned off onto one of the smaller side roads, before making a quick U-turn and pulling off beneath a canopy of trees.

He had checked as close as he could for bugs or bombs, but no one was perfect.

Seconds later, the dark sedan raced by, their lights sweeping within feet of the truck before continuing around the curve and along the main road.

He watched the lights disappear before hitting the gas and

racing back toward Trina's. Once their assassins figured out he had pulled off, he hoped they would check this side road before suspecting him and Morganna of heading back the way they had come.

"We're in a shitload of trouble, aren't we?" Morganna breathed out several minutes later as they raced past the road that led back to Trina's.

"Yep." He flipped the lights back on, breathing a sigh of relief as the illumination of the darkened road made navigating the curves easier.

Trina *would* have to live in the backcountry rather than closer to town.

"Why? We haven't even made contact with the only suspect we have. Why make a move this fast?"

"It's a setup." He glanced over at her, his chest tightening at her narrow-eyed surveillance of the empty road behind them.

She was cool as hell. He wouldn't have suspected that a week ago. Her expression was composed, determined. Her eyes sharp and intelligent, suspicious, but not frightened.

"Why is it a setup, Clint?" She still gripped the little pistol close to her thigh, her fingers curved around it easily.

But hell, he was still gripping his. He laid it carefully on the seat beside him.

"Relax. I have a friend I can borrow a car and some clothes from. It's time to get the hell out of Dodge, Morganna."

"I'll ask again. Why?" He glimpsed her from the corner of his eye, staring back at him suspiciously.

"This isn't just about the operation you're working," he told her then. "Remember the operation where Reno was shot a year ago?"

"I remember he was shot." Of course she did. She had nearly lost her brother. All of them had lost a good friend.

"We went against a man named Diego Fuentes in Colombia. Two SEAL teams, mine and Reno's, along with a six-man

Ranger team and two six-man teams of government soldiers. We went in to rescue the daughters of three senators who had been kidnapped and were being held in exchange for the safe passage of a shipment of drugs. We killed Fuentes' wife, his son, and his brother; we were told Fuentes went down with the house when it collapsed."

"He didn't?" She settled back in her chair as the truck raced to the outer edges of town. Thankfully, Trina wasn't too far from the social center she loved so much.

"Fuentes' scientist developed the date rape drug." Clint wiped his hand wearily over his face. "I would have joined Joe's team a year ago, if my CO hadn't held me back. The DEA was working to find the supplier, but another group was working to track the distributors of the videos as well as the lab creating the drug. And possibly Nathan. They were using Joe to keep the suppliers distracted from the other group's work."

She was silent. Clint grimaced. This wasn't a good thing. He flicked a look at her closed expression, grimacing at the glitter of anger in her eyes.

"I had no idea you were involved in this until it was too late," he growled. "No one suspected Fuentes was actually alive."

"And what makes you think he is?"

"Trina. She was part of Fuentes' network two years ago, and evidently still is," he snarled, wishing he could wring Trina's neck for not telling him sooner. "We have to switch vehicles, then find some place to hole up where Merino won't be able to track us. I don't trust him or his crew now, Morganna. I'll call in the rest of the team tonight. We'll take care of it."

"Convenient," she muttered. "Why didn't you do this sooner?"

"I can't save the fucking world," he snarled as he rubbed at his neck in frustration. "I do my little bit, Morganna. Me and Reno. That's the best we can do, and we have to be content with that. I agreed with the operation as it was being handled. That drug is too dangerous not to track it to its source. It has to be eliminated. Taking out a supplier in Atlanta isn't going to help the problem growing in New York, or on the West Coast. And it is growing. Find the root and you kill the vine."

"What about the women dying in the meantime?" she cried out, furious, the pain in her voice slicing through his chest.

"The alternative is worse, Morganna," he bit out. "If we just take out a few suppliers here and there, and miss the lab while it's in one place, controlled by one hand, then it goes worldwide. It will become as popular and easy to find as crack or pot. Is that better? How does that benefit the women who have already had their lives ruined or taken?"

"You could have told me," she protested furiously. "You could have worked with me when you came into this instead of hiding everything."

"I wanted you out," he bit out, the blood thundering through his veins. "For God's sake, do you think I wanted you mixed up in this any deeper than you were already?"

"Do you think you could have stopped it?" She raked her fingers through her hair, glaring at him as he looked over her, pulling to a stop as the light before him turned red.

His eyes flicked between the mirrors, checking traffic, watching for the sedan.

"I wanted to stop it," he growled. "I would have stopped it, if you hadn't been so damned stubborn."

"Dammit, Clint, you promised to work *with* me. This is information Joe needed. Information I needed."

"Joe doesn't need anything more than he has," Clint bit out. "There's a mole on that team, Morganna; admit it. I didn't give you the information because I thought the danger you faced was the damned dealers or suppliers, not the head viper."

Morganna breathed in roughly. "What do we do now?"

"We have to get to Macey's." Macey was one of the few

men Clint knew could help him now. The hacker from hell. "We'll get another car and head to the mountains—"

"That won't help—"

"The hell it won't," he snapped, staring back at her, certain that the stakes in the game Diego was playing were much higher than he had ever imagined. "I won't let Fuentes have you, Morganna. He knows you were the one that witnessed those dealers' spiking that drink. He may even know who I am. I won't give him a chance to take you."

He'd hide her as far back in the mountains as he could get her and pray to God they could catch Diego before he found them. If Fuentes' network was back in place, then they could all be screwed. Royally.

"Raven's blocking my calls to Reno," he informed her tightly. "When we get to Macey's, call her; get Reno on the phone. They could be in danger as well. He needs to know what's going on now."

"God, Raven will kill both of us for ruining her honeymoon."

"She'll live. That's what's important," he snapped back. "When you get Reno on the phone, Morganna, I want to talk to him."

"Sure. Fine. Whatever." He heard the safety click on her gun before she opened her purse and stored it inside.

God. He couldn't believe this. Years, fucking years of fighting to protect her, only to have her in danger now because of him. Flashes of the videos taken in as evidence in the past two years that drug had been sifting through the party scene had his guts tying in knots.

The women were brutalized. The thought of Morganna being taken, drugged, hurt in such a way, was more than he could stand. His hands tightened on the steering wheel in a killing grip as he drove through the late-night traffic to the seedier side of town.

Macey wasn't anyone's idea of a good ole boy. A huge bruiser with a head for electronics like nothing Clint had ever seen and a fist that packed a hurting. Pulling his cell phone from its holder, Clint punched in the number.

"We're on leave." Macey's voice was warning.

"I'm in trouble," Clint said softly. "I have Reno's sister with me and we have some bad shit going down, Mace."

"How far away are you?"

"I'm five minutes from you. I need wheels and the ones I have need to show up in an area far, far from here."

"Hell of an order," he grunted. "Pull into the back; the garage doors will be open. We'll store your beauty there until we can round everything up."

Macey wasn't one to waste words. The line disconnected just as fast as he had answered.

"We have to warn Joe," she said as Clint pocketed the cell phone.

Clint sighed deeply. She was a friend to Merino, he understood that, but she wasn't hard enough, cold enough, to understand that a friend's knife would slash your throat faster than the enemies' would.

"Clint, we can't leave him in the dark," she pressed again.

"We can't risk it, Morganna." He shook his head firmly. "I don't know who I can trust on that team, but I know one of them betrayed us. Only Joe's team knew where we were going to be ahead of time. Not even Trina knew we'd be showing up."

"It can't be Joe," she whispered. "Clint, he's lost friends in this assignment already. You haven't seen the effect it's had on him. Joe wouldn't do this."

She wasn't hard enough. God help him. And her.

"And he won't believe it was one of his team," he snapped back. "He trusts them, Morganna, just as I trust Reno. Use your head here. We don't trust anyone. Macey understands the rules. I'll get what I need and then we're out of there. Period. He screws me and he won't live to spend whatever Fuentes might have tried to bribe him with. Macey won't screw himself like that. I can't say that about Merino or his men."

She was too innocent for this. Too tender. He caught the flash of hurt that crossed her expression, the stillness of her slight body.

"I'll take care of you, Morganna." He ground the words between his teeth and looked over at her, reaching out to touch her, to cup her pale cheek. "But you have to trust me, baby. Trust me."

Clint pulled back as he neared the end of Macey's street. He pulled into the alley behind Macey's less than pristine house, then turned into the small junkyard behind it.

The garage door was open as Macey had promised. Clint drove the truck into the dark interior, the heavy doors sliding closed behind him as the overhead lights lit up the area.

There was no way to reassure her. Not yet. He had to keep her alive. He had to keep his wits about him. If he touched her, God forbid if he weakened enough to hold her, then his control would be shot. And that neither one of them could afford.

Chapter 19

MASON "MACEY" MARCH WAS HUGE. At least six feet, five inches and built like the broadside of a barn. There wasn't an inch of fat on his big body or trust in his chocolate brown eyes.

Long, thick dark blond hair was pulled back from his face and tied in a ponytail, emphasizing the broad planes and angles of his face. He was what Reno would have called a force of nature. You didn't go up against it; you moved to the side until it passed by, and breathed a sigh of relief you weren't caught in the turbulence.

Macey was waiting for them at the doors at the side of the garage, dressed in a black sleeveless T-shirt and black jeans. Biker's boots covered his feet and a rifle was slung over one powerful arm.

"Trusting today, ain't you, Mace?" Clint commented as he helped Morganna from the truck, his hands flexing against her waist before he released her. "Only one gun as a greeting?"

The behemoth grunted, a rough sound that could have been a laugh.

"Get on in here." He stood back from the doorway. "I turned on the receiver after your call. You got some serious dudes searching for that pickup, boy."

"No shit," Clint sighed as he led her to the doorway. "Mace, this is Morganna, Reno's sister. Morganna, meet Macey; he's part of my team and the best damned computer whiz I've ever laid my eyes on."

Macey's full, surprisingly sensual lips quirked at the description.

"Glad to meet you, ma'am." He nodded as he turned and

led the way into the house. "Reno's a good friend. He has a piss-poor brother-in-law, though. He should have shot him years ago."

"I suggested it," Morganna drawled, flicking Clint a laughing glance. "Reno wanted to wait. He was certain Clint would age well."

The chuckle that met her statement had Clint casting them both a brooding glare.

"Don't gang up on me with her, Mace. I'm stuck with her for a while. You're not."

"Too bad. I'd be nicer to her," Macey grunted.

The house was surprisingly neat but plain. Bare, actually. She stared around, wondering how a man as personable as Macey seemed to be had a house with nothing personal in it.

"This is the reception area, darlin'." Macey's smile was wicked as he caught her staring around. "Come on; I'll show you my home away from home."

He led them through the threadbare living room with its floor-model, ages-old television, into a kitchen with the barest essentials and then into a hallway. There he pulled a remote from the back pocket of his jeans and flipped a switch. Morganna jumped back as a section of the wall slowly slid to the side.

"Come on down. I have the radios picking up transmissions now. I finally pinpointed the boys looking for you, but they aren't giving away anything important." He loped down the cement stairs that led from the hallway.

Morganna glanced back at Clint warily as she followed slowly, catching his soothing wink as the wall slid closed once again.

"What happens if the place catches on fire?" she whispered to Clint.

"Then we peel out under the house and escape through the sewer," Macey called back. "Nasty place, though, so I'm going to hope no one decides to burn me down. I'd get pissed and have to kill someone."

Somehow, she didn't think it was an idle threat.

As she stepped into the main portion of the basement, her eyes widened. Now this was definitely lived in and taken care of. A long, comfortable upholstered couch divided the room. In front of it, on a far wall, was a wide-screen flat television hung on the wall with a state-of-the-art sound system running along the walls. A scarred wooden coffee table sat between them. On each side, a recliner, used but in good condition, sat angled to the television.

Behind the couch, an electronic madman's dream: computers, receivers, and shelves of beeping, tweeping machines that made no sense to Morganna whatsoever. Above them, several flat monitors showed the outside of the house on all four sides, giving Macey a perfect view of anyone coming up on him. Two others flipped through the rooms of the house upstairs, keeping a careful watch on each area for several seconds at a time.

"There's beans and bread on the stove." Macey flicked his fingers to the corner where a stove, refrigerator, and large sink sat. A small table and chairs occupied the wall to the side of it.

"Hungry?" Clint's hand ran up and down her back as he led her farther into the room.

"No." She shook her head. "Will the cell phone call out here? I'll try to get hold of Raven. It takes her a while to answer sometimes."

"Yeah, she's good at avoiding calls. I think she stole Reno's cell phone."

"It was one of her conditions when she agreed to the wedding," Morganna told him. "She was tired of you calling and bitching about me and making Reno leave the house all the time."

"Hmm." The noncommittal murmur had her lips twitching. "Go ahead and see if you can get hold of her. I'll see what me and Macey can find out."

"Get her a drink at least, Clint," Macey muttered. "Hell,

she looks wore out. There's beer in there, and Stacey keeps some wine coolers just to piss me off. There's lunch meat and bread and junk. Stacey's always eating something. I swear when that girl's metabolism slows down, she's going to blow up like a balloon."

"Hey, it takes energy to keep up with brothers," Morganna informed Macey, keeping her voice playfully tart. "If she's anything like me, she gets tired of you having all the fun."

She was aware of the surprise that crossed his broad face, along with his amusement.

"Stacey would like her, Clint," he laughed. "She has mouth. I bet she keeps you and Reno on your toes."

"More than you know." Clint shook his head as Morganna glanced up at him knowingly.

"Kind of surprised me when I heard you were working with Merino's crew," Macey surprised her with the announcement as she moved away from Clint and headed for the refrigerator. "A few of our guys that frequent the clubs have been keeping watch. They say you're damned fine for an amateur."

"Thanks." She caught Clint's look of disapproval as she turned back to them. "Clint wasn't too happy."

"Course he wasn't," Macey drawled. "A man likes to keep his personal sweets stashed away from hungry eyes. He's not stupid. Me and the others were getting ready to draw straws on who was going to have to tell him about it, though."

"Shut up, Macey," Clint growled.

"Yeah, like all of us didn't know you were hungry for her, Clint." Macey smiled placidly as Morganna leaned against the wall and watched in interest. Not many people had the nerve to rib Clint so blatantly. "Did he tell you about him and Reno getting into that fight in Germany over you?"

"Shut up, Mace."

Now this was some surprising news.

"No." She arched her brow in interest. "He didn't."

"Oh yeah, kept us all watching those two real wary like. We were winding down after a mission—"

"Shut up, Macey."

"Seems Clint wanted Reno to do something about some musician you were seeing at the time. Wanted it stopped before you ended up in bed with him—"

"Don't make me kill you, Macey." Clint's voice was suddenly harder, darker. "I need you right now, man. But later, we might have to talk."

Macey tilted his head and stared back at Clint with a quirk of his lips, his dark eyes dancing.

"Sure, man." He smiled slowly. "Get your ass on over here. Let that pretty thing there get herself a drink. That skirt is hot as hell, too. You wearing panties under that, Morganna?" He turned back to her, his grin rakish.

"Actually," she drawled. "I'm not. But don't tell Clint, okay? He might get upset."

A shiver worked down her spine as Clint turned back to her, his gaze starkly possessive, his expression suddenly sensual, carnal.

"Get hold of Raven," he growled. "And stay away from the one-night wonder here." He nodded to Macey. "I'd hate to have to castrate him. Or cut his damned tongue out."

Morganna continued to watch him as he stalked over to the bank of computers Macey was working at. Now wasn't this just a surprising development. The musician in question hadn't been her lover; actually, his lover had been his bass player. A very handsome young man who had idolized him. But Shawn Kevin had been desperate to uphold the image of heterosexuality. Why, Morganna had never really understood. But he had been nice and, for a while, interesting. Morganna had no idea Clint had actually been jealous of him.

Shaking her head, she pulled her purse from her shoulder and unsnapped it. Extracting the cell phone from inside, she laid the purse on the table, then returned to the refrigerator to collect a bottle of water.

Punching in Raven's number, Morganna let it ring until the messaging system came on.

"There's trouble, Raven. Reno has to call." She flipped the phone closed as she pulled out the water.

Clint was talking on his cell phone, obviously calling in the team he and Reno normally worked with. She knew from the wedding that several of them were on leave until after Reno's honeymoon.

"I can't find Markwell." Clint flipped the phone closed as he turned back to Macey. "Kell and Ian are still in town; Max headed out to Texas to catch up with some friends there. That leaves Markwell unaccounted for."

"Let's see if we can find our boy then." Maccy turned back to the computers. "I know Kell and Ian have been going between the clubs. They were the ones keeping an eye on your bit of sweets," he snickered as Clint slapped at the back of his head.

As Clint hovered over the other man's shoulder, Morganna eased closer to him. She felt chilled. Uncertain. Too much was happening too fast, and the implications of the battle facing them seemed overwhelming.

In that moment, Morganna realized the extent of her inexperience. She was trained to watch, to shoot. She wasn't prepared to go against international terrorists and drug runners such as the Fuentes Cartel was rumored to be.

As she neared him, she was surprised when Clint's arm came around her and he pulled her against him. Just like that, he tucked her against his chest, his gaze never leaving the computer Macey was working on.

"Shit. What's this?" Macey hit a key, bringing up several pictures and a text report.

Morganna recognized the picture. Devin Markwell. He was young, smiling. Beside that picture was a chalked outline of a body in a garbage-ridden alley.

"No fucking way," Macey muttered as Clint tightened beside her. "This happened this morning. He was found outside a bar in downtown." Macey shook his head before turning back to Clint, his gaze shocked. "He's dead, Clint."

"How?" Clint's voice hardened, chilled.

Macey turned back to the computer, hitting more keys, his fingers flying over the keyboard until another page came up. "They found another guy. A naturalized South American. A dealer." His voice was quiet, emotionless. "Devin was beat to death. The dealer was gutted like a fish. Santos. Wasn't Santos—"

"Part of the Fuentes Cartel. He's Roberto Maneulo's bastard brother. He was born here. But Roberto has looked after him." Clint finished for Macey before a curse sizzled from his lips. "And Roberto is a member of the Masters clubs."

Morganna stood still, staring at the picture of the dealer on the screen.

"He's one of the three men Joe arrested at Diva's," she said quietly. "He was the one dosing the drink with the date rape drug. There was Santos, Robert Lewis, and Donny Caine."

Macey typed in the names. "Dead." The report wasn't unexpected at this point. "Found this morning. Lewis and Caine were found this evening outside town. Suspected drug deal gone bad."

"Fuentes is cleaning house," Clint said. "He tried to hit me and Morganna this evening."

"Check for Roberto Manuelo," Morganna suggested. "He's our suspect at the moment in the supply of the drug. Though there was no report of a suspected connection to the cartel. I also saw him in Diva's Downstairs the night we were there."

The search took longer. Morganna nibbled at her thumbnail as Macey pounded on the keys, cursed, sweet-talked the computer, then finally grew silent.

"Manuelo is breathing," he finally said. "His cell phone number matches that of the ones I've been tracking since the search for you and Clint began. I caught your names being bandied on the receiver I use to monitor unsecured cells." He flashed her a cold smile. "He's leading the search."

"Not for long."

Morganna jerked around, staring up at Clint as he stood alone several feet from her.

"Contact the Admiral, Macey," Clint ordered, the muscles in his jaw working tensely. "We have a possible hit on our men. We need Reno's location checked, secured, and he needs to be apprised of Markwell's death."

"I'm on it." Macey turned back to the computer as Morganna stared back at Clint.

"What are you going to do?" she asked, though she sensed she already knew.

He stared back at her, his blue eyes blazing in his dark face. He seemed so remote, so self-contained. This was the Clint that worried her. Cold. Unemotional. This Clint needed no one, especially not her.

"I'm going to take care of it, Morganna," he told her softly. "However I have to."

"The Admiral is in contact with Reno as we speak." Macey's voice was clipped. "He's moving himself and Raven to an undisclosed location for the time being. He warns you to keep Morganna locked up."

There was no amusement in Macey's voice. His voice was just as hard as Clint's.

First Nathan during the operation in Colombia, now Markwell. And if Fuentes wasn't taken out, then he would come after Morganna again. He wasn't a man who gave up, but he also wasn't an easy man to take out. He surrounded himself with lackeys, with men willing to die for him, to protect him no matter the consequences.

"I have to get rid of the truck." Clint had to get out of there, he had to track down information, and he had to do it alone. "Macey, keep her down here." He turned to the other man, seeing the horror in his eyes. "If I'm not back in five hours, you know what to do."

"No!" Morganna's eyes widened in fear. "You're not leaving me here—"

"The hell I'm not," Clint growled fiercely, gripping her shoulders as she rushed up to him, clamping them tight, staring into her eyes as the rage and pain burning in his stomach threatened to overwhelm him. "You're safe here and I don't know what the hell is waiting out there. You're not trained for this, Morganna, and you know it."

"I can watch your back." She was shaking her head, her eyes filling with tears.

"No, Morganna," he snapped, the thought of her out there, in the line of fire, more than he could handle. "I have to check some sources, I have to ditch that truck and find out what the hell I'm looking at. I can't do that with you with me, baby."

He couldn't kill while she watched. She was strong, stronger than he ever imagined, but he couldn't bear for her to see him as he really was.

"Macey." He didn't have to turn to the other man.

"I got her, man," he swore. "She won't move from here. I swear it."

"I need you to do this, Morganna."

He watched the knowledge in her expression that he was right and the impotent anger that filled her eyes. She knew she wasn't experienced enough, and it was eating at her, tearing through her.

But God help him, even if she had been, he wouldn't have been able to take her with him. He was a killer. Stone cold. Without remorse when it came to the enemy. And Fuentes and any of his men were the enemy.

"Macey, find out if Markwell was into anything. If this was a personal hit. Get Kell and Ian out here; we'll need their help."

"I'm on it." Macey stood behind Morganna, prepared to stop her if she tried to follow Clint. He was terrified she would try to do just that.

He jerked her into his arms because he couldn't help himself. His lips covered hers, tasting her tears, her fear, then her heat. Pulling back, he pushed her to Macey. Clint didn't wait to be sure the other man was holding her back; he knew Macey would. Clint ignored her cry, ignored the need to touch her one more time before he moved quickly for the stairs.

"Macey, I need some hardware." He detoured to the other side of the room, moving behind the stairwell to Macey's stash.

"Take what you need."

He did. He chose quickly, pushing ammo into a small duffel before slinging the automatic rifle over his shoulder and pushing the handgun into his waistband. Ignoring Morganna's arguments, he raced up the stairs and through the open entrance.

Fuentes had caught him unaware. It wouldn't happen again He knew the monster stalking them now, and he'd be damned if he would let the bastard touch Morganna.

Chapter 20

"DAMN YOU, CLINT," MORGANNA CURSED as Clint disappeared up the stairs and left the basement.

She raced up the steps, catching the wall as it clicked shut behind Clint's exit, effectively blocking her in once again. She pounded her fist against the wall before kicking out at it furiously.

Stomping back down the stairs, she faced the quiet, somber Macey as violence surged through her.

"He can't do this alone." She had seen the grief in his eyes, soul deep, filling his being and breaking her heart. "Go with him, Macey."

"Chill out, babe," he sighed, crossing his arms over his broad chest as he glared down at her. "You're forgetting who you're dealing with here. You're a hazard out there with him, just as he said. And so am I. Let him keep his head clear; he doesn't need to come back here to find you in Fuentes' hands."

"He hasn't caught me yet," she snapped.

Macey snorted. "He hasn't really tried, darlin'. Fuentes has been playing. It's what he excels at. He'll play in earnest now. He's taken out one of our men and that's not an easy thing to do. Right now, Clint needs to do what he does best. Hunt. While I do what I do best and track."

She flinched, stepping back as helplessness washed over him.

"They killed his men," she whispered. "He's destroyed, Macey—"

"He's a SEAL, Morganna." Macey rolled his eyes at her. "He's lost more friends than you can imagine. Nathan last year and now Markwell is a heavy hit, I admit, but he's stone cold when he's in work mode; don't you doubt it. That boy is an instrument of death right now, and you don't want to see that. Hell, you don't need to see that."

"He's hurting—"

"He's out for vengeance." Macey's smile was cold. Hard. "And trust me when I say Clint knows how to do death the right way. So just chill out and let him do his thing. Staying safe is the best way you can help him."

Her gaze flicked to the monitors then, seeing Clint step into the garage, the black-and-white monitor showing more than color ever could have.

The shadows shifting around his expression sent a shiver up her spine. His eyes were cold, hard. Chips of dark ice as he moved to the truck. He looked like death.

"Yeah, hell of a change, huh?" Macey grunted as he caught her expression. "He'll be back, Morganna. I can promise you that. He knows what he's facing, and he has more than his own life to fight for. He won't fail."

She stared back at him, hating the tears falling from her own eyes, hating the helplessness that filled her.

"What does he have left?" she whispered. "All he does is fight."

He shook his head slowly. "Clint's loyal to his men, don't doubt it," he growled. "But something anyone who really knew Clint understood was that you are his soul. He fights it. He denies it, but trust me, Morganna. Clint's not fighting for friends or family now, or for himself. You're his innocence, girl. And *that* a man would fight the devil himself for."

She shook her head slowly. "He'll always fight loving me."

"He likes to think he can," Macey grunted. "There's not many of us who know Clint down deep like I know him, sweetcakes. Me and Reno. We know Clint to the bone. And we know what you mean to him. Don't doubt that."

"How can you know this?" She hoped, prayed. She kept her confidence intact when Clint was around, but he hid so much from her. Kept too much to himself.

Macey grimaced as he turned away from her for a moment, watching as the gray pickup eased from the back drive, the lights off as darkness shadowed it.

"I've seen him when he can't hide." Macey cleared his throat softly. "Me, Reno, his men. Clint was hurt pretty bad once; we didn't know if he would make it until we could get him to the pickup point. Reno, uhh, told him you were hurt. Told him you were crying for him." He shook his head as she stared back at him in shock. "He fought like a madman to live. He shouldn't have survived, but he did. And he will now."

His dark eyes bored into her as he turned back to her. "You do what that boy tells you to do and you'll stay safe. If he wants you trussed in cotton and hid in a corner, then you do it. Because if he lost you, I don't think he would survive, and maybe that's something you'd better think about."

L EAVING MORGANNA ALONE WITH MACEY was hell. Beneath the rage and pain, and the knowledge that another part of the team that he called family was gone because of Fuentes, was the knowledge that another man was protecting his woman.

Forcing the jealousy, the possessiveness, into the distant corners of his brain wasn't easy, but the violence swirling through his head made it easier. Fuentes had made a serious mistake in thinking he could strike at Morganna for any reason as long as Clint was alive. This was the reason Fuentes had fallen the first time, because he liked to play games.

Fuentes had been convinced he was the master gamesman. He'd been wrong. His wife, Carmelita, had been the true strategist. She had allowed Fuentes to believe he was the mastermind of the cartel, but that black-hearted bitch he had married had been the true mastermind. And she had wielded that power with effortless ease through the easily manipulated Fuentes.

It didn't take long for Clint to pick his tail back up or to lead the bastards where he needed them. They weren't stupid;

Clint gave them credit for that. It took him nearly an hour to "lose" them again and to make certain they spotted the pickup parked behind Diva's.

Watching from the shadows, he waited as the three men left the sedan and made their way into the club before he moved. He knew the fourth had held back; Clint had watched him slide into position along the shadows of the back of the building, with a clear view of the truck.

Yeah, they were good. Some of Fuentes' finest, and if Clint wasn't mistaken, the little prick watching the truck was one of his highest lieutenants. It was just a sad day when you had to use your best men to play trackers. But Manuelo was no place to be found.

Fuentes' soldier was good, but taking him out was easy. Clint slipped from position, careful to stay low until he was only feet away from assassin wannabe. He hefted the blade he held in his hand before drawing back slowly, then letting it go with a powerful flip of his wrist.

The body slid slowly down the side of the building without a sound. Clint moved quickly to the fallen form, rifling through pockets and shoving the contents into the pack at his side to go through later.

As quickly as he moved in, he was fading into the shadows, moving into position to wait for the other three. Taking them out wasn't much harder. They hadn't expected him to be waiting for them. He dragged each one back to their vehicle, throwing him in quickly before closing the door and patting the hood triumphantly with the pad of his thin leather gloves and connecting a small receiver to his ear.

"Macey, four down. Am I clear?"

"Clear, Ice," Macey spoke. "I have a report on Loader," he said then, his voice soft as he used Markwell's code name. "He was called out at zero hundred hours last night. A call to his cell from good ole Santos reporting information he needed to give Loader for Ice." Clint was Ice. The Iceman. "They arranged a meet and the rest is blood."

"How did he know who to contact?"

"That one's up in the air," Macey reported. "But he called Max's cell, too, left the same message. Important information for Ice and a request for a meeting. That's all we have."

Their cells and numbers were secure. Son of a bitch, how had one of Fuentes' men gotten hold of them?

"We have more than one mole," Clint murmured.

"Roger that," Macey agreed.

"I'm making a stop inside Diva's; then I'm clear," Clint reported. "Expect me in sixty. If I'm not there, contact the remainder of the teams and secure the kitten."

Morganna had to stay safe at all costs.

Pulling the receiver from his ear and tucking it into the small pack on his belt, Clint headed for the back entrance of Diva's.

The private room he kept there held a small store of cash, fake IDs, and a few credit cards. He had learned enough over the years to become one paranoid son of a bitch where protection was concerned.

The dimly lit hallway was empty as he moved inside, the hard thump of the music pounding through the walls as he strode quickly to his private room. He was under no illusion that Drage wasn't watching for him. It shouldn't have surprised him to find out the club owner was involved with Joe in this mess. Drage Masters was a sly bastard, living just on the light edge of complete criminal intent and somehow managing to keep his balance.

Clint pulled the key card from his wallet, swiped it quickly through the security bar, and watched for the green light. He kept the gun securely against his thigh as he pushed the door open and stepped inside.

Son of a bitch.

His lips thinned at the sight of the couple leaning negligently against the bar on the other side of the room. Speak of the devil and he will come, followed by his gun-toting demoness.

"I don't have time for you, Masters," Clint growled. "Clear out."

Drage sighed patiently as he turned to Jayne Smith and nodded slowly. A grin tugged at her lips as she reached to the other side of the bar and lifted a small wooden box to the top of the well-polished teak bar.

Damn. Maybe Clint's stash wasn't hidden as well as he had thought it was.

"You will find it untampered with," Drage commented softly as Clint closed the door behind him. "I assume time is of the essence, so I thought I would make it easier for you."

"What do you want?" Clint kept his weapon lowered, though his finger lingered on the trigger. A fact that his host was well aware of, if the tightening of his lips as he glanced at the gun was any indication.

"I want the bastard who's using my clubs to kill women," Drage snarled with cold fury. "Killing men who could lead me to him in my parking lot won't help my cause much, my friend."

"Find Diego Fuentes and you'll find your problem," Clint bit out, ignoring the surprise in the other man's eyes. "Now get out of my way and let me collect my little stash there and I'll head on out."

"Fuentes is dead." Drage ignored his order. "He was taken out a year ago by the Colombian army."

"Actually, his cartel was busted by mine and Reno's units," Clint sneered. "Fuentes evidently escaped. This drug was his and his little wife's brainchild. Trust me, Fuentes is alive, and I don't have a whole lot of time to get back to Morganna and get the hell out of here. One of her suspects, Roberto Manuelo, is one of his highest henchmen. Follow him, you'll find Fuentes."

"Is that wise, Clint?" Jayne Smith spoke up. "Running won't capture him; you'll always be looking over your shoulder."

"Don't fuck with me," he snapped, caressing the trigger

of the gun. "The bastard nearly ambushed us at a party earlier. He took out one of my men in Colombia and he hit another last night. I have a damned itchy trigger finger right now, so don't push me, Smith."

"Fuck!" Drage pushed his fingers roughly through his hair as he gave his head of security a pointed look before turning back to Clint. "Bring Morganna here, Clint. Let him believe you're still accessible. Draw him out where you'll have your back covered."

"Covered?" Clint arched his brow. "Aren't you the one whose men can't even catch the bastards working this drug? And don't tell me you haven't figured out that the DEA team working this little game has a mole, Drage. I thought you were quicker than that."

"We know, and we are very close to cracking his identity," Smith revealed, her voice as cold as a winter night. "Bail out now and Fuentes will go looking for you. Continue this operation and I'll cover your back personally, Clint. We find the mole and he will lead us to Fuentes. Whoever he's paying off would have direct access to him. You know the control freak he is. He wouldn't allow anyone else to work this for him. It would be too important to him."

She was right, as much as Clint hated to admit it. Because no way in hell was he putting Morganna's life on the line any further.

"No."

"Jesus, Clint, you're losing your objectivity here," Drage snarled. "You're letting your emotions cloud your judgment. You know we're right. Fuentes has stepped up his efforts to refinance his cartel. He'll take you and Morganna out the first chance he has just for the hell of it now. Let his own ego take him down. Work with me here."

"And I'm supposed to trust you for what reason?" he growled. "Weren't you the one preparing to sponsor my woman, Drage? That was confidence-inspiring."

"It got you off your ass and into her bed, though, didn't

it?" Drage shot back. "I don't believe in running from your demons, Clint. Perhaps I was helping you face yours."

"Well, thank you all to fucking hell and back," Clint snarled furiously. "Did I ask for your help?"

"Consider it a favor between friends." Drage waved off the sarcastic remark with a mocking flip of his hand as his lips flattened with his own anger. "We have the master suite downstairs. I can circulate the rumor that you have tired of her defiance and you're using the suite to complete her training. No one would doubt it except Fuentes. He would attempt to hit you here. To do so, he would have to use the mole he has within Merino's team. This way, we both get what we want, and you aren't running alone. Fuentes could have a damned army backing him. Don't be a fool with Morganna's life."

Clint had a nice little cabin deep in the mountains, secluded, sheltered. He had taken great pains to keep it secret, but he knew the information could be had. He had intended to run there with Morganna, to hide her as far from danger as possible. But would she be safer there, where he couldn't face the enemy?

"Clint, they raped and tortured friends of ours. These women they're striking have done nothing to deserve what they found at this bastard's hands," Jayne's voice echoed with a killing chill. "We would have betrayed you already if that was what we meant to do. Let's help each other."

They were right, and he fucking hated it.

"They won't expect the security system I have in place in the private rooms," Drage continued. "You'll have the suite to yourself for the week. You can make your appearance in the bar each night and taunt him with the fact that you're killing his men off and that you're unafraid of the threat he represents. If you run, you're giving him the upper hand."

"Dammit, I know that," he snarled. "This is Morganna, Drage. She's as predictable as lightning—"

"She's smart, and she's careful. You haven't watched her

the past months as I have." His lips quirked faintly. "Her brother has entrusted me with her care for nearly two years, Clint, and I am the eyes and ears that allowed her to work this operation for the past six months. Trust me, if I didn't think she could carry this off, then I would be helping you to cart her out of state."

Okay, that made better sense. Clint knew Reno was well acquainted with Drage and Jayne. He hadn't expected this, but as he thought about it, he knew he shouldn't have been surprised. Which also explained the fact that Raven was able to monitor and block the calls to Reno's cell phone. This was the only way Reno would have allowed it.

God, he was going to kill Reno. He could have at least warned him.

"Shit!" He raked his fingers through his hair in a gesture of complete frustration.

Everything inside him was screaming out in rejection of the idea. Every possessive instinct in his body was demanding that he cart his woman off and hide her as far away from this shit as possible.

"You need backup for this, Clint," Jayne inserted. "You know you do. If we work together, we can finish Fuentes for good." Bloodlust echoed in Jayne Smith's voice, causing Clint to stare back at her with hard intent.

"They nearly had me, McIntyre," she revealed, her lips tilted mockingly. "Trust me, that drug is no fun, and had they managed to get me out of the club I was in that night, I would have never lived to find vengeance. Now I want vengeance."

The flash of fury in her eyes, the cold set of her expression, combined with Drage's sudden tension, convinced Clint. He hated it. If there was anything he hated more than allowing Morganna anywhere near the danger swirling around this club, then he couldn't imagine it. But they were right. Eventually, Fuentes would find him in the mountains. He couldn't keep watch 24-7 on his own and he couldn't ask Reno to leave his sister right now and help him.

"I need a car," he bit out. "I have her hid for now. I'll collect her and bring her back here. You." He pointed his finger fiercely back at the two of them. "Had better have your shit together. Because if anything happens to Morganna, there won't be a hole you can hide in deep enough to save you. Man or woman, I'll kill you."

"He's so fierce." Jayne shivered mockingly. "I bet I could teach Morganna how to tame him, though."

"Tsk, tsk, kitten," Drage murmured. "Let's not tempt an explosion until we're in safer quarters."

Shit, they reminded Clint of Morganna. Was this where she had learned her smart-mouth tendencies or had she taught them to Smith? He didn't doubt she had.

"You can use my car." Smith pulled a set of keys free of the snug pocket of her leather pants and tossed them to him. "It's completely secure and parked in the underground garage. I'll be waiting for you at the back door when you return and we'll get her inside safe and sound. Let's do this and do it right, Clint. Then we'll all be safe."

He caught the keys in his free hand as he finally allowed himself to breathe in deeply. He didn't like admitting to the terror that had crawled through his system when he realized how easily Markwell had been taken out. He had been one of the best. A fully trained Navy SEAL warrior with the reflexes and instincts that only sheer talent for the job and hard training could instill. Fuentes wouldn't be easy to take out. If Clint could at least manage to wound his network enough to find that lab, then they could defang him for a while, if nothing else.

"How do we work Merino?" Clint asked then.

Jayne Smith smiled easily. "We tell him the truth, of course. You aren't comfortable with the attacks on Morganna or the fact that one of your men has been taken out, so you're going to work from here. We'll work with him and see what Fuentes' next move is. In the meantime, I'll have a tag put on each of Joe's men and see what happens. It won't take long."

No, it wouldn't. Fuentes had shown how desperate he was to get his hands on Morganna. He would make his move soon.

"I'll be back tomorrow night." Clint nodded his head sharply. "I need to sleep a few hours and get a few things together. Do what you have to on this end."

Drage straightened from the bar, his eyes gleaming with anticipation.

"We'll have everything in place, Clint. I look forward to working with you."

Yeah, Clint just bet he did. The son of a bitch didn't count success from the amount of money he made but rather from the contacts he could call in. Clint wasn't a man who liked to be beholden. But in this case, he was also a desperate man. Because he knew if anything happened to Morganna, if the life that burned in her eyes were to ever dim, then Fuentes wouldn't have to kill him. The grief alone would.

Chapter 21

As he drove back toward Mace's neighborhood in the leather comfort of Jayne's steel blue Z4 BMW Roadster, it wasn't the extravagance of the car, the smell of warm leather, or the ride he would have enjoyed at any other time that filled his head.

He thought of the friends he had lost to Fuentes' damned network. Nathan Malone, "Irish." He had fallen during the mission in Colombia.

His death had been a hard blow. Nathan was a good friend, but with his death Clint had seen what was left behind. Nathan's young wife had been destroyed. Clint remembered seeing her at Nathan's memorial service, her eyes vacant and hollow, her face as pale as death.

She had worshipped Nathan, just as Nathan had worshipped her.

And Devin Markwell. Hell, he was one of the best fighters the SEALs had ever produced. His body was an efficient, highly trained weapon, yet he had been taken out.

It didn't make sense. Fuentes couldn't know who had taken out his compound. That wasn't possible. Even the Navy hadn't listed their names for that mission. Unless Nathan was alive. It was the only answer.

Clint leaned his head against the backrest, feeling weariness drag at him. He was damned tired. Tired of the missions, the deaths. It had begun with Irish's death. Seeing the horror and grief on his young wife's face had started the cycle. Now— God, Clint didn't think he could do it anymore. If they managed to take Fuentes out this time, then it might be time to pack it in. Clint was thirty-five years old and felt eighty. He had two more years before he could claim his retirement. Maybe it was time he began considering that.

And then there was Morganna.

He had left her with one of the biggest womanizers he had ever laid his eyes on. Mace was dependable, a hell of a brute fighter, and loyal as hell when it came to the battle. But he liked women. Loved women. As many as he could get his hands on.

And Morganna had been madder than hell, furious that Clint had left her. He remembered clearly the fights between his parents before his father went off on a mission. Terrible screaming matches that would run for hours on end before Clint's father slammed out of the house and headed out for war. And Clint's mother headed out for a round of parties night after night, man after man.

Could he handle it? he wondered. Hell no, everything inside him screamed out in fury. If Mace touched Morganna, Clint didn't know if he could contain his rage.

His hands clenched on the steering wheel as he pulled into the open garage door and waited for the door to close and the interior lights to blaze on. He knew better than to step out of the car before Mace knew who was there.

When the lights flickered, Clint opened the door and eased his long frame out of the vehicle before moving for the door.

His fists were clenched, his jaw bunched so tight he could feel his molars grinding. Could he survive another man touching her after he'd had her? Would he lose his mind as his father had?

Clint shook his head as he moved through the house, feeling the weight of his fears bearing down on his shoulders as he fought to make sense of the soul-deep tiredness filling him.

The wall section slid open as he neared it, assuring him that no matter what may have happened through the night, Mace was watching—

"Thank God!"

Clint's hands automatically wrapped around the small body that threw itself into him no sooner than he'd stepped to the staircase landing.

As the wall slid closed, Morganna was sobbing against his chest, her hands running over his shoulders, his back.

"Are you hurt?" Her voice was hoarse as the words tumbled from her lips, demanding, fierce. "If you managed to get your ass hurt, I'll skin you alive."

"Bloodthirsty wretch." He inhaled the scent of her. He could smell his own darker scent beneath the sweet, clean smell that was so much a part of Morganna.

She still wore the skirt and corset, though she had kicked off her shoes. Leaning back from him, she let her gaze go over him, her misty eyes shadowed with worry and a hint of anger.

"I am so mad at you." She slapped at his shoulder as she pushed away from him and stalked back down the stairs. "You just run off like Rambo. . . ." Her words trailed back to him as she stomped into the main room. "All gung ho and tough and you leave me just sitting here twiddling my fingers. This is *not* going to work, Clint."

Did he smell food? Real food? Mace could cook, but what Clint smelled wafting up the staircase was pure heaven in the form of pancakes and maple syrup. But where was Mace?

Clint moved down the staircase, wary as he stepped from the enclosed stairwell. Mace was sitting across the room by his computers, his arms crossed over his chest, glaring at Clint.

Lifting his brow, Clint turned to stare back into the kitchen area where Morganna was muttering to herself.

"Everything okay?" he asked the other man.

Mace glared harder.

"Go ahead and answer him," Morganna snapped. "He's back now; I'm sure he can protect you." She sounded a bit upset.

"That woman is trouble in progress," Mace suddenly snapped. "I swear to God, you go off and leave me alone with her again and I'll kill you. You won't have to worry about Fuentes." He swung around in his chair then and hunched over the keyboard of his computer, his fingers striking the keys.

"What did you do, Morganna?" Clint sighed, moving to get a good look at her. She was flat-out furious. If possible, she was more pissed now than she had been when he left.

"I didn't do anything." She propped her hands on her hips as a feminine little sneer curled her lips. "But he doesn't seem to know where his stupid hands belong—"

"Ah hell, just get me fucking killed, why don't you." Mace jumped from his chair, staring back at Clint wild-eyed. "I swear to God, it was harmless. I didn't mean nothing by it, Clint."

Clint took a deep breath. The fury that should have been there was overshadowed by confusion. Mace looked almost scared, and Morganna was in killing mode.

"Look, you don't have to kill me. That damned little witch of yours nearly shoved my balls into my stomach. I didn't mean a damned thing by it. It was harmless."

"He patted my ass!" Her voice was a low, snarling growl as she pointed a shaking finger at him. "He patted *my* ass!" She was shaking with feminine outrage.

Clint blinked back at her, wondering if he should shake his head to get his bearings here. "Mace pets every woman's ass." He gave in and shook his head as he looked between the two of them. "He's a Romeo."

"He's an alley cat," she snapped. "And he can keep his damned hands off my ass. No one touches my ass."

"I do," Clint pointed out. Something wasn't clicking here, he just wasn't certain what it was.

Morganna lowered her chin and gave him the "moron" look, as he and Reno had always dubbed it. The droll glare, the slightest arch to her brows as her lips thinned in irritation.

"For the moment, you have permission," she said sarcastically. "He," she pointed her finger imperiously, "does not."

"Don't worry," Mace growled back with no small amount of ire. "He can keep your ass. I was just being nice."

"Then keep it to yourself." She glared back. "And the stupid pancakes are done if either of you would care to eat them. Now that Rambo has returned, I need a shower." Then she frowned again. "Did you at least bring me some clothes?"

He lifted the small duffel in his hands out to her silently. He still hadn't figured out what had happened, but her face brightened, her lips trembling just for a moment before she pounced on the bag. She pulled it from his hand and unzipped it quickly.

"Yes! Comfies," she sighed, clutching the soft cotton pj pants and the loose T-shirt to her breasts. "God, I love you."

Before he had time to comment she was rushing to the other side of the room and disappearing into the bedroom. Clint turned back to Mace, who, being no one's dummy, was tearing into the homemade pancakes with a rumble of glee.

"Want to tell me what just happened here?" Clint queried as he moved to the refrigerator and pulled out the milk before snagging a glass from the counter and sitting down at the table.

"Woman's insane," Mace muttered around a mouthful of pancakes and syrup. "Swear to God. She was crying like a baby, Clint. Damned woman can't even sob. Just these silent tears and that lip trembling. She was breaking my heart. I had to just hug her, man." His fork was poised halfway to his plate as he stared back at Clint in bemusement. "Ought to kick your ass for making her cry like that. But I just hugged her and patted her butt at the same time. Next thing I know I'm on the floor with my balls choking me." He glared at Clint again. "She's deranged. Told me to get in my damned corner and not to make the mistake of speaking to her again or she'd take a knife to me. I didn't speak." He shook his head, his expression frankly disturbed. "I haven't spoke for hours, Clint."

Clint sat back in his chair slowly. "Struck out, did you?" he asked casually.

"Struck out?" Mace blinked back in amazement. "Man, you'd have to be loose a few screws to go after that woman. Where the hell is your head? In your pants? That is not a woman you want to piss off. She is going to deball you and fry your nuts up for dinner and make you like it. Have you lost your ever-lovin' mind?"

"What were you doing touching my woman's ass to begin with, Mace?" Clint asked him carefully. "I left her here for you to protect, not to be handling."

"A woman only belongs to a man if it's what she wants." Mace grimaced. "I'm telling you, though. That woman." He pointed his fork in the general direction of the bathroom. "Ain't no man gonna own, but only one man is gonna touch. And that's at his own damned risk. You sure you didn't lose a few brain cells when you took up with that mini-volcano?"

Maybe he had, because he'd be damned if he couldn't feel something inside his chest melting.

"Oh man, you are so sunk," Mace grunted. "Get that fool grin off your face before she comes back in here. I'm telling you, that woman is dangerous."

"Yeah, she is," Clint murmured, shifting in his seat, realizing he was suddenly hard, engorged with lust. He was so damned tired that just eating was a chore, but damn if he wasn't ready to show Morganna just who that pretty ass of hers belonged to. "Eat, Mace. She'll forgive you in a few weeks."

Mace choked comically. "She racked me, man," he moaned. "And you're making jokes. I can't believe you're making jokes. And I was just trying to be nice."

Mace stuffed his mouth with pancake, sighed, and devoured his half. Evidently being racked didn't affect his appetite. It was affecting Clint's heart, though. He hadn't known a single woman who had ever rejected whatever attention Mace wanted to pay her. Women loved him, lusted after him, stood in line to be at his beck and call. To Clint's knowledge, no woman had ever kneed Mace in his sexual history.

Until Morganna.

Clint finished the pancakes Morganna had made, delicious, fluffy pancakes that damn near melted in his mouth, before he carried his plate and glass to the sink.

"Go get some rest. I'll get these dishes. I'm just running some intel on the computers right now; it will be an hour or so before I have anything worth mentioning."

Clint turned back from the sink, dragging in a weary breath before releasing the pack he still carried from his belt. The black pouch bulged with the four cell phones and a variety of matchbooks, little black books, and an assortment of receipts.

"See what you can get from these." He tossed the pouch on the table. "They came off the four men tailing me."

"Gave 'em up willing-like, did they?" Mace picked up the pouch and hefted it slowly.

Clint stared back at him directly. "It's hard to disapprove of something if you're dead, Mace," he told him softly. "Fuentes has a nice little message coming his way."

"Shit," Mace muttered. "You sure they were Fuentes' boys?"

Mace had a problem with killing first and asking questions later. Clint didn't.

"I recognized one of them right off." He shrugged. "The other three I had to study on. They were all with Fuentes, and four were looking to ambush the dumb little SEAL they were tailing. Their mommas should have raised them better."

"You're cold, man," Mace sighed. "Real cold."

"One of my men is dead and those bastards want to rape my woman," he snarled in reply. "Yeah, Mace, I'm real damned cold, and I can get colder, my friend. Don't you doubt that."

But first he intended to get warm. Real warm. He flicked a final glance at the pouch Mace was picking up before moving through the underground room to the bedroom. Mace had himself a cool little setup here. The bedroom was almost soundproof, the entrance sealed shut with another wall-like door that slid in place when he hit the switch on the inside of the bedroom.

From there, there was a trapdoor down in the bathroom that actually did lead to a sewer access tunnel. Mace was a paranoid SOB, even more so than Clint.

As the wall sealed shut behind him, Clint stripped off his shirt, then sat down in a surprisingly comfortable wing backed chair to take his boots off. He could hear the water running in the bathroom. Bathwater rather than a shower. Mace had the biggest damned sunken tub Clint had ever laid his eyes on in there. Evidently Morganna was taking advantage of it.

The thought of that had him grimacing at the hard-on swelling beneath his leather pants. The thought of her stretched out in that huge tub alone, all that sweet darkly tinted flesh, her Spanish ancestry evident just enough to tint her flesh, to give it a soft earthy glow that he loved so much. It also gave her that damned temper, he thought with a smile.

He couldn't believe she had racked Mace. As Clint placed his boots and socks beside the chair, he rose to his feet, shaking his head at the memory of Mace's bemused expression and Morganna's furious one. If there was one man on the face of the earth Clint would swear could crack any woman, it was Mace.

Morganna had racked him instead.

Clint padded to the open bathroom door, the smell of sweetened vanilla reaching his senses. She was using the bath gel he had chosen from the all-night convenience store where he had found pj's. Warm vanilla sugar. That was the scent. The name had reminded him of Morganna and made his mouth water for the taste of her. So he had bought it. He had bought the bath gel and the pajamas, even though he had no intention of allowing her to sleep in them.

He stepped into the steaming room, intent on joining her in the bathtub, until he saw her. The steamy water lapped around her slender form as she sat with her knees bent, her face buried against them as her arms covered her head.

Her shoulders were shaking, but the only sign of her sobs was the soft hitch of her breathing. Long, wet corkscrew curls floated in the water around her like a silken cape.

"Morganna." He knelt beside the raised side of the tub, fighting his shaking hands as he pushed the long strands of her hair back, over her shoulder. "Baby, why are you crying?"

She shook her head, hiding her face.

His heart was breaking. He could actually feel the splintering effect in his chest, the tightness in his throat, as she turned her head from him.

"Morganna, honey, you know I can't stand to see you cry. It makes me crazy. You have to talk to me here."

When she still didn't speak, he moved slowly, sliding into the water behind her and forcing her back against his broad chest as his heavy thighs bracketed her small body.

She flowed against him, her head turning to press into the thick expanse of his upper arm, the warmth of her tears washing over his flesh, branding him.

"I came back as soon as I could," he whispered, pressing his lips to the top of her head as he fought the need to hold her tighter.

Her hands gripped his lower arm, holding on tight to him as he heard that little broken sound that came from her throat. It wasn't exactly a gasp, a bit more than a hitch. A breathy little catch filled with sorrow and pain. Morganna didn't cry often, but when she did, it was because the hurt went too deep to contain. That was why her tears made him violent. He couldn't handle Morganna hurting that deeply.

"Did you think I was going to be upset that you racked

Mace?" he whispered, feeling the heat of the water and the warmth of her body seeping into him.

She shook her head.

"I couldn't take you with me." He closed his eyes tight, unable to resist pulling her closer to his chest, his arms holding her tighter. "I couldn't risk you like that, Morganna."

"Stop." She shook her head again. "That made me mad. . . ." Her voice hitched. "I don't cry over mad . . . Just go to bed. Rest. . . ." The keening little whimper that left her throat had terror racing through his soul. Oh God, if she started sobbing, could he survive it? Morganna had never, ever sobbed.

"I can't leave you like this, Morganna." His hands smoothed up and down her arms, everything inside him reaching out to her, desperate to comfort her. "Tell me how to make it better, sweetheart. I will."

She shook her head again.

"Sweetheart, you're breaking my heart here," he whispered against her hair. "I can't stand to see you hurt like this; you have to let me help you."

"How?" she cried, her voice rough, hoarse. "You didn't see your eyes, Clint. You didn't see the grief and sorrow, and I can't help it." Her hands clenched on his arm. "I can't do anything to take it away like I used to. I can't joke, or poke at you, because I know what he meant to you. I can't help you. . . ." One little sob. It jerked from her chest and sent a dagger stroke of pain to sear his soul.

He had thought he had a handle on it before he faced her. Had thought he was hiding the grief, the rage. He should have known better. He had never hidden anything from Morganna; it was one of the reasons he had fought to stay away from her, to push her as far from his life as possible. Because she could see into his soul.

He fought to swallow back his emotion as he sighed roughly.

"He was a friend," he said softly. "Just as Nathan was."

His jaw clenched at the thought of the hell they would awaken to. "I can't imagine waking up one day and knowing you were gone, Morganna," he said, feeling a shard of weakness filling his soul. "I don't know if I could survive. And that's all I can think about. Losing you. Never hearing you laugh, never being pissed at you again, or touching you again. It makes my gut knot with terror. And I don't like that fear. I hate it, baby. Fear makes you weak. It makes you slow. I can't afford to be slow right now."

"I need to comfort you." Her breathing hitched again. "And I don't know how. Just like a year ago, after Irish's service, I needed to do something. Anything. . . ."

And he had sent her away. Had she cried then? Had she hidden and let her misery flow in the tears she shed? He had made her cry, more than once. Him, the same son of a bitch who had broken a man's nose for making her cry.

"You're here," he told her then, knowing that was more comfort than he deserved. "Look at you, flowing against me, sweet and soft. I don't have to be alone. . . ."

He clenched his teeth tight, realizing the truth of the statement he was making. He didn't have to feel alone, because she was with him. Because something about Morganna eased him.

"You never had to be alone," she said hoarsely. "I was always here, Clint."

He lifted her then, turning her across his lap, cuddling her close to his chest as he felt his erection slipping between her thighs, resting against the silken flesh of her sex. He wanted her. Hungered for her. But for the first time in his life, his arousal was taking a backseat to something more important, something primal, insistent.

Comforting his woman.

He stared into the stormy depths of her tear-soaked eyes, her dark lashes spiked around the misty depths, her expression paler than normal.

"I knew you were waiting on me," he said as he smoothed

his thumb over her cheek, wiping away her tears. "I came back to you, desperate to feel your warmth against me. I'm cold inside, Morganna." He grimaced at the emotion she inspired within him. "Warm me."

Her eyes widened, her breath hitching again as her hand curled around his neck, her fingers pushing beneath his hair as she drew him to her.

"Warm me," he whispered again as her lips touched his. "Just for a little while."

Chapter 22

HE COULDN'T NOT TOUCH HER. The loss raging inside him, the danger surrounding her, the emotions ripping through his soul, needs and hungers, desire and feelings he couldn't define, refused to define, tore through Clint in an upheaval that threatened to destroy him.

Morganna's lips were heated satin, hungry beneath his, opening to him as he sent his tongue to taste her. And she tasted like nectar, the wine of the gods, the perfect passion. A balm to the ragged wounds he had felt shredding his very spirit with the loss of his men.

Her fingertips moved over his face with trembling caresses that had his body tightening, his mind fighting the loss of control over his emotions. He couldn't afford to feel this deeply for her. Yet he did. Here, surrounded by the steamy heat of the bathwater, the rising hunger that flared so easily between them, Clint knew he would never walk away from her easily.

"I was scared for you." Her breath hitched again as his lips slid from hers to taste her jaw, his lips sliding lower as her head fell back over his arm. "I hated you being alone."

"Shh. I'm not alone now, baby." One hand caressed her hip as the other smoothed along her shoulder. "You're right here with me. Feel me?"

"No one . . ." She gasped as his hand smoothed to her full breast, the swollen weight fitting perfectly in his hand. "Watched your back. . . ."

He had learned to watch his own back, but he couldn't tell her that. He kissed her instead. Bending her over his arm as his lips devoured her, short, stinging little kisses that flushed her face, that darkened her eyes and left her panting in his arms.

She shifted against him, the slick heat of her pussy caressing his engorged cock, sending electric fingers of sensation to race through the swollen shaft before it sizzled up his spine.

She was like a storm, whipping through his senses, drowning out his control and his sanity as he let his lips feed from hers, consuming her passion as he gave her his.

There was no time for the gentleness he wanted to give her. No room for finesse or soft words. Blood and death surrounded them both. Grief, sorrow, and a need he couldn't fight or ignore filled him until he wondered if he could survive the emotions tearing through him.

He needed her. He wouldn't survive if he didn't take her, if he didn't fill his soul with her need, his senses with her touch. With the assurance that there was something left worth fighting for. There was the innocence of true passion, Morganna's throaty moans, and the feel of her nails pricking at his scalp as she held him to her.

"You make me burn, Morganna." The words were torn from his lips as he lifted her, turning her until those long, slender legs clasped his hips and he could feel the thick head of his cock parting the tender folds between her thighs. "Inside and out."

He held her waist as her head tipped back on her shoulders, a keening moan of need whispering past her lips as he felt the head of his cock force past her tender entrance.

Being inside her wasn't easy. She was small, tight, clamping around the invading crest as her panting moans urged him to hurry. He had no intention of rushing; he wanted to feel her, needed to experience each convulsive ripple of pleasure that quaked through her slick channel.

"Clint, I need you now." Her voice was breathless, imperative.

"Shh, baby, let me feel you." His head lowered, his lips brushing over the tops of the swollen mounds of her breasts. "You're so sweet and warm, flowing over me like honey. Let me feel you, baby."

She shuddered as her breath caught and he felt the soft cream flooding her sex, washing over him, easing his way as he slid inside her. Clint was hard-pressed to go easy, to take her gently. His thighs bunched with the effort to hold back, to work inside her rather than taking her. To pull back before sinking in farther, feeling the hot, wet silk gripping him, clenching along his hard flesh as he felt his chest tighten with the arousal growing within him.

He slid farther into the tub, half-reclining as his hips raised and lowered, spearing his cock into the soft depths between her thighs as his hands held her hips prisoner.

He needed to taste her. The taste of her went to his head like the most intoxicating brew, sweet and addictive. His tongue curled around a stiffened nipple, his teeth gripping the small ring of gold piercing it as she jerked in his arms.

Lower, he could feel the ball ring piercing his foreskin rasping inside her pussy, tugging at his cock, creating a friction he wasn't certain he could bear much longer.

"Clint . . . oh God. It feels so good . . . so good. . . ." Her voice was breathless, filled with rising lust and tinged with emotion. "I love you, Clint. Oh God, I love you."

His hips jerked as her words sent a shock wave of emotion crashing through him. He heard her cry, filled with pleasure and impossible hunger as he drove the last inches of his erection fully inside her, seating her perfectly against him.

He could feel her vaginal muscles struggling to adjust to him, caressing over his thick shaft as panting little growls of sexual excess left her throat. His lips clamped over a nipple, his mouth drawing on her as he fought to hold back the words poised on his lips. Words of hunger, need, of emotion he knew he couldn't speak.

She was destroying him with her acceptance, with her pleasure. Damn her, she was ripping his guts out, stealing his convictions. Clint gripped her hips, holding her to him as he began to move. He ignored the sloshing water, ignored his own certainty that she was stealing his soul as he gave her every part of himself. Silently. Irrevocably.

Morganna felt the change in Clint the moment the unbidden words passed her lips. As though a switch had been flipped, an intensity, a heat bordering supernova, seemed to fill him, whipping into her as he lost the impeccable control she so hated.

His hips moved fiercely between her thighs, lunging against her as he buried his cock inside her over and over again. Jerky, hard thrusts that stroked inside her, building the pleasure as it rasped hidden nerve endings, the ball ring creating an additional sensation she didn't know if she could do without now.

Her hands moved from his shoulders to his head, her body arching, pressing her nipple deeper into his suckling mouth as she felt the flames of never-ending pleasure burning in her womb. Each stroke pierced more than just her vagina, filled more than just the aching depths of her sex. Her womb flexed with the driving pleasure as her heart filled with a subtle, burning emotion. Was it hers? His?

She jerked against him as she felt it building inside her, felt the change in him, the depth of his touch, the longing in his ragged groans. There was more than just the possession of her body, the sleek, thick intrusion of his cock inside her.

"God help me!" The harsh words, torn from his chest, had her womb convulsing as his thrusts became harder, deeper.

His hands held her to him, his head buried between her breasts as she felt his struggle to breathe, her struggle to breathe, felt the world darkening around her as each stroke of his cock inside her pushed her higher, burned her deeper.

"Clint. . . ." Her hands tightened in his hair as she felt her pussy tighten around his invading cock. "Oh God, yes. Deeper. Harder. Harder, Clint. Take me—"

"Mine!" The sudden, furious burst of emotion in his voice triggered her explosion. The possessiveness, the dominance, the hard, unconscious demand, swept through her, triggering an orgasm she hadn't expected.

Lights exploded behind her tightly clenched eyelids, brilliant bursts of light snapping through her head as she felt the sudden release sweeping through her body, her senses.

It overtook her, flung her into a midnight sky, and left her shuddering as aftershocks tore through her body. The feel of Clint's release, hard, heated pulses of his semen jetting inside her as his hands tightened with bruising strength at her back, held her on the edge of ecstasy, refusing to release her as another hard orgasm tore through her.

Never ending. Unstoppable. She felt his lips, his teeth, at the side of her breast, marking her, stamping his ownership onto her just as his body fought to mark her with the hard, pulsing ejaculation filling her.

How long it lasted she didn't know. She didn't care. With each shudder of pleasure tearing through her, she felt Clint own another part of her soul. As though he hadn't already possessed her heart, he was filling her very spirit.

Finally, the strength left her body. As though only the hunger and the hard spear of his erection had kept her upright, Morganna collapsed against his chest, spent, overwhelmed. Weakness flooded her, sapping the last bit of strength that had kept her conscious.

She felt sleep roll over her like a dark, warm blanket. Sheltered against Clint's chest, assured of his safety, of his passion, she gave up the fight and let it have her. Sated. Warm. In Clint's arms, she found the rest she needed.

H E WAS GOING TO HAVE to get out of the damned water. Clint breathed out raggedly as he shifted Morganna in his arms, holding her against his chest as he pulled himself to his feet, water sloshing around his calves as he stepped from the tub and jerked one of the large towels from the low shelf by the tub.

He wrapped it around Morganna, drying her quickly.

A grin quirked his lips as she muttered drowsily at being disturbed. She was sleeping in his arms, despite the awkward hold he had on her, relaxed and pliant as he clumsily dried the water from both of them.

Shaking his head at her, he padded into the bedroom and laid her gently on the bed, pulling the blankets over her before heading back to the bathroom to clean up the damp mess they had left there.

The woman was killing him. He couldn't keep himself from touching her, from taking her every chance he had, filling her with his release. Feeling each hard spurt of his semen inside her did something to him that he couldn't explain. The feeling of ownership, of possessiveness, that locked around his soul each time he marked her in such a way was starting to worry him.

It couldn't continue forever, this blinding hunger. He couldn't allow it to. When the danger was over, when she was finally safe, he would have to leave again. He had no intentions of tying her to him, of creating a bond that would tempt the violence that was so much a part of him.

Tossing the damp towels into the hamper after he cleaned up the mess, he moved back to the bedroom, sliding into the bed beside Morganna, trying to ignore how natural it felt. How right. She curled into his arms, a warm weight that his arms seemed to relish, that tightened his chest with pleasure. Had it been sexual pleasure alone, it wouldn't have worried him. But it wasn't. It was a pleasure that pierced his soul and reminded him once again of the heartache that awaited him. Because he couldn't keep her. No matter how much he wanted to. No matter how much he needed to. One day soon, he would have to let her go.

TRINA BLAKE MOVED WEARILY INTO her bedroom, ignoring the expensive furnishings, the large, empty bed. As empty as the house she had bought. As empty as her life. Walking toward the antique vanity table on the other side of the room, she pulled off the heavy silver earrings she wore, dropping them to the cherrywood vanity before sitting down on the upholstered stool and unzipping her high boots.

Her feet ached. They never ached. She had been wearing the impossibly high heels for years, moving comfortably in them, enjoying the additional stature they gave to her. The impression of height and inner strength. But lately . . . She massaged her arches, frowning at the stiffness there. Lately they had begun hurting.

She turned to the mirror, automatically uncapping a cleansing cream and spreading it over her face before cleaning the makeup off with the tissues sitting ready by her elbow. It was automatic, her nightly ritual. Cleaning off the layers of the mask she faced the world with and for a few hours, just a few hours, allowing the sensitive skin of her face to rest.

She stared into the mirror, seeing more than just the residue of the cream and makeup lifting free of her skin. There were a few fine lines at the corners of her eyes. Her skin wasn't as unblemished as it had been or as dewy as when she was in her twenties.

She was getting old. And lately, she was beginning to feel it. She was thirty-two years old, and her home, like her soul, echoed with exactly how empty her life truly was. She was a puppet, a pawn to the lifestyle and the power she had believed she coveted at one time.

Slowly she had begun distancing herself from the criminal elements she had been involved with throughout her life. With Carmelita's death, that had come much easier. The bitch from hell had been sent back to her fiery realm, leaving Trina in peace for a change. No more late-night phone calls, no more demands from the black-hearted bitch.

Until Diego had shown up. God, how she hated him, wished with every fiber of her being that he had been consumed in the same fiery battle that had taken Carmelita's life. How much easier Trina's life would have been then.

How much easier it would have been if she had never been entered into the insanity of Carmelita's life. Maybe Trina could have had a measure of peace to go with the wealth she had amassed.

A husband perhaps. Maybe a child.

A bitter smile crossed her lips at the thought of either. Such pleasures would be quickly used against her if she even considered such things. Especially now. With Carmelita's death, Diego's paranoia and psychotic tendencies were no longer contained.

As Trina wiped the last of the cleansing cream from her face and stared back at her own expression, she wondered when it had become so hard to look into her own eyes. Had it only just begun, or had it only grown over the years?

Shaking her head, she had picked up her silver-backed brush and lifted it to brush out the long mass of black hair when a shadow reflected in the mirror, moving toward the bedroom doorway.

A hard, dread-filled surge of blood rocketed through her veins. She had been expecting it. Had actually thought he would come sooner than midmorning. She should have known he would know exactly when to strike.

Laying the brush down, she turned on the stool and waited.

Two of his men moved into the room silently, their hard eyes sweeping over her before ascertaining that she had no company. She had known better than to have company. She had no desire to lose another lover to the games Diego liked to play.

Seconds later, Diego stepped into the room. He had aged much more than she had in the last two years. Gray marred the thick black hair; his brows were shaggy; his once-trim body sagged. Carmelita was no longer around to make certain he maintained the image she had demanded. Without her, Diego was a mess. Trina hoped soon he would be a dead mess. She doubted she would be around to enjoy the sight.

"Good afternoon, Diego." She kept the smooth confidence in her voice, noting the narrowing of his eyes.

He expected her to be nervous, to show her guilt. She wasn't the fool he thought she was, and she found that she wasn't as afraid of dying as she had once been.

"Trina." The dark rasp of his voice sent a chill up her spine. "My prey escaped your home last night. My men reported that it appeared perhaps my prey had been warned of their arrival. Could this be true?"

The silky menace in his tone wasn't lost on her.

She shrugged negligently. "One moment he appeared to be heading for a bedroom to screw his little whore; the next minute your men told me he had fled. He's not a predictable man, Diego. If he were, I could have killed him myself a year ago."

"Hmmm." He came farther into the room, the silk of his clothes rippling over his gaunt body as she wished she had kept her heels on. They gave her confidence.

She watched, fighting her nervousness as he paced across the expensive cream carpeting toward her, his black eyes glittering with a maniacal anger.

"He and his whore escaped from my hold, Trina. I needed to know how far Santos had betrayed me, and the very people who could tell me have now flown," he sighed, the malevolent light in his eyes sparkling with pure evil. "I will not tolerate failure from those who owe me their loyalty."

He stopped beside her, taller only because she was sitting down, but she knew better than to stand. Only by sheer force of will did she keep from flinching as he ran his hands over her thick black hair, picking up a few strands and allowing it to cascade from his fingers.

"You were Carmelita's most treasured playmate," he sighed. "She often bragged about your loyalty to her. She loved you above all others, even her family."

Only because Trina had, at one time, cherished life. She had played the game better than the others, had assured

Carmelita of her loyalty with acts that even now made Trina's soul cringe. Life didn't seem as important anymore when faced with the same choices.

"I loved Carmelita." She forced a whisper of regret into her voice. "Seeing her murderers pay means everything to me."

She stared up at him, allowing the façade of submission to enter her voice as well as her gaze. Carmelita had taught her the best way to deal with Diego's fanaticism. His insanity.

"You failed me tonight," he murmured.

Fear burned in her gut as his hand tightened in her hair, holding her head back, forcing her to meet his gaze.

"McIntyre fooled me." She swallowed tightly. "I didn't expect him to leave the house. He must have seen your men drive up—"

He reached out with his other hand to caress her cheek. "I have considered this." He smiled, the false gentleness in the curve of his lips assuring her that death would not come easy. If it came. The maniacal genius Carmelita had been successful in harnessing burned in his gaze now. Sometimes death didn't come. Diego understood that often death wasn't the greatest punishment.

"Diego, I did as you ordered," Trina whispered, hating the possible reprisals that came to mind as he towered over her.

"I have considered this as well." He released her slowly as he lifted his hand, a beckoning gesture of his fingers toward his men causing her to glance across the room.

The guards stepped from the doorway, allowing several other men to enter. Trina fought to control her breathing, her fear.

"Diego . . . please. I did as you ordered."

"You did not do it well enough, and now you must be punished." He stepped from her as the three men advanced. "Carmelita loved you, Trina; for this I will not kill you. But she also told me once how much you hated to be raped. To be held down, to be forced."

She stood to her feet, staring back at him in horror.

"I did as you ordered," she cried out furiously. "There's no reason to punish me."

There was no escape. Her eyes went around the room frantically, noticing the placement of his men, the lust glittering in their eyes.

"You failed me. Failure is not forgiven easily," he murmured as the men advanced on her. "Take your punishment, so that I may forgive you. Then we will see if you can redeem yourself in my eyes."

She jumped to avoid the hands reaching out for her, scrambling to keep them from touching her, to keep them from hurting her. Nightmares of the past rose before her eyes, the soldiers who'd held her down, grunting, sweating over her as they raped her.

God, death would have been better.

She screamed as she was tossed to the bed, hard hands tearing her clothes from her body, touching her, laughter echoing around her.

She heard herself begging. Crying. She felt the horror that took her mind as her legs were jerked apart, restrained, and her punishment began.

Was it worth McIntyre's life, she wondered hazily, this punishment? Was it worth giving the fragile emotion she saw in his gaze when he watched Morganna a chance to grow? Was it worth allowing him what she would never know?

Loyalty was earned. McIntyre had earned her loyalty. But with this act, even death would not ease her plans to see Diego fall. By her hand.

Her mind drifted, darkened. Unable to accept or to deal with the pain, the horror, of what was happening to her body. She escaped the only way she knew how, within plans for vengeance. Diego would fall by her hand.

Chapter 23

WE HAVE SOME SERIOUS INTEL moving across the Net," Mace informed Clint as he stepped into the basement fortress, his hands loaded with shopping bags Jayne Smith had arranged to have waiting for him hours before.

If Morganna was going to pull this off, then she was going to need clothes. Slipping into her house to get her clothes wasn't going to work, so Jayne had gone shopping for her. Clint worried about that one. To be honest, the two women seemed way too alike in temperament; he didn't need Morganna getting any clothing or personality tips from the other woman. Morganna was too hard to handle as it was.

"What have you found?" He set the bags on the couch, glancing toward the still-closed bedroom door.

"Don't worry; she's sleeping like an angel," Mace grunted. "I haven't heard a peep out of her."

She was exhausted. The weariness that had lined her face as she slept earlier had worried Clint. He hadn't allowed her much sleep during their stay in the hotel room, and last night hadn't exactly been relaxing.

"Intel's coming in from several sources. Trina Blake called in her personal doctor a few hours ago. One of her maids is a pretty little spy for the Feds. Seems Diego made a visit. He messed her up pretty bad."

"Shit." Clint pushed his fingers through his hair, a scowl tightening his face. "What happened?"

"Five of his men raped her." Mace's voice was tight with fury. "Diego was pissed off when you got away from his men. He made her pay for it. The maid reported extensive damage, though her physician is treating her from home rather than a hospital."

Clint prowled around the room, his muscles tight, fighting the urge to go hunting. If he did, Diego would merely go to ground; they had learned that over the years. That was why the strike against his compound had been made, to take him and his wife out together, without warning.

It was one of the reasons Trina had become so important as an informer two years before. If it hadn't been for her information, the team would have never located the senators' daughters last year and rescued them before they were brutalized.

"Any reports on Diego?"

"Nothing conclusive. There are some rumors of several of the large gangs within the South American community being pulled in to work together. I'd hazard a guess that's Fuentes getting his spy network in gear. Your and Morganna's picture is being flashed a lot, but no one is one hundred percent certain where you're hiding." Mace flashed him a triumphant grin. "Those boys just don't know how it's done; that's all I can say." Mace could find a needle in a haystack a continent away.

"You're so modest, Mace," Clint snorted. "What else have you found?"

"There's a rumor you have Morganna stashed in Diva's basement suite." Mace cast him a leer. "Now that sounds like fun. Can I come play, too?"

"Did you forget Morganna's trigger-happy knee?" Clint asked him carefully.

"Not likely," he growled, scowling. "I didn't mean with her. Jeez, Clint, not all of us have lost our minds like you have."

Boy, that one was the truth.

"Any leaks on Diego's whereabouts?"

"Nothing yet. He's staying hid real good. But we do have good ole Roberto Manuelo. He's Diego's right hand since Carmelita died. From everything I have coming in, it's ole Manuelo that has the hard-on for you." Mace stood from his chair, stretching the kinks out of his body before glancing back down at the computer. "I have some feelers out on his whereabouts. Kell and Ian are also on their way here. They'll be able to cover your and Morganna's asses after you leave here."

"Have you briefed them on the situation?" The message was clear. If anything happened to Morganna, Clint was going hunting. Everyone responsible would pay.

"It's been done." Mace nodded firmly. "I also have the info on Manuelo and several of Fuentes' current head men. Those boys need to watch their asses better. My sources have been spilling info since last night."

"Pull it up." Clint walked over to the computers. "Once we make our appearance at Diva's, then he'll make his hit. If he goes true to form, he'll not come himself, though. He'll send his best men, so we can at least slow him down for a while and hopefully get the location of the lab they're using for that drug. And Nathan's whereabouts."

Macey stilled. "Nathan wouldn't willingly give info," he said.

"And his training to resist the drugs came second only to Kell's," Clint reminded him. "He's the only one that could have given the names of the teams that took him out."

"Damn," Macey sighed wearily before turning back to the plan they were working up. "What's the chance of pedestrian casualties in this thing?"

Mace's fingers were moving over the computer keyboard as he began to pull in information.

"Almost zero," Clint sighed. "Diego doesn't hit en masse. He likes to think he's subtle. He likes to prove he's the better gamesman. He'll want to take us out personally. My guess is since I was the commander of one of the teams that struck him, he wants to make an example of me and Morganna. He can't do that if he does a wipe on the club."

Clint ran over the information that popped up beneath Mace's talented fingers. There were four listed as Fuentes' generals, Manuelo among them. There was Diego's bastard uncle Jose and his nephew Santiago as well as a smaller player from a year ago.

"When Kell and Ian get here, I'll apprise Morganna of the plan we have in place." Clint rubbed at his jaw as he read the data on the screen. "We'll get moving this evening."

"She's going to be jumping out of her skin to get started," Mace grunted. "That woman is an adrenaline junkie, Clint. Maybe even as bad as you are. She'll be raring to go."

That was what he knew, and it terrified the hell out of him.

"Kell and Ian are itching to get started as well. They'll be here soon."

"How many know about this place?" Clint frowned.

"Just the right people," Mace assured him. "Men who know to keep their damned mouths shut, that's for sure. Did you think you were my only leak? I love ya, man, but you're a rare visitor and I get lonely." He waggled his brows and pursed his lips in a comic display of utterly false affection.

"Let me have your keyboard." Clint waved Mace away from the computer. "I need to run a few checks of my own on some of the regulars I recognized at Diva's."

"Spoilsport." Mace lumbered from the chair. "You can play with my toys, but yours racks me. That's just so not right, man."

Clint's snort of laughter was followed by the sound of a door slamming. He turned, eyes narrowing, as he watched Morganna smile benignly at both of them.

"I bet Clint isn't rude enough to get inside and play with your hard drive, either, Mace." She arched a brow mockingly as she padded across the room.

Mace shifted nervously, rubbing his hand over his chin as he flashed her a bright smile.

"Sunshine. I hope you slept well?" Amusement laced his voice as he steered carefully clear of her.

Her lips twitched as her gaze flicked from Mace to meet

Clint's. Laughter lurked in the gray depths and tugged at her lips. With her hair falling in disarray around her face, the loose T-shirt and pajamas, and her bare feet, she reminded him of the precocious teenager she used to be.

"I got cold." Her gaze was warm, heating him in ways he knew he should be terrified of.

Instead, he swiveled around until he faced her fully and patted his knee in invitation. She fitted against him perfectly as her arms looped around his neck and she perched on his lap.

"He has work to do," Mace grumbled. "You should fix more pancakes."

"Give me a reason to cook, Mace," she drawled mockingly. "I do my best work after seeing grown men twitching in pain."

"Then beat up on him," he grunted, pointing to Clint. "Instead of cuddling against him like a damned kitten. Some things just ain't right."

Clint smoothed his cheek over Morganna's hair, watching Mace scowl at both of them.

"Do your thing on my computer, Mac, and get it over with. Then you can explain this harebrained scheme you've set up with Drage Masters and that balls-busting woman of his. Smith and Morganna here ought to get along just fine."

There was a triumphant glitter in Mace's eyes as he spoke, a smirk on his lips as he met Clint's gaze. Clint sighed, shaking his head as he felt Morganna tense in his arms.

"What is he talking about?" She tilted her head back to stare at him, putting his lips much too close to hers.

He couldn't help dipping his head that last inch for a kiss. She was sleep-tousled, soft in his arms, and what he was about to do was clenching his guts with dread.

When he lifted his head, bittersweet satisfaction raged through him at the misty emotion in her eyes and the flush to her cheeks.

"He's talking about taking out Fuentes." Clint grimaced, pushing her up from his lap before patting her rear and allowing his hand to linger, to enjoy the soft curve and warm flesh beneath the cotton.

"I thought that was the object all along." She crossed her arms beneath her breasts. Breasts tipped with pebble-hard nipples despite the frown on her face.

Clint stared back at her, steeling himself against the decision he had made, praying to God for a miracle.

"You have your wish," he told her. "We're going to Diva's tonight. We'll be staying in a suite in the lower level, and working with Drage Masters and his head of security, Jayne Smith. We're going to draw Fuentes' men out and see how many we can take down. Manuelo will know where the lab is; we suspect he's the head of that little operation."

"What about the mole on Joe's team?" Clint watched her eyes sharpen, watched the sense of excitement that filled her eyes even as calculated intelligence began to gleam in the stormy depths of her gaze. Damn, she could be scary sometimes.

"We're after him, too. Joe's only in so far as using his team to watch and provide backup. He's unaware we're also working to uncover the mole he doesn't want to admit he has. We're in a dual operation here, Morganna. It's not going to be easy—"

"Bullshit!" She waved the warning away. "If we're working together we can do it, Clint. I saw Masters' computer setup; his system is state-of-the-art."

"It was compromised, though." Clint explained the drugging of the girl the night before and the bastard's awareness of the cameras in place. "He's changed his camera angles and added a few, but Joe doesn't know this. He's also added a secondary surveillance point to the computers. Those in his office won't display the two additional cameras. Those will be in another room. Joe's group will be given a quick explanation of the setup and then we'll see what happens."

Morganna watched Clint closely. He was in SEAL mode now, hard-eyed, his voice firm as he laid out the operation and answered her questions. He was talking to her. He wasn't ordering her. He wasn't treating her like an extra he had to deal with. He was working with her. And the plan he and Drage had come up with was a damned good one.

"I'm pulling in two of my men on this as well." Clint turned to the computer, motioning her over as he pulled up their information. "They're regulars at Merlin's. Know them?"

She stared at the screen. "Kell and Ian. I don't know their last names. They pretty much stay to themselves, other than whatever women they have on their arms. They like to watch us dance." She waggled her brows mockingly. "They like that a lot."

"I bet they do," Clint growled, a scowl marking his face. "You know what that dance floor is, right, Morganna?"

"Of course I do." She shrugged negligently. "The droves of wolves pick their innocent little lambs from within the writhing masses of bodies. Only the, quote, unquote, subs take to the dance floor. They're out there to be seen, to be lusted over and watched."

"So why were you out there?" Clint's voice was dark, possessive. She loved it.

"Because I like to dance. If I wanted a Dom, I could pick one myself. I don't need to literally put myself up for auction to do it. Why did you think I was there?" She propped her hand on her hip as she regarded him with mocking amusement.

"You're a menace," he muttered, his hands moving over the computer keys as he followed the information Mace had pulled up.

"You say that as though you doubted it, Clint," she drawled, ambling over to the couch and the stacks of boutique bags sitting there. "Whose clothes?"

"Yours. Smith went shopping for you." He sounded less than pleased. "I haven't looked at them yet. I was afraid to."

It was a good thing he hadn't. Morganna looked into each bag, restraining her smile as she glimpsed the clothes the other woman had bought. Jayne Smith just had righteous taste. She was definitely going to have to go shopping with her soon.

"I'll go through them later then." Morganna picked up the bags and carried them into the bedroom. "Are you hungry, or have you eaten?"

"Hungry." Mace's voice was almost desperate. "Pancakes."

She rolled her eyes. She should fix bologna sandwiches instead, except she was rather hungry herself. Besides, she had a feeling she was going to definitely need her strength to work with Clint. SEAL mode was complete Dom mode. Obey me, do it my way, tough-assed alpha. She smiled slowly. Working with Clint was going to be a lot of fun.

DARK HAD SETTLED OUTSIDE THE house when Kell Krieger and Ian Richards stepped into the basement, staring back at Clint and Mace with hard expressions. Morganna had talked to them several times, had danced with them, but the steely glints in their eyes had always had her pulling back warily. These weren't men you played with, and until Clint, Morganna hadn't been interested in any sort of relationship, especially the fully committed ones she had a feeling both men would require.

"Chief." Ian nodded his dark blond head at Clint, his brown eyes assessing.

Clint stood by the couch behind Morganna's sitting position. She had drawn her legs up, regarding the two men over her upraised knees.

"I had a feeling you were hiding out with her." Ian's hazel eyes lit with a glint of laughter. "You're trouble, woman."

Her lips twitched as she glanced up at Clint. He didn't look happy.

"I thought you didn't know them very well?" he half-snarled down at her.

"I don't." She smiled. "Just enough to know to steer a wide path around them when they're hunting for a woman. They're worse than those wolves I mentioned earlier."

Kell shook his head as Ian chuckled at the description.

"We checked Markwell's body before coming here," Kell told them then. "They did a number on him, Chief."

Morganna blinked her eyes against her tears as she ducked her head. Clint wasn't talking about the man he had lost; he wasn't mentioning it. He wasn't cold, but he had grown distant over the last few hours, his dark blue eyes cool and shadowed.

"Come on over here and I'll explain what's going on." Clint led them over to the small kitchen table where the wall and surface of the table were littered with drawings and printouts.

She laid her arm on the back of the couch, watching the four men as they talked. For once, Clint wasn't dressed in leather. He wore jeans, boots, and a white cotton shirt. The clothes, rather than detracting from the strength of his body, emphasized it instead.

Black strands of hair fell over his brow as he lowered his head, discussing the operation with the other two men; the short growth of a beard and mustache gave him a rakish, wicked look. She liked it. She had especially liked the feel of it against her skin in the tub earlier.

"Your main job is to watch her." He turned then, pointing imperiously toward Morganna as she rolled her eyes. "If you know her, then you're very well aware of the fact that she's as slippery as an eel and twice as dangerous. Fuentes' men are determined to get their hands on her. If they take her, there's going to be hell to pay. From me and Reno." He stared back at the two men fiercely. "Be sure you want to take that risk."

Kell turned and winked back at her. "We've been practicing over the last two years. I think we can keep up with her."

It would have been nice if they had informed her that they

actually knew Clint and Reno. She could have managed to avoid them as well.

She caught the tightening of Clint's jaw and the flare of anger in his eyes before he hid it. A sigh slipped past her lips. Pushing him past this jealousy stuff wasn't going to be easy. It was never smart to tempt a man's beast, but in this case, he'd best keep the jealousy thing under control.

She had a feeling she now knew why she had never met the men in Reno's and Clint's units. Clint didn't want her anywhere around them.

"Be sure you do," Clint muttered. "And while you're undressing her with your eyes, try to leave enough clothes on her for decency's sake."

That one surprised her. Morganna lifted her brow as the other men chuckled, turning from her, but Clint's gaze lingered, dark, assessing. She winked back at him, pursing her lips in an airy kiss before rising from the couch.

"Have fun plotting and planning, boys." She looked at the clock on the wall. "I need to get showered and dressed if we're going to get out of here on time."

She had left it to the last possible moment. It wouldn't do to give Clint time to actually protest the clothes she had chosen to wear for the night.

"There's a duffel by the bed. Pack the rest of the clothes in there, Morganna. We'll be taking them with us," Clint stated absently as she headed for the bedroom.

"I'll be sure to, cupcake." She kept her back to him. "See you in a bit."

"Cupcake?" Ian turned back to Clint, his gaze going over the tall, lean form and the fierce scowl that creased his expression.

"Get fucked!" Clint growled, turning back to the plans they had laid out.

"Only one game in sight right now; do we take dibs?" Kell murmured.

Clint lifted his gaze, his midnight eyes turning icy, filled with a promise of retribution. "Ask Mace."

Ian turned to Mace, a smirk on his lips. "You're still alive."

"Trying out for soprano, though," Mace sighed. "That woman has a wicked knee and perfect aim. Watch your hands there, Ian my man; she can do some damage."

"And if she doesn't, I will." And there was no mistaking the intent behind that voice. Deadly. Menacing. Clint McIntyre had staked his claim. "Now get your head out of your pants and back to protocol here. We want to finish this up fast. I want this taken care of and taken care of now."

Chapter 24

CLINT DIDN'T KNOW EXACTLY WHAT he expected in the way of Morganna's clothes. Tight leather, maybe. The little schoolgirl outfit. His blood pressure could have handled either one. But what she walked out of the bedroom wearing an hour later damned near sent him into cardiac arrest.

The long-sleeved crop top and matching pants had sexy cutouts on the front and at the sides. Cutouts nothing, the hips and thighs were nothing but stretching straps of material and too damned narrow for his peace of mind. Her soft little pussy was barely concealed. Long sleeves covered her arms and fitted over the sides of her breasts. It covered her nipples. Maybe. The straps on her thighs were copied across her breasts, and the material stopped just below those full breasts. There was way too much silken skin left bare from the bottoms of her breasts to the juncture of her thighs. It was made to fit like a glove and that was exactly what it did.

The four-inch black heels made her legs look a damned mile long and fit for nothing but wrapping around his thighs.

Clint was aware of the other three men staring at her, jaws unhinged, their eyes bulging, as she paused halfway across the room, swung out a hip, and propped her hand on it and tilted her head mockingly.

"Are you going to get dressed?" Her gaze met his, jerking him back into reality rather than the fantasy of fucking her silly in the middle of Mace's basement.

"I will if you will." He forced himself to speak, though how he managed it with the lust choking him to death, he wasn't certain.

"You're funny." She smiled gently. Gently. She didn't even

bother to show the least bit of concern that he was about to cover her with a blanket and hide her in a damned closet. "But you'd better hurry. I think you said Drage was supposed to be waiting to slip us into the club."

"And leave you here alone?" He blinked back at her. Yeah, he really thought maybe he should just drag her into the bedroom and put those pajamas back on her. They were a lot better. They weren't capable of causing a riot.

"Yes, you are going to leave me in here alone with these three yahoos just waiting to make a smart comment." She arched her brow at the other men. "I'd hurry if I were you, too. Or I might end up making pancakes."

Pancakes? Oh yeah, she cooked when she was pissed.

He glared at the three men. "Touch her and I'll kill all of you. Better yet, stop looking at her. It's pissing me off."

He stomped from the room before he heard more than a snicker. He didn't pause as he passed Morganna; he couldn't. If he did, he would end up throwing her over his shoulder again and hauling her straight to the bed. Damn. Could a man die of a hard-on?

THE MUSIC WAS PUMPING FROM Diva's as Clint pulled the BMW up to the back entrance. The door opened smoothly, revealing Jayne Smith, outfitted in skintight leather, biker boots, and a pistol held close to her thigh.

"Righteous." She grinned and lifted her fist to Morganna as she glanced at the outfit.

Meeting the other woman's fist with hers, Morganna slid a look to Clint's closed expression, winking back at Jayne subtly. He hadn't said two words since he had come out of the bedroom dressed in the leather pants, shitkicker boots, and black shirt and leather jacket. He looked hot as hell, in more ways than one, Morganna thought with an inward laugh.

"Everything is in place." Jayne hid her smile as she nodded back to Clint. "The lower suite has a private entrance to it, or you can use the main entrance. We'll slip you down in the private elevator and you can come back upstairs through the main entrance. No one will know you just arrived."

She slid a key card into the elevator's security slider and ushered them inside.

"Is Joe's team in place?" Clint questioned as the doors slid closed.

"All but the tech in the van." She nodded. "I managed to get a little bug inside the vehicle, though. If he calls out to Fuentes, we'll know it."

Morganna caught the look Clint slid her way. "Where did you get your bugs?"

"I make them myself," Jayne drawled. "Want a few?"

His answer was a noncommittal grunt.

"I think he's upset with you, Jayne," Morganna sighed. "He doesn't like the outfit."

"What outfit?" he growled. "There's no outfit to it. A few strips of cloth, that's it."

Jayne lifted her brows mockingly as she glanced at Morganna. Morganna sighed. Again.

"She'll be noticed." Jayne shrugged in unconcern. "The object is to have her seen and to push Fuentes into making his move soon. If he makes it while we're prepared, we have a better chance."

Morganna glanced at Clint as he turned his gaze to Jayne. The flat, knowing glint in his eye had her lips twitching. Yeah, he was aware of all that, but that didn't mean he liked any of it.

"Here we are," Jayne announced as the elevator slid to a smooth stop. "We've had all the security pass cards into the suite changed." She handed Clint a key card, which he tucked into the front pocket of his pants. "You're fully stocked with drinks and snacks; if you want anything in the way of meals, Drage's chef will take care of you. His number is beside the phone in the kitchenette."

Morganna stepped from the elevator, entering an opulent,

richly designed sitting room the size of the lower floor of her house. A wide leather couch and matching chairs sat well back from a gas-lit fireplace. The opposite wall held a huge wall-mounted television.

The small dining room and kitchenette were open into the living room except for gleaming marble columns used as ceiling support. A wide hallway led to the bedrooms. Clint set the duffel bags he had carried from the car beside the couch and turned back to Jayne.

"I'm carrying. Make sure your men are aware of that."

Jayne grimaced. House policy was no weapons, period. The entrance and exits were equipped with advanced electronic sensors to help pick up any handguns being slipped into the club. "I assumed you were. Stay away from the entrances and we'll be fine. I've already alerted my men. The bouncers on duty tonight were handpicked by me and are trustworthy. So we should be good to go."

He nodded. "We'll be up momentarily."

Jayne's lips twitched as Morganna rolled her eyes; the invitation to leave was clear.

"I'll see you upstairs then." Jayne nodded briskly as she turned back to the elevator.

Silence filled the room as she stepped into the elevator and the door slid shut. Clint turned to Morganna, his gaze brooding as he swept over her outfit.

"I wouldn't start over the outfit again, Clint," she warned him softly, her eyes narrowing at the dangerous glint in his eyes.

He looked rakish, wicked with the new growth of beard that he hadn't shaven. His midnight blue eyes were dark, filling with lust and just a hint of danger as he advanced on her.

Morganna backed up warily.

"Do you think I'd hurt you?" His voice was a sensual rasp across her senses as she swallowed with difficulty.

Morganna shook her head slowly. "No. You would never strike me." There were other ways to hurt her. He could gain her cooperation with his touch, make her dress in a nun's habit and enjoy it, until the haze of sexual pleasure wore off. He made her weak. He made her want to give in to him, made her wonder if that would hold him to her forever, even though she knew better.

"Then why are you backing away from me?" He continued to advance on her. She continued to move backward until she came up against one of the thick column supports.

She breathed, a quick, hard inhalation as he caught her wrists, gripping both in one hand as he pulled her arms over her head, holding them against the post.

"Do you know what that outfit does to me, Morganna?" he whispered.

"Pisses you off?" she guessed, fighting to tamp down the nervousness rising within her.

"It makes me very hard. Very horny. It makes me want to prove to every moron looking at you exactly who you belong to."

"I belong to me, Clint." Oh man, God was gonna get her bad for that lie.

"And that outfit proves it," he growled, his other hand gripping her hip, jerking her against his harder body as his knees dipped, driving his erection against the soft mound of her sex. "But baby, we both know the real truth."

His lips covered hers, but rather than the fierce, dominant kiss she expected, they sank into hers instead as a hungry growl left his throat.

Morganna felt her chest tighten painfully as his eyes grew heavy lidded but still stared deep into hers. His lips moved over hers, his tongue licking at her lips, his hips moving against her, stroking the suddenly swollen, throbbing bundle of nerves between the folds of her sex through the material of their clothes.

A whimper of longing, of emotion, left her lips at the exquisite pleasure, the sense of slow-building heat, overtaking her.

Clint owned her with this kiss, and she knew it. The soft rasp of his beard against her skin, the way his lips stroked hers, his tongue tangling with hers as his eyes held her gaze.

She strained against him, feeling her heart racing in her chest as her nerve endings sensitized, heated. The extreme tenderness of the kiss was like velvet, but beneath it was steel, fire-forged, dominant.

"When I get you back here," he whispered, "what's left of those clothes you're wearing will be peeled from your body, Morganna. Slowly. And then you're mine. While you're mine . . ." He took small kisses from her, pulling at her lips, making her moan at the threat of the deeper, darker passion she could feel just beneath the surface. "I'll show you what happens to bad little girls who run around half-dressed."

"Hmm, promise?" Her teeth caught his lips as he moved to pull back, seeing the flare of surprise, of possessive dominance, that flared in his eyes.

The primal growl that rumbled in his chest was her only warning before he stole the kiss from her. Catching her closer, releasing her hands as his fingers gripped her hair and pulled her head back for the deep mating thrust of his tongue into her mouth as his lips slanted over hers.

Oh yes. This was what she liked. A powerful, convulsive clench of her womb had her breath hitching as her hands tangled in his hair to hold him closer. The rasp of his beard, the corded power in his long, leanly muscled body, combined to overwhelm her senses.

"Enough." He pulled back, his breathing as harsh, as heavy, as her own. "You would tempt a saint." His lips were pulled back from his teeth in a grimace of pain-filled hunger that echoed in her body.

"Well . . . you're not a saint . . ." she panted. "Am I tempting you anyway?"

He groaned, a snort of laughter mixing with the sound as he laid his forehead against hers and stared back at her with heated need.

"Be careful up there," he whispered. "Reno would kick my ass if anything happened to you."

And how would he feel? She smiled, knowing, feeling, the determination in him, the emotion, unspoken, undefined, but whipping from him like invisible waves of power.

"I'll keep you safe from Reno then," she promised softly. "Come on, big boy; let's go fight some bad guys."

Chapter 25

T HIS WASN'T GOING TO WORK.

Clint could feel the blood rushing through his veins, pounding beneath his flesh. A fine film of sweat covered his skin, his sensitive skin. The heavy beat of the music was almost a physical caress as the waves of sound rushed around him, heavy with the singer's strident moans, her throaty, sexual cries of passion. Cries that reminded him of Morganna's. And as he listened, he watched.

She moved to the dance floor within the first half hour in the club, joining her friends Jenna and the dark-skinned young man, Sandy.

Sandoval Mitchell was of South American descent, twenty-seven years old and a student at the university. He was a regular club-goer, though not an active part of the peripheral BDSM community.

At the moment, he was in danger of extinction. Honest to God, if he touched Morganna one more time, Clint swore he was going to rip Mitchell's hands off. Not that the other man had touched her in any way indecent. It was just the fact that he was touching her.

Touching bare skin displayed by that mockery of an outfit she wore, his eyes frankly admiring as they went over her. Of course, she had ignored Clint's request to stick close to his table as most of the women who had taken Doms as their lovers were doing.

The little witch had laughed at the order. She was there to dance, not to fetch his drinks, she had informed him.

The dance floor was the central attraction of the club. Here the submissives vying for a Dom, or to please one, danced with abandon. At least, Morganna danced with abandon. She danced like she made love, without reservation. And to this song it was the worst torture. "French Kiss." The song was pure sex. Morganna was pure carnal heat.

Her hands smoothed down her mostly naked thighs as her head tipped back, her long hair caressing her bare hips as her hands came back up her thighs, caressing slowly across her midriff as her head rose, eyes slitting open. Her gaze locked with his as her hands moved slowly, lifting until they clasped above her head as her body swayed.

The beat picked up, the moans and passionate cries echoing around him as her hips kept in time to the beat, moving side to side as her hair swept around her like a silken curtain.

Perspiration glistened on her flesh; her eyes gleamed with purpose, with desire. She beckoned him with her look, with the movements of her body. Sent shards of hunger to rip at his tortured cock as he shifted in his chair.

Damn her. Son of a bitch, he was going to tie her down and spank her bottom red. She had him ready for her now, ready to pick her up, rip those next-to-nothing pants from her body, and fill her as deep and as hard as he could go.

When the song finally came to an end, he found himself breathing in deep, relief warring with driving lust. The song might have changed, but Morganna's energy hadn't. Her love for the music was clear on her expressive face; her joy in the movement, in tempting him, making him crazy, was even more evident.

His fingers tightened around the drink sitting on the table before him as he lifted it to his lips and consumed the liquor he had ordered. Pure, raw Jack burned its way down his esophagus as he fought back the lust.

He was here to do a job, not to pant after that damned wildcat he couldn't seem to get enough of. He could barely keep the sweat of pure driving lust out of his eyes enough to do that.

Clint grimaced at the thought. He knew she was dangerous to his self-control and mental health years before. He'd had no idea how true that was until now.

"Clint, I hear you snagged our girl's apprenticeship." Timothy Wagner, the stocky Dom sitting across the table from him, lifted his drink as though in congratulations. "There are a lot of jealous men watching tonight, my friend."

Clint let his lips quirk into a facsimile of an amused grin. Truth be told, he wanted to rip Wagner's face off.

"She's a joy on the dance floor," Timothy called out again. "Watching her is better than foreplay."

Better than foreplay? Clint stared back at Timothy broodingly before dragging his gaze back to Morganna. She had retreated farther within the circle of dancers, obviously talking with Jenna and the young man, Sandy, as they all danced. The other woman had a less sophisticated style of dance. More gyration than flow with an explicit grinding of hips that did little for Clint. Morganna was like water, though, all smooth moves and swaying desire.

His cock throbbed at the memory of holding her, possessing her, as she moved like that beneath him.

His gaze moved over the dance floor farther, eyes narrowed against the clash of light coming from the strobes and the haze of smoke slowly building from the cigarette smokers. Shade and Reese were within feet of her, dancing with several of the young women on the floor. It wasn't unusual to see a Dom dancing with the women, and Clint had to admit no one could have mistaken the two Rangers for less than full alphas.

There were a lot of new dancers, which wasn't unusual. He recognized Craig making his rounds as well as Joe as he lounged lazily against the far wall. Grant Samuels was missing, called home unexpectedly.

Clint continued to survey the club, coming back every few minutes to Morganna as he listened to the pulse of music and hollow voices in the receiver at his ear punctuated with the reports coming from the technician in the van that had accessed Drage's security cameras.

Morganna continued to dance, conversing as she moved,

laughing, enjoying the freedom of movement. She was drifting farther into the crowd, which made him nervous.

"You can't take your eyes off her, Clint." Timothy's voice was smug, superior. "You're going to lose control of her at this rate."

As though anyone would ever have control of Morganna. There was no controlling her; he was learning that quickly.

"She'll do okay." He had refrained from commenting much due to the simple fact that Morganna wore the same receiver in her ear that he wore in his.

As the wave of the crowd moved around her, Clint kept his eyes on the top of her head, tensing as the dancers shifted as well. Jenna was moving farther and farther away from Morganna, as was Sandy. Clint couldn't glimpse the man dancing next to her now but had noticed the other man's fondness for her hair. He kept touching it. Kell and Ian were still close to her. Catching Kell's attention, Clint flicked his gaze deliberately on the stranger, indicating that they should stay close. Something about the man made Clint uncomfortable.

The two SEALs were on radio silence, unknown to Joe and his team. Which meant the mole couldn't mark them. Kell nodded imperceptibly before he and Ian began to move in, drawing the women dancing with them closer.

A short pulse of static at Clint's ear heralded the tech in the van.

"Boys and girls, we have an anomaly at the club's back door. Do you have that, Drage?"

"We have it," Drage answered. "Jayne is heading there. It appears the security lock is being disengaged. Can you see anything?"

"Nada, too many shadows," the tech answered.

Clint's gaze jerked to the dance floor's exit leading to the private halls and the back door. Jayne Smith was gliding smoothly through the entranceway, her shoulders straight and tense as she headed for the area.

As Timothy's voice droned in the background, Clint swung his gaze back to the dance floor. Once again Morganna had moved, and this time he had lost sight of her. Standing easily to his feet, he searched the floor, finally catching a glimpse of her on the far side with Ian and Kell moving in close synchronization with her and the stranger.

The stranger was making Clint damned nervous. He was too careful, keeping his face shadowed and out of Clint's range of vision. And he was too close to her. If it were any other woman, Clint would have felt a spurt of jealous anger. But he knew Morganna now, and he knew damned well she wouldn't allow another man to dance that closely with her.

"Who's the stranger?" Clint snapped out, moving along the edge of the dance floor.

"We can't get an ID. He's keeping himself shielded," Joe reported. "He reminds me of the bastard trying to slip that last girl the drug."

Which was exactly what Clint was thinking. "Craig, can you see anything?" he questioned, watching the taller forms of his men as they moved into combat mode. He knew the signs. Their bodies were tense, prepared, the subtle hand signals they sent back to him warning.

Morganna didn't appear to be dancing anymore; neither did the stranger. Dressed in heavy leather, a hat shielding his face, the figure led her to the edge of the dance floor; coming up quickly on the rear was the young man Sandy.

"Morganna, is everything okay?" Clint snapped the question, knowing the sensitive mic on the receiver would pick up his words.

There was no answer.

"Morganna, report."

"Her receiver is disabled," the tech suddenly reported. "We have no contact with her. I repeat, no contact."

"Kell? Report." Radio silence be damned.

"We can't get a clear look at his face, but she's scared. We have them covered for now, but he has ahold on her upper arm. I think he's heading for the exit."

"Converge." Clint snapped the word into the receiver as he headed for the back door.

"Fuck! We have a security breach at the exit. Jayne is covering. The bastard just led Morganna into a blind zone, Clint. I can't see her anymore." Drage's voice was dark with anger as Clint moved quickly along the side of the dance floor, once again losing sight of Morganna.

The bastard had somehow tagged the cameras again.

"Use camera backup, Drage; we have a problem on the floor," Clint snapped into the link.

"Backup is running, but the crowd is too thick," Drage retorted.

"She's being led to the exit at the far end of the floor. Lyons." Clint spoke to the tech. "Can you pull the van around and check out the action there?"

There was no answer.

"Lyons, report," Joe snapped into the link.

"I'm heading for the back door," Craig reported.

"I have a bouncer heading there as well," Drage came back. "Clint, do you have a sighting yet?"

"Ian. Kell. Report." Clint pushed his way through the crowd, desperate to get to Morganna now.

"Fuck!" Kell's voice was low, furious. "The bastard has a gun on her, Clint. It's hidden between his body and hers and the grip on her arm is a tight one. This is going to get sticky."

"Who the hell is that, Clint?" Joe was snarling. "What the hell is going on?"

"Backup," Clint snarled. "Concentrate on Morganna. The bastard who has hold of her is your mole, man, and since only one of your men is unaccounted for, want to bet who it is?"

Clint knew who it was.

"I have bouncers covering the door, and the outside cameras are showing action outside it."

As Drage spoke, the crowd began to surge mindlessly. Screams rose above the sound of the music as Clint jerked his revolver from the small of his back and rushed for the center of the disturbance and began to pray.

ORGANNA KNEW THE MINUTE GRANT Samuels danced up to her that something was wrong. For one thing, he wasn't wearing his trademark ball cap. But if that hadn't been a clue, the minute he reached out and quickly slipped the receiver from her ear, she had known she was in trouble.

The gun suddenly pressing into her side was a good indication as well.

"Clint isn't this stupid," she warned Grant desperately as he led her to the far side of the dance floor. "You know that, Grant."

This was Joe's mole, and the shock of it was nearly mind-numbing. At least it would have been mind-numbing if she wasn't so damned scared. Fear had a way of clearing the mind, and suddenly everything in Morganna's head was crystal clear.

"It doesn't matter now, Morganna." His voice was cold, unregretful. "They won't know it was me. That's all that matters. All I have to do is get you to the back door, and Fuentes' men will take over. No one will even know when or where you disappeared."

Oh yeah, she was just going to go peacefully here. She stared around her, catching Reese's gaze and the confidence in his face. He was aware of what was going on, covering her, but that gun in her side was pretty damned threatening.

"Are you crazy?" She tugged at the painful hold Grant had on her arm. "Do you think Clint will just sit nice and still once he loses sight of me?"

"He'll depend on Lyons' and Drage's camera abilities." Grant's voice was calm. "I know where the cameras are and how to avoid them. No problem. Lyons will be dead by now, which is regretful, but not really a problem."

God, Grant spoke so coldly of the death of a man Morganna could have sworn was his friend. Of the whole team, Grant had always seemed the most solid, the most dependable.

"Don't do this, Grant." Fear rose like a dark cloud within her mind as she fought his hold. "You know what Fuentes will do to me."

Would Clint risk a gunshot to her to keep her from being taken? Morganna knew if Grant managed to get her to that door, then she was dead.

"Do I act like I care?"

He sure as hell didn't sound as though he cared. She glanced into the stony, hard expression and knew he didn't care.

"Why are you doing this?" The gun dug harder into her back as she fought against him. "I haven't done anything to you."

"No. You didn't," he agreed, his voice benign. "I'm afraid you've been caught in a very clever trap I only meant to use against Joe. You brought yourself into it, Morganna."

"Let me go." They were getting closer to the back exit and still Kell or Ian hadn't made a move on Grant.

She had a chance of surviving a gunshot. A slim one, yes, but a chance. And if she did die, at least it would be fast. If Fuentes got hold of her, death would not come easy, nor would it come peacefully.

"I won't let you take me, Grant." She dug her feet in as they reached the wall and he began leading her to the exit light that glowed in the color of blood.

Something in her voice, in the sudden resistance of her body, had him pausing. He jerked her closer, bringing a gasp from her lips as his hand tightened around her upper arm.

"A gut shot hurts real bad, Morganna," he sneered as he pressed the gun into her abdomen. "There's no way Clint will get you to the hospital in time, and even if he did get you there before you died, you'd never survive surgery. Just think, with Clint's contacts, he might find you before Fuentes kills you. You have a chance by going peacefully."

Morganna tightened her lips in the almost certain knowledge that she was going to die there.

"Shoot me." She fought him as he began to pull her to the door. "I won't let you do this."

"Then I'll shoot a few friends of yours; how does that sound?" The pain as his grip tightened further stole her breath as her knees weakened. "Do you want to choose the first one I shoot on that dance floor, Morganna?" He turned her until she could see the dancers, most of whom she knew, at least in passing. "How many should I start with? One? Three? I have a dozen bullets in this clip just waiting to discharge. Pick out the first one."

Oh God! Morganna felt the strength leave her body, felt horror fill her soul as she saw the determination in Grant's stone-hard brown eyes. He would do it. He had nothing to lose.

"Please don't do this." The fear raging inside her left her shaking, desperate. There had to be an escape.

"Are you going to move, or do I start shooting?"

She moved. Her breathing became jerky as terror started to overwhelm her, whipping through her mind as she fought to find an escape. There had to be a way to stop this, to stop him, but as the door ahead slowly came nearer and no help arrived, hysteria began to edge at her mind.

"Hey, Morganna." Sandy stepped in her way, his dark eyes staring down at her as he smiled with an easy, engaging grin that was just a shade tighter than he normally used. "Where's your boyfriend?"

"Behind her," Grant growled. "Get out of the way."

"Hey, dude." Sandy blinked, glancing from Grant to Morganna. "He's not your boyfriend. What's up?"

Yeah, what was up? This wasn't the quiet, almost shy Sandy she knew.

"Excuse us, Sandy—"

"Are you crying, Morganna?" He tilted his head, his body shifting just enough that if Grant tried to shoot him, he would have to reveal the gun first, rather than keeping it hidden between them. "You making her cry, man?" Sandy glanced back at Grant.

"If you don't move, I'm going to make you cry," Grant snarled.

"Fine. Whatever."

Morganna had no warning of what was coming next. Before she could prepare for it, before she had any clue that Sandy was as perceptive as he was, she felt herself being torn from Grant's grasp and flung against the wall. She bounced against it, her head striking the stone as she heard the gun go off.

Somewhere, someone screamed her name. Funny, she didn't feel as though she had been shot. She shook her head as she stumbled to the floor, staring around, dazed, her eyes widening as hard hands gripped her waist and pressed her closer to the wall.

Then she saw it. Clint and Grant fighting for the gun as the crowd began to flee. Another shot went off wild, screams echoing around her as Sandy collapsed against her.

He'd been shot. She twisted around, catching the young man as he collapsed to the floor.

"I'll live." He grimaced, snarled actually, his expression twisting painfully as his hands gripped his side.

"God! Are you insane!" she raged as she pressed her hand over his, feeling the blood seeping through his fingers. "Where the hell has your mind gone, Sandy?"

"Trust you . . . to bitch . . . at me," he gasped, his face pale. "Bullet went through my side. Shit hurts."

Oh hell. There was so much blood.

Another shot rang out as she lifted her head again, staring in shock as Joe stood to the side of the two grappling men, Clint and Grant. Joe's gun was held in both hands, his expression so grief-stricken, so filled with pain, her breath caught.

Slowly, Grant slid from Clint's grasp, the gun held between them falling to the ground as Clint caught him.

The music was silenced. An eerie, pervasive absence of sound filled the club as everyone watched.

"Bastard," Grant gasped as his hand pressed to his chest. "You should be dead . . . not me. . . ." He coughed as Clint laid him on the floor. "You should be dead."

Morganna's eyes widened. They were friends. Joe treated Grant like a brother, loved him, always joked with him.

"Morganna?" Clint was beside her, pulling her to him as his hands began to move over her quickly, checking for injuries. But she couldn't take her eyes from Joe. "Are you hurt, baby?"

She shook her head slowly. "Sandy." She showed Clint the blood on her hands. "Sandy's hurt."

He moved to the younger man as Joe knelt beside Grant. They were inches apart. Joe's face was expressionless, but his eyes raged with grief.

"Why?" She saw the word pass his lips. "Why, Grant?"

"Because I hate you. . . ." Grant coughed, blood seeping from his lips. "You got the promotion; you had Maggie—"

"You married Maggie. . . ." Joe shook his head. "She has nothing to do with this."

"She does now." The smile on Grant's face was cruel, evil. "And you'll never have her. Ever, Joe. Ever. . . ." The light dimmed in his eyes as death stole over him. Slowly. Completely.

"Morganna, dammit, are you okay?" Clint's hands gripped her shoulders, shaking her fiercely as she turned her head back to him.

His face was white, his midnight blue eyes nearly black with rage as he glared down at her.

"I'm not hurt. Sandy?" She turned back to him, watching as Craig and Drage steadied the other man, applying towels to the wounds as a cacophony of voices began to surge through the club.

"Police and ambulances are on the way." Jayne slid in to Drage's side, her face bruised, her arm seeping blood beneath a hastily bandaged wound. "They hit the back door. The van tech is dead, but we managed to round up a couple of Fuentes' men. He wasn't with them."

"You're hurt." Morganna shook her head, shock rising inside her quickly as tears began to fill her eyes. God, she shouldn't be crying. They had survived. She had survived. Sandy would be okay, wouldn't he? Clint was alive.

"I'm fine." The woman's eyes were stone cold, her voice level.

"Here, baby." Clint wrapped his leather jacket around her as she realized she was shaking, shaking so hard her teeth were rattling.

"This sucks," she said tearfully, forcing the words past her chattering teeth.

"Shock. You'll get over it. And you did good, girlfriend," Jayne assured her, a small smile softening her face. "And, Sandy, babe." Jayne flashed him an approving smile. "You did good. Real good."

Sandy stayed noticeably quiet as his gaze flickered back to Morganna.

"What were you doing?" she asked the young man. "How did you know?"

A bitter smile twisted his lips. "I tracked the drug here. Fuentes' soldiers killed my mother, her husband, and my half sister in South America."

"Delores." Clint growled the name as he stared down at Sandy. Adam Delores had been one of the government employees on Fuentes' payroll. He had also been one of the DEA's inside men.

"Delores." He nodded weakly. "They raped and murdered my younger sister before killing my mother and her husband. I couldn't let them escape. I had no idea Fuentes was still alive, though."

"He's been here for more than a year tracking the drug,

trying to uncover who was behind it," Jayne added before quickly moving back and making way for the medics pushing their way to Sandy's side.

"Morganna." Clint turned her back to him, staring down at her worriedly. "Are you sure you're okay?"

"I'm fine." She was still crying, though, and she hated that. "Grant was going to kill me, Clint." She hadn't expected this. She had expected a stranger, someone she didn't know. Despite Clint's assurances that there was a mole in Joe's unit, she hadn't really believed it.

"I know, baby." Clint pushed her hair back, his fingers moving down her cheek before he pulled her into his embrace. "I know. I was right behind him. Sandy gave us the chance we needed to get you out of the line of fire."

She held on to his back, shuddering at how close Sandy had come to dying for her. "It was Grant. I thought he was Joe's friend. They were like brothers."

"No, they weren't." Clint's arms tightened around her. "Joe just thought they were. Hang on now, sweetie; the police are here and we have to sort everything out. We'll get through this."

She nodded against his shoulder. "We'll get through it." Her voice hitched as she fought her tears; then she straightened her shoulders and took a deep breath. "I'm okay."

"I know you are, but I might not be." He held her in place as she moved to push away from him. "Just hang on to me a minute, sweetheart. Let me assure myself you're still in one piece. I think I died of fear when I saw that gun at your side."

She trembled at the memory of it. He wasn't alone. It was a damned good thing she hadn't eaten dinner early, or she would have lost it on the dance floor when she realized what was going on.

"Clint. The police are here now." Joe's voice wasn't normal, but she couldn't expect it to be.

As Clint allowed her to turn from him, helping her to

her feet, she faced the sorrow-filled expression in the other man's face.

"I'm sorry," she whispered.

Joe blinked back at her. "Why?"

Her gaze moved to the dead man stretched out on the floor, the blood staining his clothes from the wound to his chest. "He was your friend."

Joe paused, his gaze flickering to the body before returning to her. "He was no friend of mine," Joe said softly before turning away and moving toward the officers rushing into the club.

Chapter 26

GROWTH SUCKED. MATURING, SEASONING, GAINING experience, whatever the title, Morganna decided it was a pain in the . . . soul.

As the investigation officers swarmed into the club, followed by the Atlanta Division of Internal Affairs, to take over the case of the betrayal and death of Agent Grant Samuels, she saw another side of the horror she was facing in the job she had chosen. And she could feel that seasoning, that growth, rising inside her. Just as she felt the hollow certainty that Clint was right. This wasn't the job for her.

It brought home a resounding crack of reality that she had been trying to avoid. The hard, cold look in Joe's eyes, minutes after he'd shot and killed his best friend, reminded her too much of the banked ice she often saw in Clint's gaze. The look of a man who had known betrayal, who had learned the price of trust. Of love. She didn't want to ever learn those lessons.

As she gave the investigators her report, she watched Clint. The customers who had filled the club had been released, leaving Joe and his remaining agents, herself, and Clint. Kell and Ian had slipped out with the crowd to preserve their cover. It wasn't over. Fuentes was still out there.

"You doing okay?" Clint moved next to her as the investigator took her signed report and moved to Joe.

She still wore Clint's jacket pulled close around her to ward off the chill she could feel moving through her very bones.

"I'm doing fine." She inhaled deeply, staring around the club with a sense of disbelief. "Any word on Fuentes?"

"Nothing." Clint shook his head. "Jayne and her men

apprehended a bastard uncle, Jose, and the nephew Santiago attempting to make their way into the private elevator that leads downstairs. They're in custody now. Manuelo managed to slip away, but Kell and Ian are looking for him."

Morganna propped her arms on the table she was sitting at and lowered her head to push her fingers through her hair.

"So what do we do now?" She stared around the club again, hearing the eerie echo of the officers' voices as they cleared up the final investigative process.

Grant had been placed in a body bag and taken away, while two officers had been sent to his home to notify his wife of his death.

"Now we wait." Clint sat down in the chair opposite her, stretching his long leather-clad legs in front of him as he watched her quietly. "And watch. He'll move again soon."

Morganna pressed her lips together as she clenched her teeth against the curse that wanted to pass her lips. She wanted this over with, now. She wanted Fuentes caught, wanted him off the streets and behind bars. She wanted to curl into Clint's arms and assure herself that the ice lurking in the back of his gaze would melt, it would thaw, and he would find a way to stay in her life.

Maybe it was just adrenaline overload, she thought, lifting her eyes back to him, staring into the midnight orbs and feeling her chest clench at the cold that shadowed the concern. He cared, she knew he did, but not where it mattered, not where it would keep him with her forever. And she knew it. When this operation was over, Clint would be gone, and it was breaking her heart.

"So what next?" She pulled her eyes from his, hating the clenching pinch of pain in her chest.

"Next, we head downstairs, eat dinner, and—"

"I'm not hungry, Clint."

"That's just too bad, darlin'," he drawled with silky warning. "Because I am, and I'm going to insist that you share a meal with me. Then we'll have a nice hot shower and go to bed. Where hopefully I'll get a chance to fuck the fight out of you so you can sleep peacefully in my arms."

She stared back at him. A grin edged at his lips, crinkled the corners of his eyes, but the hand that lay on the table was tense, almost curled into a fist.

"Don't put yourself out." Morganna rose jerkily to her feet, glaring back at him in ire.

"Morganna." He followed suit, moving to his feet to block her way. "What's wrong?"

What was wrong? She had watched a friend betray her, watched another's life destroyed, and it had brought home the glaring fact that the dreamworld she was living in was going to come crashing down around her feet any day.

It was in Clint's eyes. In the careful deliberation he used when he "handled" her. He wanted her; he craved her physically; she was woman enough to know this. Hell, it was more than that. He loved her. He loved her so much that he would never allow himself to stay with her. The house of cards she had been building in her own heart was crumbling around her.

"Nothing's wrong." Nothing except the truth.

Clint wasn't a man who changed his mind often. The vasectomy she had forced herself not to think about was a nail in the coffin of her dreams.

"Nothing's wrong." She shook her head, too worn inside to find the strength to cry. How many times had she cried? Given up? Only to turn back to him at the first opportunity. Because she continued to hope, to pray. To dream that the love she felt for him would thaw that layer of ice she felt in his heart.

"Baby." His hand cupped her cheek as he stared down at her in bafflement. "It's been a hell of a night. This business will break your soul if you let it. Don't let it do that to you, Morganna."

"Like it's broken yours?" Her lips twisted painfully. "Where's your soul, Clint?"

"Don't, Morganna." He shook his head, denying the unspoken question. "Look around you. The night has been filled with blood and betrayal. It's enough to throw a hardened man off balance. It will throw you into chaos if you let it."

Her lips trembled, but not from tears. She couldn't cry.

"I'm tired. I just want to sleep. I don't need sex tonight."

He stared back at her broodingly. "Maybe I do. Maybe I need to feel you, Morganna, convince myself you're really safe. That this time, you weren't hurt. If you continue on in this, one of these days it's going to be your body in a morgue, your life taken. Is that what you want? All your dreams blown to dust?"

She reached out, her fingers trailing over his hard jaw because she couldn't help but touch him. Couldn't help but love him. When this operation was over he would be gone and she knew it. He would walk away, and when he did her heart would follow him, just as it always had.

Each mission she would weep and worry. Each day without him would be an eternity. Each night without him would be bleak and cold. For a while. It was going to rip her heart out, but she would live, she assured herself. Just as she always had.

"Maybe you're right," she whispered, her fingers falling from the warmth of his skin. "Let's go fuck like there's no tomorrow, Clint."

She saw the edgy wince at the corner of his eyes. He didn't like the explicit term when she said it. Too bad. She was tired of making love alone.

"What are we waiting on?"

His eyes narrowed on her, a muscle ticcing in his jaw as she felt the air between them thicken with tension.

"You would drive a saint to drink," he growled as he gripped her arm and began to lead her across the dance floor.

His fingers were gentle, though, his stride restrained as they headed for the hallway.

"Good thing you're not a saint," she quipped. "So you should be just fine."

"Don't start on me, Morganna. I swear to God, I thought I'd have a stroke when I saw that bastard leading you to that back door. Do you think I enjoyed that?"

"Yeah, Reno would have been pissed if you let me get shot. I can see your problem there." She was pushing him. She was pushing herself. Grief was eating a hole in her heart, her soul, and she didn't know how to contain it. She didn't know how to deal with the loss she had seen this evening or the evil she had faced.

The look he gave her sizzled with ire.

"Oh, you're going to make me shiver with that big bad SEAL look you have going there, Clint." She tossed her head before slanting him a seductive look from the corner of her eye. "Don't go making me wet before we get to the bed now."

"Son of a bitch!" He dragged her through the entrance to the private hall before pushing her against the wall, anchoring her there with his taller, harder body as his hands clasped her face, tipping her head back and staring down at her with heated lust. No ice there. It was melting beneath the raging lust, the thin façade of control.

"Are you going to go Dom on me now, Clint?" Her hands pressed against his hard abs, her fingers luxuriating in the feel of the hard muscles beneath hot male flesh. "I might melt if you do."

The hardened length of his cock pressed against her lower stomach, sending her pulse rocketing with the assurance that at least, in his hunger for her, he couldn't yet deny her again.

"Stop this, Morganna," he gritted out, grimacing with painful pleasure as his hips pressed his erection tighter against her. "You'll destroy yourself if you aren't careful."

Her eyelids drifted closed. The feel of his hands framing her face, the pads of his fingers running slowly over her cheeks, filled her with a weakening, heated pleasure.

"I need you," she whispered bleakly. "All of you, Clint. Just one time, just this time, give me all of you."

His eyes widened just a fraction, a haunted look entering them as he stared back at her.

"You're going to destroy us both before it's over with, Morganna."

"Just once, Clint." She turned her head to press a kiss to his palm, her tongue peeking out, licking at the tough, calloused flesh before turning back to him. "Just once. I promise no one will know but the two of us. I won't let your secret out."

"Oh, baby." His sigh was bittersweet, his gaze pensive. Lowering his head, he rested his forehead against hers, their gazes connecting until she could see her reflection in the midnight depths. "What am I going to do with you?"

"Love me." Her breath hitched with emotion. "I don't need the words, Clint. You don't have to lie to me. But just once, give more than just your body. Give me something to remember."

Her breath caught in her chest, her eyelids fluttering as his hands smoothed from her face to her neck. His fingertips caressed her as his expression slowly changed.

She felt the battle-ready tension leave his body as his fingers slid around the back of her neck and his eyes, they heated, darkened until they were almost black. She had never seen his eyes like that. She had seen him furious, killing cold, worried, and grieving, but she had never seen this. Pure emotion. His expression softening, his lips fuller, as though his own strength of will had kept them restrained over the years.

"Do you know how I hunger for you, Morganna?" he whispered. "The nights I've lain on the cold ground, warmed by the thought of you?"

He lowered his head, his lips pressing at the corner of hers as her breathing increased, seductive pleasure suffusing his expression, her soul.

"I dreamed of you," she whispered, uncaring where they stood or who might see them. "I dreamed of your touch, Clint. Your voice, like it is now." She shuddered in his grip as his lips moved over her jaw, his teeth raking against the sensitive flesh.

"No more dreams, baby," he soothed the desperate ache building in her chest. "Just tonight. We'll both have what we need. Just tonight. . . ."

Just tonight. Would she survive when the night was over? Would the memory be enough?

One hand moved, his thumb running over her lips, parting them, preparing them as his eyes gleamed with a barely banked midnight blue flame that burned to the very depths of his gaze. The haunted shadows were gone, the chilly control abolished. There was only the man, his heart, his soul reaching out to her, touching her.

She would survive on this memory for the rest of her life, she decided. This one night, forever.

"Come on." He moved back slowly, his hand running down her arm to catch her fingers in his. "Downstairs."

There was a difference in him now. Something at once more dominant, and yet gentler. Warmer. As though the shields he used to hold everyone at bay had suddenly been wiped away.

As they stepped into the elevator and the doors slid shut soundlessly behind them, Morganna could feel the difference in Clint. Physically, he was more tense, his body controlled, harder. But the aura of sexuality wrapping around them was deeper, more intense. The hint of emotion she had always felt within him seemed to swamp her now, as though a bond she had never known existed between them was suddenly coming into play.

The elevator doors slid open as his hand pressed at the small of her back, pushing her into the entrance of the suite.

"I've lost my soul in you," he whispered as he drew her to a stop, staying behind her, his fingers moving to caress her stomach as he pulled her closer.

The hard length of his erection pressed into her lower back as she felt her knees weakening.

"I lost mine in you years ago." The knot of emotion clogging her throat made it hard to breathe. His voice was like rough velvet, caressing over her senses, sinking into her heart.

She felt the regret in the small hesitation of his breath behind her and fought back her tears. No regrets. She wouldn't regret this, no matter where her life went afterward.

"I want this outfit off you." He brushed her hair aside with his cheek, his lips moving to her ear. "Do you know how crazy it's made me tonight, Morganna? All I could think about was stripping it off your body. It's all any man in that damned club could think about."

She fought to drag in air as his hands moved up, cupping her swollen breasts before his fingers worked at the small clasps that anchored the strips of cloth running between them.

She needed to touch him, somehow. Someway. Her hands moved back, flattening against his thighs as she resisted the urge to bury her nails in the leather covering him.

"There, baby," he crooned before catching her earlobe in his teeth and tugging at it sensually as he peeled the top from her breasts.

"Damn, I knew you were wearing those. I love those pretty pierced nipples." His fingers caught at the small rings, tugging at them slowly, hardening her nipples further.

Pleasure mounted in her womb, convulsing it with hard spasms as she felt the tugging motion echo through her nerve endings.

"You bought them," she gasped, her eyes opening as she lowered her gaze to watch his fingers play with the violently sensitive tips.

Clint paused, stilling behind her as his hands cupped the undersides of her breasts, lifting them as he stared over her shoulder.

"You had the earrings altered," he growled, his thumbs rasping over the hard points and the small ball closures that held the rings closed. "I bought them for you, for your birthday."

Two years before. The last present he had sent to her through her brother, Reno. The implications of the rings were left silent. The fact that she belonged to him, heart and soul, wasn't in doubt. The fact that she wore his rings was no more than an outward sign of it.

Morganna bit her lip as he moved, his hands sliding from her breasts to her hips as he turned her. She stared up at him, her eyelids fluttering weakly as his hands lifted to smooth the top over her shoulders and down her arms. It fell to the floor, forgotten as velvet-soft midnight eyes watched her intently and calloused hands began to caress her.

"You're going to torture me to death?" She was panting as his fingers skimmed along the straps of material over her thighs.

"I want tonight to last forever, Morganna." His head bent, his lips moving over hers as he spoke, his eyes staring into hers. No barriers, no ice. Just Clint. "I want to hold tomorrow at bay as long as possible."

She wanted to hold it at bay forever.

Morganna lifted her arms, curling them around his neck as she moved against him, taking his kiss, his passion, with a hunger that beat through her soul in a heavy, desperate rhythm.

He ate at her lips, hard, stinging nips, followed by deep, melting kisses that had her writhing against him, her hands locked in his hair as she fought to hold him to her forever.

She was only dimly aware of him lifting her, moving the short distance to the leather couch where he laid her beneath him. Heat enveloped her as Clint came over her, his hard thigh parting her legs, pressing against the core of her as she arched against him.

"Take the shirt off." Her nipples rasped against the silk, but she needed the heat and hardness of his bare flesh, the feel of his heart beating against her.

"Not yet." He lowered his head, his lips pressing against the side of her neck just before his teeth rasped over it. "This is for you. . . ."

"For us." Her fingers went to his shirt. Forgetting finesse or any semblance of control.

Clint lifted his head, his gaze narrowing as he stared down at her, watching as she jerked the shirt from the band of his pants and finished opening it. She pushed it over his shoulders, leaving the rest to him as her hands smoothed over the hard, well-defined pectoral muscles, feeling them ripple beneath her touch as he shrugged the shirt from his arms.

The heavy thud of the gun and holster he wore in the small of his back was a reminder of the danger she had faced earlier, but it only served to heighten the arousal. Adrenaline pulsed hard and fast through her system, just as arousal burned with a sweet, all-consuming fire.

"Oh God yes," she moaned as Clint pulled her against him, feeling the heat of his skin sear the sensitive tips of her breasts as his hands pulled her closer, his rough moan caressing her senses as his hands caressed her body.

He touched her as though there were no tomorrow. Hot, liquid kisses pushed reality to the deepest corners of her mind as his hands tangled in her hair, holding her firmly beneath him.

The leg wedged between hers pressed harder between her thighs, notching against the burning flesh of her sex as her clit swelled in response. She was drowning in the sexual hunger that poured over her, through her. Lost in Clint as she savored each touch.

"I need you naked." He tore his lips from hers long moments later. "Naked and wild beneath me, Morganna."

She forced her eyes open, shocked at the brilliance of his deep blue eyes. Blue flames, so dark they were nearly black, glittering with pinpoints of brilliant light.

"Now," she whispered, her hands going to the wide leather belt that cinched his tight hips.

His chuckle as he caught her hands was wicked, seductive.

"You first." He pushed her hands aside, moving back from her as his fingers hooked into the band of her pants. The stretchy Lycra that molded to her body pulled easily from her legs as he undressed her, revealing the tiny black silk thong she wore beneath them.

"Sweet mercy," he groaned as he tossed the pants aside, his hands moving to the inside of her thighs as he spread them wider.

She was open to him now, nothing but a triangle of silk shielding her from his view, his touch. She wished she hadn't worn it.

"Touch yourself for me."

Her eyes widened at his words. It wasn't what he said; it was how he said it. His voice was nearly guttural, the demand in it sending pulsing flares of pleasure to spasm through her vagina.

"Push your fingers beneath the panties," he urged her again. "Let me watch you pleasure yourself, Morganna."

She lifted her hand from the couch, allowing her fingers first to trail slowly down her abdomen as she watched the dark flush that mantled his cheekbones

As her fingers moved closer to the narrow band of her panties, his hands tore at his belt while he still knelt between her thighs.

"Tease," he growled, watching as she ran the tips of her fingers over the elastic band before inserting them beneath it, and pausing.

"I'm the tease?" she questioned with a smile. "Come on, Clint, stop playing with your pants and get them off. Let's see how much you want me."

She was amazed she could speak, let alone tease him right now. She was so aroused she was nearly panting for breath.

"Oh, baby, have no doubt I want." His smile was tight, his eyes narrowing as her fingers moved just beneath the band of elastic silk.

Morganna watched as he jerked the belt open, then tore at the fastening of the leather pants. Within seconds, the material parted beneath his fingers as he pushed the dark gray boxer briefs lower over the straining shaft of his erection.

Her hips jerked in longing as her fingers slipped lower.

"Go on." His expression was heavy with sexual intent, his lips fuller, his cheekbones darker. "Push your fingers lower, baby. Tease me. Let me see your fingers move beneath the silk and imagine the softer flesh you're touching."

As his fingers gripped the gold ring that pierced the foreskin of his cock, her fingers slid between her own thighs, easing into the slick, saturated folds of her sex.

"Fuck yes!" His lips tightened into a grimace as his fingers curled around his cock, stroking it slowly while he watched her touch herself, watched the silk of her panties moving over her hand.

"Are you wet, baby?" he growled.

"Very wet," she breathed out roughly. "And swollen. I ache, Clint."

His teeth clenched, the muscle at the side of his jaw flexing convulsively as he reached out with his other hand, pulling the small triangle of material aside to watch her.

"Oh yeah, baby," he whispered as her fingers circled her clit, making it swell further as it throbbed in need. "Slide down further. Let me see you enter yourself. I need to see it, Morganna. Show me how you pleasure yourself when I'm not with you."

She whimpered at the dark tone, the suspicion that like her, Clint was building memories. She did as he asked, her fingers moving lower until one finger was dipping inside the hot, wet depths of her vagina.

How did she please herself when he wasn't around? Desperately. She ached and cried out his name and writhed beneath him as her finger thrust inside the aching channel. Her hips lifted, her feet digging into the leather couch as her palm raked her clit and she began a steady rhythm designed to throw her into release. Except the pleasure was stronger this time; it gave a mockery to any sensation she had ever known without his gaze upon her.

"Oh yeah." He stroked his cock as he watched her, the hard muscles of his stomach clenching as she lifted her hips to meet the thrust of her own fingers, the sound of wet flesh meeting the desperate movements colliding with their panting breaths. "Damn, that's pretty. So sweet and pretty," he growled as he began to push at his pants, jerking them over his hips before he cursed. "Damn boots."

She was close, too close to find the humor in his words or to understand what they meant.

"Clint." She whispered his name as she did when she was alone, barely able to stare up at him, fighting to keep her eyes open enough to watch his face. This would be another memory to pull out and hold close when he left. She didn't want to miss a single moment of it.

"Yes, baby," he growled, moving closer to her, his pants at his thighs as one hand gripped her wrist. "Enough now."

She cried out in protest.

"Easy, baby." He pulled her fingers free of her own wet flesh before lifting them to his mouth while bending closer to her.

He moved into position, sliding between her thighs as he came over her. His eyes were nearly black, burning with lust and emotion as she felt his cock press against the tender opening of her vagina.

One hard thrust sent his cock spearing to the very depths of her aching pussy as his lips covered her fingers, sucking them into his mouth as her vagina sucked at the thick flesh invading it.

Flames beat at her mind as a burning heat filled her core. One hand gripped her hips, lifting her closer as he braced his knees on the couch and his hips began to thrust the thick spear of his erection inside her with deep, hard movements.

It was so good. Her hands dug into the leather of the couch

as she lifted to him. Oh God, she was so close to coming, she could feel the hard clench of her womb, the fire sizzling inside it, and she knew she wouldn't last much longer.

The expression on Clint's face held her spellbound; the lust and emotion raging through his eyes would have stolen her breath if there was any left in her body.

"That's it," he groaned. "Tighten around me, baby."

His grimace was one of painful pleasure as she felt the contractions attacking her, the release overtaking her.

"Watch me." His harsh command had her eyes jerking open, staring back into his as the rhythm of his thrusts increased, his cock pumping in and out of the desperately clenching channel of her vagina as panting moans began to leave her throat.

She watched him. Watched his expression tighten, watched the violent pleasure that filled his gaze as she finally slipped over the edge.

The explosion that detonated in her womb overtook her. Mind. Body. Heart and soul. She jerked in his grip, thrusting back into him harder as the rocketing flames bloomed through her senses and overtook her nervous system.

The cataclysmic physical upheaval went beyond pleasure, beyond ecstasy. It consumed her soul as she felt his final hard thrust a second before the deep, heated spurts of his semen began to fill her.

She felt his release with a sense of bittersweet acceptance. For once, he had given her all of himself, only to deny them both the choice of her ever carrying his child.

As Clint collapsed over her, Morganna's arms lifted to his shoulders, wrapping them around him as she held him close. Their heartbeats pounded against each other fiercely, shaking their bodies as the final tremors of release eased through them.

"If I could change myself I would, for you," he whispered at her ear. "If I could change the past, I'd do it for both of us."

He was such a man. But that was okay, for now; she was

sated, replete, and warm. For now, she would let him believe whatever it was he believed. He could continue to believe he was footloose and fancy-free for the time being. He was hers. He just had yet to realize it.

"I love you anyway," she whispered. "I'll always love you, Clint."

As the words whispered from her lips, a low vibration of sound began to hum through the suite. It wasn't a piercing alarm, but her eyes widened at the knowledge that it was an alarm all the same.

Chapter 27

L ET'S GO!" CLINT JERKED FROM her the second the pulse of the alarm echoed through the suite, throwing his shirt at her before quickly fixing his pants and fastening them.

Morganna struggled into his shirt, her fingers fumbling as her eyes lifted to the entrance of the kitchen and she froze, aware of Clint doing the same as they faced the nightmare that had been haunting her.

Roberto Manuelo stood in the entrance between the living room and the kitchen, a benign smile on his face as he held the small, lethal submachine gun in one arm, his finger caressing the trigger with obvious enjoyment. At his side stood Jenna Lancaster.

"I would not bother dressing." He watched them with a fanatical gleam in his black eyes. "I would only have to undress her later, and this would only irritate me."

Morganna pulled the edges of Clint's shirt around her, staring back at the two in shock.

"I told you she would never suspect me," Jenna drawled mockingly as she propped her hand on a wide hip and tossed her dark hair from her eyes. Her gaze gleamed with a drugged intensity that was almost terrifying. "No more than Mr. Hot Ass Masters thought his private key cards could be duplicated. All it took was being at the right place at the right time. He'll never know how it easy it was to fool him and his precious security bitch."

Morganna breathed in deeply, fighting for control as she felt Clint's gun by her foot. There was no way to drop and grab it. The machine gun Manuelo carried would cut through the leather couch in seconds. The only chance they had was to hide the gun.

As the thought raked through her mind, she felt Clint shift, felt his arm come around her as he pulled her against him, subtly pushing the gun against the edge of the couch with his foot as he did so.

"The alarm is wired directly to Masters' control center, Roberto," Clint told the other man quietly. "He'll know you're here."

"My little Jenna took care of this as well." His smile was cold, cruel. "She has been quite an asset in this little venture, just as Samuels was. Of course, her little tryst with one of Drage's security personnel helped immensely. It seemed he gleaned a bit of perverse pleasure from tucking in his boss's office. All it takes to succeed, my dear, is finding the weak link. And he was so very weak when it came to the lovely Jenna."

Morganna saw the calculating gleam in Manuelo's eyes as he flicked a glance to Jenna. He would kill the other girl, and Morganna knew it. Jenna's usefulness to him was at an end.

"And what do you get out of this, Jenna?" Morganna asked bitterly.

"I get rid of you." Jenna rolled her eyes mockingly. "The darling of the office and the clubs. Every Dom wants you, or wants to be like you. You've been a thorn in my side since you showed up, bitch. I'll be Roberto's woman, as soon as all this unpleasantness is over."

Morganna shook her head in confusion. "I didn't do anything to you, Jenna."

"You didn't do anything for me, either." The other girl curled her lip in a sneer. "Every Dom I attempted to snag for myself wanted you instead. Everyone wanted to be Morganna's little friend. It was sickening. But being rid of you is only the icing on the cake. As Diego's right hand, Roberto has something you don't, sweetie, an unlimited bank account and all the power I crave."

Power she would never live to enjoy.

"He'll kill you," Morganna whispered. "You'll never enjoy the money or the power, Jenna."

Jenna frowned, her gaze moving slowly to Manuelo as she shook her head. "He needs me. Don't you, Robby?"

"Of course, sweetheart." There was a sneer in his words as his thin lips curled into a facsimile of a smile. "You are always safe."

A triumphant smile curved Jenna's fuller lips as she turned back to Morganna.

"We have Diego's uncle and nephew," Clint said. "They didn't get away."

Manuelo chuckled at that. "They are acceptable losses as far as I'm concerned. This wasn't by Fuentes' orders anyway. He won't care to kill them for being stupid."

Manuelo was as sick, as demented, as Fuentes.

"If not by Fuentes' orders, then why?" Clint narrowed his eyes on the couple.

"Revenge." Manuelo's lips twisted as a grimace shaped his expression. "Your bitch is responsible for my brother's death. When she turned him in, allowed those bastard DEA agents to arrest him, Diego killed him. Now you can both pay for it. Diego may be willing to play with you for the life of the family you killed in Colombia, but I don't play."

"Yeah." Clint's voice was cool, chilling in its complete lack of emotion. "That was a shame about your brother there, Robby, but from what I heard, he made a hell of a spy into your little organization."

Manuelo's eyes flickered with rage. "Never. Santos would never have betrayed me."

"Why do you think he was meeting with Markwell?" Clint said softly. "That's why Fuentes killed him. He contacted my man in an attempt to find me. You're a disease, Manuelo, just like your boss. Even your brother knew it."

"You lie! You bastard. I raised Adonis. He was there to kill your man."

Clint snorted. "Uh-huh. Yeah. He knew he could take on a

SEAL. Come on, Robby, you know better than that. That's why Fuentes killed him for you. Gutted him like a fish, because he was giving Markwell information."

"He's picking at you, Robby," Jenna whispered at his side, her hand gripping his arm imperatively. "Don't let him make you angry, sweetie."

"He lies." Manuelo jerked his arm from her. "My brother would never do such a thing."

"Evidently you don't really believe that," Clint chuckled mockingly as the other man glared back at them, a gleam of insanity filling his eyes. "Why else was a member of my team killed with him? Diego was watching him; he knew Santos was a weak link."

"Shut up!" Manuelo raised the barrel of the gun, fury contorting his features as he glared at Clint.

"Robby, sweetie, don't let him push you like this." Jenna was worried now, but hell, Morganna thought, so was she. Had Clint lost his ever-lovin' mind?

She kept her eyes on Fuentes, her gaze flickering nervously to the finger caressing the trigger.

"Yeah. Kill the messenger." Clint was tense, despite the relaxed, confident sound of his voice. "It must suck knowing your baby brother was trying to get you killed. Didn't you raise him, Robby? Sacrifice for him?"

"No. Not my brother." He shook his head desperately, his lips twisting in grief. "He wouldn't do such a thing."

"He was a mole, just as Grant was yours. Didn't you wonder why he was released from jail so quickly?" The insidious suggestion in Clint's voice had the other man's head lifting sharply. "Hell, Robby. Joe needed his source of information on the outside, not stuck in jail."

It wasn't true, Morganna knew. Clint was playing with Manuelo, working on his emotions, his rage. His instability. It was easy to see that Fuentes' general wasn't as stable as he could have been.

His brother was even less stable. He and the men arrested

with him had been released on the hopes that they would
lead the DEA back to the labs or to their supplier, not so they
could ferret out more information.

"No!" The gun lifted, his finger tightening on the trigger.
"Santos would have never done such a thing. You lie."

"No, Robby, this wasn't our plan," Jenna snapped furiously at his side. "Your revenge will not come this way and
neither will Fuentes'. He'll punish you for not bringing them
to him as he ordered."

Manuelo shuddered, his jaw clenching as she dug her fingers into the opposite arm.

"You're letting him maneuver you, push you—"

"Another controlling female, Robby?" Clint mocked.
"She reminds me of Carmelita. Boy, that woman had a mean
streak, didn't she? Wasn't she the one that got Santos hooked
on drugs to begin with?"

Manuelo's eyes flickered to Jenna.

God, Morganna hoped Clint knew what he was doing.
She could feel his hand at her back, soothing her, reassuring
her, as he picked at the other man's last threads of sanity.

"Shut up before I kill you myself." Jenna lifted the pistol
she carried at her side.

"Looks like guilt to me, Robby," Clint murmured. "She's
awful desperate to see us shut up. I bet Carmelita even
trained her."

"You want to run your mouth, McIntyre? You can scream
for mercy while Diego's men rape your bitch. How will you
like seeing her beg to be fucked as his soldiers get in line to
try her out?" Jenna grimaced with rage.

Clint sighed heavily. "Don't bore me with threats, Jenna.
You're a very small little bug trailing after Robby here.
Now, Carmelita, she was an animal. She would have had a
bullet in our heads first thing and made excuses later. She
would have never let Diego see her trying to take over. Better watch her, Robby. You might have more woman than you
can hold on to."

Manuelo shook his head, his straight black hair falling over his brow as he stared back at Clint furiously.

"Sweetie, he's just working on you." Jenna was frantic now. "Santos loved you. Don't let him do this."

"Like you love him, Jenna?" Clint mocked. "Does he beat you until you're bloody? Or does he prefer to let you lie in a lonely bed while he plays his games with his other women like Fuentes does? I bet the latter. Hell, I know because I saw him in a window room just last week. That little blonde he was fucking sure as hell wasn't you."

"Shut up!" Manuelo stalked furiously across the room, moving around the couch until he was only feet from them, the gun pointed straight at Morganna's heart. "You will shut up or I will kill this whore now."

Clint was silent. She could feel the satisfaction flowing from him, though, just as she felt the complete readiness of his body. That he thought he knew what he was doing, Morganna had no doubt. But that black weapon wasn't pointing at him; it was pointing at her. She stared down the barrel warily.

"You're going to let him defeat you," Jenna hissed at Diego's ear. "This wasn't the plan. Give me the syringe and we'll take her out of here."

"Over my dead body," Clint drawled.

"That can be arranged." The anger building in Jenna was clear. She was livid.

"Naw, Robby wants me alive and so does Diego," Clint told her confidently. "He wants to hear me screaming while he rapes my woman. Unfortunately, he's smart enough to know he can't haul both of us out of here drugged."

"All we need is the bitch," Manuelo snapped.

"You'll have to kill me to take her, and you know it. So how do you intend to resolve it?"

Manuelo was breathing heavily now, a fine film of perspiration glistening on his dark forehead as he stared back at Clint with enraged eyes. Small tremors tore through Manuelo's body as Jenna watched him worriedly.

"What you say about my brother. It is untrue." His voice was hoarse, his finger pressed a little too snugly against the trigger of the gun.

Jenna moved to Manuelo's side, her gaze definitely nervous now as Diego began to tremble with rage.

Clint shrugged. "We spent two years investigating Fuentes' organization before we hit his compound in Colombia. We had spies everywhere. Santos was one of our best."

The fury that overwhelmed the other man would have been terrifying if Morganna had the time to be terrified. As Maneulo brought the gun up, Clint moved.

Before she could do more than gasp, he had gripped the barrel, tearing it away from her as he backhanded Jenna and jerked her gun out of her hand at the same time.

Morganna didn't think; she went after the other woman. As long as Jenna was moving, she was a danger, and Morganna had a feeling Clint was going to have his hands full with Manuelo.

As Jenna snapped back from the force of Clint's blow— no such luck that it would have knocked her out—Morganna came up with the palm of her hand, aiming for the other woman's nose.

Jenna wasn't quite as lazy as her attitude led others to believe, though. Before Morganna could deliver the blow, Jenna snapped her head back, causing the blow to glance off her chin. But it gave Morganna the chance she needed.

A roundhouse kick knocked Jenna farther back from where Clint and Fuentes were exchanging blows with a force that sounded like two mules kicking each other.

"You fucking whore!" Jenna screamed as blood flowed from her nose, her expression twisting with maniacal rage as she kicked her shoes off and raised her fists. "Come on, bitch."

Oh yeah, she was going to fistfight, Morganna thought sarcastically. She didn't think so. She kicked out again, catching Jenna in the gut and throwing her farther back.

Balancing on the balls of her feet, Morganna was thankful she had managed a few of the buttons on Clint's shirt before she caught sight of Manuelo and Jenna. Otherwise, she would have had to flash the other woman, and Morganna just hated giving the bisexual Jenna that pleasure.

"Come on, Jenna." Morganna motioned to the other woman with a flick of her fingers. "Come and get me if you can. I'm going to kick your ass for this; then I'm going to watch you hauled away in cuffs when Drage gets down here."

"Drage won't be here," Jenna sneered. "I told you, I disabled everything."

"And he'll see it, if he hasn't already. And he'll know," she assured Jenna with a cool smile as they circled each other. "He'll know, Jenna, and when he looks at you, he's going to give you that little sneer you've always hated so much. Won't that suck?"

Behind her, she could hear Clint and Manuelo grunting between blows. Dammit, she wished Clint would finish off the little prick. Morganna hated fighting.

"Bitch, I'll fuck you myself," Jenna snarled, spit dribbling from the corner of her mouth and mixing with the blood on her lip. "You and your boyfriend."

Morganna imitated Drage's sneer. The little curl at the corner of the lips, the knowing, cynical expression. The other woman screamed in fury before she rushed her. Unfortunately, she caught Morganna off guard. Just a little bit, Morganna assured herself. But the blow Jenna delivered to Morganna's face snapped her head back a second before Jenna tackled her.

"Dammit." Morganna went to the floor as she slammed her knee into Jenna's pelvis, causing the other woman to double over in pain.

A sharp blow to the side of her face, and Jenna collapsed to the floor as Morganna rolled to her knees and scrambled for the couch. She could see the gun just beneath the edge, still holstered, as Clint and Manuelo grappled with each other.

They were both bloody. And Manuelo had a knife. Blood marred Clint's chest from a shallow cut at his breastbone and again low on his abdomen. Manuelo was wielding the knife like a demon, despite the obvious broken and bleeding nose. As the other man struck out with the knife again, Clint delivered a sharp kick to Manuelo's knee, obviously intending to send him to the floor. Which might have worked if he hadn't managed to somehow bring Clint down with him.

As Morganna jerked the gun from beneath the couch and tore it from the holster, fingers clawed at her hair, jerking her back.

Damn Jenna. Morganna slammed her elbow back, hearing the other woman's pain-filled grunt with an edge of satisfaction a second before she turned to Jenna, doubled her fist, and laid into her face.

Jenna's eyes rolled back in her head as she toppled backward. Gripping the gun, Morganna flipped around, staring back in horror at the sight of Manuelo straddling Clint, the knife between them as they struggled for it.

Morganna lifted the gun, her hands shaking as fear tore through her system. As her finger tightened on the trigger, a sharp blow to her back knocked her off balance.

"I'm going to blow your fucking head off!" Morganna screamed, jerking around as another blow knocked the gun from her hands.

Jenna was wobbling on her feet, blood smeared across her face, and her eyes were dazed. As she drew back her foot and let loose with a kick, Morganna gripped her ankle and jerked.

Jenna went down with a thud, but she wasn't out. Dammit, Morganna didn't have all day to fuck with this. As she scrambled to hold the other woman in place, Morganna felt for the vase she had seen seconds earlier. Where the hell . . . ? There it was. Her fingers wrapped around the neck as she lifted it and, with a surge of strength, swung it to the larger woman's head.

It shattered as it connected. Jenna's eyes widened, dimmed; then she toppled to the floor again. God, she needed to stay there. Morganna crawled across the floor to the gun, her head lifting, her eyes widening.

As Manuelo and Clint struggled for the knife, Morganna watched Clint bending the other man's wrists, turning the knife slowly toward its owner, the point driving home just beneath his chest. But it was the shadow that moved behind Maneulo that held her gaze. The dark visage of death that jerked the South American's head back and slid a deadly blade across it.

Blood gushed from the wound as an animal snarl of rage left Kell Krieger's lips. His electric green eyes were narrowed, fierce, predatory, and filled with satisfaction as he stepped back and watched his victim topple to Clint's side.

"Clint." Morganna stumbled to her feet, her gaze centering on his chest. It was rising and falling; he was breathing. That was all that mattered. He was breathing.

"Shit. Is Jenna still alive?" He caught Kell's hand and pulled himself to his feet.

"She's unconscious," Kell stated, his voice cold.

"Shit, son!" Clint was staring back at him in shock.

Kell's green eyes were calm, his expression filled with satisfaction. "Looks like we got him." His lips kicked up in a grin.

"You got him." Clint glanced at the corpse now lying on the floor as he shook his head. "Damn, did you get him."

Morganna stood to the side, staring around her in shock as the elevators slid open. Drage, Jayne, Reno, Raven, and Joe rushed into the room, guns drawn, expressions filled with horror as they stared around at the destruction.

"Looks like we showed up a bit late." Drage winced at the blood staining the carpet.

"Morganna." Reno rushed to her side as Raven moved for her brother.

"You managed to drag me home from my honeymoon,

Clint." Raven was chastising him, though her voice was filled with worry.

Voices raged around Morganna, hammered at her skull, and no matter how hard she tried to break free of her brother to get to Clint, Reno refused to let her go.

She could feel the tears washing down her face as reaction set in. She needed Clint, just for one more minute.

"Let me go!" She pushed against Reno, staring around her, looking for Clint.

"Morganna." She swung to the other side as she heard his voice, her eyes widening as Clint suddenly pulled her into his arms. There he was. Oh God, he was okay. Bloody, his eye was blackened, his lips swollen, but he was okay.

She ran her hands over his face, his bare shoulders, his chest, skirting the sharp, bloody line where Manuelo's knife had torn the skin.

"It's not too deep." Clint touched the bruise on her cheek, his eyes dark, swirling with shadows and, beneath them, the chill he always carried. "Are you okay, baby?"

CLINT RAN HIS HANDS OVER Morganna's arms, her back. He ignored the disapproval in Reno's gaze, the concern in Raven's. God, Morganna had fought like a little wildcat. He had caught glimpses of her, hence the few times Manuelo had caught him with that damned knife, and she had kicked ass. Literally.

"I'm fine." She was dazed, shaking, in shock. "Are you sure you're okay?"

"I'm fine, baby. But the debriefing on this one is going to be a killer." Clint sighed. He didn't want to let her go. He didn't want to leave her. But it was better now than later. If he left her now and just didn't return, then her chances of getting over it, of getting over him, were better.

"Don't leave." She stared back at him knowingly.

God help him, he could drown in her eyes, even now. She was like a drug he couldn't get out of his system, one he had come to depend on as much as he depended on breathing. And he couldn't keep her. He knew he couldn't keep her. He loved her. Loved her until everything in his heart, his soul, his world, was consumed by Morganna. And it scared the shit out of him. What if he *was* like his father? How could he live with hurting her?

"I have to, baby—"

"If you leave me, don't come back." She stepped away from him as he stared back at her, surprised by the sudden core of steel he saw in her eyes.

"Morganna . . ." He didn't know what to say. He hated the pain he saw blooming in the velvet gray depths of her eyes, the betrayal that flashed across her expression.

"If you're not back in my bed soon, then you'll never share it with me again, Clint McIntyre," she told him fiercely. "You do your debriefing; you tie up your loose ends—" Her breathing hitched, her eyes blinking furiously at her tears. "If you leave me, don't come back."

He breathed in roughly, and damn her, he could feel his hands shaking. The look in her eyes wasn't much different from the look he'd seen just before she tore into Jenna.

"I know you," Morganna whispered, her hands digging into his forearms as she glared back at him. "If you think you're going to run away, then come limping back when you can't stand it any longer, like you've done for years, then you've lost your mind. I'll cut your heart out and feed it to my cat."

"You don't have a cat, Morganna," he told her softly.

"I'll buy one," she snapped. "Then I'll go to the biggest, baddest honky-tonk I can find and marry the biggest, meanest redneck so he can kick your ass." A single tear fell down her cheek. "Don't you do it, Clint."

What the hell was he going to do about her?

"McIntyre, we need you with us," the investigator called out as he loaded Manuelo's dead body and Jenna's unconscious one.

"I'm coming." Clint nodded tightly before turning back to Morganna.

"I mean it, Clint," she snarled, her finger poking into his chest as her expression turned fierce. "I'm going home, and if you aren't there when this is all said and done, then don't bother ever coming into my life again."

"You're better off without me," he whispered. "You know you are, Morganna."

She breathed in deeply; the fight to hold back her tears was breaking his heart.

"You heard me," she repeated huskily as she stepped back from his arms. "If you don't love me, if you can't fight with me, *for me,* then by God, I don't need you and I sure as hell don't want you. Think about that one."

He let her go. His arms tightened at his sides as he fought the need to pull her back, fought every instinct inside him that had the vow to return hovering on his lips.

"I have to go," he finally growled as someone called his name again.

"Go," she whispered. "I'm going home. And I expect to see you there. Soon, Clint. Very soon."

He knew Morganna. He knew her moods and he knew her stubbornness, and he knew she was serious. If he didn't come back as soon as possible, then he could kiss his ass good-bye. And if he did return? The thought of ever hurting her, of turning on her as his father had turned on him, terrified him.

And the vasectomy wasn't the safety net he had thought it would be. He knew his woman, inside and out; it wouldn't be long before he would be trying to reverse it, before he would give in to the need she had for children, for a family. Hell, keeping her barefoot and pregnant would be the only way to keep her out of trouble and to send him to hell.

Clint made himself turn away and move to where Kell waited for him. The other man's green eyes watched Morganna thoughtfully before turning back to Clint.

"Hey, we got the bad guys. That's all that matters. Right?"

The knowing glint in Kell's eyes had Clint tamping down the protest rising to his lips.

No, that wasn't all that mattered. There was more to life than catching bad guys. There was getting the girl. Clint looked back to Morganna and met Reno's hard gaze instead.

It wasn't all that mattered, and Clint knew it, just as Kell did. But Clint left anyway. He turned, following Joe to the elevator, and moved inside with him and the rest of the team as Kell followed.

Clint's last sight of Morganna was her eyes meeting his as the elevator doors closed, and he felt the certainty that if he didn't return soon, then he would lose her forever. And if he did return . . . ? He could lose her anyway.

Chapter 28
TWO DAYS LATER

H E MISSED MORGANNA. AS CLINT pulled his pickup truck out of the Federal Building parking lot, he finally admitted the truth to himself. He hadn't slept worth shit in his apartment the night before. The bed, normally the height of comfort, had developed lumps. He couldn't get comfortable, no matter how hard he tried.

And every time he'd drifted off he had awakened reaching for Morganna. Only Morganna wasn't there. And she wasn't answering her phone. Though the message on the phone was telling.

"If this is you, Clint, I'm checking out honky-tonks now."

She was home. He knew she was home because Reno was answering his cell phone and he had been there twice when Clint had called to check up on Morganna.

"Between me and you, ole buddy," Reno had snorted the day before, "she came home with a cat today. That worries me."

Clint shook his head as he negotiated downtown Atlanta's traffic and headed for his mother's home, just outside the city limits. He hadn't seen her in years. He called, checked up on her, but bringing himself to actually walk into her home and pretend a bond that had never been there wasn't something he had been able to bring himself to do since he had joined the SEALs. Now he had no other choice.

Admitting he was a coward wasn't something a man did easily, but as Clint negotiated the traffic through town, he admitted that was exactly what he was when it came to Morganna. He had held himself as far from her as possible until he had no choice but to keep her close to him. And just as he had always known, she had wormed her way so deep into his soul that he couldn't pull free.

He loved her. But until he faced his past, as well as himself, then he would never be the man he knew she needed. The man he needed to be.

He couldn't imagine being a part of Morganna's life and not having children with her. Not immediately maybe, but in the next few years. A little girl with Morganna's laughing smile and dove-gray eyes. A little minx determined to take on the world and drive all sane males crazy. Or a little boy . . . Clint swallowed tightly at the thought of a son.

Reno's dad had taught Clint to play ball, to shoot, to be a man. Clint's father had taught him the wrong side of his fist and nothing else. What would Clint teach his son? The thought of it terrified him.

He pulled into his mother's driveway, turned off the truck, and stared at the small two-story home silently. It wasn't much different from the house he had been raised in, though the neighborhood was slightly better. She had lived in an apartment until recently, hoarding the money Clint sent her as she waited for her retirement and the small nest egg his father had begun when they first married.

Raven said Linda McIntyre was proud of the house. She talked often about grandkids and visits and holiday meals. That wasn't the mother he remembered. But then again, she had always been different with Raven, just as their father had been.

And now that Clint was here, what the hell was he going to say? He hadn't seen Linda in five years and damn if he wasn't ready to turn around now and just leave. As his fingers tightened on the keys, the door opened and there she was.

She was smaller than he remembered, older. Her hair was gray, her face lined, and her eyes, so like his own, were staring straight back at him. Clint pulled the keys slowly from the ignition before opening the door.

Damn, he should have just kept driving. He should gone straight to Morganna's. This was a mistake. But he forced himself from the truck, standing beside it silently, awkwardly.

As he stared back at Linda, he remembered the woman she had been twenty years before. Slender, beautiful, with long black hair, soft gray eyes. Clint had taken his facial features and his broad, muscular body from his father, but his coloring had come from his mother, as had Raven's.

"Raven just left." Linda's voice was the same as always—bitter, rough. "You may as well come in."

She turned, leaving the door open for him as she reentered the house. It was a hell of a welcome, but he hadn't come here for a welcome. He wasn't certain why he had come, but a welcoming might have been too shocking for him to survive.

Pocketing his keys, he breathed out roughly before heading up the flower-lined sidewalk to the small brick home. The door opened into a small entryway, then a classically pretty living room. His mother had always been a stickler for everything looking just right, color coordinated and prissy.

She was waiting for him in the middle of the room, standing stiff and silent as she stared back at him.

"How's Raven doing?" he finally asked as he closed the door and faced Linda with none of the anger he remembered feeling the last time they had been in the same room together.

"As forgetful as ever," she sighed. "She left the door cracked when she left. That girl never did understand how to close and lock doors. It's a wonder she hasn't been raped and murdered in her own home."

Linda was nervous. Clint heard the slight quiver in her voice, saw the wary look in her eyes. It was her habitual look whenever she saw him, as though she expected him to strike her at any time. He had never laid a hand on her, had never wanted to.

"I admit I bought the house with the money you gave me,"

she spoke up with a spark of anger. "You didn't say how I was to use it. So if you're here because I'm not in that dinky little apartment—"

"The house is nice, Mother."

"I was tired of the apartment—"

"I didn't come to argue with you. I don't care what you do with the money," he finally told her softly. "I just . . ."

He just what? He dipped his head, sighing wearily. This was a hell of a mistake.

"You haven't been around in more than five years." She clasped her hands in front of her as she lifted her chin in challenge. "Why now?"

He shifted, wondering what the hell to say, to do. Jeez, he was a glutton for punishment, wasn't he? In the years since his father's death, Clint had rarely visited and whenever he did, it was never for more than a few minutes. He saw her and the past swirled in his mind like a furious cloud. The beatings, his pleas each time his mother went out, how he would cry and beg her not let his father catch her. She would pat Clint's head and tell him to be a big boy. God, she had been as fucking crazy as his father had been.

"I'm thinking about getting married." Fuck. Okay, yeah, he had been thinking about it, but he hadn't been thinking about telling her about it.

She blinked back at him. "Anyone I know?"

"Yeah. . . ." He nodded slightly. "Look, I don't know why the hell I'm even here." He pushed his hands over his head wearily before dropping his arms to his sides once again. "I'm sorry I bothered you." He turned to leave, to get the hell away from her and the memories that rose like a black cloud in his mind every time he saw her.

"He didn't believe you belonged to him."

The words stopped Clint as he headed for the door. He froze in his tracks for a long second before turning back to her.

"What did you say?" He shook his head in confusion.

She squared her shoulders and for the first time that he

could remember, she looked him in the eye. Not that the look was in any way comforting. There was no regret there, no warmth. Just the same cool gray gaze he had always known.

"He didn't believe you belonged to him." There was a curious light in her eyes, almost one of interest, as though she wondered how he would react.

He didn't react at all. He didn't give a shit one way or the other what the bastard thought of him, but he was curious as to whether or not he shared blood with the man he had known as his biological father.

"Did I?"

"Of course you did. I may have been a whore, Clinton, but I was a careful one. You were his."

The mocking quirk at the corner of her lips no longer had the power to hurt him or to make him angry. It served instead to emphasize the fact that she really didn't give a damn.

"So why did he believe otherwise?"

She sighed as though tired, turning away from him and pacing to a tall shelf on the other side of the room. There, numerous picture frames graced the shelves. There were a few family pictures, but most of them were of Raven, Raven and their father, Raven and their mother. There were very few of Clint.

"I never claimed to be a good mother." Her lips flattened as she stared back at him. "But lately, as I've realized how quickly age is creeping up on me, I've regretted many things. I let him believe it, because it hurt him. It hurt him the way it hurt me each time he went to another woman. Each time he came home and spent his nights away from the house. So I let him believe it."

"You let him beat the hell out of me."

"You survived."

He had the impression she would have rolled her eyes if she weren't too scared to.

"I survived?" he snapped. "I could barely move for days, damn you. He took that fucking belt of his and beat the shit out of me and you didn't even care enough to keep him from catching you whenever you screwed around. I was a child."

"And you're a man now," she shot back, as cold and unfeeling as she had ever been. "Your father was raised to believe the strap was the only answer to anything. He never broke your bones; he didn't leave scars. It wasn't my fault he blamed my infidelities on you."

"It was your place to protect your children." His fists clenched at his sides, not because he wanted to strike her, but because in that moment he realized how much of his life he had wasted caring one way or the other why his parents had done anything.

"He was a hard man, but he provided for you." She finally shrugged. "You and I, we were never close. Even when you were a baby, you didn't care much for me." Her lips twisted bitterly, accusingly. "You didn't want to be held and cuddled like Raven did. You were always content to be alone, unless you needed to be fed or changed. You didn't want a mother; you wanted a caretaker."

He blinked back at her in surprise.

"You're as crazy as he was," he finally said softly, not really surprised or shocked.

"I'm not crazy, Clinton." Her smile was mocking. "I didn't want children; your father did. He forced me to conceive you, and then he convinced himself you didn't belong to him. I didn't claim I was right or wrong, but I knew he would never kill you, nor maim you. You grew up fine."

He grew up to hate his parents; he grew up with a cynicism and distrust that had shadowed his every move, his every relationship.

"You're more like him than you know." She crossed her arms over her breasts and watched him with calculated interest. "A Navy SEAL. He lived for the service, for his men. You even look like him now. He would have been proud of you had he lived."

Joy-joy. The distaste Clint felt as he watched her filled

his mouth with a sour taste. This woman had borne him, nothing more. She hadn't been a mother then, and she wasn't a mother now.

"So, are you marrying the Chavez girl?" she asked curiously. "She's been flipping her tail around you for years. Did you know she came to see me the other day?"

He watched Linda closely. "No, I didn't know that."

"Yes." She smiled coolly. "She was upset. She tore into me quite furiously, actually. I'm surprised you told her about the beatings. You were always very aware of family loyalty, even as a child. You've changed over the years."

"Family loyalty," he murmured mockingly. "There would have to be a family first, Mother."

Her lips tightened in irritation. "As I said, she was upset. Very protective." Rather than the sneer he expected, there was a slight softening to her lips, a glimmer of respect in her eyes. But her next words came close to pissing him off. "Did she finally manage to get you to knock her up? Is that why you're getting married?"

He shook his head, admitting that maybe he *was* in shock. His mother had more nerve than he gave her credit for.

"She isn't pregnant," he said, dazed when he knew he shouldn't be.

The knowledge that Morganna had been there shouldn't have surprised him. He should have expected it. She was like a tigress. It didn't matter that in this, he needed no protection; he had been defending himself against his family most of his life.

For all her makeup, girlie-girl habits, and social skills, Morganna had a core of pure steel. He would never get anything over on her, not that he would want to, but she would never allow it. No more than she had allowed his mother to.

"Of course she's pregnant." His mother laughed softly. "You loathe the idea of marriage. You always have. She's obviously trapped you and thought she could cement it by appearing here and raging at me over motherhood and protection. It was an obvious ploy of some sort."

"No, Mother," he said gently. "There was no ploy, just as there is no pregnancy. Because I had a vasectomy years ago to ensure I never fucked up like you and that bastard you married did." He ignored the surprise in her gaze. "I'm sorry I bothered you today. I'll be leaving now."

"I would have liked grandchildren." The sudden regret in her eyes sickened him. Regret, from a woman who had never allowed her son an iota of hope that he could escape the next beating, that he would ever have a father.

"Then hope Raven never learns how cold you can be," he sighed. "Because God as my witness, I could never trust you with a child of mine."

He turned from her, stalking to the door and jerking it open as he felt the regret sinking into his bones. What had he expected after all this time? June Cleaver?

He pulled the door shut as he dug the keys from his pocket and moved to his truck. Hell, he had wasted enough time on this, enough time letting the past and his own fears ruin the one dream that had clung to his soul no matter how hard he had fought to be rid of it.

Morganna. And if there was one thing he was damned certain of, even if the monster of his father did lurk within him, Morganna would make sure it was kicked out fast, while she kicked his ass to hell and back. No one would ever threaten a child of hers.

He wiped his hand over his face before unlocking the truck and moving into the driver's seat. It was time to find his future, rather than fearing his past. And his future was with Morganna.

A S CLINT'S PICKUP REVERSED FROM the driveway and accelerated down the street, Raven stepped slowly down the stairs. She wasn't supposed to have been there. The cab had arrived on time, but she had forgotten some pictures she wanted upstairs. Pictures of her father. The man who had sung to her, laughed with her, who had treasured her. The monster who had beaten Clint. She had sent the cab back and re-entered the house, never thinking that her mother hadn't heard her.

As she had listened to the conversation downstairs, the past flashed before her eyes. Clint as a young teenager, no more than fifteen, claiming he was sick, pale and weak after his father returned home, every time his father returned home. How he would stay in bed for days, sometimes not even eating unless Raven badgered him. He had left when she was still a child. The night her brother had turned seventeen he had walked out of the house and joined the Army. He hadn't even finished high school.

She had been young, too young to understand, but the guilt ate at her anyway.

She stepped into the living room, watching as her mother turned from the large window, where she had watched Clint leave. Her cool gray eyes widened, darkened, then filled with wary fear.

The emotion Raven saw in her mother's eyes as she realized she had overheard every word should have made her feel better. Raven had been the princess. The treasured child. She had been spoiled and loved and had felt nothing more than a strong resentment to her mother for driving her father away. Raven had never known about the affairs or Clint's pain. And she hated herself for that. Hated the fact that she hadn't seen how Clint had suffered.

Raven laid the pictures on the table beside the door and stared back at the other woman as pain rose within her.

"I knew you were cold-hearted." She could barely force the words past her lips. "I knew that somewhere, somehow, there was something missing in you that could have allowed you to love—"

"This isn't your business," her mother snapped, her gray

eyes darkening in anger. "You weren't supposed to be here. And I have always loved you, Raven. Always."

Raven lowered her head and stared down at the picture that lay on top of the small stack she had chosen. Her father. He looked so much like Clint. He had been so gentle to her; he had loved her. Hadn't he? She shook her head. You can't love one child and nearly destroy another. It couldn't be possible.

"I can't see you for a while, Mother," she whispered painfully as she laid her hand on her stomach, resting her palm against the child she suspected grew there. Her child. Hers and Reno's. A child who would never, ever know the fear Clint had lived through.

"It's all his fault," her mother snarled as Raven lifted her eyes. "That damned Clinton's. He was always ruining things. If he had learned to lie when he was a boy he wouldn't have been beaten near as often. All he had to do was lie to his father."

"He was your son."

Her mother's face was twisted into a grimace as her eyes narrowed with icy warning. "He has always been a thorn in my side. I won't allow him to ruin what we're finally rebuilding."

Their relationship had deteriorated after Raven's father's death. She had believed the fights revolved around her father's career, the danger it represented, and many had. But the underlying reasons were suddenly clearer. It wasn't because he'd gone to war; it was because of her mother's own selfishness and her father's cold determination to punish someone for it. Anyone but the woman he had married.

"We were rebuilding nothing," Raven finally told her hoarsely. "Maybe, later, I'll be able to look at you without remembering all the years Clint suffered. One day, maybe. But I'll never forgive you for what you and Father did to him. I'll never forgive either of you."

She left the pictures where she had laid them, opened the door, and walked out. She ignored her mother's cry, the sound of her name echoing from inside the house as she pulled her cell phone from the fanny pack she wore and dialed her husband's number.

"Hey, baby, are you home yet?" His voice came over the line as she began walking down the sidewalk.

"Reno—" Her breath caught as the tears began.

"Raven? Baby, what's wrong?" She heard the alarm in his voice, the fear.

"I'm fine. I'm safe. I need you to come get me."

"Where are you?"

She stared around her. There was a deli at the end of the street. She could wait there. She told him where she was, breathing in roughly, fighting to hold back her tears as she wiped her fingers over her damp cheeks.

"I need you," she whispered as she ducked her head, forcing herself to put one foot in front of the other. "I need you now."

"I'm heading your way." Of course he would be. She could hear the squeal of his tires, the concern that radiated over the line. "Stay on the phone with me, baby. I'm twenty minutes away. I'm coming."

"Do you know I love you?" She had to tell him. "How sorry I am that I ran from you for so long?"

"I'll spank you again for that later. How does that sound?" The forced teasing in his tone had a smile trembling on her lips.

"Promise?"

"Always, baby. Forever. You sure you're okay, Raven? You're crying." His voice was tight, and though he was holding back, she could hear the dread in his tone.

"I've been at Mother's." Not "Mom's." Never "Mom" again.

"Yeah. I knew that. Did you argue?"

"No."

"Are you hurt?"

"Not physically."

His muttered curse was filled with regret.

"Just come get me, Reno." Her breathing hitched as she entered the thankfully nearly deserted deli. "I just want to go home."

She wanted to lie beside him, feel the warmth of his arms holding her, and let her tears fall. She needed to cry, not just for herself or the shattered image of the father she had loved, but for Clint.

At least she had known the fantasy of a loving parent. Her mother had always been cool, disinterested, but her father— She breathed in jerkily. She had thought he was a hero. Clint had never been given the chance to know the love of either parent, and it was breaking her heart.

She just wanted to go home, find solace in her husband's arms, then kick her brother's ass for keeping such secrets from her. That was, if Morganna didn't kick his ass first just for being a stubborn male.

Chapter 29

CLINT SLIPPED INTO MORGANNA'S HOUSE several days later using the spare key that had been kept hidden at the bottom of the mailbox. She was mad, steaming mad, but clearing up the mess of the date rape drug hadn't been easy. He had no more left his mother's home than Joe Merino called. Jenna had talked, and they had the location of the lab.

Clint had been damned surprised to learn that Morganna wasn't a part of breaking down the lab. Even more surprised to find out that she had accepted a position training to work in the local intelligence-gathering office.

Yeah, she would be good at that. She was as nosy as a damned cat. And it would keep her out of the line of fire for the next two years at least. Until he could retire. Until he could devote himself to her and maybe raising a kid or two.

The sound of the shower running upstairs caught his attention as he closed the door carefully and relocked it. He had been five days returning to her. Five days of hell. Sleeping wasn't an option; all he thought of was Morganna. He missed the warmth of her, missed the sound of her laughter, her smart-assed comments. Hell, he craved the sound of her whispered moans, the feel of her lips beneath his. Her presence.

He shook his head as he walked into the living room, drawn to the pictures Morganna kept on the light wood shelves. Unlike the pictures his mother kept, these were filled with laughter, with family. And even some who weren't family. There were several small frames of Rory Chavez with his son, Reno, and with Clint. Rory was between the two boys, his arms around both of them.

There were similar pictures of Lisa with Morganna and

Raven. Pictures of both parents with their children, as well as the two Chavez children.

Rory Chavez had been a good man, and Lisa, God she had loved her kids. They had birthday parties every year, went to the beach on summer weekends, and damn, would Lisa chase after them all while they were around the water. She never let her kids out of her sight, and if the kids brought company, then they were as cherished and well loved as the Chavez kids were.

What the hell had he done with his life?

As he stared at the pictures, he thought of Lisa and Rory, their strength, their love for each other, their children, and even children who weren't their own. They had taught him more than he had realized. Too bad he had forgotten it in his determination to run from the only person he couldn't defend himself against.

Morganna.

As the sound of the shower shut off, his head lifted, turning toward the staircase at the entryway. Just that quickly his body hardened, his erection filling his jeans with a sudden, intense demand.

Clint grimaced at the hunger that spiked through his body. Damn her. In a matter of days she had anchored herself inside his soul tighter than she had ever been. Why?

His lips quirked as he turned on his heel, moving silently through the living room as he headed for the entryway and the stairs.

She was more than he had ever imagined. For so many years he had allowed his mother's actions to taint his view of women. Morganna loved to look pretty, to dance, to laugh and enjoy people, just as his mother had when she was younger.

That slim resemblance to the woman who had helped make his childhood so miserable had kept him running from the one woman he had ever truly loved.

Morganna would die and go to hell before she would ever

allow anyone to hurt a child of hers. The thought of children scared the hell out of him, Clint admitted, but he had been a fool to allow the past to mar the feelings he had never been able to truly run from where Morganna was concerned.

As he took the first step upstairs, he heard her in her bedroom. Dresser drawers were slamming and she was muttering angrily to herself. She would be pissed that it had taken him so long to return, but he could handle pissed.

Morganna was like a fire in winter, heated, capable of burning a man clear to his soul even as she renewed the life within him.

He could do this.

He kept his steps silent as he moved to the landing, easing his way toward her bedroom, feeling the fires she lit within his body burning higher with each step he took toward her.

"Kitty Chesney, I've about had it." He rolled his eyes as he heard her talking to what could only be the cat Reno said she had acquired. She *would* call the damned thing Kitty Chesney. For all her love of the hard-pounding music in the clubs, Morganna still had a soft spot for one particular country artist.

He heard a distinct little meow.

"Stubborn men." Another drawer slammed. "Tell me again why I decided he was worth waiting on. He's not worth kicking anymore."

He could hear the pain in her voice, felt it clenching in his heart as disillusionment colored her tone.

"That's okay. Who the hell needs him?"

He winced at her monologue.

"I can live without him."

His eyes narrowed.

"And the captain was very pleased with how well I handled that assignment. So happy that he gave me my pick of positions."

Her voice was growing angrier.

"Screw him. He's a pain in the ass, arrogant, take-over

male, and I don't need that. Do I? Tell me I don't need that, Kitty."

Meow.

"Exactly."

He could imagine the sharp little toss of her head, the narrowing of her eyes.

"You know, Kitty, the next time I see him, he better be wearing a protective cup."

Meow.

His lips quirked almost in amusement.

"Kitty," Morganna sighed. "He's not coming back, is he?"

His chest tightened at the pain in her voice.

Shaking his head, he moved into the doorway, then came to a cold, hard stop. Sweet merciful heaven grant him strength, because the sight of her took his breath.

She had her back to him, dressed in a black silk thong, her back covered by the long, silken fall of her hair. Rounded smooth buttocks tempted his hands, caused his erection to jerk in sudden, hungry demand.

"Sometimes, he's just a little slow." Clint spoke softly, leaning against the doorjamb, as Morganna whirled around to face him.

Whew. Damn. He was going to keep his head, he promised himself he would, but the small triangle of silk covering her mound and the sheer lace of the bra covering her full, firm breasts were stealing his sanity.

"You're late." Slender arms crossed over those heaving mounds as her irritated voice snapped through his lust-dazed senses.

"I see you got the cat." He cleared his throat, watching Morganna carefully.

Her eyes were storm-dark, fierce, and narrowed. Her pouty lips were thinned, her cheeks flushed. Oh, she was pissed. Pissed he could deal with.

"And tonight, I'm going to find a redneck," she snapped back at him. "I'm done with you, Clint. Go away." She waved him away with a mocking little flip of her hand. "Me and Kitty Chesney have decided to just cut our losses and deal. You're not wanted now."

She turned away from him, stalked to the closet, and disappeared inside the clothing-filled depths. Clint waited. Following her into that closet would be like following a she-wolf into her lair. He was lust-crazed and so in love with her he couldn't breathe for the hunger rising inside him, but SEAL training was tough, and every instinct he possessed warned him to tread carefully where Morganna was concerned right now.

A minute later she stalked out. It was possible she was a bit angrier than when she'd gone in. She carried a pair of jeans and some kind of white top. It didn't look like there was much to the top. And she carried boots.

"I have a date. Go away." She flashed him a glare.

Clint hid a grin. "You little liar. You have a meeting with Joe later."

A little moue of displeasure pouted her lips as her gray eyes flashed back at him.

"You think you're so smart." She tossed the clothes on the bed as the cat watched them curiously.

"I think I know you." He arched his brow. Morganna could fool a lot of people, but he knew her. Well. Too well, he was starting to realize.

She rolled her eyes. "Well, maybe I have a date after I meet with Joe." She picked up the blue jeans.

"Do you like those pants, Morganna?" Clint asked curiously as she pulled the first leg over her ankle.

"Would I be wearing them otherwise?"

"Finish putting them on and I'm going to cut them off you later," he informed her gently. "I'd hate to have to ruin a good pair of jeans."

"I'd hate to have to hurt you, Clint." Her smile was tight, hard, as she finished putting the jeans on.

She stared back at him defiantly, challenging. He chuckled

at the deliberate dare in her expression. He watched as she dressed. She buttoned the jeans, then reached to the bed for the white sleeveless blouse. Not that she should have bothered. It barely reached her navel, flashing that little gold ring that pierced it.

He shook his head, braced his feet apart, and pushed his thumbs in the pockets of his jeans as he watched her. Yeah, she was really mad.

"It's only been a few days, baby," he murmured.

"It's been five days, Clint. You left; you walked out again—"

"I love you, Morganna."

She shut up, staring back at him with wide eyes a long second before she blinked.

"What?"

"I love you," he repeated. "I knew I loved you five days ago. I knew I loved you more than ten years ago."

"And you're just now telling me?" Her breasts were moving faster now, harder. Tight little nipples pressed against the layers of bra and blouse, assuring him that her arousal was burning just as hot, just as high, as his.

Facing her with the truth, though, that was harder. Admitting to a weakness wasn't easy for him, especially the cowardly way he had allowed the past to nearly destroy what had always been between him and Morganna.

"Yeah, I'm just now telling you." He breathed out heavily. "Because you made me feel, Morganna. You made me dream. Dream of me and you together." He glanced at her belly. "Dreams of you beneath me, growing round with my child. Dreams that were destroying me because I was terrified I was my father's son."

"You thought you would beat your child?" She stared back at him incredulously.

"Dammit, Morganna, don't stare at me like that," he growled. "His father beat him, just as his father before him did. I was concerned—"

"You are so full of bullshit!" She stomped her foot.

Now that really wasn't a good sign. Morganna was approaching eruption level when she stomped her foot.

He narrowed his eyes on her, wondering what the hell she had in her mind now. This was what he got for trying to bare his soul to her? Next time he'd just fuck her and have done with it.

"You ran because you thought you'd beat your baby? Because you thought because I wore makeup and flirted and had fun, I'd screw around on you?" Her eyes began to brighten with tears. No. Hell no. She was not going to start crying.

"You ran because the big tough he-man, the Conan of the block, couldn't make one little girl obey him like everyone else in the damned world did." She was yelling before she finished, in his face, her finger poking into his chest. "Can your bullshit, Clint. You ran because you cared. Because when you were with me, I made you feel. I made you love and you hated it."

And she was right, which he hated more. Or did he? She knew him. She had always known him. What made him angry, what made him laugh, what could make him pull his hair out in frustration. Morganna knew, like the little witch she was.

"You still don't obey. Anyone." He rubbed the back of his neck in frustration. "You drive me fucking crazy. You've always driven me crazy. You make me want to fuck you silly and at the same time I want to paddle your ass for not listening to good sense."

"Good sense being whatever you want me to do?" she argued, her eyes blazing, her breasts heaving. His dick was throbbing like an open wound even as his own frustration began to rise.

Damn, nothing turned him on faster than Morganna when she decided to get defiant.

"For God's sake, Morganna, you drove us crazy all your

damned life," he snarled. "Slipping out of your room to follow me and Reno—"

"You were always catting around." She pouted. "God only knows what kind of disease you would have ended up with if you hadn't had to deal with me following you instead."

Surprise narrowed his eyes.

"The parties?"

She rolled her eyes. "Oh really, Clint, you came looking for me, didn't you?"

His lips flattened. "The flirting? The boyfriends?"

She breathed in mockingly as she lifted her hand, glanced at her nails, then placed her fingers on her hip as she gazed back up at him archly. "Now, Clint, would you have paid half as much attention to me over the past few years if I had sat at home and waited on you? You would have forgotten I existed."

"You little minx." Astonished amusement underlay the irritation in his voice.

"Hey, a girl has to do what a girl has to do." She shrugged negligently. "But I've stopped chasing after you, Clint. I'll be damned if I'll waste any more of my time on a man who continues to run from me. Go play SEAL games or something; I have a life to get on with, and living that life doesn't include watching you leave every time you figure out that you can't control me. And it sure as hell doesn't include waiting on you to decide if I'm worthy of loving every time you get in a little snit."

"A little snit?" he growled, feeling the loss of control he always felt around her. Damn her, she could tie his guts into knots with no more than a look. "Wanting to keep that pretty little ass of yours alive doesn't constitute being in a snit, Morganna."

"You're too controlling—"

"You're too damned wild," he accused in return. "Left on your own, only God knows the chaos you'll cause. You're trouble in progress, dammit, and you know it."

She tossed her head; the seductive, sensual little movement had every instinct in his body howling to take her down. He wanted her on her knees, that pert little ass lifted to him as he plowed into her from behind.

"Whatever, SEAL-boy. Now just go away. I'm certain I'll manage fine without you."

The last parting shot should have pissed him off. Hell, he had just bared his heart to her and she came out fighting. But he saw the pain in her eyes, the hope and the dreams. Yeah, he knew Morganna way too well. She was a woman, with a woman's strange thoughts and illogical demands, a beautiful, challenging little witch, and by God, he was going to get the upper hand here if it killed him. She was daring him to do it, and he wasn't about to pass up the opportunity.

"And you think I'm just going to turn and walk out that door now?" he asked her curiously. "It's hard to believe you're giving up so easily, Morganna. You've been fighting to get me into your bed for years. I thought you were more stubborn than that."

He moved his fingers to the buttons of his shirt while he talked, flicking the little discs free as he watched her. Her eyes were locked on each movement, her cheeks flushing further as her gaze took on a hungry little gleam.

Of course she was more stubborn than that. He resisted the urge to smile, to shake his head, as he finished unbuttoning his shirt, as he pulled the hem from his jeans. Her gaze was almost a physical touch, licking over his bare chest as he shrugged from the material.

"Don't make me cut the clothes off you, baby," he warned her gently. "Take them off."

Excitement flickered in her eyes.

"I told you, I have an appointment." She crossed her arms over her breasts. "If you think getting back into my bed is going to be this easy—"

"I went to see my mother." He sat down on Morganna's

bed, lifting one foot to place it on his knee as he began un-lacing his hiking boots.

He watched Morganna. She became still, wary.

"Oh yeah?" she finally asked when he said nothing more.

"She said you came to visit." He pulled his boot free of his foot before lifting his other foot and working on the laces of that boot.

"Is there a point to this subject?"

He dropped the boot and stared up at her. She looked frag-ile, delicate, and despite her ferocity, she was just a woman. Created to be protected, cherished.

"Why did you go see her?"

Her lips firmed as the irritation in her gaze turned to anger.

"She pretends to be so caring," Morganna snarled. "She had the nerve to call here, to see if I knew where you were. Pretending to be worried because she hadn't heard from you." She swiped at the tear that fell from her eye. "I wanted to face her. I wanted to see the monster I knew she was."

"And what did you see?"

She looked away, her lower lip trembling.

"You didn't see a monster," he told her softly. "You just saw an old, very selfish woman. You saw something you couldn't fix."

Another tear tracked down her cheek.

"I love you, Morganna," he whispered. "I'm not hiding from that any longer. I'm not running anymore. I'm scared shitless, though; I'll tell you that right now. The thought of destroying that love, of destroying your belief in me, terri-fies me."

He watched her swallow tightly as she gazed back at him, her face becoming damper with her tears. He rose from the bed, unable to stand those tears, to bear the pain in her eyes.

Clint reached out to her, fighting the trembling in his hands as he clasped her face, his thumbs easing the dampness from her cheeks.

"I'll never leave you again," he swore, knowing that running was no longer an option. "You'll drive me crazy, I'll go gray early, but I'll always love you, Morganna. With everything inside me, I'll love you . . . and any children you allow me to father."

She gasped, a shudder working through her as her lips parted, the tears running faster.

"I love you." Her whispered sob ripped through his heart with a joy and a hope that filled every particle of his being. "Oh God, Clint, I love you."

Chapter 30

E HAD SAID THE C-WORD. "Children." The L-word. "Love." Morganna felt the aching, desolate emptiness that had held her for the past five days ease from her body as Clint's lips covered hers.

The feel of his lips moving on hers, his tongue licking, teeth nipping, had her reaching for more, wishing she could crawl into his body and hold on to him forever.

"The clothes are coming off, Morganna," he growled a second before his hands moved, his fingers curling into the low neckline of the shirt and tearing it apart.

Buttons scattered as she felt him pulling her arms from his shoulders before he jerked the material from them.

"I should tie you down and cut those jeans off." His hands tore at the metal buttons. "But damn, they look good on you, baby. I might want to see you in them again sometime."

"I might let you." Morganna fought to pant for breath as Clint knelt in front of her, slowly drawing the jeans down her thighs, lifting one ankle, then the other until he was tossing the material away.

"You take my breath away." He laid his head against her stomach, his lips pressing against her skin, his tongue flickering against her belly ring, tasting her skin as she shuddered in his grip.

Calloused fingertips rotated against her outer thighs, smoothed over her flesh, sent razor-sharp explosions of need echoing through her womb. She could feel the pleasure racing through her nerve endings, his touch, heated, moving deeper than flesh alone as his fingers moved slowly closer to the aching center of her body.

"You're making my knees weak," she whispered breath-
lessly, her fingers clenching in his shoulders as the slow-
building burn began to encompass her body.

Morganna could feel the heated slide of dampness from
her vagina, the swollen nub of her clitoris, her nipples sensi-
tizing. Each touch of his fingertips, each slow, sensual drag
drawing closer to the small triangle of silk covering her sex,
had the veil of sensuality thickening around her.

She could feel the perspiration gathering on her body, between her breasts. Each panting breath rasped her nipples
against the delicate lace of her bra; each suspended moment
brought Clint closer to his goal.

"You bewitch me," he breathed against the moist silk between her thighs, sending shards of incredible pleasure to
tear through her body.

"Clint." Whether her whispered plea was a protest or a
whimper for more, she couldn't say.

His hand moved, his fingertips rasping against the silk
covering the swollen folds of her sex as she shivered before
him. The other moved to her rear, curving beneath a rounded
buttock in support.

"You smell like summer." He nuzzled his lips against the
damp material as a broken cry fell from her lips. She was
shaking in need, perched on the edge of an arousal so intense
she wasn't certain she could survive it.

"I love your touch," she panted. "Your hands, your
lips . . ." She was almost sobbing with the need for more,
the need to feel him against her, surrounding her, penetrat-
ing her.

"Ah, baby, no more than I love touching." He drew the
silk aside before giving the slick flesh a long, loving lick,
drawing her moisture to him, feasting on the taste of her.

Her thighs parted further at the urging of his hands,
her legs shaking as she fought for the strength to stand before him.

His tongue rasped over the delicate, tender bud at the apex of her mound, licking around it, drawing it into his mouth before suckling at it with greedy pulls of his mouth.

Her womb rippled with the incredible pleasure; her vagina convulsed with the need to be filled. Her hips pressed closer to his lips as her hands moved to his head, fingers burying into the silk of her hair as she opened herself further for him, pleading for release.

"As intoxicating as the finest wine," he whispered against her saturated flesh before kissing at her clit with gentle suction. "Come for me now, baby. Fill me with sweetness."

Two long, broad fingers slid inside the hungry depths of her vagina as his lips circled her clitoris, drew on it, his tongue flickering over it with devastating results.

She came apart beneath the onslaught, her body tightening, arching, suspended within a pleasure that sent starbursts shattering through her mind.

The world tilted as the quakes of pleasure tore through her. The feel of the mattress at her back was quickly followed by the rending of the silk between her thighs. Morganna opened her eyes, staring into the brilliance of Clint's dark blue eyes as he pushed her thighs up, back, then filled her.

The burning pleasure tore through her vagina, clenched her womb, and had her arching closer. Her hips writhed as he worked inside her, spearing the depths of her sex with such incredible rapture that she was screaming with it.

Her nails bit into his shoulders, her back arched.

"There, baby . . . so sweet, so tight." Clint strained against her, pushing inside her with greedy thrusts, stroking nerve endings so sensitized that the next orgasm sent her screaming with the pleasure.

"More," he groaned, his voice hoarse, desperate, as he pushed her further, sending her peaking again, hard tremors shuddering through her as she felt him tighten above her.

Three hard, fierce thrusts heralded his release. He drove

inside her with a near-violent surge before catching her orgasm at its peak as his own release joined hers. She felt the hard spurts of semen filling her, the rich heat, a bonding as she melded into him, as he melded to her.

"I love you. . . ." His voice was a strangled vow at her ear. "With all I am, Morganna, I love you. . . ."

Epilogue

DIEGO FUENTES SAT SILENTLY behind his desk, staring at the waves breaking over the California coast below the mountainside home.

His steepled fingers rested against his chin, his eyes narrowed thoughtfully at the sun setting in the distance. Behind him, the report that had been faxed in was crumpled on his desk from the fury that had driven into his brain as he read it.

The lab had been destroyed. The potent date rape drug known on the streets as Whores Dust was gone forever. The stupid scientist had refused to give Diego the recipe for it, and it was so complicated that so far the others he had working on it had yet to duplicate it properly.

It had something to do not so much with the ingredients as it did with the production of those ingredients.

Ah well. He had quite a bit stocked in a little-known warehouse, and though it wasn't enough to make available on the streets, it would be enough for other uses perhaps.

"Don Diego." His new general knocked briefly at the door before stepping inside. "More reports have come in."

Diego turned in his chair to watch as the older man entered the room.

Saul had at one time been Diego's father's advisor. He had returned this past year to advise Diego and now, with Roberto's death, had agreed to take the helm as Diego's second.

Saul was a good man. A cold, merciless man.

"Come in, Saul." Diego smiled benignly. "What more could those bastard DEA agents have taken from me?"

"Grant Samuels' journal," Saul answered. "Our men have found only those filled with his lurid imaginings of his wife.

We have not yet found the one that reveals the secrets Carmelita gave him."

Carmelita. Diego sighed. He had loved her. Loved her until there was no reasoning involved. And she had betrayed him so many times and with so many men.

"What of our SEAL?" There was another loose end. "He is still secure?"

"He's secure." Saul's lips lifted into a cruel smile. "The latest batch of the drug that Dr. Germano created seems to have promise. We'll break him yet."

Breaking the SEAL had become a compulsion. He was strong. So strong that he had resisted the Whores Dust for over a year now. He had yet to take any of the women locked into his cell with him. Though Diego could tell it was wearing away at the man's sanity. Soon the SEAL would find his release in a body other than his wife's, and then Diego could kill him.

But until then, they had that damned journal to deal with.

"Samuel's wife would know," Diego said pensively. "Take her and question her. If she does not talk, then you can give her to your men for their trouble. Watch Merino as well. He will not give up until he finds the journal. If the wife does not know where it is, then Merino will find it."

"Those were my thoughts as well." Saul nodded. "His daily journals speak of the secret one often. Merino will not be able to resist searching for it."

Diego smiled at that. The journals spoke often of Grant's wife and betrayed her with every stroke of his pen. Not that she knew a damned thing her husband was involved in, but Grant had planned carefully in the event of his arrest. Too bad the bastard had not planned for his death.

"Take the wife. And please arrange for an accident for the faithless Jenna. A painful one."

"It will be arranged." Saul nodded. "I've also finalized the plans to draw in your son, my friend. Striking the senator's daughter once again should pull him in. We should have no problems now that the spies within your organization are gone. Once we secure the journal, we can then proceed with our plan to acquire his loyalty. Everything will run smoothly from here on out."

Yes, it would. Saul was now in charge, and he trusted no one. Least of all a woman. Perhaps he had a chance, though, with his son. The boy he had been unaware of for much too long.

Women. They could not be trusted. They were, as his father had warned him, traitorous whores who were less than the dogs who served them. At least the dogs, animals though they were, knew loyalty. But sons, true sons, a son with the power, strength, and honor this one possessed. Such a son would be an asset.

"Yes," Diego whispered, aware of Saul slowly leaving the room. "Yes, now we bring in my son." The son Carmelita and his father had not told him of.

Diego's heart still ached for her even as fury ate at his soul. How he had trusted her, loved her. She had been the light in his world, and her death had nearly destroyed him. Until he found the pictures. Until he learned of her vile lusts and her betrayals. Until he learned how many times she had nearly succeeded in murdering his true child.

If he missed her at times, he pushed the traitorous feelings back and found one of her special pets to punish. Such as Trina.

Carmelita had taught him much. Lessons he would not forget.

He tapped the glossy wood surface of his desk as he considered his more immediate problems, though. Grant Samuels' journal must be found. And then his pet SEAL must be broken.

The SEALs, they were resilient if nothing else. A true challenge to a man such as him. Clinton McIntyre had survived Roberto, which Diego had anticipated. It was but another link in the chain to acquire his dream. And the girl, the Chavez girl, Morganna. They had escaped Roberto's plans.

Poor Roberto. Diego had warned him about using Santos for such an important operation, but the man had been insistent. It had only made it easier for Diego to kill Santos.

Diego still couldn't believe the boy was stupid enough to contact those SEALs, to believe he could trade the information on the pet Diego kept in exchange for the SEALs' getting his charges dropped. Santos had known of the prosecutor's ties with Diego, the location of the lab, and the location of the SEALs' missing friend.

Such betrayal could only be met with death. Thankfully Saul had been smart enough to keep a tail on Santos and to bring in a team when he realized what the younger man was up to.

Roberto had blamed the deaths on McIntyre and the woman. Instead of placing the blame on Santos' shoulders where it belonged. Such family loyalty weakened a man. Love for anything other than oneself or one's child was a grave mistake. Roberto's need for vengeance had been the death of him.

Ah well. Killing McIntyre and the Chavez girl had not been Diego's idea, so he did not suffer it. The lab, that had been a loss, but not worth seeking vengeance over for now.

For now, he had more important matters to deal with. . . .